DAUGHTERS OF THE MOON

DAUGHTERS OF THE MOON

BOOK FOUR
the secret scroll

BOOK FIVE
the sacrifice

BOOK SIX
the lost one

LYNNE EWING

HYPERION
NEW YORK

This edition, 2011
1 3 5 7 9 10 8 6 4 2
ISBN 978-1-4231-4239-3
V567-9638-5-11015
Printed in the United States of America

Visit www.hyperionteens.com

THIS LABEL APPLIES TO TEXT STOCK

For Lyla, Lyandra, Maitea, and Camila

BOOK FOUR

the secret scroll

PROLOGUE

Long ago, darkness reigned over the night. People were afraid and remained inside their shelters from sundown until sunrise. The goddess Selene saw their fear and gave light to their nocturnal world by driving her moon chariot across the starry sky. She followed her brother Helios, who rode the sun and caught his shining rays on her magnificent silver chariot, then cast them down to earth as moonbeams. She felt pride in the way the earthlings were comforted by her light.

But one night when she had abandoned her chariot to walk upon the earth, she noticed that in times of trouble many people lost all hope. Their despair bewildered her. After considering their plight, she knew how she could make her moon the greatest gift from the gods.

From then on she drove around the earth and each night caught her brother's rays from a different angle. This way the face of the moon was everchanging. People watched the moon decrease in light every night, until it could no longer be seen from the earth. Then after three nights of darkness, a crescent sliver returned and the moon increased in light until it was fully illuminated as before. Selene did this to remind people that their darkest times can lead them to their brightest.

The ancients understood Selene's gift in the lunar phases. Each night when they gazed at the moon, they knew Selene was telling them to never give up hope.

CHAPTER ONE

CATTY STOPPED ON the cement step and stared at the lettering on the side of the building. She wanted to turn and run, but Kendra took her hand to reassure her. The traffic from the nearby freeway filled the hot afternoon with a constant drone like surf rushing to shore. She wished she were at the beach. Anyplace but here.

It had been the most terrible day ever even before the phone call. She had laughingly told Kendra that the only good thing about it was that it couldn't get any worse. Then the phone rang.

Now all her problems at school suddenly seemed unimportant.

"We better go in," Kendra coaxed. She pressed her lips tightly together, resolute, and adjusted her purse over her shoulder. The phone call had upset her, too, but her way to handle anything bad was to take action.

Catty nodded and started toward the Los Angeles County Coroner's office.

Kendra gently touched her arm. "It's probably not your mother anyway."

Catty looked down at the brown envelope on which she had scrawled the woman's name. Zoe Reese. Was that her mother? She whispered the name again, hoping it would jog a memory. It didn't.

"I'm sure it's a mistake." Kendra frowned behind her dark glasses. She was a large woman with high cheekbones and long brown hair streaked with gray.

Catty loved her. Kendra was the only mother she had ever known. She had often wondered what her life had been before Kendra had found her walking along the highway in the Arizona desert when she was six years old. She hadn't even known her name when Kendra had stopped the car that day and asked if she was okay. "Catty" was the name Kendra had given her. She only had two memories of the time before that moment: one of a crash, the other of an explosion. None of her real mother. Would she finally have some answers now? She wondered if she would be able to see herself in her mother's face.

Maybe now she'd be able to piece together her past and find out where she came from. Then, unexpectedly, a feeling of hurt surged through her, reopening a childhood wound. If her mother had lived in Los Angeles all these years, why had she never contacted her?

Catty followed Kendra across a long cement slab that led to the double glass doors. When they stepped inside the coroner's office, a rush of cold air and the alcohol smell of antiseptics closed tightly around them. Catty's hands began to tremble, and she pushed them deep inside her jeans pockets.

Kendra's shoes squeaked on the highly polished floor as she stepped past the case of citations and plaques to the reception window. She slid her sunglasses on top of her head and pulled on her red-framed reading glasses, then tapped her finger impatiently on the glass partition. Her gold rings flashed and bracelets jangled on her thick wrist.

"Your office called my daughter," Kendra started.

The receptionist looked up with a practiced expression somewhere between a smile and pity, then she saw Catty and her face changed. "They called her?"

Kendra nodded. "To inform my daughter that her mother had died."

The receptionist's pale face went blank.

Kendra cleared her throat. "I'm not her biological mother," she explained.

"Oh," the receptionist answered, and that same sad and pleasant expression returned to her face. "You'll need to contact a funeral home and make arrangements with them to claim the body."

Kendra pressed her hand against the glass. Her nails were long and painted red. "But I don't understand what makes you think that woman is her mother. I spoke with the person on the phone and all they gave me was a name and an address—"

"They never call without proof," the receptionist asserted calmly.

"Maybe if you'd let us see her," Kendra suggested. "Perhaps we'd be able to see a resemblance."

Catty started. She didn't think she had the courage to look at the woman's face. Tears pressed into her eyes. She tried to swallow, but her mouth was too dry and her tongue made an odd click in the back of her throat. She had always thought about seeing her mother someday, but this was not the way she had imagined it.

"I'm sorry." The receptionist seemed truly concerned. "We're not designed to accommodate viewing. You'll have to make arrangements with a funeral home. They'll let you view—"

"You're not understanding." Kendra tried to

keep a smile on her face to hide her frustration. She clasped the beads hanging around her neck, and Catty knew she was mentally reciting her mantra, searching for calm. When she spoke again, her voice seemed more serene. "I have no proof that this woman is my daughter's biological mother, so why should we make arrangements for her?"

"They had to have had proof." The receptionist's voice had taken on a defensive tone. "They wouldn't randomly call someone."

"I understand. All I am asking is that you show me that same proof." Kendra's arm reached out and pulled Catty tight against her. The scents of sandalwood and heather clung sweetly to Kendra's dress. "Why don't you have a seat while I get some answers?" Kendra whispered to her.

Catty nodded and headed for one of the purple chairs lined against the wall. She sat down and tried to concentrate on the day, hoping her problems at school might distract her from the argument Kendra was having with the receptionist.

Her stomach pinched just thinking about her new boyfriend, Chris. She had thought everything was perfect between them, and then today at school he had seemed so distant. She wondered if he had been trying to find the words to break up with her. What had happened to the attentive guy who was so open with her? At lunch he had shrugged and said he couldn't stay with her. And they always ate in the cafeteria together. After school he had acted indifferent about meeting her at Planet Bang. He told her he would call. But he hadn't so far.

That alone was enough to make the day a disaster. But even earlier, it had started badly. During first period, Mr. Hall had passed back the last geometry tests. She had received a D.

Then right after class her best friend Vanessa had gotten mad at her because Catty had said some nice things about Michael Saratoga and his band in front of Vanessa's creepy new boyfriend, Toby. Everyone knew Vanessa still liked Michael, so why was she wasting time with Toby, anyway? There was no way Vanessa could convince Catty that she really liked him. When Vanessa flirted with him her eyes seemed to be looking for someone else, someone like Michael. And when Toby tried to hold her close, she never looked totally comfortable with it. Vanessa had only become more angry when Catty pointed this out to her. Too bad Toby had been standing nearby and listening.

Catty sighed. Before the phone call from the coroner's office, she had planned to smooth things over with Vanessa tonight at Planet Bang. They had been best friends for a long time, and no way was she going to let a guy come between them.

But then Kendra had surprised her. She wouldn't relent and take her off restriction. Since Kendra had started teaching the night Latin class at UCLA, she had relied on Catty to watch her bookstore in the evenings and punctuality had suddenly become very important to her. Twice Catty had made Kendra late, and the third time Kendra did the unthinkable and actually put her on restriction. Restriction was something new for

Catty. Kendra had always let her do whatever she wanted because she knew Catty wasn't like other kids.

She glanced at Kendra now and felt a surge of gratitude. Kendra continually tried to help Catty understand her strange ability. She had even encouraged Catty to use what Kendra called her gift. What would have happened to her if someone else had stopped that day at the desert? She hated to imagine what her life could have been. She might have ended up in some sideshow or as an exhibit in the Smithsonian.

From the beginning, Kendra had assumed that Catty was from some distant planet and that her extraordinary power was actually a form of teleportation used by her people. She had cautioned Catty not to tell anyone about her unusual skill. And Catty hadn't until she met Vanessa. She had known immediately that Vanessa was different, too, when she saw the silver moon amulet hanging around her neck. It was identical to the one Catty wore. Catty looked down at her amulet now and studied the face of the moon etched in the metal. She had been wearing the charm when Kendra found her. Now, sparkling in the fluorescent lights, it didn't look silver, but opalescent. She never took it off.

Kendra turned and glanced at her, her eyes asking if she was okay. Catty tried to smile back, but her lips curled in a sad imitation of one.

She wished she could find the courage to tell Kendra the truth. She hated keeping any secret from her. But the words never came. It was probably easier to believe in people from outer space than to accept what Catty really was, anyway. She sometimes thought Kendra would feel disappointed if she learned the truth. Kendra was always on the Internet trying to find out more about UFO sightings, Area 51, and Roswell. She seemed to enjoy the research.

Catty studied Kendra now. Her cheeks had taken on an angry red blush and her fingers frantically worked at the beads hanging around her neck. Would Kendra even believe her if she did tell her the truth . . . that she was a goddess, a

Daughter of the Moon, on Earth to protect people from the Followers of an ancient evil called the Atrox?

Who she was had remained a mystery to her until just a few months ago, when she had been kidnapped by Followers, before she even knew what they were. Fortunately, Vanessa and two other Daughters, Jimena and Serena, had rescued her. Vanessa had told her the truth then, but Catty hadn't believed it until she had met Maggie Craven, a retired schoolteacher.

"Tu es dea, filia lunae," Maggie had told her in Latin. Catty had been surprised she understood the words, but she had. "You are a Goddess, a Daughter of the Moon." The words still sent a thrill of excitement through her.

Kendra's voice pulled her back from her thoughts.

"What is your proof?" Kendra raised her voice in exasperation, and the words echoed around the small room.

Catty stood and walked back to Kendra, hoping her presence might calm her.

The receptionist picked up a pencil and began twirling it nervously between her fingers. "The person who called you should have answered all of your questions."

"We won't leave until you show us proof." Kendra's voice was firm.

Catty rested her hand on Kendra's arm. The muscles felt tense.

"I'll call Security," the receptionist threatened.

Wrong thing to say, Catty thought and shot a warning look at Kendra.

"Call Security." Kendra smiled broadly. She knew how to make a scene. She relished the opportunity.

The receptionist must have had a lot of experience with the public. She seemed to sense that Kendra's challenge was not a bluff. Instead of reaching for the phone, she set her pencil down with a sudden snap and stood. She marched from her enclosure to a door marked *property release*, knocked briefly, then stepped inside.

Kendra gave Catty a questioning look. "Should we follow?" But her shoes were already squeaking across the floor after the receptionist. She caught the door before it closed and propped it open.

Catty followed into the overly cooled room.

The receptionist spoke in whispers to a shorter woman. The smaller woman gathered a brown envelope from a filing cabinet and handed it to the receptionist, who pulled something from deep inside.

"Here." The receptionist showed Kendra and Catty a worn piece of notebook paper. "This was found in the woman's pocket."

Kendra held it in her large hands.

"It's a geometry test," Catty muttered. "My geometry test."

Kendra readjusted her reading glasses and examined the paper closely. Catty looked over her shoulder.

Catty's name and address were hurriedly written on the back of the paper in Catty's handwriting. Above that was written in another person's penmanship, *in case of emergency contact my daughter.*

Kendra turned the paper over and over.

Catty knew it was her writing, but since when had she gotten an A in geometry? Then she saw the date on the test paper. It was a week away. Her heart started pounding rapidly.

A look of astonishment crossed Kendra's face as well, and she moved her thumb to cover the date. Kendra glanced at Catty, her mouth open in surprise.

"What?" Catty asked, wondering if Kendra had seen something more.

"Your moon amulet. It's changing colors." She seemed spellbound. "Maybe it is your mother," she suggested in a voice too low for the receptionist to hear. "Perhaps because you're close to your real mother, it's glowing." Kendra thought the amulet was a homing device that would someday guide Catty back to her home in space.

Catty clasped her hand around the amulet. It resonated against her palm. The amulet only glowed when Followers of the Atrox were nearby. Did that mean she was in danger? She looked quickly behind her, but nothing was there. She wished Vanessa were here.

Kendra's eyes widened and she put her hand on Catty's shoulder. Had she noticed something that Catty hadn't seen? Then Catty felt it. The air changed. She had a curious sensation of an electric charge building around her as if she had brushed a giant balloon vigorously back and forth across her clothing.

Overhead the fluorescent lights buzzed, then flickered, only to come back brighter.

"It must be a power surge," the receptionist offered in explanation, but Catty didn't think so.

The tiny hairs on her arm stood on end as if electrons were flowing through the air charging it with electricity, but that was impossible. A current of electricity needed a conductor and a source of energy. It couldn't just exist in the air. She might get Ds in geometry, but she always knew her science.

She touched Kendra's arm and a spark flew between them.

Kendra eyed her curiously. "What is it?" she whispered.

That's when the front entrance door opened

and three men walked slowly inside. They were distinguished-looking, with graying hair and deep, clear eyes. All three wore neatly pressed black suits.

When Kendra looked up and saw the men, she edged in front of Catty as if she were trying to protect her.

Catty peeked at the men from behind Kendra. The oldest had a thick mustache and held himself overly erect, as if he were wearing a brace. The shorter one had a broad, handsome face. He turned and smiled, his white, even teeth clenched tightly. When his black eyes met Catty's, she became suddenly aware of how frightened she felt. The third one seemed almost too good-looking. Catty wondered if he was wearing stage makeup. His skin and hair looked flawless.

If there hadn't been such a strange electrical aura surrounding them, and if her amulet hadn't been thrumming against her clenched fist, Catty might have thought they were undertakers from a mortuary that was patronized by only the rich and famous people in Los Angeles. But now she was certain the men were Followers, only different from any she had seen before. They were older, for one thing, and they looked too perfect, more like wax figures than real people.

Most of the Followers Catty met were Initiates. Kids who had turned to the Atrox, hoping to prove themselves worthy of becoming Followers. They were no threat to her, unless a large group of them caught her. But there were other Followers, like these, who were powerful and treacherous.

"I have to go," the receptionist announced. "Be sure to give the paper back before you leave."

The men turned to greet her as she walked back to the reception cubicle.

The oldest stepped forward. "We've come to claim the body of Zoe Reese," he said in a smooth voice.

Catty clutched Kendra's hand. Why would Followers want her mother's body?

The receptionist sighed. "Who notified *you?*"

"No one," he answered. "I am . . . *was* her neighbor. I called the police and informed them that I had found her body in the backyard. I knew she was alone in the world and I was hoping to make arrangements for her." He smiled coldly and leaned closer to the glass. "That is, of course, unless you were able to find a next of kin."

"The next of kin has already been notified." The receptionist glanced at Kendra and Catty but didn't say more.

"Perhaps, then . . ." He stopped and pressed a finger against his lips as if he were carefully considering his words before he continued. "Perhaps you could give me their address so that I might help them."

"I'm sorry," the receptionist answered solemnly. "I can't give you that information."

Kendra suddenly jerked Catty's arm and pulled her from the property release room. They marched quickly across the polished floor to the door and outside into the sunshine.

When they had passed two utility vans parked side by side, Kendra spoke quickly. "Don't look back until we're inside the car."

"You know who they are?" Catty felt surprised.

"They're from Area 51, I'm sure." Kendra quickened her pace. "That superclean military look. You'd think G-men would try to blend in rather than stand out. Did you see how polished their shoes were? That's not the first time I've had to hide you from their kind."

"Their kind?" Catty wondered if Kendra had seen Followers like these before.

"Government agents looking for space aliens," Kendra replied. The words came out in a single breath.

They climbed into the car and Kendra quickly rolled down her window. The air outside rushed in but did little to cool the interior.

"I've tried to protect you from government officials like those." Kendra sighed. "I'm sure they've taken others like you and dissected them. They'd just love to find out about your power.

Why do some scientists have this irrational need to dissect God's creatures? Can't they just admire their beauty?"

Catty shuddered. She wondered if some scientists really would dissect her in order to find out where her power came from.

Kendra started the car and turned on the air-conditioning.

"You've seen them before?" Catty asked nervously.

"Not for a long while. It was especially bad the day I found you on the desert . . ." Her words trailed away.

"They were there?" Catty didn't remember seeing them that day.

Kendra shook her head. "No, that night when we stopped in Yuma, the town was swarming with them. It was so obvious they were looking for you. That's why we didn't spend the night there but drove on to Palm Springs."

Catty remembered the night travel and how Kendra had sung songs to her, trying to keep her calm. She also remembered the strange way

Kendra had spoken to her at first, saying each word as if it contained three syllables and talking too loudly because she hadn't known if Catty understood English.

"You remember the day I picked you up at the side of the highway?" Kendra began and looked at Catty.

Catty nodded.

"You were such a precious little thing I couldn't imagine anyone abandoning you. I asked you your name, and you didn't seem to understand."

Catty recalled the moment. She had been unable to remember her name. Like everything that had occurred in her life before that day, she had no memory of it. She didn't even know if she had ever had one.

"When you didn't answer," Kendra continued, "I told you that you were as cute as a cat. That made you giggle, so I decided to call you Catty. You seemed to like the name."

Catty grinned. She did like the name.

Kendra smiled tenderly. "It was a good choice. It fits your personality." Then she glanced back at the building and continued her story. "I had planned to stop at the Department of Social Services in Yuma and turn you over to them, but then you did something extraordinary."

When Catty was little she had always encouraged Kendra to complete the story. "What made you think I was from outer space?" she would ask and cuddle closer. The story had both pleased and frightened her. She liked to think she had descended from some super race of creatures who traveled across galaxies, but at the same time she was afraid they might return and take her away from Kendra.

Kendra no longer needed coaxing to finish the story. "When we started to drive off, you grabbed my shoulder; and without warning, we were traveling through another dimension. It was like floating inside a dark endless tunnel, and then suddenly we were back on the road where I had picked you up, but now we were outside the car. I was terrified but I knew there had to be a rational explanation. That's when I decided you must come from another planet. I assumed that what we had done was some kind of teleportation."

Kendra never understood that Catty's gift was actually the ability to time-travel. Catty wondered what she would think if she knew.

"I figured that for a civilization that could travel across galaxies, the speed of light would be an archaic measure," Kendra went on. "So merely walking would probably seem as antiquated. I decided that when we went through that tunnel, you were actually trying to reconnect with your family. It made me feel so sad for you." She shook her head and stared at her hands. "Later when you told me about your memories of the crash and fire, I assumed that your spaceship had probably smashed into Earth, maybe killing your family and leaving you wandering on the desert."

Catty bit her lower lip. She should tell Kendra right now. "Kendra, there's something about me," she started, but then the three men left the coroner's office.

Kendra stared at them. "What do you think they were doing inside all this time?"

"Shouldn't we go?" Catty could feel her moon amulet pulsing against her chest and knew it was dangerous to stay.

Kendra put the car in reverse, but her movements were frustratingly slow as if she were debating whether to stay or leave.

Finally she spoke. "The woman must be your mother, Catty, and that's why the men are trying to claim her body without arousing suspicion. They can't afford another Roswell."

She squinted against the glaring sun, then remembered her sunglasses and brought them down from the top of her head to her nose. "We should have taken the envelope with the rest of her belongings. There might have been something important in it." Kendra pulled the geometry test from her purse and handed it to Catty.

Catty hadn't realized that Kendra had kept the paper until now.

"Government agents." Kendra spit out the words as if they left a bad taste in her mouth. "After all these years, they're back. You'll need to be careful, Catty. More careful than usual. I wonder if it's even safe for us to stay. Maybe we should leave Los Angeles."

Kendra's words left an uneasy foreboding in the air.

CHAPTER TWO

THAT NIGHT, CATTY awakened with a start, her heart beating as if she had been running. She tried to bring the dream into focus, but the more she did, the more it seemed to slip away, leaving her with only a nagging feeling that there was something important she should be doing.

Moonlight streamed through the windows, giving her walls and furniture an eerie silver glow. Glancing at the butterfly chair next to her bed, she had the strangest impression that someone had been sitting in it, not just talking to her, but warning her about something. What had they said?

She rubbed her eyes. Her apprehension felt so real. It must mean something.

She tossed back her covers and rolled to the side of the bed. She tried to reassure herself that no one had been in the room. Her easel stood in the corner with her latest painting of a moonscape. The sketchpads and pencils on her desk looked the same as she had left them.

She listened to the silence for a long moment, then stood and walked to the chair. Her hand hovered above it. Finally, to convince herself that no one had been in the chair, she touched the seat. The faux-fur cover felt warm. She jerked her hand back as if it had been burned and scanned the room in disbelief. The warmth had to be stored heat, leftover from the day, but when she touched the edge of the chair, it felt cool.

Then she thought of Kendra and relaxed. How many nights had Kendra sat by her bed to comfort her? Kendra had probably come into her room to check on her, then sat down. Maybe she had even voiced her concerns about the "government men."

Catty took a deep breath and decided to go downstairs for a glass of milk.

In the hallway, the gray moonlight dissolved into total blackness. She waited until her eyes adjusted to the dark, then she continued to the stairs. She gripped the banister, and with quiet, even steps she made her way down to the living room.

At the entrance to the kitchen she stopped, suddenly aware of a cold draft. The back door was open and hanging on its hinges. Had an intruder come into the house? But why would a trespasser leave without shutting the door? Then she thought of Kendra upstairs and alone. Suddenly, she felt afraid for her. She rushed back through the dark house, stumbling up the stairs. Her breathing was hoarse by the time she opened the door to Kendra's room and switched on the light.

Kendra jerked awake and sat up in bed. "What's wrong?"

Catty walked slowly into the room. "I'm sorry to wake you." She slumped onto the bed and took deep breaths.

"What happened?" Kendra asked. "Are you all right?"

Catty shook her head. "I had this unbelievably crazy idea that you were in danger."

"I was," Kendra said softly.

"You were?" Catty looked quickly around the room. She didn't see anything that suggested danger.

"I was having one of those horrible nightmares." Kendra laughed softly, but the look in her eyes told Catty that the dream had truly frightened her. "You know the kind in which you can't wake up?"

Catty nodded. "What were you dreaming?"

"About those government men we saw in the coroner's office today." Kendra brushed her hands through her long hair and stretched.

"What were they doing?" Catty asked.

"They were chasing me because they wanted to find you." Kendra put her hand in front of her mouth to hide a yawn, then laughed. "They were demanding to see my memories, but I closed my mind to them." She shook her head. "I guess all that meditation makes me too focused," she joked. "Then they thought they could make me tell them where you were by force. It felt so real. One grabbed my arm and wouldn't let go. I'm glad you woke me."

Kendra must have seen something on Catty's face because she reached forward and patted Catty's cheek. "Don't be so concerned. It was only a dream."

When Catty didn't smile back at her, she continued. "Besides, the dream was probably only an expression of my very real fear that government officials *will* find you."

"Probably," Catty agreed, but secretly she wondered if these new Followers had a power she hadn't encountered before. Could they somehow go into dreams? Or was it only a strange coincidence that Kendra had dreamed about them? She grabbed Kendra's hand as if to protect her.

Kendra squeezed Catty's hand in return. "I love you, baby."

"I love you, too," Catty murmured.

Kendra got up and went to her bathroom,

splashed water on her face, then stared back at her raw-boned reflection in the mirror over the sink. Her eyes still held a charm, and her nose and cheekbones had an attractiveness, but nothing like the pictures that sat in the frames on her dresser.

Then Kendra looked down at her arm. "Odd."

"What?" Catty asked.

"Look at this." Kendra walked toward her, holding out her arm.

Catty stood and examined it. Four circular bruises colored the skin.

"I must have done this to myself while I was sleeping," Kendra announced, bemused.

Catty nodded. But she knew with a certainty that made her stomach curl that Kendra had not done that to herself. Somehow the Followers had found her in her dreams.

"Maybe I'll sleep in here for the rest of the night," Catty suggested.

"Okay," Kendra answered.

Catty knew from the quickness of her response that Kendra felt edgy about being alone.

She suddenly remembered the back door was still open.

"I'll get us some milk." Catty started to leave the bedroom. She didn't want to alarm Kendra about the open door. Besides, maybe the wind had blown it open.

"Good idea," Kendra called after her.

Catty hurried downstairs and closed the back door. As she slipped the dead bolt in place, she saw last year's Christmas pictures of Kendra's nieces and nephews on the refrigerator. She realized suddenly how much Kendra had sacrificed to protect her. Kendra rarely saw her family because she was afraid they might guess that Catty was a space alien. She also never dated for fear of exposing her. But Kendra never seemed to have any regrets for what she had had to give up to take care of Catty. Catty felt grateful, but also sad. Kendra loved her nieces and nephews and had always wanted a large family of her own. Catty hoped she wasn't going to repay her by putting her in danger.

CHAPTER THREE

THE DAY STARTED with a fire in the Sepulveda pass. By the time Catty walked to school, three new brushfires had begun burning in the hills surrounding Los Angeles. Newscasters blamed the continued drought and hot, dry weather. The air smelled of smoke, and gray ash drifted over La Brea High School.

Catty saw Vanessa leaning against the bank of lockers outside the classroom. She waved and hurried toward her. Like Catty, Vanessa had a special gift. She could expand her molecules and become invisible. But she didn't have complete control over it. If she became too upset or excited, her molecules acted on their own. That had made it difficult to date Michael at first, because every time he had tried to kiss her, she had started to go invisible. Catty wondered if she was having any trouble kissing Toby. Vanessa usually shared everything with her, but she had been closemouthed about him.

"Hi." Vanessa smiled. Her long blond hair shimmered in the morning sun.

"Hi," Catty answered and glanced down at Vanessa's flat, tanned stomach. White boxer shorts peeked over the top of her black, hip-hugging slacks. Catty wondered briefly if the boxers belonged to Toby.

Vanessa's blue eyes looked at Catty with concern. "Why weren't you at Planet Bang last night?"

Catty took in a deep breath. "It's a long story." She was glad Vanessa was no longer upset about what she had said yesterday.

"So tell me." Vanessa shifted her books.

"Hey." Jimena joined them. She was wearing a red tank top and jeans. Catty had tattooed the crescent moon and star on Jimena's arm. Jimena also had two teardrops tattooed under her eye. Her other tattoos, remnants from her gang days, were hidden under her clothes. She, too, had a gift. She received premonitions about the future.

Jimena glanced at Vanessa's outfit and playfully snapped the boxer's band. "Still trying to make Michael jealous?" she teased. "Or have you become somebody's *chavala*?"

"It's just a style," Vanessa huffed.

"Do the shorts belong to Toby?" Jimena smiled and brushed her luxurious black hair away from her face.

"So what if they do?" Vanessa muttered and looked away.

Jimena whooped. "I want to hear the whole story." But then she caught Catty's eyes, and her smile faded.

"It's just a style," Vanessa repeated, but Jimena didn't seem to hear her now, she was staring at Catty.

"What's wrong?" Jimena put a comforting

hand on Catty's shoulder. "Something big is bothering you. I don't need a premonition to know that, I can see it in your face."

Catty started to tell them about yesterday, when Serena ran up, carrying her cello case and geometry book.

"Hi, guys," she shouted. She was wearing a gold ring in her nose pierce. Her hair, curled and long, bounced on her shoulders. Serena and Jimena were best friends now, but their relationship had started uneasily. They hadn't become close until after they had fought a group of Followers together. That's when they had begun to trust each other.

Serena glanced at Vanessa and gave a loud laugh. "Are you wearing Toby's underwear?"

Vanessa looked around quickly. "Do you want everyone to hear?"

Serena set down her cello case. "It's only natural—people are going to talk."

Vanessa blushed.

"Come on, I'm kidding!" Serena said. "So

why is everyone so quiet?" Then she glanced at Catty. "What's wrong?"

Catty started to speak but couldn't find the words at first. "I'm not even sure where to begin."

They gathered close around her.

Catty rubbed her forehead and slowly began to tell them everything that had happened the day before at the coroner's office.

"Why do you think Followers would come to the coroner's office to claim my mother's body?" she asked finally.

"Maybe it's just another group of Followers we have to deal with and it has nothing to do with your mother," Serena suggested.

"Yeah," Vanessa agreed. "If they knew about your mother, maybe they went there hoping to catch you off guard."

Catty shuddered. "I hope they never get me again."

Jimena continued. "Remember what Maggie told us? Ambitious Followers come to Los Angeles because the Daughters of the Moon live here."

"We're the biggest prize," Serena added. "If they get one of us, the Atrox rewards them by allowing them into the Inner Circle."

Catty nodded but she still wondered if her mother had had some kind of association with these Followers.

"They didn't seem like ordinary Followers," Catty continued slowly. "They were old, for one thing, and then they had this high-voltage aura."

"You mean there was an evil feeling in the room?" Vanessa asked.

Catty shook her head. "No, the room felt like . . ." She thought for a moment. "You know when you brush your hand in front of the TV or the screen on your computer monitor?"

They nodded.

"Like that," Catty explained. "The air felt fuzzy as if it were filled with static electricity."

She sensed Serena entering her mind to try and get a better understanding of what she was saying. Like the rest of them, Serena hadn't understood her power when she was little. She only knew then that she was different. Sometimes, she forgot that people weren't speaking aloud and she would answer their thoughts. She did it even now if she became too happy or excited.

Catty looked at her three best friends. Maggie had brought them all together and was still showing them how to use their special powers to fight the Atrox and its Followers. She called them an unstoppable force, but more often they felt as if their powers controlled them. Of all the Daughters, Catty had the strangest power. She missed a lot of school because she was always twisting time. Vanessa was the only one who had time-traveled with Catty so far.

A few moments later, Serena left Catty's mind and stared at her. "Freaky."

"There's more," Catty added.

"What?" Vanessa asked.

"The receptionist in the coroner's office gave us this from my mother's belongings." Catty pulled out the wrinkled and worn geometry test.

Jimena took it. Vanessa and Serena studied it over her shoulder.

"Look at the date," Serena whispered.

"Wow," Vanessa breathed.

"But we don't have a test scheduled for next week, do we?" Jimena asked.

"No," Vanessa said.

"You've never gotten an A in geometry before," Serena teased.

Catty rolled her eyes. "I know."

Vanessa seemed puzzled. "How could your mother get something from the future if she's already dead?"

"Weird," Serena commented.

"Did you get the rest of your mother's things?" Jimena asked.

Catty shook her head.

"Maybe if you could have looked through all of her things, you'd have some answers," Vanessa suggested. "There could be something important that you missed."

"Yeah, some clue," Jimena agreed.

"Maybe we should ask Stanton," Serena put in. "I'm sure he'd know about these new Followers."

The others turned and stared at her.

"Well, he might," Serena answered defensively.

Catty knew Serena wanted an excuse to find Stanton. She still liked him, even though she tried to act like she didn't. Stanton was a powerful Follower who could read minds, manipulate thoughts, and even imprison people in his memories. Serena had fallen in love with him. She didn't think he was evil, but Catty had never gotten used to Serena being with a Follower. She didn't trust Stanton and thought Serena was putting them all in danger by seeing him. Then unexpectedly Stanton had ended their relationship. He had told her it was too dangerous, because if the Atrox found out about them, it would send Regulators to destroy them. Serena thought that proved how much Stanton cared for her, but Catty wondered if it was only another trick to gain even more of her trust.

"So why is everyone being so quiet?" Serena looked from one to the other suspiciously as if she knew they were feeling sorry for her.

"It's not a good idea," Catty answered bluntly.

"It's dangerous for you to hang around with Stanton."

Serena started to say something back, but Vanessa interrupted her. "Mr. Hall is coming."

Mr. Hall swung on old leather briefcase in one hand and jangled his keys in the other. He shaved his head, wore tiny black-rimmed glasses and had a beak nose that he was always wiping with his handkerchief.

"So everyone be extra careful until we can see Maggie," Vanessa warned. "Especially you, Catty. Promise?"

Catty nodded.

Vanessa gave her a worried look. "I mean, *really* promise."

Catty looked at her. "Why?"

"Because you always go off on your own even when it's dangerous," Vanessa complained.

"That's true," Serena agreed.

I do not, Catty started to say. But she knew they were right. "Okay, I promise."

Mr. Hall unlocked the classroom door, and

the girls followed him inside and took their seats.

He set his briefcase on the desk, then took a piece of chalk and wrote a date on the black-board. He pulled a handkerchief from his back pocket and swiped it under his nose as he clicked the chalk against the board. "Next week we'll have a midterm," he announced.

Catty glanced down at the worn geometry test paper. The date on the paper matched the date on the blackboard.

She turned and looked at Vanessa. Her eyes were wide with astonishment.

"The same date," Jimena whispered with surprise.

"What do you suppose it means?" Serena asked.

"Girls," Mr. Hall cautioned.

Catty stared down at the paper. Her heart pounded rapidly. She wondered if maybe she would finally be able to go back in time to the day when Kendra had found her walking along the highway. So far when she had tried to go back to that day, she had become stuck in the tunnel. It was a horrible claustrophobic sensation; floating for hours in the black void before she was able to free herself. But she kept risking it, because more than anything, she wanted to see her mother.

CHAPTER FOUR

AFTER CLASS, CATTY threw her geometry book into her locker. She was about to pick up her Spanish book when someone ran down the hallway and grabbed her waist. She twirled around. Chris stood behind her. He was a good-looking guy with an adorable smile and spiky hair. He wore bagged-out jeans and his red leather Reeboks.

She stared into his clear eyes and wondered how she could like him so much.

"I've been trying to find you since last night. You weren't at Planet Bang." He pulled her closer, and she let him. She liked the feel of his body next to hers.

"Things came up." Another time she might have told him everything, but since yesterday, she felt guarded.

"Missed you," he confessed.

She felt a smile crawl uninvited across her face. She didn't want him to see how much she cared for him.

"A guy in the school band is having a party," he announced.

She loved the way a smile made his eyes shine.

"I was hoping you'd go with me," he continued.

She felt a thrill of excitement and almost said yes, but at that moment he glanced down the hallway as if suddenly worried that someone might see them together. Then he slammed her locker and pulled Catty around the corner, his eyes drifting over her head as he scanned the crowd of kids walking down the corridor behind them.

"Who are you looking for?" she asked.

A light blush rose under his tanned cheeks, and his eyes shot back to hers. "Looking? What do you mean?"

"Your eyes keep wandering," she accused him.

"No they don't," he argued.

"Yeah." She nodded. "Like you're afraid someone is going to catch us together."

He laughed it off, but she wasn't convinced. She'd heard about guys who tried to have three and four girlfriends at a time, like it was some kind of sport, but Chris didn't seem like that kind of guy. Still, the way he was acting made her wonder. Then another thought came to her. He had just transferred to La Brea High, so it was also possible that he still had a girlfriend at his old school. Maybe someone here knew his old girlfriend, and he didn't want that person seeing him with Catty.

"Do you have a girlfriend?" she asked boldly. She tilted her head and watched his eyes closely.

"No." His eyes remained steady on hers, and she believed him. Then he touched her cheek, and a sweet shock of delight rushed through her. "Why would you think that?"

"Just wondering," she answered.

He smiled and she began to relax. How could she ever think such things about Chris?

"It's going to be a great party," he coaxed. "Lots of garage bands are going to play, and everyone is going to be there."

She started to say yes, but then his eyes left hers again.

"I don't know," Catty muttered.

He glanced back, and she hated the wounded look on his face. She wanted to tell him yes, but first she needed to find out what was going on.

"Why not?" he asked. "You know we'll have a good time. We always have a great time together."

"Chris, there's something I've been wanting to talk to you about since yesterday."

"Sure." He took her hand. She loved the feel of his hand, holding hers. Was there another girl who felt the same way? "Tell me," he encouraged her.

"You've seemed . . ." She stumbled, trying to find the right words. She decided to just say it. "You've changed." She caught something in his eyes then, a sudden nervousness. So he *had* been acting different, and he was also aware of it. "Is something wrong between us?"

"No, everything's fine." She sensed a lie in his words.

"Tell me the truth," she said matter-of-factly. "I thought we always shared everything."

His lips started to move, but before he could say anything, Jimena, Serena, and Vanessa ran up to them.

Jimena spoke first, and there was real concern in her voice. "You disappeared so quickly, we were afraid something had happened."

"What could happen at school?" Chris asked with a smile.

"Things." Vanessa looked at Catty. "One minute you're at your locker, the next you're gone."

"I pulled Catty away," Chris answered. "Sorry, I didn't know it would cause such a big commotion."

Serena cocked her head to the side and tried to smile but her tongue pierce clicked nervously against her teeth. "We just thought maybe someone had kidnapped her," she joked, but Catty knew they were worried that the new Followers might have captured her.

Chris smiled. "I was just asking her to a party one of the guys who plays in the school band is having," he explained. "You guys want to come, too?"

"Sure," Jimena answered quickly.

"It could take our mind off other things." Serena looked pointedly at Catty.

"Yeah." Vanessa seemed really eager. "I can't wait to show off all the new dance sequences I've learned with Toby."

Catty was surprised. That was so unlike Vanessa. She used to be nervous about dancing.

"Well?" Chris looked at Catty. "What do you say?"

"All right, I'll go." Catty sighed. She wasn't sure she was doing the right thing.

"Great." Chris kissed her cheek. "See ya." He

darted away toward the music room for band practice. He played tuba in the marching band.

"What's up with Chris?" Jimena asked.

"Yeah," Serena added. "I thought you liked him."

Catty sighed. "I did—I mean I really do like him a lot, but he's acting so . . ." She shrugged. "I just get the feeling that he's seeing someone else. Whenever we're together, he's always looking over my shoulder like he doesn't want anyone to see us together."

"No way," Jimena disagreed. "He's such a sweet guy."

"He's really cool and funny, too," Serena added.

"You worry too much," Vanessa offered. "Besides maybe it's other things. Maybe you've been acting weird and it makes him feel unsure."

"Me?" Catty said in disbelief.

"It's not like you don't have a lot going on," Serena declared. "You said yourself that yesterday was the worst day of your life."

"De veras," Jimena agreed.

Catty nodded and considered what they were saying. She didn't think her problems were making her believe Chris was seeing someone else. Besides, she knew him well enough to know something was going on.

The bell rang.

"I can't be late again," Serena complained.

"Come on," Jimena yelled.

Serena and Jimena ran down the hallway. Vanessa started after them, but Catty grabbed her arm and held her back.

Vanessa looked at her curiously. "What? I'm going to be late."

"I'm sorry," Catty cut in. "But I need to talk to you."

"Can't it wait?" Vanessa asked and started edging away. "You know how much I hate to be late for class."

Catty shook her head.

Vanessa seemed suddenly worried and stepped back to Catty. "What is it?"

"I want you to go back in time with me," Catty pleaded.

"No," Vanessa answered firmly and started to walk away.

Catty clasped her hand and pulled her close. "Please—I know you hate it, but I want to go back to the coroner's office and get my mother's things."

Vanessa shook her head.

"You're the one who said I should have looked through all of her stuff," Catty reminded her. "I might have missed something important that could give me answers."

"But you don't need me for that," Vanessa argued. "I'd just be in the way."

"The Followers will be there."

"Go back earlier before they get there," Vanessa suggested. "You'll be safe then."

"The property release room won't be open yet." Catty stared intently into Vanessa's eyes, hoping to see some sign that she was relenting.

"So? Go back and land inside the property release room," Vanessa advised.

"My landings have never been that accurate,"

Catty pointed out. "You say that all the time."

"Just call them up then." There was rising impatience in Vanessa's voice. "They have to release her things to you. Kendra can help you."

"That could take months," Catty answered. "And what if Kendra and I take the forms in or do whatever we have to do and the Followers are waiting for us to show up again? I could get kid-napped."

"Going back now is just as risky," Vanessa argued.

"You made me promise not to go off and do anything on my own." Catty folded her arms across her chest. "But I guess I'll have to."

Vanessa's eyes widened. "It's too dan-gerous."

Catty knew she had her now. "Not if you make us invisible so we can sneak past the Followers and the receptionist and steal my mother's things from the property room."

"I'm sure it's against the law," Vanessa objected. "Can't you do it the right way for once?"

"I already explained why I can't," Catty told her. "Besides, it's not like we'd really be stealing anything. Whatever is in the envelope belonged to my mother and should go to me. Think how you'd feel."

"All right," Vanessa agreed reluctantly.

"Great!" Catty grabbed her hand.

"But not here," Vanessa complained. "Someone might see us."

"All right." But it was too late. Catty could feel the power surging in her mind and pressing outward against her skull.

Vanessa had an astonished look on her face. She knew what was happening.

Catty glanced down. The hands on her watch began turning backward, and an abnormal heaviness crackled through the air. Vanessa shrieked and dropped her books as the school roared away with a burst of white light. Sucked into the tunnel that opened behind them, they whirled downward in air that felt dry and at the same time seemed to feel fizzy and effervescent.

Vanessa choked and coughed. She could

barely breathe in the thick foul air. Catty had gotten used to it.

She glanced down at her watch.

"Now!" she shouted in warning. Vanessa also hated the landings.

They fell back into time. In her mind's eye, Catty saw herself landing softly on two feet, but instead she fell and skidded across the parking lot in front of the coroner's office. Her chin hit the ground with a sharp crack. "Ow!"

Vanessa landed next to her.

"Sorry," Catty muttered and stood, brushing off her clothes.

Vanessa shook her head. "That one was worse than normal."

Catty stared at the building. "I know," she confessed, rubbing her chin. "I'm nervous."

A horn honked. Catty turned. A car was coming slowly toward them.

"Yikes," Vanessa said and grabbed Catty's hand. "We're in the middle of the parking lot. I hope no one saw us land."

"Too late now," Catty commented.

They dove between two utility vans parked side by side.

Catty started laughing. "Can you imagine what the driver must have thought if he saw us falling from the air?"

"How would we have explained ourselves?" Vanessa asked, but then she started laughing, too. "Hello, sir, we were just dropping from the sky."

Finally, Catty stopped laughing and turned to Vanessa. "Ready?"

"Okay." Vanessa stared at the two buildings connected by a broad cement walkway. She seemed more apprehensive than usual. "Which building do we go into?"

Catty pointed. "That one."

Vanessa read the words on the side of the building. *"Department of Coroner. Medical Examiner. Forensic Laboratories."* She shuddered. "Is that where they keep . . ." Vanessa stopped, then started again. "Is that where they keep the bodies?"

Catty looked at her. "In the basement. We don't have to go down there."

Vanessa took in a deep breath. "All right

then, but it still creeps me out."

"Let's get it over with," Catty urged.

Vanessa grabbed Catty tightly around her waist and pulled her close. Catty breathed through her lips trying to suppress her nervousness. Almost immediately her molecules began to stir and a pleasant ache spread through her body. She glanced down at her hands and watched in amazement as skin, muscle, and bone began to separate into innumerable specks. In a few seconds she was able to see through her hand. Finally there was nothing to look at, only air.

They caught a breeze and drifted toward the coroner's office.

Catty didn't glance back. She was afraid if she did she might see Kendra and herself sitting in the car staring back at the building.

There was a large crack between the two glass doors, and Vanessa sifted through it, taking Catty with her. If Catty had been able to scream, she would have. She wondered how Vanessa could be so afraid of the tunnel. Being invisible was far spookier.

Inside, the cool air seeped through them. The cold was bad, but worse was the electrical charge that hovered around the three Followers standing near the reception window.

Vanessa paused. Catty pushed her molecules in the direction of the property release door and they started floating that way.

Then Catty sensed something odd. What was happening? She experienced a sharp pain like a pin-prick, quickly followed by another and another. Her molecules were colliding. She glanced where she thought her hands would be and saw a mass of dots. Was she becoming visible? She looked ner-vously at Vanessa. Her face was forming.

"Oops," Vanessa mouthed.

Catty's molecules clashed together with an abruptness that left her skin tingling. She fell to the floor and landed on top of Vanessa.

"What happened?" she whispered.

"Sorry," Vanessa answered. "I got so spooked thinking about all the dead people in here that I lost control."

"That's the least of our problems." Catty

glanced up as the Followers turned languidly and stared down at them.

"Do they know who we are?" Vanessa asked.

"Let's not take any chances." Catty scrambled to her feet and bolted for the door, dragging Vanessa with her. But before she could reach it the Follower with the broad face stepped in front of her and blocked her way.

"Is there a problem?" he spoke in a polite voice.

"No, none at all," Catty answered with a nervous smile as Vanessa tugged her arm and pulled her in the opposite direction.

They dodged around the other two Followers and ran down the hallway, past a sign that read ATTENTION VISITORS, LAW ENFORCEMENT ID BADGE MUST BE WORN BEYOND THIS POINT.

"I think we're trespassing," Vanessa said. "I swear, Catty, someday you're going to get me arrested."

"Not as long as I can change time," Catty smirked.

Their feet pounded heavily on the floor.

"You can't go down there!" the receptionist yelled after them.

Catty and Vanessa darted around a corner and pressed against a door.

"You hide," Vanessa ordered.

"Me?" Catty peered back down the hallway. The Followers were coming at a slow even pace. "Why not both of us?"

"I'll let the Followers chase after me, then I'll go invisible so they'll lose my trail and you'll have time to find what you're looking for."

"I don't know." Catty felt reluctant to leave her. "It could be dangerous. Maybe it's better if we stay together and try to fight them."

The plodding footsteps of the Followers grew steadily louder.

"Just do it. We'll meet in the basement," Vanessa called over her shoulder as she started to run.

Catty slipped into a utility room behind her and watched through a crack in the door as the three men followed Vanessa.

When they passed, she started to leave the

room but other footfalls made her pause.

The receptionist and a security guard hurried down the corridor. After they went by, Catty eased back into the hallway. She had promised to meet Vanessa in the basement, but there was something she had to do first.

She crept back to the property-release room. The door was still open. She peeked inside. The clerk was humming, her back to Catty.

The brown envelope with her mother's belongings sat on a small file cabinet. She held her breath and tiptoed forward. Glancing up, she saw her reflection in the huge convex mirror that hung in the corner like a giant bug eye. If the woman looked up, she would see her.

Catty steadied herself and took another step forward. She picked up the envelope. The paper crinkled and something inside moved across the bottom.

The clerk stopped humming and cocked her head, listening, then hunched back over a pile of papers and began ruffling through them.

Catty turned and started silently back to the

door. She had only gone a little way, when she heard footsteps behind her.

She glanced back. The clerk was walking toward her. Catty's heart pounded so loudly she was sure the clerk could hear it.

"You still here?" the clerk questioned. It was the same woman from yesterday. "I thought you'd left." She didn't seem to notice that Catty was wearing different clothes.

Catty nodded.

"Did you put the paper back in the envelope?" She looked at the envelope in Catty's hands.

"The receptionist still has it," Catty lied.

"Make sure she brings it back," she ordered.

"Yes, ma'am."

The clerk inclined her head and studied Catty briefly, then satisfied, she returned to the pile of papers she had been sorting in the corner.

Catty left the room. The reception area was still empty. She turned, hurried down the hallway, and found an elevator. She pressed the button impatiently. The metal doors slowly scraped open. She rushed in and immediately pushed another button. When the doors finally closed, she let out a long sigh of relief.

As the elevator trundled down, she opened the envelope and peered inside.

She lifted out a chain and held it up. Her breath caught. Dangling from the end was a moon amulet that matched her own, except for the odd coloring. It looked tarnished and blackened as if it had been in a fire. She studied the face of the moon etched in the metal. Had her mother been a Daughter of the Moon?

CHAPTER FIVE

THE ELEVATOR DOORS opened with a rasping sound, and Catty peeked out at the hallway. When she didn't see anyone, she took a cautious step forward, stopped, and listened. Overhead the fluorescent lights buzzed, then dimmed and lit again as if there had been a power surge. She glanced up and wondered if the Followers had caused it.

"Vanessa?" she called tentatively and slipped her mother's moon amulet into her pocket. She tossed the envelope into a tall white trash cylinder.

She took a few more steps when the lights flickered and went out. She stood in complete darkness before the emergency lighting came on behind her. Slowly her eyes became accustomed to the dim light and she started again.

As she passed the numbered rooms, she drew in a deep long breath and immediately regretted it. The smell was too antiseptic. Her stomach felt suddenly queasy.

"Where are you, Vanessa?" she called softly.

She looked at the long line of doors in front of her and wondered what she would see if she ventured into one of the rooms. She tried not to think about it and crept farther down the hallway.

The door to the next room was partly open. She tiptoed past it.

The utter silence seemed too deep and unnatural but then, she reasoned, if the electricity had gone off, there would be no sounds from air conditioners or buzzing lights that normally filled any large office building.

She stepped into the heavy shadow near an open door and wished that Vanessa would hurry.

"Where is she?" she whispered with rising anxiety.

A sound from behind her made her alert. She took an uncertain step into the deeper shadows inside the room.

"Vanessa!" She tried again. "Now's not the time to play games."

Silence answered her.

"That's it. I'm leaving."

She started to turn to go back to the elevator when a hand reached out from behind her and touched her shoulder.

CHAPTER SIX

A LONG HISS OF AIR escaped Catty's lungs. She stood motionless, waiting for the person to speak. When they didn't she rushed to give an explanation. "I'm sorry," she said, assuming the person was a security guard. "I took the elevator, then the lights went out and I got lost."

The person didn't answer.

She tried to turn her head to see who stood behind her, but when she did a gloved hand stopped her.

"What?" Catty whispered nervously.

"Don't turn," the person whispered. The

voice was magnetic, and it was definitely a guy. It also seemed familiar.

"Who are you?" she asked, still trying to identify the voice.

"Catty." He spoke her name quietly.

A shock ran through her. "Yes," she answered with a quiver in her voice. "How do you know my name? Do I know you?"

"I have something for you," he said, ignoring her questions.

There was a rustling behind her and then the gloved hand reached over her shoulder and gave her something that looked like a thick piece of paper.

She took it and recognized the feel of parchment. She held it close to her eyes. It was a lavishly decorated medieval manuscript or something that looked like one. The first letters caught the light from the hallway and sparkled in gold. Strange birds and exotic animals hidden in a tangle of foliage and fairy-tale landscapes lined the borders.

"You're giving this to me?" Catty asked. If it

were authentic it would be priceless. "Is it stolen?"

There was a pause, followed by a chuckle. "It belongs to you."

"Me?" She smoothed her hand over the swirling script.

"Take the manuscript and use it," he instructed.

"Use it how?"

"The manuscript contains the answers to your questions."

She wondered who he was. She wanted to turn and see his face but every time she tried, his hand would stop her again.

"I don't understand," she murmured at last. "What questions should I have?"

He paused for a long moment.

"Read the manuscript," he answered. "Then you will know."

"Know what?" Catty asked. "What am I supposed to know?"

She could feel him take a step away from her.

"Don't try to follow me," he warned.

"Please don't go, not yet," she pleaded. She wanted to find out more about him.

She hadn't even realized he had left until she heard his footsteps echoing down the hallway behind her.

She stood motionless, staring at the manuscript. Should she follow him? He had said not to, but she didn't understand why. A devious smile crossed her face. She had always hated rules. She turned suddenly and ran to the doorway. She didn't see him in the long deserted corridor, but he had to be someplace nearby. She hurried in the way he had gone, her feet slapping loudly. She glanced at the closed doors, wondering where he had hidden.

Ahead of her a door was open. She stopped and peeked cautiously inside. It looked like a huge storage room. She took two stealthy steps inside. The shadows seemed deep and foreboding. She didn't even want to consider what was resting on the gurney, wrapped in plastic.

A harsh voice spoke behind her. "You must never try to discover who I am, do you understand?"

She nodded.

"That is essential," he warned. "Your very existence could depend on it, Catty." He spoke her name with tenderness as if he had known her for a long time. "Do you understand?"

"Why?" she asked in a hushed tone. "Why should knowing you put me in danger?"

"Simply accept that it is true."

She believed him but she wanted to know why. Before she could ask again, his gloved hand took her hand. She tried to see him from the corner of her eyes, but darkness kept him hidden.

"Trust me," he whispered.

"Yes," she answered. "I trust you." And at the same time she wondered how she could trust a complete stranger.

"Good-bye." He spoke the word against the side of her neck and it sent a pleasing shiver down her back.

Now more than anything she wanted to know who he was. She turned abruptly, expecting to be face-to-face with him. But the room was empty.

Suddenly she heard footsteps echoing in the corridor. Excitement rushed through her. If he were in the corridor, she would have enough light to see who he was.

She ran out the door and collided into Vanessa.

"There you are." Vanessa sounded angry. "How could you leave me alone in this place for so long? I'd rather face the Followers than creep around these passageways."

Catty started to show Vanessa the manuscript, but a noise made her stop.

At the end of the hallway, two Followers pushed open a large metal door and stepped from the stairwell.

They turned and started walking toward Vanessa and Catty. The air took on an odd fuzziness, and Catty could feel the hairs on the back of her neck rise as static electricity whisked around them.

"Why are there only two?" Vanessa asked nervously. "What happened to the third one?"

Catty shook her head. "I don't know."

"Take us back, Catty," Vanessa urged. She clutched Catty's hand. "Hurry."

"I can't," Catty answered, feeling too flustered to attempt opening the tunnel. "Can't you make us invisible?"

"Are you kidding? I can barely breathe."

"We better try to fight them off." Catty braced herself. "That takes less energy."

Catty and Vanessa stood together, concentrated, and sent their mental energy spiraling at the Followers. The hallway filled with a gleaming light. Catty felt the power rise up in her, but the Followers didn't stop their slow steady advance and they didn't respond with an attack of their own. Instead, they smiled at Catty and Vanessa as if they found their efforts amusing.

"What's with them?" Catty asked. Her nerves were raw, but nothing was happening.

"Take us back to the present," Vanessa urged. "This is getting too totally spooky."

"I'll try." Catty took Vanessa's hand but her energy felt drained. She couldn't concentrate. "I don't think I can. I don't have enough power right now."

"You have to. Hurry!"

Catty struggled to open the tunnel. "I can't. But I've got a plan."

"What?"

Catty grabbed Vanessa's hand. "Run!"

They turned and ran down the corridor as the third Follower suddenly appeared at that end and began walking toward them.

Vanessa clasped Catty's hand. "Please, Catty, now. Just try."

Catty clutched the manuscript tightly against her chest and squeezed her eyes shut. Nothing happened.

The Followers pressed closer.

"Never again," Vanessa whimpered. "I am never doing this again."

"You're being optimistic," Catty tried to joke in spite of her rising fear. "You think we get another chance?"

The Follower with the thick mustache reached out to touch Catty. A flurry of blue sparks shot in the air like miniature forked lightning bolts.

"I'm sorry, Vanessa," Catty sighed. "So sorry."

CHAPTER SEVEN

ABRUPTLY, VANESSA wrapped her arms around Catty.

"Relax," she ordered.

"Right."

Catty's molecules began spreading outward, and she watched in wonder as her body started to dissolve. Instantly Catty and Vanessa were both invisible, rising above the hallway. They drifted over the heads of the Followers, and continued in an easy flow up the stairwell, through the brightly polished upstairs corridors and then out into the hot afternoon.

Vanessa didn't make them visible again until they were in the back of the building near the freeway, then they became whole. Catty tumbled to the ground.

"Can you take us back now?" Vanessa seemed nervous and tired.

"Sure." Catty stood slowly and smoothed her hands down her body. Her skin still prickled and she felt shaky. She had almost forgotten the manuscript. She picked it off the ground. "How did you make us invisible?"

"It doesn't matter," Vanessa grumbled.

"Tell me." Catty offered Vanessa a hand and pulled her up.

"Okay, but it doesn't mean anything." Vanessa hesitated a moment. "I thought of Michael."

"What?" Catty smirked. "I thought you were through with him."

"I told you it doesn't mean anything," Vanessa argued, but Catty wondered if she was just trying to convince herself. "Just take us back, okay?"

Catty nodded and concentrated. She held the manuscript in one hand and Vanessa's hand in the other. She could feel her power growing. At once the hot afternoon burst away and they were falling into cool blackness. It took a few seconds for Catty's eyes to adjust and by then it was time to fall back into the present. They landed in Catty's backyard.

Catty glanced at her watch. "Sorry. School's over. I hope you didn't have anything important today."

Vanessa lay in the grass with her arms spread. "I don't care right now. I've never been so grateful to be back in the present," she paused. "Those Followers were the creepiest we've ever come across. Why didn't our powers work against them?"

Catty waved the manuscript over her.

Vanessa blinked. "What's that?" She stood and brushed her hands through her hair.

"Come inside, and I'll show you." Catty started across the patio. She opened the sliding glass door and they stepped into the kitchen.

Catty set the manuscript in the middle of the kitchen table. She and Vanessa leaned over it and studied the rich illuminated borders, the enlarged first letter ornamented with interlaced patterns in gold, red, and blue and the detailed miniature within the first letter of someone locking the jaws of hell. The figure looked like a goddess, but there was something disturbing about her eyes. They looked phosphorescent, like the eyes of a Follower in moonlight.

"What does it say?" Vanessa wondered.

Catty ran her finger along the words and tried to translate the Latin. When she couldn't, she looked at Vanessa. "I don't get it. We can speak and understand Latin, so why can't I read it?"

Vanessa pointed to the framed medieval manuscript page that hung on the wall between two of Catty's watercolors. It was Kendra's prized possession. Even though it wasn't a valuable piece, Kendra loved the old Latin script.

"Remember what Kendra said? Old Latin manuscripts are difficult to translate even for scholars because the scribes had their own personal quirks and distinct way of writing, and different regions had their own types of script."

Catty remembered how Kendra became frustrated with the translations until she could get used to each scribe's individual style. But that was also what Kendra liked about translating the old documents; she felt as if she got to know the scribe's personality after studying his work. "I guess it's no wonder I can't read it."

"Hey, maybe Kendra will do it for us," Vanessa suggested.

"Kendra will do what for you?" Kendra walked into the kitchen, holding a pile of newspapers. She dumped them in the paper recycle bin. She was wearing a black sports bra and leggings.

Catty glanced up, happy to see her. On Wednesdays she always closed the shop early. Catty held up the manuscript. "Maybe you can translate this for us."

Kendra took the reading glasses hanging from the chain around her neck, slipped them on, and studied the manuscript. She was awestruck. "How did you get such a priceless piece of work?"

Catty told her about the mysterious stranger. Both Kendra and Vanessa were spellbound. When she finished, Kendra studied the manuscript again.

"This is highly unusual." She took off her reading glasses and tapped them gently in the palm of her hand. "So often in medieval pieces the scribe's work is mechanical, typical of the armies of transcribers who didn't know Latin, but labored in the scriptoriums copying books word by word, letter by letter onto the parchment. But this manuscript is different. I think it might even be older than that."

"What do you mean?" Catty asked.

"There's a fluidity in the lettering at the beginning, but then toward the end, the writing looks more rushed."

"Does it mention the moon?" Vanessa asked.

Kendra nodded. "Yes it does, and it also mentions a curse."

Catty and Vanessa stared at each other. "A curse?" they said together.

Kendra nodded. "There's a curse for anyone who holds the manuscript." She put her reading glasses back on, then looked down and translated the warning. *"To hold the manuscript is to capture misery and death."*

She continued translating the first line. *"The Atrox arose from primal darkness."* She stopped and looked back at Catty and Vanessa. "What in the world is an Atrox?"

Vanessa and Catty exchanged frightened looks. Had the mystery man actually given her something dangerous?

"Atrox," Kendra repeated. "It's probably one of the scribe's little quirks. Some word he either misspells or doesn't know." She glanced at the clock. "Time for my yoga. Will you excuse me?" No matter what was going on, Kendra always stopped for her yoga and meditation. It could be frustrating at times.

Catty waited until she heard Kendra rolling out her mats in the living room, then she turned to Vanessa. "I think we better call Serena and Jimena and take the manuscript to Maggie tomorrow."

Vanessa nodded in agreement.

CHAPTER EIGHT

THE NEXT DAY after school, Catty crawled into the backseat of Jimena's brother's car. Jimena didn't have her driver's license yet but when her brother visited from San Diego, he let her use his '81 Oldsmobile. She had learned how to drive when she was in a gang and jacking cars.

"Why are we going to Westwood?" Catty asked.

"Not Westwood," Serena corrected from the passenger seat. "The Federal Building."

Jimena gripped the steering wheel. "Maggie's taking part in a demonstration," she answered as she pulled away from the curb with a squeal of rubber.

"Yeah," Serena winked. "She said she'd be in the crowd. Just find her."

"What do you suppose she's protesting?" Vanessa wondered.

Jimena zipped the car into the traffic on Doheny. The muffler rumbled against the street with a deep throaty sound that Catty liked.

"They protest everything there," Catty put in. "It's like a party. Kendra says it's a great place to meet people."

"Maybe Maggie's getting lonely and wants to meet some guy," Jimena added with a wry smile.

Serena shook her head. "Maggie's upset that the tuna industry is still harming dolphins."

Jimena eyed Catty in the rearview mirror. "Did you bring the manuscript?"

Catty nodded. "It's in my messenger bag."

"I can't believe we're treating a priceless manuscript like that." Vanessa shook her head.

"We don't know that it's worth anything to anyone but the Atrox." Catty pulled off her sunglasses and then she noticed something different about Vanessa. "You're not wearing your moon amulet."

Serena and Jimena both turned to look at Vanessa. Jimena's eyes shifted back to the road. She buzzed around a bus, then made a sweeping left-hand turn.

Vanessa rubbed a rough patch of red skin on her chest. "It was giving me a rash. Mom said it probably wasn't the amulet but some cream that reacted with the metal."

"You never take it off." Catty looked at her curiously.

Vanessa stared out the window as if she didn't want to continue the conversation. "I know, but I couldn't stand the itching."

Jimena parked in the lot behind the Federal Building. The girls climbed out, and walked toward Wilshire Boulevard. Sunlight filtered through the smoky sky and cast a surreal orange glow across the hot afternoon.

A gathering of people lined the street protesting global warming, abortion, animal rights, and INS violations. A smaller group stood at the edge of the curb, waving placards at passing motorists. Maggie twirled a sign that read SAVE THE DOLPHINS. She was a thin short woman with long gray hair curled into a bun on top of her head. She wore dangling earrings, a flowing orange and purple dress, and a large canvas bag hung from her shoulder. Her temples were beaded with perspiration.

The girls approached her and she hugged each in turn. A man with a full beard stood next to her. He set down his sign and nodded at the girls in greeting.

"You have lovely granddaughters, Maggie." He extended his hand to Catty. "I'm George."

"George is a dear old friend." Maggie looked at him with warm caring eyes. "You'll excuse us for a moment, George?" She handed him her placard and he went back to the curb, holding both signs high in the air.

Maggie threaded through the other protesters. The girls followed after her.

Finally she stopped in the shade near the

building. A security guard eyed them suspiciously.

"Now, my dears, what is going on?" Maggie took a Kleenex from her pocket and patted it across her forehead.

Catty opened her messenger bag and handed the manuscript to Maggie.

Maggie touched the brittle parchment reverentially. "The Secret Scroll," she muttered with amazement.

"You recognize it?" Catty asked.

Maggie nodded, still too stunned to say more. When she was finally able to speak, her voice seemed filled with awe. "I had always thought the existence of the Secret Scroll was only a legend. I never imagined it was real. Tradition maintains that the manuscript was hidden to protect the ultimate secret forever."

"What secret?" Serena asked.

Maggie hesitated. "The Path of the Manuscript," she breathed. "It reveals how to destroy the Atrox."

"How?" Vanessa asked and peered over

Maggie's shoulder as if she could read the spiraling script.

"That's amazing," Catty voiced the excitement for all of them.

"What do we do first?" Jimena asked eagerly.

"Have patience," Maggie warned. "You must not rush forward. Every act has good and evil consequences. I need time to read the manuscript and consider all its possibilities."

"Why was it given to me?" Catty wondered.

Maggie looked at her solemnly. "According to the legend, it would mean that you are the designated heir." Her voice sounded filled with sadness and Catty wondered what Maggie wasn't telling her. Maggie seemed to read her concern. "The heir is the one chosen to follow the Path of the Manuscript."

Catty felt new anxiety take hold. "But how can I follow the Path when I can't even read the manuscript?"

"Don't worry, Catty." Maggie touched her gently. "It wouldn't have been given to you if you weren't up to the task."

The words provided little comfort. Catty knew Maggie was holding back.

"Tell Maggie about the Followers you saw," Jimena reminded her.

Maggie looked up, her eyes questioning.

"They looked older than any Followers I've seen before and they were too perfect-looking," Catty said.

Maggie glanced at her oddly. "What do you mean *perfect-looking*?"

"They looked like they'd just spent an hour in makeup on some movie set. You know, like politicians going on TV for a debate. Every hair in perfect order. Clothes perfectly pressed. They also had this strange electrical aura."

Maggie raised a quizzical eyebrow.

"The room seemed to fill with an electrical charge when they came in," Catty explained. "Their presence even affected the lights."

Maggie nodded in understanding. "Don't be deceived by their appearance. They weren't Followers."

"But I'm positive they were," Catty answered.

"Me, too," Vanessa agreed.

Maggie held up her hand. "They weren't Followers. They were Regulators."

"Regulators," Serena repeated with a worried expression. She tried to hide her concern, but Catty knew it was there. Her relationship with Stanton was forbidden, and the Atrox punished Followers who violated the taboo by sending Regulators to terminate them. Stanton had been willing to risk everything for Serena until he realized he was also putting her in danger.

Maggie looked at Serena as if she knew what she was thinking. "Yes, but I am confident that these Regulators are here for the manuscript. The Atrox wants it destroyed."

"Are you sure?" Serena asked apprehensively.

"The Regulators Catty has described are the fiercest class," Maggie continued. "They are so committed to the Atrox, that their very appearance becomes distorted and twisted by its evil until they look monstrous."

"But they looked perfect." Catty seemed confused.

"Yes, dear." Maggie touched her arm gently. "They looked perfect because they can conceal their hideous appearance. Most choose to appear like distinguished adults because it is easier to gain trust that way. They can just as easily appear as a younger person. But altering their appearance takes tremendous energy and fortunately they are weaker when disguised."

"But what about when they're not disguised?" Jimena wondered.

Maggie sighed. "They are extremely powerful. Their greatest power is their ability to enter dreams."

"Dreams?" Vanessa asked uneasily and pulled at a strand of hair.

Maggie nodded. "These Regulators are free to travel about the dreamland. Every night they scan the dreamscape, searching. In fact, most people have seen them in their dreams but they think they've only had a nightmare."

Catty thought of the number of times she had awakened in the morning and found her lights still blazing because a nightmare had made her too afraid to sleep in the dark. Had the Regulators frightened her? Then she thought of Kendra's dream and another chill passed through her.

"The dream realm is an easy way for the Regulators to find a person who is trying to escape the Atrox," Maggie went on.

"How?" Serena asked uneasily.

"Once in a person's dream, they can scan a person's memories," Maggie explained. "Memories are like fingerprints, unique to the individual, and an infallible way to identify someone. These Regulators can also use dreams to enter a person's conscience and control them."

Maggie studied the manuscript again. "I'm confident that the sudden arrival of these Regulators is somehow associated with the manuscript, even though all Regulators are terrified by it."

"Why would they be afraid of it?" Vanessa asked.

"Because Regulators believe in the manuscript's curse, and yet their allegiance to the Atrox demands that they search for it and destroy it. I don't need to remind you to be alert and careful. The Atrox will do anything to destroy the manuscript. We'll meet after I've had a chance to study it."

"Shouldn't we follow the first step?" Jimena asked.

Maggie smiled. "I admire the way you are always ready to act. But let me spend some time with the manuscript first. After all, I had always believed it was only legend."

Maggie stuffed the manuscript into her canvas bag. She walked away from them and didn't look back.

Jimena sighed. "Let's go over to Westwood and get something to eat."

"I'll catch up with you." Catty suddenly remembered the moon amulet that had belonged to her mother. She ran after Maggie.

Maggie turned and placed a hand on Catty's shoulder.

"I forgot to show you this," Catty announced and pulled the amulet from her pocket. The metal was dull and blackened and didn't reflect the light.

Maggie gasped and tried to cover her reaction.

"Well?" Catty asked impatiently.

"I'm afraid the amulet belongs to a Daughter who turned to the Atrox," Maggie answered.

CHAPTER NINE

CATTY HURRIED AWAY, pushing into the crowd of protesters. She didn't want Maggie to see the tears building in her eyes.

Maggie called after her but she pretended not to hear. When she was sure Maggie wasn't following her, she stopped and glanced down at the amulet in her hand. Now more than ever she wanted to see her mother. She clenched the tarnished silver charm tightly. If she could find a way to go that far back in time, perhaps she could help her.

Catty made an effort to compose herself as

she hurried toward Westwood Village below the UCLA campus. Normally she loved looking at the spires, domes, and minarets on the old buildings but right now she was too busy searching for her friends. She found them sitting around a table at a sidewalk cafe.

Jimena was adjusting her ankle bracelets. She looked unhappy. Serena sipped a glass of water, frowning in concentration. Vanessa nervously bit her fingernails.

Catty sat down. "What's up? I thought everyone would be really excited about the Scroll. It's what we've been waiting for."

"Listen up." Jimena nodded toward Serena.

"I was able to go inside Maggie's mind," Serena said simply.

"You've never been able to read Maggie's thoughts," Catty argued.

"I know," Serena agreed. "I didn't even really mean to, but I guess she was so distracted by the Scroll that her guard was down."

"Tell her what you read," Jimena urged.

"Maggie thinks the manuscript is sending

her to her death," Serena spoke the words slowly.

"No way," Catty exclaimed. "Why would Maggie think she's being sent to her death if the manuscript is the key to destroying the Atrox?"

"She wouldn't," Jimena answered.

"Not unless Maggie has somehow deceived us," Vanessa added quietly.

They stared at her in silence.

"How do you figure that?" Jimena picked up a menu, then set it back on the table with a slap.

Vanessa sipped her water, then finally answered. "Maybe she's really part of the Atrox and has been conning us. If that were true, then if the Atrox is destroyed, she'd be destroyed."

"How could you even think that?" Serena said angrily.

"Think about it," Vanessa stated. "Maggie stops us from acting. I mean, our instincts tell us to do the dangerous thing, but she always cautions against it."

"Because she cares for us," Jimena reminded her.

"And besides," Serena put in. "If we do something that she's asked us not to do, she's never upset. In fact, she usually says that it was exactly what she wanted us to do anyway."

"So maybe she tells us not to do something," Catty suggested, "because she's really testing us to see if we have what it takes."

Vanessa shrugged. "It's a possibility."

"But you're thinking something else." Jimena sounded exasperated.

"Come on," Vanessa continued. "Catty was given the manuscript. She's the only person who can follow the Path, and yet Maggie takes it from her. Shouldn't it stay with Catty?"

"She took it because she's going to study it," Catty protested.

Vanessa started to say something more, but a deep voice interrupted. "Hey, how's my girl?"

They turned. Toby stood behind them. "I didn't know you guys liked to hang out in

Westwood. What are you talking about?"

"It's private," Serena snapped.

Toby smiled. "I could hear you guys arguing all the way inside, so it couldn't have been too private. What's this manuscript that you're talking about?"

"Nothing," Catty and Jimena said together.

Vanessa stood suddenly, and Toby's eyes admired her body. "You look great," he cooed and kissed her cheek.

"Let's go over to the campus." Vanessa took his arm. "I love to walk around there."

"Sure." He tried to pull her closer, but when he did, her hands went automatically to her chest in a protective way as if she were trying to make a barricade between them.

The gesture baffled Catty. Vanessa said she liked him, and yet her body language revealed the opposite.

"I'll call you tonight." Vanessa waved and left with Toby.

Catty watched Vanessa and Toby walk away

arm-in-arm down Westwood Boulevard. She reached for her water and accidentally touched Serena. A spark flew between them. "How'd that happen?"

"Dry, hot weather," Serena remarked blandly.

"I thought it was dry, cold weather," Catty offered.

"Does Toby creep you guys out as much as he does me?" Serena asked.

Catty nodded. "He's cute with that dark goatee and great bod, but his smile makes me uneasy. I don't know why Vanessa likes him so much."

"He's too clean cut," Jimena interrupted. "I like guys who are a little roughed up."

"You better," Serena joked. "Collin always has a peeling nose and sand in his ears."

Jimena laughed. "Yeah, but he's the best-looking guy I've ever met." Collin was Serena's surf rat brother and Jimena's boyfriend. "I'm counting the days until he gets back from Hawaii."

Catty glanced down at her watch. "Could

you give me a ride over to the bookshop? I can't be late again."

Twenty minutes later, Catty pushed through the front door of the Darma Bookstore on Third Street. Brass bells on leather cords tingled in harmony as she closed the door behind her. Books, candles, prayer beads, crystals, and essence oils sat on white shelves in neat arrays.

"Hi, Mom," Catty called. Incense curled sinuously around her and filled the air with a pungent scent.

Kendra glanced at her watch and a smile crossed her face. "Thanks for being on time." She picked up a stack of papers and started for the back door. "What should I pick up for dinner?"

"Anything," Catty answered.

"That's dangerous." Kendra gave her a teasing grin.

"No health food," Catty added. "Something with lots of fat and calories."

"Order pizza, then," Kendra called over her shoulder.

"Sounds good," Catty answered.

After Kendra left, Catty wandered around the bookstore. It always made her feel tranquil. Water bubbled from fountains set in stone planters near the door, and soothing guitar music played from the speakers.

Catty pushed through the blue curtains separating the back room from the store and went into the small kitchen. She sat down at the oak table. A blurred photo of a flying saucer hovering over the Arizona desert hung on the wall next to posters of deep space taken from the Hubble telescope. Kendra thought the pictures would comfort Catty.

Catty pulled out her mother's moon amulet and set it on the table in front of her. She wondered if Maggie was right. Could her mother have turned to the Atrox? Or was there some other reason the amulet was with her mother's belongings? She wished she could go into the past and see her mother right now. Then she remembered what Serena had said about Maggie. Before she could consider it more, the bells hanging on the front door tingled. She put the amulet back in her pocket and walked into the shop.

Chris stood near a counter, looking at a pack of green candles.

"Hi," he called when he saw her.

"I didn't know you were coming by." She felt happy to see him, but she couldn't spend time with him right now. She had too many things she needed to sort out. Plus it was against Kendra's new rules to have guys visit while Catty watched the shop, and she didn't want to chance getting in trouble again.

"I missed you after school," he said with a flirtatious smile. "You didn't stick around."

She was surprised that he had noticed, but she was glad that he had. She shrugged. "I had to go someplace."

"Anywhere special?"

She cocked her head and looked at him. If she hadn't known better, she'd think he was jealous. "Just out," she answered lightly.

"Not with someone else, I hope." He tried to

make it sound like he was teasing, but she sensed his worry.

"Not with another guy, if that's what you mean." She looked at him curiously.

He took her hand. "Is that what you think I mean?"

"Look, I really am busy." She wanted him to leave. What if Kendra suddenly came back? "I have a lot of things I need to do."

He acted like he hadn't heard her. He stepped closer and with the tip of his finger, he turned her face up to his. His breath was sweet and tickled across her cheek. He rested his hands on her shoulders, then slid them down her arms to her elbows. He pulled her to him and placed her hands behind his back.

He draped his arms around her. "I really am sorry about the way I acted at school. Can you just trust me for now?"

"Can't you tell me what's going on?" She glanced at his sensuous lips.

He shook his head. "I want to tell you. I will someday. I promise."

She looked into his alluring eyes. She wanted to believe him. More than anything, and if she were only going by the way her heart felt, she would trust him.

"I really like you." He spoke softly and the words floated around her in a dreamy way. "More than I've ever liked anyone and if you knew everything about me, you'd know that means a lot."

She started to ask him to explain, but before she could he bent down. She thought he was going to kiss her, but he let his lips tease, hovering inches from hers. Their breath mingled. When his lips finally touched hers, a pleasant shock went through her.

All the worries that had been building inside her seemed to vanish and there was only Chris and the sensations of her body. She had imagined so often what it must feel like to kiss a guy, but even in her wildest fantasies a kiss had never felt as good as the ones Chris gave her.

When he pulled back, she opened her eyes quickly and caught a look of intense longing in his eyes, and then it was gone. Was it only her imagination?

"Chris . . ." She started to ask him what was bothering him, but he closed her mouth with another kiss.

CHAPTER TEN

CATTY SAT IN geometry class nervously waiting for Mr. Hall to hand back the test papers. He stepped down the aisle and paused in front of her desk, tapping his toe. He gazed suspiciously at her through the lens of his small black-framed glasses, then set a paper on her desk.

A large red *A* looped across of the top. She tried to pick up the paper but her hands trembled so badly that kids sitting on either side of her were starting to stare. She had been the first one to finish the test the day before, not because she had studied, but because the test questions were a duplicate of the ones on the test found in her mother's belongings.

She stared at the paper and took a deep breath. She wanted to compare the new and old tests, but she knew if she pulled out the old one, Mr. Hall would see and accuse her of cheating.

Finally, she couldn't take the wondering any longer. She grabbed her bag and the new test paper and went up to Mr. Hall's desk.

"Can I have the hall pass?" she whispered.

He scowled and wiped his handkerchief across his nose. "Class just began."

"Girl stuff," she confided in an even lower whisper.

Mr. Hall dug the large wood board from his desk and handed it to her. "Don't lose it this time, Catty."

"I promise I won't." She grinned nervously. How could she ever explain that she had lost the last hall pass somewhere in time?

She hurried from the room. Jimena, Serena, and Vanessa all cast worried looks after her.

In the corridor, she walked quickly past open

doors. Teachers' voices drifted into the hallway after her. She went outside to the back of the school and found a cement bench near the weed-infested corridor between the gym and music building. The rays from the morning sun dusted the side of the stucco wall but did little to warm her. She sat down and spread the first paper in front of her, then searched for the old one in her bag, found it, and smoothed it next to the new one. She let out a long hiss. They were identical. Even the red As were a perfect match.

She stared at the papers for a long time, wondering what it meant. She was about to go back to class when a shadow slid over the papers.

Even as she was turning to see who it was, she could feel her moon amulet pulsing against her chest. Her body became vigilant and tense.

Stanton stood behind her, dressed in black, his shaggy blond hair hanging in his eyes. He was handsome in a dangerous way that made her want to stare forever in his intense blue eyes.

"Catty." His voice sounded annoyed.

"What?" she answered coldly. She grabbed her bag and took a step backward.

Catty often wondered what evil act Stanton had committed to receive the gift of immortality from the Atrox. It didn't matter that Serena liked him. Catty saw him as purely evil. Besides, she never believed that Stanton really cared about Serena. She assumed he was only using her. There was immense competition among Followers for a place of power in the Atrox hierarchy and the biggest prize for any Followers was the seduction of a Daughter of the Moon or the theft of her powers.

She stuffed the two test papers back in her bag and stood to face him. Before she was even aware that his hand had moved, he ripped the bag from her.

"Give it back." She started to reach for it but already he had opened it and was digging inside.

When he didn't find what he wanted, he tossed the bag back to her. "I've been told you possess the Secret Scroll." His voice rumbled with anger. "Where is it?"

Catty felt her body preparing to fight. She

stood taller, anticipating his attack. "Like I'm going to give you that."

"The manuscript belongs to my family," Stanton spoke calmly. She tried not to look in his eyes but it was hard not to stare at their haunting beauty.

"What makes you think it belonged to your family?" she challenged. "I'm the heir."

A darkness seemed to pass over his face. "There was a quest for the Secret Scroll at the end of the thirteenth century. My father found it. It belongs to me now."

Without warning, his mind was in hers before she could deflect it. Her heart beat nervously, but it didn't feel as if he meant to harm her. He seemed to be holding back as if he didn't want to frighten her. Abruptly his memories came in a fast-moving torrent, spinning and swirling around her in an ever increasing speed until she had to reach out and clutch his arm to keep from falling. Finally, the dizzy motion stopped and she focused on one memory.

It opened before her, and Catty hesitatingly

stepped forward. Stanton had once trapped Vanessa in one of his memories but while there she had tried to save a younger Stanton from the Atrox. For that act he could never harm Vanessa, but Catty had no guarantee. Stanton was capable of trapping her forever in his memories. Still, she felt awed by what was happening, but she didn't feel afraid.

She stepped onto a hard floor and almost tripped on an animal skin. Crosses and candles were placed around the small room. Tapestries hung on the stone walls and a fire crackled in a corner. Three men sat around a table that was covered with a delicately woven cloth. Two of the men wore the cowled robe of monks. Catty couldn't see their faces. Then she saw what held their attention. The Secret Scroll lay in the middle of the table.

The third man glanced at the fire. He resembled Stanton. Vanessa had told her that Stanton's father had been a great prince of western Europe during the thirteenth century. He had raised an army to go on a crusade against the Atrox, but then the Atrox had kidnapped Stanton to stop his father.

At first, she couldn't understand their language, but Stanton must have done something, because suddenly she grasped what they were saying.

"My mission has always been to combat evil by force of arms." Stanton's father spoke quietly. "Not by prayers." His voice was gentle and kind, and it stirred something inside of Catty.

"The Path of the Manuscript is the only way," said one of the monks.

Stanton's father nodded. "I've already chosen my path." He walked to the fireplace and stared at the flames. "But the manuscript must be guarded until an heir is found. Someone of pure heart who can fight the Atrox if I fail." He turned back suddenly and faced the monks again. "And even if the Atrox takes me, you are not to exchange the manuscript for my freedom."

The monks nodded again.

Stanton's father continued, "I have two sons.

One surely will survive and when he is of age you will give the manuscript to him."

The monks turned toward the corner of the room. Seated on a tall chair sat a small boy with blond hair. She knew he must be Stanton at a younger age. Even then his blue eyes were alluring. He looked frightened by what was going on around him.

"We've already named a keeper for the manuscript," the one monk asserted. "A knight who is strong and noble, and will risk his life to guard it."

Stanton's father sat back at the table. "That is all then."

The monks wrapped the parchment in a leather pouch and slowly left the room.

The memory began to fade, but Catty didn't want to leave this man. She wanted to talk to him. The edges of her vision shimmered, and then she was back in La Brea High facing Stanton.

"Now you see that it is mine," he said bluntly. "And I expect its return."

Catty shook her head and took one step away from him. "I was given the manuscript—"

"Its curse brings horrible danger to its owner," he warned. "Are you prepared for that?"

She hadn't really thought about the curse. Both Maggie and Kendra had mentioned it, but it had seemed more superstition than reality until now.

"It's not real?" She had meant for the words to form a statement but instead it sounded like a question.

"Throughout its history the manuscript has cursed its possessor."

Catty hesitated. Was that why Maggie had seemed so frightened by the manuscript?

"The Daughters of the Moon should stay as far away from the Secret Scroll as possible," Stanton cautioned.

Catty considered his warning, but she didn't trust Stanton, so how could she believe anything he told her? "You only want the manuscript so you can turn it over to the Atrox and win a place of honor in the Inner Circle."

"Inner Circle," Stanton repeated with obvious

disdain. "How little you know." His mouth opened as if he were going to say more, but then he turned his head, seeming to sense something.

He reached for Catty and she took a quick step away from him.

"Come with me," he ordered and held out his hand.

"I'm not going anywhere with you," Catty answered.

"I warned you," he said, and then he slipped around the music building and peeked back at her. "Hurry. Can't you feel it?"

She clutched her bag against her chest. There was an unusual stillness in the air. "What's happening?"

"The Regulators." He motioned for her to join him. "Come on, we have to escape into time."

She shook her head. "Why should I take you back in time and save you? I don't care if Regulators terminate you. It's just one less Follower I have to worry about."

"You understand nothing." The scorn in his voice made her hesitate. "There's still time," he continued. "Take us back to the day you were abandoned on the side of the road."

Catty felt a chill pass through her. "How do you know I was abandoned?" Then she remembered Serena and felt suddenly irritated. How many secrets had Serena shared with him?

Footsteps pounded on the cement behind her. She turned. The three Regulators from the coroner's office walked toward her. She glanced the other way and saw Stanton disappear down the corridor.

"Wait for me," she whispered and started running. When she was at the end of the corridor, she looked for Stanton.

He grabbed her hand and pulled her into the boy's restroom, then into one of the stalls. She was pushed up against him.

"Take us back," he ordered.

"You don't understand," Catty confessed. "I've never been able to time-travel that far back without getting stuck."

Footsteps sounded near the bathroom door.

"Take my hand," Stanton ordered.

"Why?" she asked.

"We have no time left." He held out his hand. "Do you want to escape?"

She stared at Stanton. Could she trust him?

CHAPTER ELEVEN

CATTY TOOK STANTON'S hand and his tremendous power surged through her. The bathroom stall wavered, then broke apart before exploding into a flash of white light. Stanton's hand clasped hers tightly, and they were sucked into the tunnel. His speed was much greater than hers. The free fall made her stomach ripple and she had difficulty breathing. She now knew why Vanessa hated time travel. Catty couldn't pull air into her lungs and at the moment when she thought she might pass out, they fell from the tunnel back into time.

Stanton landed on his feet, but Catty skidded across scorched dusty ground. She lay in the hot sand, gasping for air. Stanton paced, his shadow brushing back and forth over her. The blazing sun stung her arms and face.

Suddenly she sat up with a jerk. Tall spiny cacti surrounded her.

She stood abruptly in spite of her dizziness and wiped the sand and dirt from her face. She took an awkward step backward and surveyed the vast landscape. Wisps of black smoke came from a nearby arroyo. She ran to the edge of the craggy embankment and peered over. The air was filled with the stench of burning rubber and oil.

The charred skeleton of a crashed car sat on the rocky bottom. The sight jogged a memory. She remembered the crash and the fire. Only now she realized she hadn't been inside the car, but outside watching from the ledge as she was now.

Stanton gently touched her arm and pointed.

Her heart caught. There she was at age six,

wandering down the highway in her sandals, baggy red shorts, and a large floppy hat that kept trying to blow off her head.

Tears burned into her eyes. Stanton put his hand on her shoulder as the tears fell down her cheeks.

"Stanton," a voice called with sudden urgency.

Catty sucked in her breath. "My mother?"

"Yes," he said.

Her heart beat crazily. She turned slowly.

A slender woman with large brown eyes and thick sun-kissed hair walked toward them. She wore cutoff jeans and a man's white T-shirt. Her knees and hands were scraped and bleeding.

"Stanton," her mother repeated.

"She knows you?" Catty glanced at Stanton. How could her mother know him?

"Please, Stanton." Her mother pointed to the smaller Catty walking in the distance. "Take my daughter's memories from her so she'll be safe."

"I can't, Zoe," he whispered.

Catty glanced from Stanton to her mother.

He even knew her name. How was that possible?

"Please," Zoe pleaded again. "If she has no memories, the Regulators won't be able to find her. You must save her."

In spite of the heat, Catty began trembling. Why had Regulators been after her when she was only a child?

Stanton stared off at the younger Catty walking down the roadway.

"Do you want what happened to you, to happen to her?" Zoe spoke in a low tone. "She's only a child like you were."

Stanton hesitated, then took three steps forward. Catty watched his eyes focus and narrow.

"Thank you." Zoe sighed with relief and closed her eyes.

"It's done." Stanton turned back and Zoe seemed to relax then.

"Maybe now she'll even be able to live a normal life." Zoe wiped at her eyes.

Catty heard the whisper of tires on the hot

pavement and turned. Kendra's old Impala pulled to the side of the road. She couldn't hear what Kendra was saying to the younger Catty, but she knew she was asking Catty if she was okay.

Catty watched Zoe's reaction. "Be good to her," Zoe whispered, and then she fell against Stanton.

Little Catty climbed into the car with Kendra.

"Why aren't they leaving?" Zoe asked nervously.

"Be patient, Zoe," Stanton murmured.

Catty climbed over several boulders and perched on the top of a small hill so she could watch both her mother and Kendra's car.

The sun was at a lower angle and the saguaro cacti cast long shadows across the desert floor when Kendra's car finally pulled away. Catty climbed down from her perch on the hill. Her face prickled with the feel of sunburn.

"She's safe now." Zoe blinked away the tears forming in the corner of her eyes. She turned to

Stanton with a smile that did little to conceal her sadness. Then she seemed to notice Catty for the first time.

"Who's your friend?" Zoe asked Stanton. She glanced at Catty's moon amulet and then her eyes bore into Catty's.

"Zoe," Stanton said. "I want you to meet your daughter."

Zoe glanced at Stanton in disbelief, then stared at Catty in openmouthed wonder. Her hand reached out and caressed Catty's cheek, touched her lips, and smoothed back her hair. "I see your father in your face," she uttered more to herself than to Catty. Then a slight smile crossed her lips. "I give you away and you return to me the same day. At least I know you do make it safely into the future." She started to embrace Catty.

Catty closed her eyes waiting for her mother's hug. She had imagined this so many times—but Zoe pulled back suddenly.

"This is too dangerous," she declared, and new anxiety filled her eyes. "You must leave. The

Regulators are always watching me."

Then she turned to Stanton. "Why did you bring her here?"

Catty glanced at Stanton and wondered if it had been a trap after all.

"I wanted you to tell her about the Secret Scroll," Stanton replied smoothly.

"She's received it already?" Zoe asked and seemed surprised; then her shoulders slumped in anguish, and she raked her fingers through her hair. "How can that be?"

Catty wondered why her mother was so distressed.

Zoe's eyes nervously studied the horizon. "You must take her back before the Regulators come."

"But . . ." Catty began. "Why have Regulators always been after me? I thought Regulators only terminated Followers who rebelled against the Atrox, or didn't follow the Atrox's orders? What would they want with me?"

Zoe scanned the desert, then turned back to

Catty. "There's no time for me to explain now. Give me your address and I'll find you in the future. That's the best I can do."

Catty fumbled in her bag for a piece of paper, found one, pulled it out, and scribbled her name and address across the top. She handed the paper to her mother.

"I'll find you, later, when it's safe. I promise." She hugged Catty, then gently pushed her back to Stanton. "Take her now."

Catty looked at the paper in her mother's hands and with a shock realized she had written her name and address on today's geometry test paper.

Stanton grabbed her wrist and the air shimmered.

"Wait," Catty yelled. She reached into her bag and pulled out the blackened moon amulet and gave it to her mother. "Here."

"You have it?" Her mother seemed shocked. "I thought it had been taken from me." She held it tenderly and fastened it around her neck.

Catty smiled at her. "See you in the future."

Her mother looked up and smiled back. "See you."

Stanton reached for Catty's hand and his energy rushed through her.

Her mother looked desperate. "Don't trust Maggie," Zoe yelled after them and then she mouthed, "I love you," as her face contorted with sadness.

The desert landscape wiggled, then broke apart as if it were a sheet of glass. They were whisked into the tunnel as an explosion of brilliant light filled the air. Catty squinted her eyes, emotions roiling through her. She thought about her mother and then about Maggie. Why would her mother tell her not to trust Maggie?

They landed on a quiet street near Catty's house. It was already dark and the only sound was that of sprinklers watering a nearby lawn. Stanton caught her before she fell to the ground.

"So now you know that the Scroll has put you in grave danger," Stanton stated.

Catty nodded.

"If you'll give it to me," he offered, "you'll be safe."

Catty couldn't bring herself to trust him. "Why aren't you afraid of the curse?"

He smiled bitterly. "Because I am already cursed."

The words chilled her. She almost felt sorry for him.

"My offer stands," he whispered and then he dissolved into shadow.

She stood in the darkness and wondered why he so desperately wanted the manuscript if not to give it to the Atrox. Still he didn't seem as bad as she had once thought. She could almost understand why Serena liked him so much.

Catty wondered what it was that made her mother trust Stanton. She held the memory of her mother's face in her mind and started walking home.

A few minutes later, Catty brushed against the pink oleanders that grew in front of their redwood fence. She crossed the porch as a gentle breeze stirred and the wind chimes tingled.

She opened the door, went inside, and locked the door behind her. She had expected Kendra to be waiting for her, having fits because she hadn't gotten home in time to watch the store, but the house was as silent as a tomb and dark, except for the light coming through the windows from the street lamps.

For just a fleeting second she felt as if Stanton hadn't transported them far enough into the future and that she could run up the stairs as she had when she was younger and find Kendra in bed, reading. Then Kendra would run her bathwater and she could fall into her own bed without a worry. She wished things were still that easy.

She sighed and walked into the kitchen. She switched on the overhead lights. The clock read nine o'clock.

She reached for the telephone to call Vanessa. Her mother answered.

"Is Vanessa there?" Catty spoke into the receiver.

"Hi, Catty," Vanessa's mother greeted her.

"Vanessa's at the party with Toby. Aren't you going?"

Catty had forgotten the party.

The doorbell rang. She knew that it would be Chris.

CHAPTER TWELVE

CATTY OPENED THE door. Chris smiled at her. He smelled of spicy aftershave and looked cuter than ever.

"I've been trying to call you all afternoon." He walked into the house and handed her a bouquet of red roses.

"Thanks." As they walked into the kitchen, she breathed in the scent of the roses.

In the brighter light he glanced at her, then took a longer look, lingering on her clothes and feet. An odd expression crossed his face. She suddenly became aware that she was covered with desert dust, sunburned, and sweating. She could only imagine what she must look like. She touched her cheek and wondered if it was still covered with sand.

"I've been working in the yard," she lied and took a vase from under the sink.

"At nine o'clock at night?" he asked with a wry smile.

She ran water into the vase. "Chris, I really can't go to the party with you tonight."

He leaned over the breakfast bar and smiled at her. This time she noticed his clean, even teeth, so white and healthy as if he had been eating apples all his life. She wanted to kiss him but instead she turned away.

"Why not?" he asked. "All you need to do is take a quick shower. You don't have to dress up. No one is."

She slipped the flowers into the water and set the vase on the counter. "I feel too tired. And I just need time to think. Don't you ever want to be alone sometimes?"

"Sure." He stepped around the counter and stopped close to her. She glanced up and saw herself reflected in his pupils. His fingers played on her shoulders.

"I'd like to be alone with you," he whispered slowly. "We could stay here and watch videos." His hands smoothed down her arms and then he held both of her hands. He didn't seem to mind that they were dirty.

"That's not what I had in mind," she answered.

"But I don't want you to miss the party." His words rustled across her right ear. He took one more step and this time he was close enough to kiss her. His thigh rubbed against hers. She shivered with pleasure.

"Please come." The word fell on her ears like a caress and he looked at her in a dreamy sort of way that made her feel giddy. "Come to the party with me, Catty."

He leaned over and traced one finger gently over her chin and down her throat. She leaned back and let him kiss her.

"Come to the party," he said between his kisses.

She hated to think that she was the kind of girl who would do things just because she liked the way a guy kissed her.

Finally, she pulled away from him. "I'll take a quick shower."

"Great." He grinned.

They drove over to the hills in Brentwood. The smoky smell from the fires was stronger here, and Catty's eyes burned. Finally, at the top of the hill, Chris pulled his battered Volvo to the curb and got out. Catty heard the music as she stepped from the car. Chris took her hand and they walked up to a huge house with massive columns and an ornate iron fence.

"Whose house is it?" she asked as they walked through the front room.

"Jerome's," Chris answered. "The guy who plays drums in the marching band. His uncle's an entertainment lawyer."

She followed Chris through French doors that led to a large patio. It was already crowded with kids dancing. On the other side of the pool, a band played on a cement terrace. A heavy metal band hammered out notes with complete recklessness. Kids in black pressed against the platform, head-banging in time to the hard rock music.

"The music will change soon," Chris spoke into her ear. "Then we can dance."

She leaned against Chris. She liked the feel of his arm around her waist. Now she was glad she had come to the party.

She started to say *Let's go look at the view,* when Chris suddenly withdrew his arm.

"What's wrong?" she asked.

He shook his head but he didn't look at her. His eyes searched through the crowd of dancers, jostling around them. She followed his look and wondered if he had recognized someone.

"Listen." He took a quick step away from her. "Would you like something to eat?"

She shook her head. "I'm fine."

But he was already stepping away from her. "I'll just get us a couple of Cokes." He turned and left her without looking back.

She sighed and sat down on a patio chair that had been moved out to the grass under the jacaranda trees. Chris ran around the pool and across the lawn to a metal table that was piled high with soft drinks and ice. He took two Cokes, but instead of coming back to her, he went inside the house.

She wondered briefly what he was doing. She sat back and waited impatiently. By the time Chris returned, the heavy metal band had finished playing and three guys from La Brea High took the terrace and started rapping. Their footwork was fast. Their right arms punched down as their left legs kicked back.

"Here."

She turned back. Chris handed her a Coke, then sat on the lawn next to her chair. He opened a napkin filled with cookies.

"Try a cookie," he offered and bit into an oatmeal raisin.

She hesitated a moment, then spoke clearly, "Chris, maybe you should just take me home."

"Home?" He looked wounded.

"Well, you're not acting like you want to be with me or you wouldn't have run off as soon as we got here."

"I thought you'd want something to eat," he protested.

"I told you I didn't."

"I want to spend the evening with you," he explained. "Why else would I have asked you? I thought we could have a good time." But even as he spoke, his eyes started scanning the kids standing around the terrace.

"Look," Catty continued. "I don't want to share you with anyone else."

His eyes shot back to her.

"You're always looking around like you're afraid someone is going to see us together. That means only one thing to me."

"What?" He looked confused.

"That you have another girlfriend."

He looked at her in disbelief. "Thanks," he whispered.

"Thanks?" she repeated. Now it was her turn to feel surprised. "What do you mean, *thanks*?"

"Thanks because it means you think we shouldn't see other people." He looked happy.

"I didn't say that," she protested.

"But it implies you want us to be exclusive."

"I said I didn't want to share you." She thought a moment, then smiled. "Okay, it means exclusive, but something has been bothering you. You've been acting so—"

He jumped up. "I'll be right back," he interrupted. "I forgot to get pizza." He ran toward the house.

Catty cursed. It had been a big mistake to come to the party. She should have stayed home as she had originally planned. She looked up.

Jimena and Serena walked through the back gate on the other side of the pool. They were dressed in leather like biker chicks. Serena had on platform boots, a tight-fitting motorcycle jacket, and a mini. Jimena wore studded ankle boots, a bareback leather halter top, and a hip-hugging matching skirt.

Catty pushed through the crowd of kids dancing near the edge of the pool and joined them.

"Where'd you get the clothes?" she asked.

"Vanessa's mom," Serena answered. "You should have come."

Vanessa's mother worked as a costume designer for the movies. She wore clothes before anyone even knew they were in style. That was her job. She had to be a year or two ahead of everyone else. Sometimes it embarrassed Vanessa to have a mother so overly trendy. But Catty loved to go over to their house and try on her mother's designs.

"I wish I could have." Catty admired the slinky outfits. "But I went back in time. I need to talk to all of you about it. It's really important. Where's Vanessa?"

"Check it out." Jimena motioned to the patio where kids were dancing.

In the middle of the bobbing bodies, Vanessa moved sinuously against Toby. She wore a black leather skirt with a long slit up the side and a cropped leather jacket. Her midriff was bare and looked incredibly good with the gold chains that hung around her waist.

"Vanessa," Catty gasped.

Serena stared at Vanessa. "What do you think?"

"Since when does she dress like that?" Catty asked. Vanessa always dressed stylishly, but conservatively. "This is very un-Vanessa."

"Toby picked it out for her," Jimena put in.

Vanessa rolled her head and looked up at Toby. Maybe she did like him, Catty thought.

Toby's fingers kept running over her bare waist, and whenever he pulled her close to him his lips moved to her cheek as if they were sharing secrets. Still, Catty couldn't erase the feeling that something was wrong. Vanessa kept looking away.

Catty glanced around the room and found Michael. He was watching Vanessa and he wasn't even bothering to hide his jealousy. Other girls were coming up to him and flirting with him, but his eyes kept going back to her.

The music stopped, and Vanessa ran over to them.

"So where were you?" Vanessa asked. "You missed all the fun."

"I went back to see my mother," Catty announced.

The girls stared at her in disbelief.

Jimena was the first to speak. "Let's go back by the refreshment table," Jimena suggested. "So we can talk in private."

"How did you go back that far?" Serena asked as they walked past a row of azalea bushes.

"Stanton took me," Catty replied.

"Stanton?" Serena's eyes widened. "You saw him? Is he okay?"

Catty nodded. "He's fine. He helped me escape the Regulators and then get back to see my mother."

Serena smiled sadly. "I'm glad he's okay." But her expression told Catty that she also still missed him.

When they were next to the metal table, Jimena picked up a Pepsi and snapped the top, then turned to Catty. "So what happened?"

Catty told them everything about the afternoon. Serena kept interrupting to ask more questions about Stanton, but finally Catty finished. Then she hesitated and added, "I think it was a mistake to give the manuscript to Maggie."

"Why?" Vanessa looked surprised and worried.

Catty spoke carefully. "Just as I was leaving my mother told me not to trust Maggie."

"Maybe you didn't hear her correctly," Serena offered.

Catty shook her head. "I know that's what she said."

Jimena pondered. "But I trust Maggie."

"Me, too," Catty said. "But I'm worried. I want to get the manuscript back from her."

Jimena shook her head. "It's better if we leave it with Maggie."

"Why?" Catty asked.

"Because," Jimena said slowly. "I had a premonition."

"What did you see?" Vanessa asked.

Jimena stared at Catty. "I saw Catty destroy the manuscript."

Catty gasped. "Me? Are you sure? But I'm the heir."

Jimena nodded gravely.

"Your premonitions aren't always how they appear," Serena suggested. "So maybe it's not as bad as it seems."

Catty looked at Jimena. She believed Jimena, but she had a strange feeling of intuition of her own. She felt something treacherous in the air and somehow it was associated with the manuscript and Maggie.

"But." Vanessa was thinking as she spoke. "If the manuscript is evil it needs to be destroyed."

"What do you mean evil?" Serena asked. "If it's supposed to help us destroy the Atrox, it can't be evil."

"But we don't know if that's true yet," Vanessa argued. "We don't really know anything about the manuscript or the guy who gave it to Catty."

"He didn't seem evil," Catty explained, thinking of the mysterious guy. "He seemed . . ." She searched for a word. "Magnanimous."

"What if the Path is actually a fraud?" Vanessa pointed out. "Maybe it's a trick from the Atrox."

"What's the Atrox?" a voice said.

They stopped talking and turned. Toby stood behind them, smiling and sipping on a Coke. Had he been listening to their entire conversation?

Catty glared at Vanessa and pulled her to the other side of the table. Serena and Jimena followed. Toby leaned against the fence and watched them. "Why is your boyfriend always eavesdropping on our conversations?" Catty demanded.

"He's not." Vanessa seemed indignant. "He's just trying to be friendly."

"You were complaining about Michael not giving you space," Catty accused. "Toby doesn't even let you breathe."

"Well, if you like Michael so much," Vanessa answered coldly, "then you date him."

"Catty's not the only person who's getting bugged by the way Toby is always around," Serena added.

"Look," Vanessa explained. "Just give him a chance. I feel really connected to him."

Serena and Jimena exchanged surprised looks.

"Vanessa." Catty hesitated before continuing. "To everyone else, it seems like you still like Michael. You're always looking to see where he is—"

Vanessa shook her head. "I like Toby. I can't get him out of my mind."

"Hey, are you talking about me?" Toby was beside them again. How had he crept up so quietly?

The new band began to play a swing tune.

Toby took Vanessa's hand. "Let's go show them what we learned in class."

"Okay," Vanessa squealed. "Come on. You guys gotta come back to the patio so you can see what I can do now."

As they started back, Catty's hand brushed against the table. A spark connected between her fingers and the metal edge of the table. Her hand shot back in surprise. "Weird," she muttered to herself.

"Look at Vanessa." Jimena pointed.

Toby and Vanessa started dancing the Lindy. Vanessa turned beneath Toby's raised arm, then he pulled her close against his body before he swung her out again. They kicked sideways. Toby grabbed Vanessa, hooked her over his arm, and she seemed to fly over his back.

Kids applauded.

"Can you believe it?" Serena asked.

"She looks good," Catty agreed.

"Not her dancing," Serena explained. "I'm talking about the retro underwear she's wearing. Garters and all. So extremely cool."

Jimena laughed. "I guess love has really changed her."

"The only person Vanessa is fooling is herself," Catty said.

CHAPTER THIRTEEN

CATTY BACKED AWAY from the crowd and edged to the side of the house. The noise and music pounded through her head. Maybe it was the heat or the smoky smell from the lingering fires, because she didn't feel well. She wanted to go home, but she didn't see Chris anywhere and she didn't feel like walking or trying to catch a bus.

She strolled over wide stone steps, slipped past a hedge of oleanders and found a small rose garden that looked out over the city. Streetlights made a geometric pattern across the land below.

She sat on a small wrought-iron bench, breathed in deeply, and glanced at the moon.

She rubbed her forehead against the pain starting to spread through her head and tried to put everything that had happened that day in order. She was just starting to relax when a rustle of grass behind her made her start.

When the stealthy sound repeated, her head whipped around but a gloved hand stopped her.

"Don't look back." It was the voice of the mysterious man from the coroner's office.

Her heart raced. She hadn't known how badly she had wanted him to visit her again until she heard his voice. She wondered if she could actually be falling for a guy she didn't really know.

"Why haven't you acted?" His voice sounded angry and she caught something familiar in it. She concentrated, trying to identify it. "You're supposed to follow the Path of the manuscript."

"I gave the manuscript to someone," she explained.

"What?" Again she detected something in the voice that she had heard before, but where?

"I gave the manuscript to someone who guides me—" She tried to justify herself.

"You were never supposed to give it away. Don't you understand how dangerous that is?" Then his voice softened. "No, it's my fault. I should have explained more to you."

"What should you have explained?"

"I gave the manuscript to you because you are the heir, not someone else." His voice soothed her and she wondered if she was ever going to see his face. Then he continued, "The Secret Scroll can be dangerous in another person's hands."

"I'll get it back," Catty said with determination. "I promise."

"Good." He paused and she felt he wanted to say something more. She waited with rising anticipation but then his footsteps whispered through the grass behind her.

She knew he was leaving and she turned quickly, but he was gone.

"There you are." Chris brushed the oleanders aside, stumbled through the rosebushes, and sat on the bench next to her.

In the darkness she couldn't see the expression on his face clearly, but she hoped he couldn't see the irritation on hers.

She sighed and looked back at the moon, thinking about the mystery guy. Everything about him appealed to her. She was sure she could talk to him about all the things that had happened to her today. It was hard not being able to share those things with Chris.

"A penny for your thoughts." Chris rested his arm around her waist.

"Nothing." She shrugged.

"Tell me," he whispered.

She slowly shook her head.

"The way you're looking at the moon I'd say you have something really important on your mind."

"Maybe," she replied. "Can you take me home?"

She sensed his disappointment, but she didn't see any reason to stay. He'd just keep making excuses to leave her alone. Besides, she wanted to be home so she could think through her problems.

"Okay," he answered softly.

Chris walked her back through the party. As they started into the house, Jimena and Serena ran up to them and pulled her away from Chris.

"What did you decide?" Jimena asked.

"I'm going to leave the manuscript with Maggie," Catty lied. "You're right. It's safer if we let her keep it."

She hoped they couldn't read the lie in her words.

CHAPTER FOURTEEN

The next morning, Catty awoke to the ringing telephone. She let the answering machine pick up. It was Vanessa, and her voice sounded anxious. Catty debated picking up the receiver, then decided against it. She had her own plans for the day. Maybe it was better if she didn't speak to Vanessa yet. Besides, she thought Vanessa probably only wanted to talk about Toby.

Chris called twice while she dressed in jeans and a comfy sweater. She didn't wait to hear his messages but left the house and walked down to the bus stop.

She rode the bus over to Cedars-Sinai Hospital, got off, and walked west on Alden Street until she came to Maggie's apartment. She nervously buzzed the security panel and wondered what she would say if Maggie answered. When Maggie's voice didn't come over the intercom, she knew she was in luck.

She randomly pressed five buzzers. Two voices answered.

"I locked myself out again," she lied and hoped no one inside would bother to come down to the entrance and see who it was.

Before she had even finished the sentence a loud hum opened the magnetic lock.

"Thanks," she yelled over her shoulder. She opened the door, hurried inside, and crossed the mirrored lobby. She kept her face down away from the security cameras although she doubted Maggie would ever report her crime to authorities. She stepped onto the elevator and pressed a button. The metal doors closed and the elevator carried her up to the fourth floor. The door opened with a loud grate that set her on edge.

Her heart pounded as she got off the elevator and walked down the narrow balcony that hung over a courtyard four stories below. A hummingbird hovered over the ivy growing around the iron railing.

She glanced behind her, then quickly removed the screen from the front window and set it aside. She pressed her hands flat against the glass and pushed upward and over. It worked. She'd learned that trick in sixth grade when she had been locked out of her own house.

Catty lifted one leg over the sill, then climbed in, closing and locking the window behind her. She walked quickly through the apartment and then back to the front door. After looking both ways, she hurried outside to the window and replaced the screen before going back into Maggie's apartment. She closed the door and rested against it, trying to will her heart to slow its beat.

The apartment loomed before her. It seemed so ordinary without its magical inhabitant. The walls were a grayish white and the lace panels hung lifeless over the sliding glass door that led to a private balcony. Maggie had no electrical appliances so there was no hum of a refrigerator or air conditioner.

She stepped down the narrow hallway and started exploring. She turned into the living room and a reflection in the mirror over the fireplace startled her. What she saw worried her. Her moon amulet was glowing. Why would it be glowing in Maggie's apartment? Was it trying to warn her of some danger? She looked quickly around the apartment. The air seemed to become thicker and then she heard a soft clicking of metal. She turned sharply around. The sound came from the front door. She took three steps back as the doorknob slowly began to turn. She pressed against the wall and peered around the corner.

Maggie entered the apartment followed by the same Regulators who had been at the coroner's office.

Catty jerked her head back and covered her

mouth as an involuntary gasp came from her throat.

"Come in then," Maggie spoke in a dry voice. Catty didn't detect any fear in her speech. "It will only be a moment."

Maggie's footsteps started down the short hallway, the three Regulators following silently. It would only be seconds before she turned and saw Catty.

Catty glanced quickly around, looking for a place to hide. They were so close now, she could hear the labored breathing of one of the Regulators. She hurried toward a corridor that led from the living room. She waited there and tried to regain her composure.

The air around her began to prickle with the feel of static electricity.

She would have to time-travel if she was going to escape, but she didn't know if she could focus her thoughts. She pictured the tunnel and tried to concentrate. Power surged in her brain. Her surroundings began to blur and waver as her eyes dilated. She glanced down at her watch. The hand started to move backward. She felt relief flow through her and then suddenly the hands on her watch stopped. She blinked, then concentrated and tried again. Her head throbbed, but nothing happened.

"Damn," she muttered and took three long breaths to calm herself and tried again. But all she succeeded in doing was giving herself a headache.

She had to do something. A sound made her alert. Was one of them coming to the corridor? She glanced warily at a closed door. She didn't know Maggie's apartment, but whatever lay inside couldn't be as dangerous as waiting until she was discovered.

She put her hand on the knob, twisted it cautiously, and winced as the spring latch scraped softly. With great care, she pushed the door opened, entered the room, and closed it behind her.

The room was empty except for a small ornately carved table in the corner. The manuscript sat on top of the table. She walked over to it and picked it up.

She was deep in thought when behind her, she heard the soft sound of a latch releasing. She dropped the manuscript, jerked around, and stared at the turning doorknob.

CHAPTER FIFTEEN

RESIGNED, CATTY WATCHED the door slowly open.

No one was there.

She let out a sigh of relief. Maybe a draft had opened the door or perhaps she hadn't closed it securely.

She leaned back against the wall and then watched in amazement as the door languidly swung shut.

A dusty cloud formed in front of her, then thickened. Vanessa became visible.

"Vanessa," Catty whispered in astonishment.

"What are you doing here?"

Vanessa glanced cautiously at the door, then walked over to Catty and spoke in hushed tones. "We've been watching you."

"We?"

"Serena read your mind last night at the party," Vanessa continued in a low voice. "She knew you'd decided to sneak into Maggie's apartment to steal back the manuscript. So we decided we'd try to talk you out of it. I called this morning but I guess you'd already left to come here."

Catty remembered Vanessa's early-morning call. "But why did you sneak inside the apartment?" Catty asked. "Don't you know how risky that was?"

"Just as we drove up we saw Maggie and the Regulators." Vanessa nervously brushed her hands through her hair. "We knew if you were inside, you were going to be in big trouble."

Catty looked at her friend with appreciation. "Let's get out of here then. Do you think you can make me invisible?"

"I'll do my best."

Catty walked over to the table and picked up the manuscript. "You'll have to make this invisible, too." Catty held it up. "No way am I leaving it here for Maggie to give to the Regulators."

"I can't believe she'd actually betray us." Vanessa said sadly. "Well, at least we know."

Vanessa put both arms around Catty. Almost immediately the change started. Soon, Catty's feet, legs, and arms elongated and became like clouds of coarse sand. Then she disappeared entirely. She felt Vanessa lightly guiding her, but it was more a sensation of the softest breeze. She loved the lightness of being invisible and the way she could float on the air or spin and twirl with a breeze.

They stopped at the door. Vanessa had learned how to move objects while she was invisible. The door swung open and then they flowed from the room into the corridor.

She followed Vanessa up to the ceiling, and they fluttered over the heads of Maggie and the Regulators.

Catty could feel Vanessa's heartbeat accelerate.

The Regulators seemed suddenly tense and alert as if they could hear it.

She felt the pull of gravity and then she knew what was happening. Vanessa had become too nervous again.

Catty looked in front of her. Vanessa was becoming dense.

Then she glanced down sharply. The molecules of her hand were swirling into formation. Any second she would become too heavy for Vanessa to hold and she'd fall, right on top of the Regulators.

Her molecules began to connect one by one. If the Regulators happened to look up, they'd see a hazy partially formed girl floating above them.

She felt Vanessa tug at her, and then she sensed herself tumbling, head over heels. When she was able to look up again she was at the door, her molecules re-forming rapidly.

"What's that?" one of the Regulators asked.

"What?" Maggie's voice seemed unperturbed. "I didn't hear anything."

A chair pushed back. "Yes, something at the

door. I'll see what it was."

Then another chair scraped back. "I'll check," Maggie announced. "This is an apartment building after all. Noises aren't that unusual."

Maggie's footsteps sounded on the floor.

Catty froze. "Do something!"

"I'm trying," Vanessa shot back in a low voice.

"Come on," Catty glanced down. She was no more than a cloud of dancing dust. She tried to concentrate to make herself invisible again, but it was no use. It required Vanessa's power.

As Maggie turned the corner, Vanessa opened the door a crack and she and Catty rippled outside onto the balcony.

The door started to swing open behind them, and Catty's heart sunk. They were completely solid now and there was nowhere to hide. They couldn't even pretend that they had just stopped by to visit, because Catty held the manuscript in her hands.

Chapter Sixteen

SUDDENLY, VANESSA grabbed Catty and plunged over the railing. Startled, Catty clutched for the iron banister. She caught a handful of ivy and fell. Just as she was about to scream, her molecules spread and melded with the air. Invisible again, she and Vanessa swirled up in a lazy curl, then drifted gently down and landed safely on the ground.

Vanessa dropped her hold and Catty's molecules collided together in icy pain. The manuscript flapped crazily in her hands as tiny specks pulled tightly into place.

"Sorry." Vanessa rubbed her arms.

Catty looked back up at the balcony. "Don't ever do that again," she said in a raspy voice.

"I had no choice," Vanessa answered, looking somewhat pleased with her powers. "Did you want Maggie to see you?"

"What if you hadn't made us invisible in time?" Catty pointed out. "We'd be splattered all over the patio."

Vanessa had a smug smile on her face. "But I *did* make us invisible in time." Then her smile faded. "What are we going to do about Maggie?

Catty shook her head. "I don't know."

Vanessa started walking. "We better tell Jimena and Serena."

They went outside, then turned the corner. Jimena was resting on the hood of the car. Serena was pacing on the sidewalk.

"Well?" Jimena sat up.

Vanessa shook her head. "It's not good news."

Jimena jumped off the car. She and Serena gathered close around Vanessa and Catty, and listened as they explained what had happened inside.

"Why do you think Regulators are with Maggie?" Jimena asked. "Was she really going to give them the manuscript?"

"Yes," Vanessa answered.

"Let's go," Catty interrupted. She had a chilling sense that something bad would happen if they stayed. "Let's go someplace safer before we discuss it more."

She closed her eyes and let a breeze curl around her. She didn't detect any electrical charge in the air, not yet anyway.

They piled into Jimena's car and drove away.

Twenty minutes later, they sat in Catty's kitchen, staring down at the manuscript.

"Any ideas?" Catty asked again.

Serena shook her head. Vanessa sighed.

"I think we need to clear our minds for a while," Jimena said suddenly. "Let's go to Planet Bang and forget about the manuscript for now."

"But what about Maggie?" Vanessa asked.

"It's not like we're coming up with any

brilliant ideas here," Serena remarked.

Catty ran her finger along the edge of the Scroll. "How can I follow the Path of the manuscript, when I can't even read it?"

"Maybe that's what Maggie was supposed to do," Jimena pointed out. "Maybe she was supposed to translate it for you."

"But look at what she did." Vanessa complained.

Catty studied the curling letters. "The answers are all here. All we have to do is find another person to translate it."

"What about Kendra?" Vanessa asked.

Catty felt uneasy. "Do you think it's safe? What about the curse?"

"You don't really believe in the curse, do you?" Jimena asked.

"It's just superstition," Serena put in.

"You're probably right," Catty agreed. "I'll leave it here for Kendra."

"Let's dress up and make it over to Planet Bang." Jimena urged as if she were trying to lift everyone's spirits.

Vanessa hesitated. "I don't know. Toby might—"

"Toby might what?" Serena interrupted with a teasing voice.

Vanessa shrugged.

Catty glanced at Vanessa. Why was she acting so serious? Was she that concerned about upsetting Toby?

Vanessa smiled. "You're right. Let's go!"

Then they all stared at Catty.

"What?" she asked.

"Can we raid Kendra's closet?" Jimena asked.

Catty looked at her friends. Kendra had saved everything from her hippie and disco days. The closets in the spare bedroom were full of her old clothes. She never seemed to mind when Catty and Vanessa borrowed her things. Her clothes fit them nicely. Even though she was tall, she had been extremely thin when she was young, and they could wear most everything in the closet.

"Why not?" Catty laughed.

When they finished dressing, Jimena wore

racy red hot pants, a silky blouse with a star-burst pattern, and crazy ankle boots with thin chains draped around her ankles.

"Too cool." Serena admired Jimena's outfit, then she twirled to show off her own shoulder-baring top that exposed her midriff. She had pasted a crystal in her belly button. Kendra's bell-bottoms had been too long, but when she stepped into a pair of gold '70s platform shoes the length became just right.

Catty wore a backless halter top and a pair of lacy bell-bottoms. She held up some stencils. "Kendra is going to start selling these at the shop. Anyone want to try one?" She had two dragons in one hand and a lacy snowflake pattern in the other.

Jimena and Serena started to examine them, when Vanessa walked into the room. She was wearing a pinstripe shirt unbuttoned over a black leather bra top. Kendra's mini-skirt was too big and the waist fell around Vanessa's hips. Her skin looked golden bronze and she had applied one of the snowflake stencils on her stomach.

"Wow," Serena said.

"Talk about going for the jugular," Jimena teased.

"You like it?" she asked and took off the shirt. "It's too hot to wear." She hung it back on a hanger.

"Let's go, then." Jimena started for the door.

The strobe light flashed and blue lasers swept over the girls as they entered Planet Bang. The club was crowded already. The DJ turned the music and a loud beat vibrated through the haze.

A hand touched Catty's back. She turned quickly. Chris stood behind her. He smiled at her and she liked the feel of his hand on her bare back.

"Let's dance," he whispered.

She nodded.

He took her hand, but instead of taking her out to the dance floor he pulled her back to the shadows.

Catty stopped. "Why do you want to dance over here?"

He leaned next to her. "I don't want to share you with anyone."

She smiled back at him and followed him into a far corner. Both his hands held her waist, and a pleasant warmth ran through her body. He danced slow against her and stared down at her, his eyes lingering on her lips. She parted her mouth slightly and waited.

"You look so beautiful, Catty." His eyes did not leave hers. "I wish we could be together always."

His fingers wandered up her back and rested on her shoulders, then he cupped her face in his hands and bent down. He gave her a light kiss and murmured against her, "I like you a lot, Catty. Always believe that, even if I act strangely. It doesn't have anything to do with the way I feel about you. That's real. I just have a lot going on right now that I can't talk about."

He pulled away and she stared back at him, feeling suddenly guilty. So many kids had bad things going on in their lives. She wondered if his parents were going through a divorce or having money problems.

"I'm here for you if you want to talk," she offered. "Anytime. Just call me or come over."

"Thanks." His hands brushed down her arms and he pulled her tight against him.

She closed her eyes and let her arms slowly wrap around his neck. She had never imagined that it could feel this good to dance with a guy. Her lips moved across his cheek, searching for his. She needed a kiss. Then his lips found hers and softly traced the outline of her mouth. His kiss tasted even sweeter than she remembered and the feel of his hands on her back made her light-headed and breathless.

They stood motionless in the shadows, and then she felt him pull back. She didn't want him to stop.

"Promise you'll trust me," he whispered. "Promise, no matter what happens."

She nodded. How could she not trust him? And yet the way he was asking made her think that something really bad had happened to him or his family. And then she realized with a shock that she had never heard him mention his parents or any brothers or sisters.

"Maybe we should go someplace and talk," she suggested.

She felt him shake his head, then he leaned in to kiss her again when a commotion made them turn.

Michael was dancing with Vanessa, and Toby was picking a fight with him.

"What's he doing now?" Catty asked and started to run over to find out what was going on.

Chris grabbed her arm and pulled her back. "Who's the guy with Michael?"

Chris's eyes held hers and he pointed behind her. "That guy. He doesn't go to our school. Who is he?"

"You're right," Catty answered and wondered why Chris would care. "That's Toby. He goes to Fairfax High, I think. I'm not really sure. He's some guy that Vanessa met in dance class."

She thought he would let her go now, but he didn't. His hand squeezed tighter and he stared at Toby as if he sensed something.

"I have to help Vanessa." Catty started to pull away. "Come on, Toby is just a hundred percent creep."

She ran out to the dance floor, expecting Chris to follow her. She pushed through the ring of kids who had circled Toby, Michael, and Vanessa. She reached a hand back for Chris, but he wasn't there. She didn't see him anywhere. Where had he gone? She didn't have time to look for him now.

Toby glared at Michael.

"Toby?" Vanessa grabbed his arm as he started to lunge forward. "Stop. You want to get us kicked out?"

Toby laughed and the sound made Catty's scalp tingle.

Suddenly he charged forward and swung at Michael. Michael ducked, and Toby lost his balance.

Kids laughed at his clumsiness. Toby looked enraged.

Michael put both hands up and shook his head. "Vanessa and I are just friends, okay? I only asked a friend to dance."

Toby answered with a shove at Michael's chest. Michael took two quick steps backward to regain his balance, then shrugged and smiled crookedly. Catty could tell he was starting to become angry and that was dangerous.

"Sorry," Michael said sarcastically. "I didn't know you were so insecure about Vanessa. I thought things were solid between the two of you."

Toby started to swing, but Jimena suddenly appeared from the crowd and grabbed his wrist. He turned, ready to fight. But she tilted her head in a flirty way and smiled up at him as only Jimena could do.

"Stop making an ass of yourself," she whispered in a coy voice. "He just danced with her. You want to get a reputation for being weak?"

Toby glanced at Michael, then back at Jimena.

She leaned in close to him, a hand on her hip. "Yeah, if you believe your girl is yours, then there's no way some *vato* is going to steal her love with a dance. *No seas un payaso.*"

Toby seemed to understand everything she was saying. He considered Jimena, then glanced at Vanessa. Abruptly he took Vanessa's hand, smiled, and pulled her tightly against his chest. She gazed up in his eyes, and they started dancing as if nothing had happened.

Catty stared in amazement. "Can't she see how gross he is?"

"Love is blind," Michael said grimly.

Serena shook her head. "Are you okay, Michael?"

He looked at her. "I'm fine. I never would have asked Vanessa to dance if I'd known Toby would freak out."

Jimena shook her head. "Why did he get so mad?"

"Because," Catty explained, "Vanessa still likes Michael and he knows it."

Michael tossed his head and shook the wild black curls away from his face. "You couldn't tell by the way she's acting." He had a wounded look on his face.

"I know she does," Catty assured him.

He shrugged and grabbed Serena's hand as the beat of the music changed. A spark flew between them. Michael looked surprised, then smiled at Serena. "Let's dance." They walked out to the dance floor. Jimena began dancing with them.

Catty watched for a moment, then looked around the room, wondering where Chris had gone. She sighed heavily. She didn't see him anywhere and she didn't want to stay alone. She walked outside, hoping she might find him there. A long line of kids was still waiting to go inside.

The moon was high in the night sky, and she decided against taking the bus. She turned down a side street and started the long walk home.

A breeze soughed through the palm trees overhead. The night air felt cool against her face. She thought of Chris and wondered what had happened to him. She wished he would talk to her. Problems were always easier to bear when they were shared.

On the opposite side of the street, the trees blocked the light, making the shadows dense and thick. As she stepped onto the sidewalk, she heard something that made her stop and turn. It sounded like a footstep.

Her body felt suddenly tense and watchful. She looked behind her. The road was empty. Maybe it had only been someone walking around their house, taking out the trash or fixing a water sprinkler. She shrugged and began walking again, but now an odd sensation overcame her. Someone was following her.

She slowed her steps and wondered if it could be the guy who had given her the manuscript.

"Hello," she called and turned slowly, watching for any movement in the shadows around her.

Silence answered her.

She waited, hoping that if it were the mystery man he would step forward and show himself. She wanted to meet him, to see his face, and ask him about the manuscript.

"I know you're there," she spoke softly. "I can feel your presence."

Again silence answered her.

Finally she started walking, her shoes tapping nicely on the cement walk.

When she got to her house, she unlocked the door and entered, then without turning on the lights, she tiptoed to the picture window in the front room and looked out, searching for whoever had followed her home. Disappointed, she turned and walked through the dark house to the kitchen. She was about to switch on the light, when she sensed someone in the room with her.

CHAPTER SEVENTEEN

KENDRA SAT AT THE kitchen table, holding the manuscript. She stared silently at Catty with the wide-eyed look of an insomniac. Her hair was wet and matted against her skull as if she were burning with a high fever. Beads of sweat clung to her upper lip.

The manuscript fluttered in her hands. Kendra was shaking too violently to hold it steady.

"You," Kendra whispered.

"Are you all right?" Catty asked, taking a step forward. Kendra looked seriously ill.

Kendra stood abruptly. Her chair fell back and crashed to the floor. She stepped around it and eased to the back of the kitchen. Her eyes never left Catty.

"Kendra, what's wrong?" Catty started for her again, but stopped when she realized Kendra was afraid of her.

"I finished translating it." Kendra tapped the manuscript. "And now I know the truth."

"The truth about what?"

Kendra held the manuscript up and it flapped in her hands. *"Demere personam tuam atque ad dominum tuum se referre!"* she shouted roughly.

Catty stared at her in disbelief. She knew the words were Latin. She repeated the sound of the words to herself, trying to find their meaning. "Day-mair-eh pear-so-nahm too-ahm aht-kweh ahd dom-in-oom too-oom say reh-fair-reh."

Kendra seemed empowered when she spoke the words. She repeated them, the words scraping from her throat. *"Demere personam tuam atque ad dominum tuum se referre."*

Catty was totally confused now. "Take off

my mask? Return to my master? What's that supposed to mean?"

Kendra collapsed against the back wall. Silent tears rolled down her cheeks. "Who are you?" she asked in a low voice.

Catty shook her head. "I don't understand."

"What are you?" Kendra demanded.

Catty didn't know what to say.

Kendra's head lolled against the wall. Her eyes were only half-open. "All these years I thought I had been protecting a space alien from the government." She laughed and it was dry and filled with sadness. "And now I find out that I've been protecting something evil."

Catty started shaking. "What did you read?"

Kendra looked down at the manuscript. Her finger ran across a line as she translated it. *"The child of a fallen goddess and an evil spirit will take possession of the Secret Scroll without fear of its curse."*

"You think that's me?" Catty asked nervously. Could she be the daughter of a fallen goddess and an evil spirit?

Catty slumped into a chair and stared at

nothing. "I'm not evil. I'm a goddess," she confessed softly. "I didn't know until this year. When I found out, I tried to tell you. I started to tell you." Her voice trailed off.

Kendra dragged a chair to the table and sat down facing Catty.

"Tell me now." Kendra started to shiver again but Catty suspected that this time it was from fever, not fear.

Right now, sitting across from Kendra, Catty believed that the manuscript did have a curse and she had to do something to find out how to free Kendra from its spell.

Catty began slowly, repeating what Maggie had told her. "In ancient times when Pandora's box was opened—"

"Pandora?" Kendra interrupted. "Are you talking about the myth?"

Catty nodded solemnly. "It isn't a myth," she stated firmly and continued, "The last thing to leave the box was hope. Only Selene, the goddess of the moon, saw the creature that had been sent by the Atrox to devour hope. Selene took pity on the people of earth and gave her Daughters, like guardian angels, to perpetuate hope. I'm one of those Daughters. A goddess."

"And the Atrox?" Kendra asked.

"The Atrox and its Followers have sworn to destroy the Daughters of the Moon because once we're gone, the Atrox will succeed." She looked at Kendra. "I'm a source of good."

Kendra's lips trembled. Her eyes searched over the text of the manuscript and then she found what she was looking for and translated, *"A soulless creature who defied God and gave itself life."* Her voice seemed haunted. *"The Atrox."*

The room suddenly felt crowded with hostile forces as if saying its name had summoned it. The temperature dropped, and a chill tingled up Catty's spine.

"And your gift?" It seemed to pain Kendra to speak.

"It's not teleportation. It's a form of time travel. It's part of what I need to fight the Atrox," Catty explained.

"An entity that has existed since before

creation." Kendra spoke more to herself than to Catty. "And this." She held the manuscript more tightly. "This tells how to destroy it, and . . ." She looked back at Catty now. "You're the one chosen to destroy it."

Catty nodded, then looked down self-consciously.

Kendra regarded her in admiration. "What can I do to help?"

"I need to see my mother," Catty started. "I need to go back in time before her death and talk to her so that I can find out who my father is and why I was the one given the manuscript." She didn't add that she hoped her mother would also know how to free Kendra from the curse.

Kendra nodded and stood on shaky feet, set the Scroll on her chair, then walked slowly to the kitchen cupboard where she kept messages, notes, and telephone numbers. She pulled out a scrap of paper. When she turned back, her eyes held Catty's. "It's the curse of the manuscript, isn't it? That's why I'm so ill."

"No," Catty lied. "I'm sure it's the just the

flu. You don't believe in curses anyway, do you?" She tried to laugh but it sounded forced.

Kendra smiled weakly. "I do now." She handed the piece of paper to Catty. "This is the address the coroner's office gave me."

She leaned back against the counter as if standing for such a short time had weakened her.

Catty prayed that she had enough time. "Maybe I should take you to the doctor before I go," she offered.

Kendra shook her head. "I don't think modern medicine can cure what I have." Her hand touched Catty's cheek and her tired eyes filled with love. "I'll have to rely on you, Catty." She hesitated a moment. "And to think that all this time I thought you were a space alien."

"No regrets?" Catty asked.

"Of course I have regrets." Kendra tried to chuckle but burst into a hacking cough. Finally she was able to speak again. "I had always hoped you were going to take me to another planet someday so I could see what outer space really looked like."

She leaned over and kissed Catty's cheek. Her skin felt too hot and dry.

Catty watched Kendra wave good-bye as a glaring white explosion burned the kitchen away and Catty zoomed into the tunnel at a speed faster than light.

CHAPTER EIGHTEEN

CATTY RECOGNIZED THE street with all the magnolia trees and suddenly she became aware of how close her mother had lived to her all these years. The knowledge filled her with deep sadness and longing. She stopped in front of a narrow house with a pitched roof, took a deep breath, and headed up the brick path. Roses in every color lined the walkway and perfumed the night with their sweet fragrance. A rake rested on the porch step next to a paper bag filled with leaves and a pair of gardening gloves. Catty knocked on the door hesitantly, then rang the doorbell.

The door opened with a suddenness that surprised her. A hand reached out, grabbed her wrist, and pulled her inside.

Catty started to speak but warm fingers pressed against her lips to silence her. The sudden touch surprised her.

"Mom?" she whispered.

"Yes," Zoe whispered back. Her hand lingered on Catty's lips and the touch brought tears to Catty's eyes.

Zoe switched off the lights before she pulled Catty into the living room.

"Stay here," she ordered softly. She walked to the picture window and held back the lace panel with the side of her hand. She studied the outside for a long time, then finally satisfied, she drew the drapes, turned on a small lamp, and sat on a sofa filled with quilted pillows. She smiled at Catty. She had a pretty smile.

"So," she said quietly. "I'm sorry for the intrigue. There are Regulators watching me from the corner house. I guess they think their disguise has fooled me. I had to make sure they hadn't seen you come here. Very sloppy of them not to have seen you turn the corner."

"I didn't come *that way*," Catty answered.

"No?" Zoe patted the sofa for Catty to sit next to her. "Of course not. You have special powers of your own."

Catty started to join her, but then she looked down and saw the geometry test she had hurriedly written on and given to Zoe that day on the desert.

Zoe caught her look and picked up the test from the coffee table. "I always keep it with me," she explained. "It's the only thing of yours I own." She folded it gently and tucked it in her pocket. "Besides, I can't chance having a Regulator discover it."

"Don't they know where I live already since I'm a Daughter?" Catty wondered.

"Possibly," Zoe answered. "But I'm sure they don't know you're *my* daughter or you wouldn't be here."

Catty felt a chill run up her back.

"Right now they may think it's Serena or Jimena or not have a clue at all. They're extremely evil and powerful, but putting so much energy into their disguise makes them a bit sluggish sometimes."

Catty hated to think what one of the Regulators would be like without a disguise but then she thought of something else. "You know about Serena and Jimena?"

"Yes, I know most everything about your life."

A warm feeling spread through Catty's chest. "Everything?"

"All that I could learn." She smiled, then became serious and continued. "So I suppose something important has happened for you to find me? Who told you where I live?"

Catty sat down and started to tell her but stopped. How could she explain to her that she had gotten the address from the coroner's office?

"So you can't tell me," Zoe concluded. "Or won't, because it's something I shouldn't know or wouldn't want to know." She shrugged. "But you can at least tell me why you are here."

"I've received the Secret Scroll." Catty's voice

caught. "I was hoping you could explain why all this is happening to me. Why was I given the Scroll? I can't even read it."

Zoe leaned back on a pillow and looked at the ceiling. "I had planned on telling you before now. I should have but I was too ashamed."

Catty cast a brief look at Zoe. "Ashamed of what?"

"I had been a Daughter of the Moon like you. I had a special power, too. I could move objects with my mind." Zoe's words seemed filled with regret. "But I became too frightened of the change."

Catty nodded. She didn't like to think about the change. Their gifts only lasted until they were seventeen and then there was metamorphosis. They lost their powers and their memory of what they had been, or they disappeared. The ones who disappeared became something else but no one, not even Maggie, knew what that was.

She continued softly. "So I turned to the Atrox."

Catty's eyes widened.

Zoe drew her moon amulet from beneath her blouse for Catty to see. It still looked dull and blackened.

"The Atrox promised to give me immortality," she continued. "But it tricked me. I had failed to ask for perpetual youth and now I'm doomed to age for eternity. It's not a problem now but eventually . . . Can you imagine what it will feel like to continue aging until the end of time?"

Catty shook her head.

"The Atrox must have sensed that I made my commitment out of fear." Zoe stared off for a long while, then finally she spoke again. "That day on the desert, I was still blaming Maggie for what had happened to me. I thought for a long time that if Maggie could have told me more about the transformation, then I wouldn't have been afraid and I wouldn't have turned to the Atrox. But I know now that it was my own lack of courage that made me do what I did. I wish I had listened to her." Zoe shrugged. "But then maybe all things have a purpose."

She stared at Catty and Catty could tell from the look in her eyes that she didn't want to hear what she was going to say next.

"You never would have come into the world if I hadn't become a Follower," Zoe uttered softly.

"I don't understand." Catty tried to catch her breath.

"I fell in love with a Follower." Zoe smiled sadly. "A member of the Inner Circle."

Catty felt devastated. "But members of the Inner Circle are renowned for their evil." She tried to keep her voice steady but the words felt like bricks falling from her tongue. "They're incapable of loving."

"Yes," Zoe agreed. "But they're also very seductive and captivating."

"Who?" The simple question scraped from her throat. Did she really want to know?

Zoe stared at her as if considering, then she shook her head slightly. "You'll know who your father is only when it is essential for you to find out."

Catty could feel hot tears pressing into her

eyes. She fought to keep them from rolling down her cheeks.

Zoe continued. "I feared that you were the destined heir to the Secret Scroll because of the prophecy."

"What prophecy?" Catty hated the tremor that had crept into her voice.

"Only the child of a fallen goddess and an evil spirit will inherit the Scroll," Zoe recited.

Catty's heart sunk. Her mother was a Follower, her father an evil member of the Inner Circle. She suddenly felt damned. How could she overcome such a birthright?

Zoe took Catty's hand. "You must never worry that you are evil because of your heritage. The manuscript can only be given to someone with a pure heart and the strength to fight the Atrox."

Catty looked at Zoe's hand holding her own. Finally she had the courage to ask her the question that had been bothering her all these years. "Why did you leave me by the side of the road?"

Zoe waited a long moment before she

answered. “It was the only way I could think of to save you.”

Catty looked up at her and saw that Zoe’s eyes were shimmering with tears.

“When I heard about the legend of the Secret Scroll, I assumed that you were its heir. I couldn’t know for sure but I lived in terror. I feared that if you were given the manuscript, the Atrox would destroy you and the Scroll. I had to do something. I would have preferred to never see you again and know you were safe than to let the Atrox have you. So I abandoned you. I crashed the car and set it on fire, planning to say that I had lost consciousness and that you must have wandered off.”

“But in the desert,” Catty said accusingly, “I could have died so easily.”

Zoe reassured her. “I assumed that anyone seeing a child walking along the road in a deserted stretch of highway would stop.” Then she quickly added, “Besides, you know that I was watching over you until someone did stop.”

“But why didn’t the Regulators find me?

They could have found me through my dreams." She stopped. She was remembering what her mother had said to Stanton that day in the desert. She had begged him to take Catty's memories from her so she'd be safe.

"That's right," Zoe said as if she understood what Catty was thinking. "Without your memories, it would be hard for the Regulators to find you and destroy you."

"But you didn't know Stanton would show up."

"No, I didn't. Until he showed up my plan was risky, I know, but I'd hoped that if a stranger reared you, you'd be safe. I hadn't counted on Stanton. I don't have the powers he has. I knew then that my plan might work. Without memories for the Regulators to explore, they wouldn't be able to find you."

Catty suddenly understood that Stanton had saved her. It was hard for her to imagine that he would do anything to help her. "Why would Stanton help me?"

"You don't understand how valuable the

Secret Scroll is and how many people want it," Zoe answered. "I'm sure he hoped that if he took you back in time to see me that I would convince you to give the manuscript to him."

"But you didn't."

"No." Zoe brushed her hand against Catty's cheek.

"I'll find a way to release you from what the Atrox has done to you," Catty promised suddenly.

"It's too late for that," Zoe acknowledged.

"Let me try at least," Catty urged. "I know I can do something."

Zoe shook her head. "I've been dreaming about the goddess Selene. She comes to me in my dreams and offers me a second chance because I've done so much to protect you."

"Are you going to accept her offer?" Catty instantly felt reassured.

"Yes." Zoe nodded.

"Then why haven't you?"

"Because I know that when I accept her offer, I'll leave this body behind and become something different. I've only been waiting to talk to you again before I go."

Catty looked at Zoe and felt a terrible ache and yearning. "Why didn't you ever try to see me? You live so close. It hurts to know you were always right here and never even called me."

"I did see you," Zoe confessed. "When it was safe and I knew the Regulators weren't following me, I watched you. Sometimes I was even bold enough to go into your room at night and sit by your bed. I would speak to you while you were sleeping."

Catty was startled and wondered if the presence she had sometimes felt had been her mother.

"I'm sure I'll be able to continue to visit you after." Zoe grinned. "But you won't be able to see me. I think of how much I feared the transition when I was young, but now I'm eager for it. I think we become guardian spirits so I'll always be watching over you." Zoe stood abruptly. "I'm ready." She held out her hand. "Stay with me until Selene comes."

Catty stood and followed Zoe through a

back bedroom to a door that led to a small enclosed garden. Catty saw a small ornate mirror on the dresser. She wanted to have something that had belonged to her mother. She slipped it into her pocket, then held her hand protectively against it.

They sat outside in the backyard. They hadn't been there long when the lunar glow began to brighten. Soon an eerie whiteness covered the lawn. A blazing light stretched from the moon and Zoe lifted her hand as if she could see something in the frosty beam. When her hand fell back, the light twirled up and up, scattering stars.

Then the yard was dark again and only her mother's body remained.

CHAPTER NINETEEN

CATTY RETURNED TO the present. She dropped from the tunnel back into time and landed hard in the geranium bed at the side of her house. She jumped up, brushed the dirt and petals from her clothes, and started walking to the back of her house. She wanted nothing more than to climb in bed and sleep. She felt exhausted.

She took one step forward and felt a hand touch her gently.

"Catty." The voice of the mysterious stranger made her stop.

“What now?” She didn’t bother to hide the irritation in her voice.

“Why are you delaying?” His tone sounded urgent.

“The Scroll has a curse,” Catty reminded him and slipped her hand into her pocket. She curled her fingers around the mirror she had taken from the dresser in her mother’s house.

“Every second you delay gives the Atrox more of a chance to find the Scroll.”

“It’s not as simple as you make it sound,” Catty responded angrily and slowly inched the mirror from her pocket.

“It is your destiny as heir.” His voice sounded as angry as hers now.

“Well, it’s not exactly as if I’m not trying,” Catty answered and eased the mirror upward. “But I’ve had to deal with Regulators and the death of my birth mother.”

Abruptly she brought the mirror up high enough to see the reflection of the person who stood behind her. She gasped and quickly turned. “Chris?” Her heart beat so rapidly she thought it would leave her body. She dropped the mirror back in her pocket. She felt totally confused, now. How could Chris be the one who had given her the Secret Scroll?

Then she started laughing. She felt mentally exhausted and supertired. No way was Chris the mysterious stranger. She must have misunderstood what he had said to her or maybe she had even fallen asleep in the geraniums and he had just now awakened her.

But when Chris spoke she knew with certainty that she had not been dreaming.

"I guess I'm glad I don't have to pretend anymore." His real voice was neither the one Chris had used with her before, or that of the mysterious stranger, but a pleasant tone in between. "It's been really hard."

She shook her head. Her thoughts whirled. Could it be true? "You gave me the Secret Scroll?"

He nodded.

"Why didn't you just hand it to me?" Catty asked with mounting exasperation. "Why all the mystery?"

"I had to hide who I really was," Chris insisted. "So I could succeed in accomplishing the task I have been ordained to do."

Catty folded her arms over her chest. "Which is?"

"To protect the Scroll," Chris explained. "The Keeper must always hide his identity."

"Keeper?"

Chris stepped closer to her. "The one who protects the manuscript until it can be given to the heir."

She exhaled. "I believed your act. You convinced me and my friends."

His hand went up and gently touched her cheek. "I hated deceiving you, Catty. I really care about you. You gave me back emotions I hadn't felt in years."

She felt her heart skid away from her.

"What is it?" He seemed to sense her distress.

She cocked her head and stared at him. "You're not just some guy I'm going to go to the prom with, are you?"

He shook his head.

"Why did you let me like you then?" She hated how desperate her voice sounded.

His hands rested on her shoulders and even in the faint lighting she could see the regret in his eyes. "I didn't mean for it to happen this way. When I first met you I had no idea you were the one I'd be giving the Scroll to."

"Why not?"

"Normally, I know who is going to be heir to the Scroll from the moment of their birth, but when your mother hid you from the Regulators she also hid you from me."

"But you're in Los Angeles now," she stated. "Why did you come here?"

"I discovered that Maggie was in Los Angeles, so I assumed the Daughters were also here. When I saw the four of you go into Maggie's apartment, I knew one of you was the heir, but that was already after I had met you. I really liked you. I still do, but I couldn't chance having the Regulators see us together."

Then another thought came to her and she

pulled back. "Is this the way you really look or have I been kissing some decrepit old man?"

He laughed. "No, this is me."

At least she hadn't been kissing some old geezer. She sighed.

"What?" he asked and pulled her closer to him.

"I'm living in a nightmare," she answered. "And it just keeps getting worse."

"I'm sorry. It's my fault. I knew I had to give up seeing you for the sake of the manuscript but I couldn't. I never thought I would feel what it's like to be in love again."

She looked up at him, startled. Had he said *in love*? She couldn't control the foolish smile spreading across her cheeks.

"Maybe we can be together someday," he whispered.

"Someday?" she asked.

"You don't stay in this form forever," he said. "And if the Atrox is defeated . . ." He didn't complete the sentence. He leaned forward and started to press his lips against hers.

"If the Atrox is defeated what?" she asked, her lips brushing the words against his mouth.

"Then we can be together." He started to press against her but pulled back suddenly. "You're too young to understand how much you mean to me."

"Well, I'm not centuries old yet," she added defensively.

"Not yet," he chuckled and pulled her close against him.

He felt like flesh and bone. She opened her eyes. His skin looked young. His eyes were bright and clear.

"Have you finished checking?" he asked, his breath caressing her cheeks.

She closed her eyes and he kissed her. She parted her lips and felt his tongue brush lightly against hers. She leaned against him, forgetting all her problems and let herself feel the comfort of his arms around her. Maybe everything would turn out all right.

And then Chris reluctantly released her. "I can't stay with you, Catty. The Regulators don't know who I am yet, and they don't know for sure which one of you is the heir. It's safer if we don't see each other for now."

He walked backward until he was at the corner of the house, then he turned and walked away.

She felt suddenly optimistic, better than she had in days. With a sudden impulse she decided to share the news about Chris with Vanessa. Everything was going to work out now. She was sure of it.

CHAPTER TWENTY

CATTY RAN INSIDE and checked on Kendra. She was sleeping, a bottle of aspirin beside her bed. "You're going to be all right, Kendra," Catty promised her. "I know I'll find a way to help you." She kissed her forehead. The skin felt hot and dry. She took another blanket from the closet and placed it around Kendra, then she called a cab.

Twenty minutes later, she was running up the walk to Vanessa's small Craftsman-style house. She hurried past the twisted olive tree in the front yard and went around to the back. Even before she opened the door, she could smell popcorn.

She walked in, calling Vanessa's name.

"It's me, Vanessa," she called. "Please be home."

Vanessa crossed the kitchen. Normally, a smile burst across her face when she saw Catty, but her face seemed solemn. Her hair was tangled, and she was rubbing her eyes.

"Something wrong?" Catty asked and pinched a kernel of popcorn from the bowl on the table. She threw it up in the air and caught it with her mouth.

Vanessa smiled sluggishly. "I must have fallen asleep on the couch."

"Guess what?" Catty opened the refrigerator and pulled out a Coke. She popped the top and took a drink.

Vanessa only stared at her.

"Well, you could show some enthusiasm," Catty squealed. "I'm about to tell you one of the most exciting stories of my life!"

"What?" Vanessa was suddenly interested.

"Chris!" Catty shouted. "He's not seeing anyone else."

"I never thought he was," Vanessa answered. "Is that what you came over to tell me?"

"But guess what else?" Catty set the Coke aside. She felt too excited to drink it now.

Vanessa got a surprised look on her face. "You didn't . . ."

"Of course, we didn't," Catty interrupted her and sat down at the table. "This is way more exciting."

Vanessa looked puzzled. She pulled out a chair, sat down, and faced Catty. "More exciting than *that*?"

Catty leaned forward. "He's the mysterious stranger."

A worried look flashed across Vanessa's face and then it was gone. "What do you mean?" she whispered as if she were afraid someone would hear.

"The person who gave me the manuscript," Catty announced. "It was Chris all along."

Vanessa's hand clasped Catty's and her face looked confused as if she were fighting conflicting emotions.

"What's wrong?" Catty turned.

Toby walked quietly into the kitchen, his eyes glaring.

"Do you always listen to private conversations?" Catty practically yelled, then she turned to Vanessa. "You should have told me that Toby was here."

Vanessa didn't respond. She seemed almost unaware that anyone was in the room with them, her eyes were glazed and her mind seemed far away.

Catty glanced back at Toby. He smiled at her smugly. "Now I know who the Keeper is."

Catty felt her heart sink. "A Regulator." As Catty said the word the room seemed to come alive with an electrical charge. The small hairs on her arms and neck rose, and she suddenly understood why she and Jimena and Serena were always getting tiny shocks when Toby was around.

"You liked my disguise?" Toby grinned maliciously and his eyes became clouded, rheumy with age, and yellowed. The skin on his face fell into wrinkles as the flesh turned a sickly green color. His perfectly cut hair grew into thick tangles. But worse was his smell, and the bluish mold that gathered on his clothes and skin.

Catty stood suddenly. The chair legs scraped across the kitchen floor with a horrible scream. She backed away from him. Her hand rose automatically and covered her nose.

"Now you two can see the real me." His mouth stretched into a ghoulish wound and his fingers grew longer, the nails yellowing and splitting.

Toby crouched over Vanessa, his breathing labored, and kissed the top of her head.

Catty wondered how Vanessa didn't cringe from him. She didn't even seem to notice the way Toby looked now, or his putrid smell.

Toby stood up again, his clawlike hands resting on Vanessa's shoulders. "Vanessa can only see me the way I want her to see me," he bragged in an ugly rasping voice. "I've gone into her dreams every night and influenced all of her thoughts." He patted Vanessa. "You see me as quite charming, don't you, Vanessa?"

Catty felt ill. She looked at Vanessa and

wondered what she could do to save her friend. She felt too rattled to think clearly.

Toby cleared his throat and when she looked back at him, he was again in his high-school-boy disguise.

"I will take care of Chris," he spoke with assurance. "All that remains is for you to destroy the manuscript."

"No chance of that." Catty folded her arms across her chest.

"Is that so?" Toby asked. "All right, then." He turned to Vanessa. "Do you want to go away with me, Vanessa?"

Vanessa stood quickly and placed her arms around him. "Yes," she answered without hesitation, but Catty thought she saw a flicker of doubt cross Vanessa's eyes.

"Come, then." Toby took her hand and started to lead her out the back door.

"Wait!" Catty yelled.

Toby glanced back at her.

"I'll get rid of the manuscript," she offered. "Just let Vanessa stay with me."

"You'll get rid of it?"

She nodded.

He considered her for a long moment.

"Meet me tomorrow night in Griffith Park before the full moon rises. Bring the manuscript with you, and I'll show you how to destroy it."

"Where in the park?" Catty asked.

"Near the carousel." He started to lead Vanessa out the door again.

"Wait." Catty ran after them and grabbed Vanessa's hand. "Vanessa stays with me."

Vanessa cast Catty a strange look and jerked her hand away. "What are you doing, Catty?"

"I want you to stay with me," Catty urged.

"Why?" Vanessa looked perplexed.

Catty grabbed Vanessa and held her tightly. "Please, I'll give you the manuscript right now," Catty told him. "Just let Vanessa stay."

"That's not what I want," he assured her. "The manuscript cannot be destroyed by ordinary means. It can only be destroyed by the destined heir." He looked at her maliciously. "Bring it to the park tomorrow night and then you can have Vanessa back."

Catty nodded her agreement but she knew intuitively that there was no way Toby was going to surrender Vanessa once Catty had surrendered the manuscript. The Regulators would destroy them, or worse, change them both into Followers.

Before she was even aware that she was speaking, words spilled from her mouth. *"O Mater Luna, Regina nocis, adiuvo me nunc."* The prayer was only said in times of grave danger.

Catty watched Vanessa leave. She felt totally hopeless.

CHAPTER TWENTY-ONE

AT HOME, CATTY sat on the front porch steps and gazed up at the western sky. Veils of smoke wreathed around the moon. The fire in the hills behind her home had been contained but a larger one had started in the chaparral in another area.

She didn't see any way to outwit Toby. She thought about calling Serena and Jimena, but that felt too dangerous. She'd only be inviting them to their doom, and she didn't want more people harmed by the manuscript.

Maybe it was best to destroy it. That might

save Chris and Kendra at least. Why would Regulators need to go after Chris if there was no manuscript to protect? And if the manuscript were destroyed, then perhaps Kendra would be free of the curse as well.

The night had fallen quiet but for a fleeting moment, she thought she heard someone call her name. She listened carefully wondering if it was Kendra.

Then soft steps crossed the porch and she turned expecting to see Kendra, but instead a woman walked toward her with slow, easy steps. Was she a neighbor searching for a lost pet? Catty didn't recognize her and she didn't feel like talking with a stranger.

"Can I help you?" Catty asked.

"You help me?" the woman answered and a wry smile crossed her face as if she thought the idea was funny. She sat down on the porch stoop next to Catty and stared up at the moon.

The woman sighed and looked at Catty. "How can you lose hope now, when it is most important?"

Catty shook her head. She didn't know what

the woman was talking about, and just as quickly the woman answered her thoughts.

"You know very well what I'm talking about," the woman said. "That's all you've been thinking."

Catty studied her. She had an inexplicable feeling that the woman sitting beside her wasn't just a neighbor. Serena and Jimena had each told her about visits from a moon goddess when they were desperate. Could the woman beside her be the goddess Selene in disguise? Catty felt a wrinkle of irritation. Her situation really was hopeless. "This is the end," Catty said. "There's no escape. I don't have any choices left."

Again the woman smiled as if she found humor in Catty's answer. "You always have a choice."

"Right," Catty answered sarcastically.

"No situation is ever completely hopeless," the woman insisted. "You're just not seeing the alternatives."

"Get real," Catty said.

"Maybe if you told me your problem—"

"I thought you already knew about my problems," Catty cut in.

"Suit yourself." The woman stood to leave.

Catty sighed heavily and spoke in a weary voice. "I don't even know if the manuscript is worth saving, because it has hurt so many people. It turned Maggie against me, and the curse is so powerful that even the Regulators are afraid to touch it."

The woman sat down again. "Maggie never betrayed you."

"She didn't?" Catty turned sharply and stared at the woman. "How do you know?"

"Trust me." The woman smiled. "Maggie believes in the curse, and she thought she was protecting you."

"But why were the Regulators in her apartment, then?" Catty desperately wanted to believe in Maggie, still. "She was going to give the manuscript to them."

"Yes," the woman nodded. "She wanted to see the manuscript destroyed, so that the Atrox would think it was safe. She didn't know the manuscript could only be destroyed by the heir. If the Atrox believed it was safe, it would be less cautious. Only then would she send her beloved Daughters to fight it."

Catty's heart pounded.

The woman tilted her head and looked at Catty. "Maggie had memorized the Path of the manuscript before she offered to surrender it to the Regulators, but then . . ." Her eyes twinkled and she shrugged. "The manuscript mysteriously disappeared from her apartment."

"I stole it," Catty confessed.

"Of course you did." The woman smiled kindly.

"Did . . . did they harm her?" Catty's voice was shaky and her hands trembled. She couldn't bare it if one more person were harmed because of her stupidity.

"No. After all, she was going to give them the manuscript. They wrongly consider her an ally."

Catty felt relieved. She didn't know what she would have done if the Regulators had hurt

Maggie. The woman glanced at the moon. It was beginning to set. "Well, my time is up." She stood and started to leave, then turned and looked back at Catty. "It's strange," she started.

"What?" Catty asked.

"Just that you've never followed the rules before," the woman explained. "And so now I'm wondering, why are you going to follow them when you are dealing with the most deceitful being in creation?"

Catty watched the woman leave. What she said was true. Catty hated rules.

A slow smile crept across her face.

"Thank you," Catty said. First she'd sleep, and then she'd act.

CHAPTER TWENTY-TWO

THE NEXT MORNING Catty awoke to the sound of sirens and the low rumble of fire trucks speeding down her street. She was surprised she had slept so long. Sunlight slanted through her windows in thick gold bars. She checked on Kendra, showered, and dressed, then crept downstairs to the kitchen. She took down the framed manuscript from the kitchen wall. It was Kendra's prized possession, and part of her felt guilty for what she planned, but it had to be done. She carefully removed the parchment from its frame, then searched through the piles of translations and notes on the kitchen table. Finally she found the Secret Scroll on the chair where Kendra had been sitting the night before. She carried both manuscripts upstairs and set them on her desk.

Next she gathered paints and brushes and sat down. She studied the artwork on the Secret Scroll, then slowly began copying its rich patterns of gold, red, and blue onto Kendra's old manuscript.

It was late afternoon when she finished. She studied her work. She had managed to copy the exotic birds and animals hidden in the foliage on the borders, and even the detailed picture of the goddess locking the jaws of hell. Her work was rough, but at a distance it would fool Toby or any of the Regulators, especially since they were afraid to touch it.

Satisfied, she went to her closet. She searched through her clothes until she found the strapless top with the slit in the front. She slipped it over her head, then grabbed a silky black skirt and stepped into it. She carried her stiletto boots to the bed and tugged them on.

At last she drew black liquid eyeliner over her top lid, added green glitter shadow, rolled thick mascara on her lashes, and brushed her hair. She added gloss to her lips and rubbed sparkle lotion over her arms and chest. Then she remembered the dragon stencils. Soon, she had a sinuous dragon adorning her thigh between the bottom of her skirt and the top of her boots. She liked the look. She turned in front of the full-length mirror behind the bathroom door.

"Dynamite," she whispered. Her reflection thrilled her. She looked vamped-out and mystical. At once, she sensed the fierce power of the dragon rising in her. She felt like an invincible goddess-warrior.

She crept down the hallway and stairs, her heels clicking on the wood floors, then paused over Kendra, who was now curled on the couch, breathing uneasily. She kissed her forehead. The kiss was her seal; tonight she would release Kendra from the curse.

She started to leave when the doorbell rang. She opened the door.

Jimena and Serena stepped inside, their eyes smoky with makeup, star glitter on their arms and cheeks and hair. They were mysterious creatures of the night, now.

"We knew you'd need our help," Jimena said.

"Thanks," Catty answered, smiling.

"She saw you next to a carousel with Toby." Serena seemed unsure. "Does that make sense?"

Catty nodded. "Toby asked me to meet him at the carousel in Griffith Park. He's a Regulator. He's got Vanessa and he won't let her go until I destroy the Secret Scroll." Then Catty told them the details of what had happened.

Neither Jimena nor Serena seemed surprised.

"Do you think all the Regulators will be there?" Serena glanced down at her moon amulet as she opened the door.

"No, just Toby," Catty answered. "I don't think he'll want to share the glory with the others."

Jimena nodded and followed Serena.

Catty stepped outside and saw Jimena's brother's blue-and-white '81 Oldsmobile parked at the curb. That took care of one problem at least. They had transportation.

She glanced up at the Hollywood sign. Smoke billowed into the evening sky, close to the huge white letters. Another fire. It felt like an omen. She suddenly stopped and wondered if they shouldn't turn back.

"*¡Vayamos!*" Jimena squealed and slid behind the steering wheel.

"Come on," Serena called back to Catty. "Let's go."

Catty reluctantly climbed in the backseat. A feeling of foreboding twisted through her as the car shot away from the curb. She hoped she wasn't leading her friends to their deaths.

CHAPTER TWENTY-THREE

HEAT FROM THE DAY intensified the pungent smell of smoke from the fire in the hills near Griffith Park. The acrid fumes stung Catty's eyes and the back of her throat as she stepped away from the car. Overhead, the smoke-clouded sky reflected the setting sun with a golden cast.

"We're early," Jimena announced and jumped on the carousel. She patted the neck of an outside horse and smoothed her hand over the glass jewels set in the bridle, then she threaded her way through the first and second row of ponies. "I used to love riding this carousel," she announced.

"Me, too," Serena agreed. She climbed on and swung her leg over a black steed.

Jimena and Catty laughed as Serena pretended to gallop away, but their laughter suddenly stopped. The silence in the park became overwhelming and the length of Catty's back shivered with anticipation.

Jimena crouched beside a white horse. "What is it?"

The air felt permeated with a negative charge, as it had in the coroner's office when the Regulators had entered the reception area.

"It's Toby," Catty said.

A security light unexpectedly blinked on. In the sudden brightness the wooden horses seemed to come to life. Their glass eyes blazed yellow and their shiny muscles seemed strained, as if the horses were trying to escape from whatever was coming.

"Did he do that?" Serena whispered in awe.

"What?" Catty asked.

"Make the light go on," Jimena spoke in a low voice.

Catty shrugged.

The air became heavier and more electric. The small hairs on her arms rose and her skin prickled.

Then, the carousel creaked and groaned as if struggling against inertia. A cascade of sparks fell from the generator.

Serena let out a soft hiss of air. "Freaky."

"*¿Qué hay que hacer?*" Jimena asked quietly. "Should we be doing anything?"

Catty shook her head. "Wait."

Gears squeaked, and then the horses rose and fell. Serena climbed off hers in quick, jerking motions and stood beside it in awe.

They watched in amazement as the platform circled. Then the band organ pinged. Music sputtered and stopped. A trumpet squawked, then continued to play. Finally, cymbals and drums joined the brass. The horses moved up and down.

Serena and Jimena jumped off the slow-moving carousel and stood with Catty.

After the first rotation the platform circled with ever increasing speed, stirring a breeze that rushed over them. The manuscript flapped back and forth in Catty's hands.

"Stay back," Catty ordered suddenly. "He'll know you're here, but I don't want him to think we came to have a standoff."

Jimena and Serena stepped back until their faces were hidden in darkness.

"Catty," Jimena warned and pointed.

Beneath the bulking trees, purple shadows clustered and grew thicker. Leaves on the bottom branches quivered. Suddenly Catty knew it had been a mistake to come here with the fake manuscript, a foolish, impulsive mistake. How could she fight something whose aura alone was strong enough to give a carousel life? She had put her friends needlessly in danger and there was little chance of success. She turned to tell Jimena and Serena to run; but before she could, the face in the shadows became whole.

Toby emerged in his disguise, holding Vanessa behind him. The whirling lights from the carousel cast a kaleidoscope of everchanging patterns over them. The breeze ruffled Vanessa's hair, but Toby's stayed rigidly in place.

He walked slowly forward. His feet made no sound in the dry grass. He stopped before he reached Catty. His eyes were the same as the wooden horses, lacking warmth and light of their own, but stealing it from the environment and reflecting it back.

"You have it." He glanced at the parchment in her hands but did not come closer to examine it.

Catty held it up. Was it only her imagination or had he glanced away? Could he be that frightened of the manuscript and its curse? But why? He seemed so all-powerful.

"Take off your moon amulet," he ordered.

She hesitated. She never took off her amulet. Was it a trick? She glanced at Vanessa, hoping for some clue. But Vanessa didn't appear to have heard Toby. She didn't seem to even be aware of where she was. She was too deep inside herself. Toby sensed what Catty was thinking and pushed a strand of hair away from Vanessa's face, then bent and kissed her lips.

Vanessa jerked back.

Toby glanced at Catty and smiled. "My beautiful moon goddess doesn't appreciate my kisses now, but she will learn to. Won't you, Vanessa?" He rubbed the back of Vanessa's neck and placed a possessive arm around her.

Vanessa began trembling.

Catty yanked off the moon amulet. "As soon as the manuscript is destroyed, you let Vanessa free."

Toby nudged Vanessa gently. "Go wait under the tree."

She obediently stepped back under the branches.

He turned to Catty, satisfied. "When the moon rises," he commanded, "reflect the light of the moon from your amulet onto the manuscript."

Catty gazed at the night sky. The moon

edged over the jagged tops of the trees. She glanced at Toby to see if the time was right, then lifted the amulet and reflected the milky glow of the moon onto the manuscript. For a moment Catty worried that if Toby looked closely, he would know it wasn't the real Secret Scroll. Then the parchment began to bubble and foam and she relaxed.

At last, a streak of purple light shot from her amulet. The manuscript pulsated, then exploded into a thousand fragments that rained down on the night.

Tiny wisps of white smoke curled in the air where the sparks had been.

Toby smirked.

"Now," Catty shouted.

Serena and Jimena suddenly ran from the shadows. They quickly grabbed Vanessa and pulled her back to Catty.

"Go," Jimena ordered. She and Serena held Vanessa's hands and latched on to Catty's shoulders.

Catty concentrated, trying to use her power

of time travel for them to escape. Instantly, the carousel and trees roared away from them in a blinding shaft of light and they were falling into the tunnel.

Catty whooped as she clasped her moon amulet around her neck. "We did it!"

Jimena yelled, "We fooled him."

"I can't believe it was so easy," Serena added.

Catty looked at Vanessa. Her eyes were blank and she didn't seem to realize where she was. "Do you think Vanessa will be okay?"

"Claro," Jimena reassured her and gave Vanessa's hand to Catty. "We'll take her to Maggie."

Catty clasped Vanessa's hand tightly.

As they drifted deeper into the tunnel, Catty became aware that something was wrong. She glanced down at her watch. The hands had stopped moving. Panic seized her. They were no longer traveling from one time to another but hovering. This had only happened before when she had tried to go too far back into the past.

"What's wrong?" Jimena asked.

"I don't know," Catty answered. And then she felt a presence. She wrenched her head around.

Toby appeared behind her, grinning. "The tunnel is my realm," he said.

Catty struggled to leave the tunnel and fall back into time, but her power wasn't working.

Toby seemed to understand what she was trying to do. "I have even more power here. You can't escape me now."

Catty drew in a huge gulp of air. How was she going to save her friends? She felt as if she had led them into a trap.

Jimena tugged at her. "Drop back into time."

"I can't," Catty answered. "He's not letting me. He has more power than I do."

The tunnel seemed to be heating. Catty could feel beads of perspiration gathering on her forehead.

"Is the tunnel always this hot?" Serena asked.

Catty shook her head. "No. It's Toby. He's building a huge electrical charge."

"Look." Serena pointed.

Blue and orange sparks crackled around the tunnel walls.

"You think he's building a charge so he can zap us with electricity?" Jimena asked.

"Why not?" Catty answered. "We've all gotten electric shocks when he was around."

"But that was static electricity," Serena replied.

"Lightning is the same thing," Catty explained. "Just static electricity suddenly discharging between clouds and the ground."

Jimena turned quickly to Serena. "Maybe you can go into his mind and try to stop him."

"I'll try." Serena concentrated. Her eyes began to dilate and then suddenly her body jerked. "Ouch!" she yelled.

Toby's laughter filled the tunnel.

"What?" Catty and Jimena asked together.

"He shocked me." Serena looked surprised. "It was like hitting an electric fence. He's got some kind of shield."

Catty watched Toby. The smile on his face

told her that he had something horrible planned for them.

The friends squeezed together and waited for the end.

CHAPTER TWENTY-FOUR

UNEXPECTEDLY, TOBY grabbed Catty's shoulder. The coldness of his fingers seemed to sink deep inside her, making her body cold in spite of the heat.

"Did you really think you were the only one with the ability to escape into a different dimension?" he sneered.

Catty closed her eyes in concentration and tried one last time to escape the tunnel. This time when she opened her eyes, she was surprised to find herself standing alone in a dreamscape.

Rolling mists circled her feet and the horizon had the same pinkish cast and line of craggy mountains that she remembered from a repeated nightmare. Only now forks of lightning cut across the sky. She knew if she took a step forward she would find herself sucked down into quicksand and suffocated. That was the way it had always happened in her terrifying dream. How many times had she awakened from it, gasping for air? Except now she wasn't dreaming. She was awake.

She cautiously turned. She didn't see her friends.

"Jimena!" she called. "Serena!" Her words echoed peculiarly around her, disturbing the mists as if her voice had become three-dimensional.

When no one answered, she turned back. Were they still in the tunnel? Or without her power, had they been forced back into time? She hoped they were safe.

She stared ahead. Something hidden in the mists was watching her, something malevolent.

The feeling was not new to her. She had felt it in this dream before. Now she wondered if it had always been Toby or one of the other Regulators.

A fine tremor started in her legs and traveled up her spine. She feared what would happen next. She took a deep breath and waited. Was there any way she could exit the nightmare? She had to find some way. If she didn't, Serena and Vanessa and Jimena might be trapped in the tunnel or worse, lost in another time with no way to get back to the present, and it would be her fault.

But she was awake. Maybe that meant she could do something. Perhaps she could turn and run away from the quicksand.

Slowly, she took one step backward. When nothing stopped her, she quickly removed her boots, and then spun around and ran. As she sped across the dreamscape, her steps became lighter, and soon she was sweeping over the dream world like a wind. She felt suddenly optimistic. Maybe because she was awake she would be capable of changing the outcome. If she concentrated hard enough, could she create an opening in the dream?

One that would lead her back to the tunnel?

Without warning, lightning crackled and split the air in front of her. In the jagged light, grotesque faces formed and surged around her. She tried to press through them but she felt herself being turned in the direction of the quicksand. Were these the undisguised faces of the Regulators? She struggled against their roiling faces, but in the end, their strength was too great.

As she was thrust closer and closer to the oozing quicksand, she tried to convince herself that even though she was awake what was happening to her was only an illusion. Nothing here could really hurt her.

She was only inches from the quicksand now. Her heart hammered inside her rib cage. Would she suffocate?

As if to answer her question, Toby abruptly appeared beside her. "I came to watch the end."

His disguise was completely gone now. His face was cruelly distorted, eyes evil and piercing. "This isn't a dream, Catty," he smirked. "If you fall in the quicksand here, you die."

Already she could feel the cold swampy waters lapping at her toes.

She tried to keep her feet from moving but they seemed to have an intent of their own.

"Just one step," his voice urged.

Against her will, her feet inched forward, compelled by Toby's voice. The sucking water and sand swirled around her toes and crept up to her ankles. Immediately, she started to sink as she had done so many times before in the dream.

The slimy waters quickly reached the top of her knees and edged up her thighs.

Her body tensed in an involuntary scream that came painfully and silently from her throat. She pressed her eyes closed against the nightmare and waited for death to take her.

She thought of the manuscript. At least the manuscript hadn't been destroyed. It would be safe until another heir was born. That was the only thing she had managed to do right. She had failed miserably at everything else. If only Serena, Jimena, and Vanessa could be saved.

All at once Toby grabbed her arm. "What

did you say?" His words breathed against her ear and she turned her face away from his fetid smell.

"I said nothing," she answered and watched in horror as the spongy quicksand pulled her deeper and the sandy mire lapped at the top of her thighs.

"About the manuscript," he yelled in frustration. "You said something about the manuscript."

"No." She shook her head.

"In dreams, thoughts are expressed aloud," he warned. "You said *'at least the manuscript hasn't been destroyed.'* "

Toby's monstrous eyes flared and she watched in bewilderment as a jagged hole tore the dreamscape apart.

Suddenly she was back in the tunnel, clasping hands with Jimena and Serena. Jimena was holding Vanessa tightly against her.

"What happened?" Jimena asked.

"He took me into a dream," Catty answered, and before she could say more, they tumbled from the tunnel back into time.

Toby was in a rage. He quickly reworked his

features, changing nose, eyes, and hair until he resembled the schoolboy Toby.

"Where are we?" Jimena stared at the land around them.

"It looks normal enough," Catty examined the nearby eucalyptus trees. "Maybe we're back in Griffith Park." But the feel of the air was too heavy and the silence surrounding them too complete.

"Are we in another dream?" Serena asked and pointed up.

Giant sparks of heat lightning split across the night sky. Terrible thunder followed, shaking the ground beneath them.

Catty shook her head. "I don't know."

Then she saw Vanessa, lying on the ground. She got up and went to her. She knelt beside her, cradled her, and held her tightly. In the flashing glow from the lightning, Vanessa's face looked pallid and sickly. Her eyes no longer focused and her heartbeat felt weak and slow.

Catty stared back at Toby as he paced angrily around them. Nothing was taking Vanessa from her. Not death. Not Toby. But even as she made the promise to herself, she felt Vanessa weaken and slip away. Tenderly she stroked Vanessa's hair and kissed the top of her head.

Toby walked slowly toward her.

CHAPTER TWENTY-FIVE

CATTY STARED AT Toby as he paced silently around her.

"I understand your trickery now," he said.

Catty remained motionless, paralyzed with intense fear, not for herself, but for Vanessa.

His voice was deadly when he spoke again. "You didn't destroy the Secret Scroll."

"I did," Catty lied.

"That was a forgery you destroyed." His hand whipped out and he yanked Vanessa from her arms. Catty threw herself at Toby and tried to pry her from him. Sparks of electricity stung her, but still her fingers worked to free Vanessa.

"Confess," he ordered.

"Let Vanessa go with Jimena and Serena and I'll tell you," she answered.

He smiled mockingly, as if her bravery amused him. He dropped Vanessa, and she crumpled to the ground. Jimena and Serena pulled her away.

"I took another old manuscript and painted it to make it look like the Secret Scroll," Catty admitted. "I didn't think you'd look at it closely."

His eyes narrowed into slits but not before she caught a flicker of uneasiness. "Take me to the real manuscript," he spoke more calmly now.

Catty looked around her. "How? I don't even know where we are."

"Where is the manuscript?" he demanded.

"My house," she said quietly and hoped that Kendra was sleeping. She didn't need to add her into the mix.

He touched her shoulder and her body

began to shiver. "Take the hands of your friends," he ordered.

As soon as she did, lightning flared around them. They were lifted into a vortex of white light and soon they were standing in Catty's backyard.

"Get the manuscript," Toby ordered. "The correct one. No trickery." He pressed one menacing hand around Vanessa's neck in warning.

"I understand." Catty hurried toward her house. But as she walked across the patio and opened the sliding glass door, she remembered what Maggie had told them. Regulators were afraid of the Secret Scroll. There had to be a reason. Something more than the curse. If the Path of the manuscript described the way to vanquish the Atrox, then surely it must also tell how to destroy the Regulators.

She dashed across the kitchen, her heart beating with renewed hope, and climbed the stairs. Maybe the manuscript could protect them!

She walked into her bedroom and started to grab the manuscript from her desk. Her hand stopped in midair.

The manuscript was gone.

She glanced at the hallway. Had Kendra come into her room and taken it? What if she had tried to destroy the manuscript herself? That would be so like Kendra.

Catty rushed down the hallway and paused at the door to Kendra's room. A dim night-light cast an orange glow across the room. Catty entered silently, the thick oriental carpet absorbing her footsteps, and sat on the edge of the bed. Kendra's breathing was thick and heavy. Her eyes opened and she smiled thinly. Catty knew without asking that she was feeling worse.

"I need the manuscript, Kendra," Catty spoke softly. "Where is it?"

"The kitchen." Her breath hitched and broke the words apart. "I was double-checking my translations. I wanted to find some clue."

Catty suddenly remembered the incantation that Kendra had yelled at her the night before. That had to be the answer. She started to ask, but Kendra had fallen back into a deep sleep.

She bolted from the room and ran down the

stairs to the kitchen. She searched quickly through the scribbled pages scattered about the table. Finally she found what she was looking for. The words were underlined in bold red slashes. That was exactly what she needed.

She read it quickly, then grabbed the manuscript and went back outside to face Toby.

CHAPTER TWENTY-SIX

CATTY STEPPED FORWARD, holding the Secret Scroll high in the air as Kendra had done the night before.

Toby glanced at her, a smile of triumph on his face. Then Catty spoke and his smile vanished.

"Demere personam tuam atque ad dominum tuum se referre." Catty recited the incantation clearly. The words empowered her and the Scroll seemed to come to life, its force throbbing through her.

Toby hesitated, then backed up slowly. Blue sparks fluttered around his body.

Catty started to repeat the incantation but before she could, white clouds pushed into her vision. Was he taking her into another dream? She shuddered. He controlled her in the dreamland. Once there, he could force her to destroy the Scroll.

Desperately, she lifted the manuscript and tried to say the words but her voice had become useless. She struggled to speak and now her lips refused to move.

Her vision cleared suddenly and she was back in the same nightmare. The jagged mountains from her dream came into clear focus. Toby stepped through the churning mists.

"You'll never be able to use the incantation in my world," he said with a terrible smile. "Destroy the Secret Scroll."

She forced her lips to move. "I won't destroy it." She was resolute, but already her free hand was reaching for her amulet. As her hand started to yank the amulet from its chain, a searing pain stabbed her back. She looked at Toby to see why he had hurt her, but his eyes looked as confused as she felt.

Another spike of pain dug into her and as it did, the dream broke apart like a thousand birds scattering into flight.

She shook her head. She was standing back in her yard, clutching the manuscript. Jimena and Serena held her arms.

"Sorry." Jimena smiled deviously. "I had to hit you." She rubbed Catty's back.

"We figured pain would jar you out of the dream-trance," Serena explained, massaging Catty's shoulder.

Toby glared at them and took a step forward.

"Thanks, I guess." Catty grinned in spite of the pain twisting through her.

Toby took another trudging step toward them.

"Here," Catty whispered and pointed to the lines in the manuscript. "Maybe we'll have more power if we say the incantation together."

They grasped the manuscript and repeated the incantation after Catty. *"Demere personam tuam atque ad dominum tuum se referre."*

A brilliant white flash stung their eyes and

filled the yard with a strange light. Then another flare as bright as lightning roared around Toby.

"We did it!" Serena squealed and let go of the manuscript.

"Wait," Catty cautioned. "Something feels wrong." And then she knew. They hadn't destroyed Toby. He was escaping into the tunnel.

Before they could react, Toby grabbed Vanessa and took her with him.

"No!" Catty screamed.

"Follow him," Jimena yelled.

"Hold on to me," Catty ordered.

Jimena and Serena grabbed onto Catty's arms, then she opened the tunnel and they fell in after Toby and Vanessa. Catty was going dangerously fast but she needed to catch up to them. She wouldn't be able to go as far back in time as Toby could go, so her only chance to save Vanessa was now.

"Say the words together," Catty urged and held up the manuscript.

Jimena and Serena each put one hand on the manuscript while their other hand clasped Catty tightly. Then they repeated the incantation.

Finally, Jimena stopped. *"Mira."* She pointed.

Toby's appearance began to change. His features twisted and melted. His mouth stretched into a brutal slash of scar tissue. Cartilage curled irregularly around two holes where his nose had been. He crouched over, his breathing labored. Air rattled from his throat. What remained of him seemed to fall into a deep sleep. Toby began to tumble away from them, carrying Vanessa with him.

"We have to save Vanessa!" Jimena shouted. "Catch up to him."

"I don't know if I can," Catty answered, straining her power.

"Try," Serena yelled.

Vanessa stirred.

"Vanessa!" Catty yelled.

Vanessa glanced at her weakly, then a baffled look crossed her face. She seemed to become aware of her surroundings again. She gasped when she saw the monstrous creature who was holding her. She struggled to free herself from the clawlike hands but they held her tightly. She reached toward Catty.

Catty grabbed Vanessa and wrenched her free. As she did, the manuscript fell from her hands.

Jimena started to go after it.

"Don't," Catty warned. "If you let go of me, you'll fall back into time, and who knows where you'll land."

"I wish you'd mentioned that earlier." Serena held more tightly to Catty's arm.

They watched the Secret Scroll fall into the void and disappear. Then they landed back in time.

"Where are we?" Serena asked and looked around. "I hope this is real life and not someone's dream."

CHAPTER TWENTY-SEVEN

CATTY LOOKED UP at the hills and saw the Hollywood sign. "We're in L.A.," she answered with a surge of happiness.

"When?" Jimena asked urgently and looked around her.

"Yeah," Serena wondered. "What day is it?"

Catty glanced down at her watch and looked at the date display. "It's the same night we left."

"Great, let's go get the car," Serena suggested.

"Yeah," Jimena said. "Then let's get something to eat. *Tengo hambre.*"

"Isn't anyone going to tell me what's going on?" Vanessa asked. "What was that monster?"

"You tell her," Serena told Catty.

"It's a long story," Catty began as they started walking toward a bus stop.

An hour later, they were in Jimena's car, driving through the park. Cool air smelling of pine and eucalyptus rushed through the windows. The fires had been put out and the winds from the ocean had driven the smoke away.

Catty rested her head on the backseat and looked out at the night.

"I almost got us all destroyed," Vanessa remarked. "None of this would have happened if I hadn't been trying to make Michael jealous." She shook her body. "Yuck. Did you see what Toby really looked like?"

Catty nodded. "A putrid monster. I tried to tell you."

"We all did," Jimena put in.

Vanessa sighed and looked out the window. "Tell me I didn't kiss him when he looked like that."

"You kissed him," Catty teased.

"No way." Vanessa covered her face.

"Yes way," Serena laughed.

"With tongue," Jimena added with glee.

"I wonder what Michael is doing tonight?" Vanessa leaned back against the seat and laughed. "I hope I didn't make him too jealous."

They all laughed.

"I got my one and only," Jimena remarked. "Collin *es mi todo.* Only two more days and he'll be back from Hawaii."

"I had my guy," Catty sighed. "Too bad."

Serena turned and looked at her. "You're not going to break up with Chris, are you?"

"He's so cool," Jimena added. "You'll be sorry."

Vanessa smiled slyly. "Wait until you hear about Chris."

"What's with Chris now?" Serena asked.

"Well, he's a few hundred years old for one thing," Vanessa began.

Then Catty explained.

By the time Catty arrived home, Kendra was up, sitting at the kitchen table in her robe and big furry slippers.

"I must have been delirious," she said. "I hope I didn't frighten you."

Catty shook her head.

Kendra's hand sifted through the piles of papers on the table. "You'll never believe the things I thought I read in that manuscript." She paused, her eyes fearful, and looked at Catty. "It was all true, wasn't it?"

Catty hesitated, wondering if she should tell Kendra the truth.

Then Kendra took her hand and Catty began to speak. There was a lot she still didn't understand, but what she knew, she told her.

CHAPTER TWENTY-EIGHT

AFTER SCHOOL ON Monday, Catty sat alone in the kitchen. Memories from the days before weighed down on her. There was no awakening from what had happened but it felt more like a nightmare now than real. It had been difficult to sleep and she felt tired. She wondered how long the fear of dreaming would stay with her.

Shadows stretched and seemed to move and shift as if the setting sun were giving them life. Catty looked behind her, trying to reassure herself that there was nothing in the dark but her own imagination. Toby and the manuscript were gone. She was safe.

For a moment she imagined she heard someone walking slowly in the living room. She tensed and listened intently. Then she caught movement in the corner of her eye. She gasped.

When she turned, Chris stepped out of the doorway and into the fading light. His smile delighted her. He was beautiful, and yet there was a difference in his appearance, a confidence and strength that he no longer had to hide.

She felt surprised and happy to see him.

"I can't stay long." He sat beside her. "I have to find the manuscript."

"Sorry. It's all my fault."

"Sorry?" He shook his head. "You protected the manuscript and saved Vanessa. You did the right thing."

He stared at her, a look of longing in his eyes, and she knew intuitively that he liked her as much as she liked him. It was more than like, it was a deep friendship with mutual respect, but sadly she knew that they could never have a relationship.

But she did know she wanted one last kiss. She leaned forward, wondering if she dared kiss him.

He stood suddenly and she pulled back abruptly. "Sorry," she whispered as a blush spread across her face.

"About what now?" he asked softly and then he took her hand and pulled her up against him. He looked down at her and smiled. It was a warm smile, but with an air of sadness.

She sighed. She would never meet anyone so perfect for her again. His hand brushed through her hair.

"We'll be together again someday," he assured her, and she knew it wasn't a wish but a promise.

Then his lips were on hers and he held her tightly.

"Someday," she whispered.

BOOK FIVE

the sacrifice

PROLOGUE

A.D. 1239

The boy's eyes could not adjust to the dark. It was as if he had been blinded in his sleep. He called for the knight who had been charged with guarding him, but no one answered. Why had his guard allowed the hearth fire to go out? The boy listened. He could no longer hear the urgent voices of his father and the other knights in the banqueting hall. Had they left already on their crusade?

Then a strange presence filled the room, and the boy knew he was not alone. He had heard his father and the priests whispering about an ancient evil. He felt his thumb for the ring his father had given him for protection. It was gone. Had it fallen off while he slept? He smoothed his hands under the pillows and down the bedcovers, searching for the comforting stone and metal.

The door to his room slowly opened. He squinted against the sudden light from the lamp torches in the hallway. A girl stood in the doorframe. She looked more goddess than human, the way her skin seemed to glow.

Abruptly cold air made him turn from her and look up. Threatening shadows gathered above him, whirling into a monstrous form. Then, without warning, the darkness rushed over him. He screamed for his guardian knight, but it was the goddesslike girl who fought through the thickening blackness and rescued him. She held him tight against her and ran. The demon shadow raged after them with a force that shook the castle's stone walls.

The girl fell, and the darkness kidnapped the boy.

CHAPTER ONE

STANTON HID IN the shadows as trick-or-treating children ran past him, their small feet crunching gravel and stone. He didn't want vigilant parents to see him sneaking behind the houses and call the police. His problems were already complicated enough. He waited until he could no longer hear the happy squeals before he left his hiding place and continued down the alley, silent as a night predator.

He stopped in a backyard lined with beech trees and breathed the bitter smoke from chimney fires as he studied the house where Serena lived.

He had gone looking for her tonight because he had felt something bad in the air, like the first tremor of premonition. She hadn't been at the Halloween party with her friends. That had surprised him. Now he saw no reassuring light in her bedroom window.

He had always been careful. What they had done was forbidden. Only the Followers he most trusted had even seen them together. That had been his first mistake. He couldn't trust his kind. He should have known.

He looked around to see if anyone was watching, then searched with his mind in the cool air to make sure no one was there in the dark unseen. At last he released his body and let it blend into the night until he became no more than a phantom form among the many sinuous shades of darkness flowing beneath the swaying trees. He glided among the shadows to the motionless black one near Serena's house, then slid up the wall and slipped through the crack between the French doors on her balcony.

The air inside her room was thick with the

scent of eucalyptus and lemon. He materialized near her dresser. His hand automatically turned her alarm clock to face the wall, then brushed across a tray filled with Vicks, cough syrup, aspirin, and a thermometer. He tenderly touched the lemon slices near an empty teacup. Could a simple illness have filled him with so much fear that he had risked coming to see her?

A dim light from a purple Lava lamp cast an amber glow across the bed where Serena lay, the leopard-print sheets twisted in a knot beside her leg. Her long curly hair was half caught in a scrunchy that matched her flannel pajamas. The words *Diamonds are a girl's best friend—they're sharper than knives* curled around a dozen marching Marilyns in army fatigues on the blue fabric. Stanton had been with her when she bought the Sergeant Marilyn pajamas three months back.

The amulet hanging on a thin silver chain around her neck began to glow. Her moon charm was warning her that danger was near. He edged around her cello to the bed, then knelt beside her and touched the dark curls on her pillow. He had been drawn to her from the first moment he saw her. She had clicked her tongue ring nervously against her teeth and smiled at him. That was just moments before she understood what he was. He had known her secret immediately; she was here to protect people from his kind.

He was a Follower, but an *invitus,* one taken against his will. He had been kidnapped from his family when he was only six and consecrated to an ancient evil called the Atrox. Because it had been done against his will, he still had memories of what he had once been. Over time he had learned that both love and death were denied him, but Serena had surprised him and offered him acceptance and affection.

He traced a finger down her arm to her hand. Her fingers uncurled as if they welcomed his touch. He wanted desperately to take her hand, but he held back. Their relationship was beyond hope. He could never change what he had become. He might struggle against it for a while, but the longer he defied what he was, the stronger the pressure became to surrender to his dark urges.

She stirred as if she sensed his presence. He stared at her beautiful face. She was wearing a small diamond in her nose piercing. He had given it to her the day he told her they had to stop seeing each other. He had lied and said it was because their love was forbidden and Regulators would destroy them both if their secret were discovered. He did not let her into his mind that day for fear she would uncover the truth. The real danger had always been from him. Even now he felt the pressure building. His darker side was close to the surface tonight. He could feel it pacing, eager to escape and hunt.

Serena's arm moved and the pajama top pulled up, revealing her flat, tanned stomach. His hand hovered over the tiny gold hoop piercing the flesh above her belly button. Her skin radiated sweet warmth.

Without warning, she sat up in bed. "Stanton?"

He jerked his hand back and released his body to the darkness, then curled inside the shadows around her bed before sliding into the corner.

She kicked back the covers and sat on the edge of her bed. "Show yourself," she whispered.

He was stunned.

"I can feel you." She turned and surveyed the room again. "I know you're here. Please."

He coiled between the French doors and escaped to the outside, then drifted to the yard below. He materialized again and stood in the falling leaves, wanting her.

Serena opened the doors and stepped on her balcony. Low-hanging clouds reflected the city lights, and in the strange illumination he was awed by how perfect she looked. He fought the urge to show himself to her. It was the dark of the moon and on this night it was even more dangerous to spend time with her. His allegiance to the Atrox was strongest when the moon was dead.

"Stanton." She stared beneath the trees as if she knew he was there.

Her thoughts pressed into the air. That was her gift. She could read minds almost as well as he could. But he had never needed to go into her mind to know how much she cared for him. He could easily read her emotions in her large expressive eyes.

"Tu es dea, filia lunae," he whispered in Latin. She was a goddess, a Daughter of the Moon, and he had sworn to destroy her kind.

CHAPTER TWO

THE CAR MUFFLER RUMBLED against the pavement as Stanton raced to West Hollywood. He sped around the corner and streetlights reflected off his polished hood in a dizzy show of color. His car was black, low to the ground, and filled with music. He had the goods: a Clarion 6540 CD player with two Clarion 6x9 speakers, a tube amp in the trunk, and more speakers hidden in the doors. The rhythm pounded through his chest. He was ready to party.

He parked under a jacaranda tree. The music vibrated the tips of the branches, sending a shower of pale purple flowers over the car. He switched off the ignition, and the music died. The moonless night shuddered with silence. He climbed from the car and started walking. It was time for some real rock and roll.

He hurried through the gloomy residential neighborhood to Santa Monica Boulevard, then stepped around the barricades and patrol cars that closed the street to traffic. Young and old were already parading in costume, blowing whistles and carrying signs with slogans like NO ONE PARTIES HARDER THAN THE DEAD. The smells of popcorn and cotton candy filled the air.

A line of stick skeletons connected on one pole greeted him. "Par-tee," said the man, waving the spiky skeletons.

A Spiderman jumped in front of Stanton. He smiled at the man's meager attempt to scare him. Three people on stilts, white sheets flowing behind them, raced around him, their eyes painted with black squares. Then a small boy dressed as Count Dracula ran up to him, exposing sharp canine teeth. He growled, one hand hooked in a claw, the other grasping an orange bag filled with candy.

Stanton let his thoughts turn silky. His question slid into the boy's head, *Do you want to meet someone more evil than a vampire?*

The boy's eyes widened and he dropped his bag of candy. "Mama!" he yelled. He turned and knocked into a ski-masked terrorist. The boy scrambled away.

Stanton grinned at the terrorist, then picked up the orange bag and stole a caramel apple. He bit into the crisp fruit. Sweet and tart flavors burst in his mouth.

The boy returned with his mother and pointed at Stanton with an accusing finger. His mother had a gentle look.

Stanton grinned. "I was looking for you," he said with forced cheeriness. "You dropped your bag of candy."

He handed the bag to the boy's mother. She gave Stanton a guarded look as if she sensed something sinister behind his smiling face. She took the bag and stroked her son's head in reassurance. Then she took his hand and pulled him away.

The dark desire rose inside Stanton, demanding release. If he waited much longer the desire would become a need and the physical compulsion would be more than he could bear. He stared after mother and son, his mind following as they pushed through the crowd.

His thoughts were broken by a sudden sense that someone was staring at him. He turned sharply. Two girls dressed in flowing robes and steeple-crowned hats blushed and laughed. Glitter covered their faces and curling sequin designs had replaced their eyebrows for the night.

The one wearing the purple robe tapped him lightly with her wand.

"Why aren't you in costume?" the girl in the lime-green robe asked. Her sultry lips pouted as she brushed back her thick golden hair, trying to work a magic of her own.

"I am in costume," Stanton answered, his voice melodic and more in her mind than the air.

"You are not," she teased back. There was a slight tremor in her voice that hadn't been there before. "Not unless you turn into a pumpkin at midnight."

"Maybe I do." He stepped closer, enjoying the fear he had awakened in her. What would she do if she knew what he really was? Would she even believe him if he told her about his evil powers? He let his mind tease around her thoughts, savoring her fear.

The girl in purple sensed the predator in him. She pulled on the other one's sleeve. "Come on, Maryann, let's go."

"Wait," Maryann answered. "I want to hear what his costume is."

But her friend was already drifting away, leaving Stanton alone with his prey. Stanton smirked. What made Maryann stay? He tilted his head closer to hers. Her breath was wintermint-sweet.

"Use your imagination," he whispered. "Can't you see what I look like when I'm not in costume?"

He weaved into her mind and planted an

image of Frankenstein. Terror shuddered through her. She sucked in air in a long draw, then let it out in sprays of laughter against his cheek.

"You're no monster," she said as Stanton moved through her memories. Her thoughts were a tangled net. He sensed she'd been drinking. Already her eyes were dreamy and lost. It would be a crime against the Atrox to turn someone like her away. She was ready to cross over.

"If you look too long in my eyes," he said, daring her, "you'll lose yourself."

She stared blissfully at him, her eyes saying yes, as if she understood his unspoken offer.

A sudden white flash made him leave her mind, but not before he read one last thought. She thought him handsome but also frightening. The danger and risk of him attracted her.

The light flashed again. A boy dressed as a pirate held up a camera. "Gotcha," he squealed and ran off, a plastic parrot bobbing on his shoulder.

"Do you go to my school?" Maryann asked, her attitude too eager. "You seem so familiar."

Already he had left his image in her memories. "I don't go to school," he answered. "I live on the streets in Hollywood."

"Homeless?" He could feel her pity and interest.

"Rebel."

Her body thrummed and pressed against him in invitation. His eyes lingered over her. As he eased inside her mind again, she giggled. Why was she trying so hard? He pushed deeper into her memories. Then he knew. She was angry with her father and wanted to bring home a guy who would displease him. He snapped out of her mind.

She looked surprised and disappointed.

He wasn't going to serve her cause. "Maybe we'll see each other around." He moved quickly away from her.

He continued past the Haunted House. General admission was ten dollars. He thought idly about going inside and making somebody's ten-dollar adventure worthwhile, but then he sniffed something floating on the air. Something portentous. He concentrated. It was the same ominous feeling he had had earlier in the day, only it was stronger now, like the warning rolls of thunder before a violent storm.

"Hey," Maryann yelled behind him.

He turned. She smiled shyly, then took his hand and held it tight against her chest as she wrote her telephone number on the palm. "Call me."

A derisive grin crossed his face. He would never call the number. He never did. Tomorrow she would be embarrassed by the way she had acted tonight, but she would continue to think about him anyway. Sometimes the ones he didn't harm came back, looking for him with a hunger of their own.

A band began to play. He recognized the feel-good music at once.

"It's Michael Saratoga," Maryann squealed. She pushed in front of a man and woman dressed as a king and queen with blunted sword and coronet.

Michael played bass guitar on a stage lined

with jack-o'-lanterns. His black hair fell into his face as his fingers ran up and down the fingerboard. There was fire in his music, even Stanton could feel it.

Around the stage girls waved their hands over their heads in time to the beat. When the song ended, the same girls screamed and stretched their arms, reaching for Michael, their hair and costumes dangerously close to the twitching flames inside the pumpkins.

Maryann gave a loud *woo-hoo* and turned to Stanton. "Isn't it great music? I love Michael's band."

"Why?" Stanton didn't wait for an answer. He entered her mind, turning through a labyrinth of Bible study and Sunday school. He hadn't seen this part of her before. She did volunteer work and played piano for her church choir. Her goodness awakened something inside him. He touched her cheek. Maybe he would take this one after all. The Atrox valued a righteous soul over one already tainted. He liked to bend this kind.

The band played a faster song. Maryann

turned away, Stanton's spell broken. He glared at the stage. Had the music broken the trance he had held over her?

Maryann grabbed his hand. "Come on," she coaxed, her hips swaying temptingly. "Don't you want to dance?"

People in costumes began to twist and clap, all spellbound by Michael's music. Two clowns standing nearby slapped their big floppy shoes on the concrete, raising small clouds of dust.

"Enough," Stanton announced. He started to walk away, but a chorus of squeals made him turn back. Vanessa stood on the stage now giving out CDs and T-shirts to outstretched hands. She was dressed as a devil, in slinky red dress. Glitter made her perfect tanned skin shine. Her blond hair was held back by devil horns and a long sinuous tail twitched behind her. She had lined her large blue eyes with tiny silver gems for this night.

He watched her carefully, but no matter how enticing she was, he could never harm her. He had trapped her once in his memory of the night the Atrox had stolen him from his father's castle.

While imprisoned there, she had tried to save his younger self from the Atrox. After that act of kindness he could never harm her.

Like Serena, she was a Daughter of the Moon, but instead of mind reading, she had the gift of invisibility. It wasn't a power that she could fully control. Right now her power seemed more to control her. He considered her, thinking how ironic it was that as a Follower he could never harm a person who did him an act of kindness, but he could destroy someone he desperately loved.

Abruptly, the night shifted. Something cruel and dangerous was near. He was bewildered by what he felt. The Halloween celebration took on a sinister feel. The laughter, yells, and whistle calls blended with the music until the noise became one whirling, ominous sound. His heart beat wildly. Instinct told him to run.

He didn't understand his need to flee, but he started to walk cautiously away. It was as if his body had sensed the approach of something that his eyes had not yet seen. With his mind, he began searching for the danger.

He had only gone a little way when someone grabbed his elbow. His breath caught in his throat. He turned.

Maryann again. She stared boldly into his eyes. "Don't go."

"Something's come up," he murmured. He tore away from Maryann and left her standing in the middle of the dancers.

"You didn't even tell me your name," she yelled angrily after him.

He ignored her.

An unpleasant heaviness filled the air. It came over him in waves. His muscles tensed as his mind searched frantically for the source of the electrical sensation. Regulators were coming. The knowledge pierced him with a certainty he could not deny. Had they discovered him after all? His first thought was of protecting Serena, but already sinuous streams of static electricity stirred through the crowd with a strange pale-blue glow. He knew it was too late. He studied the masked faces, looking for a disguise from another world.

A surge in current made the streetlights glow

brighter. No one seemed to notice. He stepped behind two men dressed as a large pink-and-green dragon and raked his fingers through his hair. The Regulators were closer. Once he was discovered their chase would be relentless. Had they gone after Serena, too?

He became aware of movement in the crowd. The stick skeletons turned as the ghosts on stilts stepped back. Now screams joined the jangle of other sounds. A halo of tiny jagged sparks surrounded whoever walked through the crowd toward him.

"Serena," he whispered. He had to see Serena one last time. He started to release his body and become one with the shadows when powerful hands clasped his back.

CHAPTER THREE

PIERCING BLACK EYES stared back at Stanton from a scarred face. He had never met Malcolm before, but he had seen him many times and heard stories of his depravity and his fearlessness. His butchery was legend. He belonged to the fiercest class of Regulators, those so committed to the Atrox that over time their faces and bodies became distorted, as if continual contact with such unthinkable evil made their flesh decay.

Normally, Malcolm looked human, tall, slender, and striking. He had the power to transform his ugliness into handsome features. All Regulators did. So Stanton didn't understand why he wasn't wearing his disguise tonight.

Malcolm's monstrous appearance had changed since the last time Stanton had seen him without his disguise. Oozing red sores now covered one side of his face and a translucent blue mold coated his scalp near the few matted tangles of hair that remained by his ears. His breath had a dead-fish smell, as if evil were rotting his insides as well.

"Stanton?" Malcolm barked from deep in his throat.

"I accept my fate," Stanton answered boldly, and stood tall, his heart racing. Then he closed his eyes and waited. When nothing happened, he blinked.

Malcolm moved his tongue over the angry slash of red skin around his lips as if he were trying to speak again. His few remaining teeth were black with decay. His electrical aura, so strong only moments before, was diminishing rapidly. Sparks fluttered and died. Finally, his tongue curled back in his mouth and with a rasping voice, he whispered, "Help me."

It was hard for Stanton to understand what Malcolm had said, not because he hadn't heard him, but because his request was so unexpected. As Malcolm's words penetrated his confusion, he realized that Malcolm wasn't there to destroy him after all. Relief and bewilderment flooded through him.

"How can I help you?" Stanton asked, his heart beating even more rapidly than it had only moments before. This was unheard of—a Regulator coming to a Follower for help.

"Take me away from here." The words rattled from deep inside Malcolm. "Some place where we can talk."

Stanton nodded, then glanced at Malcolm's body. His spine was bent at an impossible angle and his muscular legs were twisted painfully at the knees. Stanton didn't think Malcolm would be able to walk anywhere.

"Why aren't you concealing your appearance?" Stanton asked as he tried to shield

Malcolm from the curious stares of the people who had gathered around them.

Malcolm heaved in air and let it out with a harsh burst of breath. "I can't. I'm losing my strength."

"Then why have you come to me?" Stanton asked nervously and glanced back at the growing crowd. They didn't look afraid. Behind their masks and makeup they seemed to be staring at Malcolm in awe. "You should have gone to the Cincti. I'll take you there."

"No. You. I must see only you." The words came out loud and urgent.

"I can't do anything to help you," Stanton cautioned. "I don't have that kind of power."

Malcolm cleared his throat. "I need to warn you."

The words made Stanton wary. A warning—this troubled Stanton more than if Malcolm had come to destroy him. Regulators were like an internal police. They terminated Followers who rebelled against the Atrox or displeased it in any way. They never helped Followers, or warned them. What could be so bad that a Regulator would need to caution him?

"Warn me about what?" Stanton asked. "What do you need to say? Tell me now."

Malcolm stared at him and tried to communicate telepathically, but his power had weakened too much. Instead of words, Stanton felt only a sluggish swirling in his brain.

"Sorry," Malcolm said finally as he sensed his failure and pulled back.

Stanton's apprehension deepened. He needed to know now, especially if the warning involved Serena. He slowly slid into Malcolm's mind. The horrific memories of centuries gathered around him. There was no way he could find what Malcolm needed to say. His thoughts and feelings were as twisted as his body. He would have to wait and hear what Malcolm wanted to tell him. He untangled himself from Malcolm's memories.

Immediately, a brilliant white light blinded him, followed quickly by another and another. Each flash made Malcolm shudder.

Stanton turned.

The boy in the pirate costume yelled, "Gotcha seven times."

People were admiring what they thought was Malcolm's costume. They still stood too far back to smell the foul odor coming from his body, but soon the more curious would step forward. Stanton had to take Malcolm somewhere quickly before the crowd became too bold.

"That's great makeup," the pirate-boy squealed. "Do you work for the studios?" He took a daring step forward, studying the way Malcolm's body was contorted. The boy's nose crinkled, but the smell didn't stop him from edging closer. "How'd you make the body anyway? With pillows?" He poked at the exposed stomach. A strange look came over him.

Stanton knew the boy had touched what felt like warm, soft flesh. Stanton narrowed his eyes and sunk into the boy's mind to silence the scream gathering in his throat. *Don't even think about it,* he barked into the boy's head.

The startled boy looked at Stanton. His mouth dropped open and the camera tumbled from his hands and hit the pavement. The flash snapped before the camera lens shattered. The boy turned and ran, the plastic parrot jogging on his shoulder.

Stanton lifted Malcolm against him. He wanted to leave before someone else dared to touch him. That's when he noticed the cruel way Malcolm's feet were misshapen, his toes curled at odd angles.

"Can you walk?" Stanton asked, wondering how Malcolm had made the journey to find him.

"I'll try." Malcolm leaned heavily on Stanton's shoulder and breathed against his neck as Stanton pushed through the crowd.

"Hurry," Malcolm urged. "Before it's too late."

CHAPTER FOUR

STANTON PRESSED HIS foot hard on the accelerator and drove down Hollywood Boulevard. When he swerved around a bus, Malcolm slid in the seat beside him, slumping lower. It had been difficult to pull him through the curious crowd, and when they had finally reached the car, Malcolm had been too shaken to speak. He kept staring at the shadows as if sensing a presence in the night, then he had begun trembling violently. The Atrox was always near and watchful, sending shadows to be its eyes.

The squat was only a block away. He honked

twice to warn pedestrians out of the street, then zigzagged around them. Tires squealed as he slammed to a halt at the curb in front of what looked like an abandoned building. He jumped from the car, ran to the passenger side and eased Malcolm out to the curb as a gang of homeless punkers sauntered down the street. They dressed as though every day of the year were Halloween, and tonight alcohol made them brave.

"Trick or treat," the leader said, smirking. He hesitated for a second when he saw Malcolm's face, then stepped brazenly forward.

One of his friends circled near. "Yeah, what do you have for treats?" His face looked hollow in the white light from the security lamp overhead.

A third punker boldly reached for Stanton's pocket. "You got any money in there?"

Stanton let go of Malcolm and turned with a suddenness that made them duck. The leader stumbled drunkenly and fell. He got up and started forward, his combat boots beating the sidewalk. "Let's see what you got."

Stanton stood protectively in front of

Malcolm and sent the force of his mind spinning through the air. It hit the punker and slammed him against the wall. Then Stanton shot into the punker's mind and pulled slumber from the back of his head.

"What?" the punker wheezed in confusion as a grin slipped across his face and his eyes closed in sleep.

The others looked at Stanton with fear in their eyes and inched back. They turned and ran, their footsteps echoing into the night as Stanton pulled Malcolm across his back and carried him into the alley. Stanton was strong, but Malcolm was heavy and all dead weight.

By the time he reached the door at the end of the alley, the muscles in his back and legs were burning. He kicked it hard. The wood protested with a loud crack and the door popped open.

He stepped inside. Normally the squat was filled with Followers, but tonight everyone was celebrating Halloween. Neon lights from outside shone through cracks in the boarded windows and cast thin bars of pink and blue across the floor. The only sound came from Malcolm's breathing and a distant dripping faucet.

Stanton walked around inflated air mattresses and piles of blankets where the Initiates slept. Initiates were kids who had been led to the Atrox by Followers. They lived here now with the hope of someday being accepted into its congregation, but they needed to prove themselves worthy first.

The ones accepted by the Atrox, the Followers, slept on the second floor. All of them had been apprenticed to Stanton to perfect their evil. He taught them how to read minds, manipulate other people's thoughts, and imprison people in their memories. He also showed them how to bring victims to the Atrox.

Stanton had crossed over so many kids now that it was impossible for him to recall exactly how many, but he hadn't recruited anyone recently. Not since meeting Serena. He didn't think any of the Followers suspected. They seemed in awe of him. He was an Immortal after all, and none of the other Followers apprenticed to him had been granted that gift. But there was endless competition among the Followers to please the Atrox and gain favor. It made trust impossible. He had to be careful.

Stanton carried Malcolm up the stairs and into the room where he slept. He set Malcolm on a futon, then covered him with blankets. He went to the table in the corner and traced his fingers over the surface, touching a can opener, plastic forks, and a jar of instant coffee until he found a box of matches. He popped a match with the tip of his thumb. A flame flared; he lit three candles on the table and four more set on a wooden box on the floor. He knelt beside Malcolm.

"Shouldn't I take you to the Cincti?" Stanton said quietly. "Maybe the Atrox could help." He couldn't imagine what had happened to Malcolm. Maybe he had battled some force and lost.

Malcolm shook his head slowly. His chest labored to pull in a breath. "I'm dying," he muttered at last.

The words shocked Stanton. It couldn't be true. "You're an Immortal," Stanton said. "How can you die?"

"I did the unthinkable." Malcolm tried to twist his scarred lips into a smile, but failed.

Stanton's heart started pounding against his chest. He glanced around the room. The twitching candle flames made shadows tremble on the wall. He leaned closer to Malcolm in spite of the smell. "What unthinkable thing did you do?"

Malcolm shook his head. "Later . . ." He tried to keep his eyes open but only the whites were showing now. *"Caveas Lamp . . ."* he whispered.

"*Caveas Lamp?* Beware of Lamp?" Stanton asked. The name meant nothing to him. "Who is Lamp?"

But instead of answering, Malcolm eyes fluttered open as he prayed, "Glorious Goddess of the dark moon, take my soul now and guide it through the night to the light . . ." His lips continued moving in silent prayer.

Stanton flinched. The prayer was treason. Over the centuries he had heard whispers about the ancient goddess who received the dead and guided them to rebirth, but he thought they were only stories. Why would Malcolm pray to her? The Atrox was his god.

He felt desperate to know. "Tell me what you did and what does it have to do with warning me about Lamp?"

Malcolm's head fell to the side. The scarred skin on his face shriveled and tightened over his skull, then dried to brittle leather. His body continued to disintegrate until there was nothing left but yellow bone and dust.

Stanton pulled back and watched as a deadly chill inside him grew and he began to shudder. An Immortal couldn't die. Impossible—yet Malcolm was gone.

A ring fell from a finger bone and rolled across the wood floor.

Stanton picked it up and studied the purple stone set in the clawed prongs in front of the candle flame. His heart beat wildly as he turned it back and forth. The gemstone gave off a dazzling fire. A kaleidoscope of color shot across the room.

He held it close to his face in awe. It was the ring that had disappeared the night he had been kidnapped from his home. He read the inscription, *Protegas et deleas,* on the inner band. *Protect and destroy*. It was the ring his father had given him centuries before to protect him from the Atrox.

He turned and looked down at what remained of Malcolm. Where had Malcolm found the ring? He wondered if it was connected to the warning. He tried to slip it onto his finger, but the metal band burned his skin. He quickly removed it, but already his flesh was singed. He studied the red blister and wondered how Malcolm had been able to wear it. As he placed the ring into his jeans pocket, a thought came to him with a terrifying jolt. He had helped a Regulator who had turned from the Atrox. He didn't know what Malcolm had done, but whatever it was, it must have been unpardonable.

He needed to hide Malcolm's remains before anyone saw and asked questions. He had started to fold the blanket around the bones and dust when the door slammed downstairs and the hardwood floor strained under someone's footsteps.

CHAPTER FIVE

A CLAMMY COLD HAD crept in from the ocean and settled over the city by the time Stanton walked down the empty streets near the Catholic cemetery in East Los Angeles. Behind him traffic buzzed down the freeway.

Back at the squat, he had easily carried his bundle past the two Initiates who had come home early from their Halloween celebration. They had glanced at the blanket, but in the gloomy light they couldn't have seen anything to make them wonder. Besides, no one would have thought he carried the remains of a Regulator.

He breathed deeply and stopped at the locked gates. He didn't think the Atrox or the Regulators could enter this sacred ground. Malcolm's remains would be safe from discovery here. It would be the same as inside a church. But would he be allowed inside? He tentatively touched the iron bars, expecting a jolt of lightning to deny him entry. When nothing happened, he smoothed his hand over the cold metal. He felt no threat, only soothing comfort. He slid his bundle through the iron bars and released his body to the shadows. He curled into the night, then became whole again on the other side of the fence, picked up the blanket, and began walking among the headstones.

A sudden light rolled over the markers, sweeping toward him. He pressed against a large tree before the headlights from a slow moving car beamed over him. He waited as a patrol car edged slowly by, its rotating beacon flashing red light over trees, stones, and concrete benches. It was private security, probably hired especially for Halloween to guard against vandalism.

When the car had passed and its taillights were only distant beads, Stanton continued on. He tiptoed through the overgrown grass behind a square, dank-smelling mausoleum, then cut across the lawn to the older tombstones. Granite angels dusted with fine cobwebs guarded the farthest end of the cemetery. He read weathered inscriptions and epitaphs as he looped around the graves.

Finally, he found a headstone whose inscription had been erased by time. He gently laid Malcolm's bones on top of the grave. He wanted to say something important, but all that came to mind were words he had heard said too many times. Finally, he took the ring from his pocket and scratched PRIMUS APUD PECCATORES, PRIMUS APUD AFFLICTOS into the weathered stone. First among sinners, first among sufferers.

He wondered what Malcolm had needed to tell him. Instinct told him that it hadn't been about Serena. He had considered that at first, but finally dismissed it. If Malcolm had known about their relationship, other Regulators would have also, and both he and Serena would have been terminated without warning. It had to have been a greater threat, but Stanton couldn't imagine what could be worse.

"Unthinkable," he whispered into the cool air. In his world of dark, nothing was unthinkable, but it was still difficult to imagine anything that could impel a Regulator to warn a Follower. A Regulator's job was to destroy renegades, not aid them.

He was about to leave when he caught movement from the corner of his eye. The whisper of stealthy footsteps followed and a shadow glided across the gravestone.

CHAPTER SIX

A YOUNG GIRL STOOD behind him, not more than fourteen. She wore a velvet cape lined in red silk over a dress with lacing across the bodice that looked like something a vampiress might wear in a movie. She stared at him and brushed nervously at the blond hair held away from her face by a row of downy black feathers. She had painted a spiderweb around one blue eye.

"Aren't you afraid to be out here alone?" she whispered in a haunting voice.

Stanton smiled at her attempt to play vampire on this night and wondered how she had gotten into the cemetery; she had probably squeezed between the bars. She looked small enough.

"Well?" she asked with more daring, and spread the edges of her cape wide like bat wings.

"Should I be afraid of you?" he asked.

She seemed upset that he wasn't. She cocked her head and looked around him at the headstone. "Is that Spanish?"

"It's Latin."

She laughed briefly. "No one knows Latin anymore. You just made it up."

"It means 'First among sinners, first among sufferers.'"

She giggled. "Yeah, but what does *that* mean?"

He studied her, alone, vulnerable. The thought of making her a Follower and showing her the darker mysteries of life excited him. The desire pulsed through him. He spoke softly, daring her to look in his eyes. "It means that if you sin, no matter how evil you are, you always suffer for it."

She put her hands on her hips. "That's an odd thing to write. Are you joking? I don't get it."

"Why would I joke about sin?" The urge to cross her over became a sweet and intense pain.

"Because you think it's cool or something." She glanced up at him and smiled, then caught his eyes and started as if she had finally seen the danger there.

He loved the fear he now saw on her face. He wanted to turn that fear into jagged terror.

"Sin and suffer," he whispered and brushed her hair away from her neck, exposing the rapid pulse of vein.

She sucked in air and took a quick step backward, her hand smoothing her throat.

He wanted her to turn and run. Above all, he enjoyed the chase.

She eyed him oddly. Terror shimmered near the top of her mind, cool and inviting. Then he laughed at what he read there.

"No," he said. "I'm not a vampire."

"I knew you weren't." She tried to sound annoyed, but her feet betrayed her. She backed away until a wobbly headstone stopped her.

"There aren't many legends about my kind," he whispered, stepping toward her, breathing in her panic. The dark impulse had taken over. His desire to please the Atrox was no longer a want, but a physical need.

"The stories haven't survived," he continued.

She smiled thinly. "You're teasing, aren't you?" But the tone of her voice said that she knew he wasn't.

"Don't you want to know what happened to all the tales about others like me?" He touched her lightly.

Her hands grasped the tombstone behind her. She stepped around it until the stone was a barrier between them. "All right, tell me your Halloween stories."

He loved the way she tried to be so brave. "The church destroyed them as heresy. That's why you haven't read about me in any of the books you sneak home from the library and hide in your closet from your mother."

She gasped. "How do you know about that?"

"I have my way of knowing." He held the ribbon that tied her bodice. "You like to read about vampires but your mother thinks it's unhealthy. Do you really want so desperately to become aligned with the night?"

She frantically shook her head.

"I can show you a more ancient evil," he promised in a soothing voice. He tugged on the ribbon, untying the bow. "One that has existed since the beginning of time."

"Right." She tried to force the word out with a sarcastic tone, but failed.

"Not many people know about the Atrox and its Followers, but you will," he assured her.

"You're not being funny anymore," she answered with more whimper than anger.

He let his finger trace up her body to her chin and lifted her face until she was forced to look in his eyes. "I was never trying to be. I was only trying to explain what I am."

She looked quickly behind her as if searching for a way to escape.

He paused for a moment, hoping she would run. When she didn't, he continued, "I can dissolve into shadow. Stay that way for days if I want. It's one of my powers."

"Stop teasing me," she whined. "You're scaring me now."

He leaned closer. "I can also enter your mind and take you into mine. Do you want me to show you?"

"No," she pleaded. It wasn't the strange light in the graveyard that gave her face such an unnatural pallor now. The true beauty of fear shimmered in her eyes.

"Let me show you." He seeped into her mind and brought her back into his. He could feel her struggle and then stop. He let her feel what he was, the emptiness and evil.

He released her again. He wanted her to run, but she only stumbled backward as if she had lost her balance.

He wrapped his hand around the back of her neck. The skin felt soft and warm. Her pulse fluttered rapidly beneath his fingers.

She tried to pull away but his hand held her firmly. Tears gathered in the corners of her eyes, making them brighter. He held her face close to his own. He yearned for the momentary peace that turning her to the Atrox could give him.

He cupped his hands around her sad beautiful face and inhaled her sweet breath. Her eyes stared sightless, the pupils large but unseeing. She was lost in his memories now. Soon he would show her the face of evil and take all of her tomorrows for himself.

"Now you believe, don't you?" he asked. "You see with other eyes than your own and know. Turn and see the Atrox."

She nodded, but as she did, he caught his reflection in her pupils and was filled with self-loathing. He felt hatred for what he had become and the raw hate broke the trance he held over her. He felt her shudder in his hands, but was surprised that she seemed reluctant to let him go. Maybe what she had seen and felt had made her feel loved.

"It's a lie," he whispered harshly. "There's no love there."

He brushed the loose hair away from her face and eased her down beside the gravestone. She would awaken tomorrow, believing it had all been a dream. But he knew her kind. She would go to the library and search until she found the obscure piece written by Herodotus that most scholars thought was only an embellishment on the Pandora myth.

He slowly walked away from her and tried to calm the part of him that felt denied. It hovered impatiently near the surface, demanding release. He had failed the Atrox. It was a crime to let Maryann and the girl go free. Worst of all, he had broken a greater taboo in helping Malcolm. He clenched his hands and stared at the black shadows twisting around the headstones. The Atrox had its spies. He wondered how long it would be before he was discovered.

Then he tested the air to see if the omen he had felt hovering around him earlier that night had been Malcolm. Instead of being reassured, he felt a shudder of dread.

It had not been Malcolm. Whatever it was, it had not reached him yet.

CHAPTER SEVEN

BY THE SLANT OF sunlight across his blankets, Stanton knew it was late morning. He pushed aside the covers and strode barefoot to the small window looking over the alley. A piece of cardboard taped over one pane flapped softly as a cool breeze seeped into the room, bringing the smells of coffee and bacon from Gorky's café.

He stared up at the morning sky and remembered another time when he had lived in a castle and his father had been a great prince. That had been so long ago, and yet he still remembered it clearly. His father would feel ashamed if he could see his son now. He felt ashamed himself.

When he had been a boy, he had dreamed of becoming a greater prince than his father. He had already been a skilled rider by age six. His future was clear. Then the priests had come. Stanton remembered the haunted look on their faces when they placed the manuscript on the table. He had never seen such fear in the eyes of grown men before.

He turned from the memory and slipped into jeans and shirt, then stepped into shoes and left his room. He stood at the top of the stairs. A thin haze of cigarette smoke rose from the floor below. His eyes traveled over mattresses and blanket. Where was everyone? The room seemed strangely deserted and silent. Something was wrong. Usually, after a holiday like Halloween, there was an uproar of boasting about what had been done the night before.

Then he heard laughter. In a far corner, Tymmie, Kelly, and Murray sat on a worn green couch. The flickering lights from the television strobed over their faces as they watched a Sony

TV, looted during the Los Angeles riots. Behind the TV, a thick orange cord snaked to an outside plug at the liquor store next door.

Stanton eased his way down the stairs.

Kelly waved. "Come see. This is just too hilarious."

"Breaking news?" he asked.

"Better," Tymmie answered. His white-blond hair was moussed into jagged spikes. Three hoops pierced his nose and one his lip. Even with so many piercings he looked like a student at La Brea High. Stanton trained his Followers to be secretive and to blend in. But now there were other newer Followers who flaunted their allegiance to evil. They liked guns, knives, and fists. Several had even been in jail.

"How's tricks?" Murray shouted, then turned back to the TV. He drew a black comb from his pocket and brushed his blond hair into a ducktail. Murray had crossed over in the fifties and still tried to look the same as he had then. His appearance got him parts as an extra in period movies.

Stanton walked over to the couch. He liked these three. They understood his example and obeyed. Kelly could have been a cheerleader or class president, but instead of attending high school, she spent her days drifting up and down Hollywood Boulevard. She was cautious and Stanton liked that. He didn't want to draw attention from the LAPD.

He glanced down at the screen. They were watching another vampire movie.

"Do you believe what he's doing with his eyes?" Kelly screamed. "And can you imagine sleeping in dirt? Yuck. How uncool is that?"

Stanton glanced at the squalor around him.

Kelly caught his look and shrugged. "Well, at least it's not dirt," she muttered.

His Followers laughed at vampire movies, but what would they do if people armed with religious faith ceaselessly hunted them down?

Stanton slumped onto the couch. Murray stood up with a snap to make room for Stanton to sprawl.

"Where is everyone?" Stanton asked.

Kelly hushed him as the vampire on the TV screen stalked his victim, then caught herself. "Sorry," she said.

Stanton frowned. He could feel Murray's thoughts, the wordless accusation *Where was Stanton last night?* "You do not question me even in your thoughts," he growled.

Murray nodded. "It's just that—"

"It's just that what?" Stanton snapped. He was stronger, more powerful. He felt Murray's fear.

"We wanted you at the celebration." Tymmie turned his head away from the TV screen.

"You don't need me to show you how to party on Halloween," Stanton answered abruptly.

"Not Halloween," Murray said, nervously searching in a pocket for his comb.

"This one's important." Tymmie clicked off the TV. "Yvonne asked me to find you, but you told me to never wake you up."

The urgency in Tymmie's voice made Stanton wonder if something had occurred the night before while he was helping Malcolm.

"What happened?" Stanton asked at last.

"It's the time of transition," Tymmie continued.

"Evil's going to dominate," Kelly interrupted in her high voice.

Murray tried to give him a high five but Stanton didn't raise his hand.

"I'm tired of all these plans," Stanton said. This wasn't the first time some Follower had claimed to have a plan to make it evil's turn to rule. Over the centuries he had heard too many schemes.

Tymmie stood as if energized. "It's not just another excuse to party this time."

"How can you be so sure?" Stanton sneered.

"It's different." Tymmie looked at him seriously. "I feel it. Everyone does."

Stanton eyed him. He had known Tymmie long enough to know that he was able to pick things from the air, the same way Stanton could. Now Stanton wondered if the transition was what he had been sensing. It could mean trouble for him. He needed to find out who his rival was this time. There was intense competition and the victors always stripped the power from those who had previously been their opposition. He definitely didn't want to go back to what his life had been before he had become a leader. He stared at the mattresses on the floor and shook his head.

Tymmie sensed what he was thinking. "That's why I'm here."

"*We're* here," Kelly corrected him.

"We'll find out more at the celebration," Tymmie suggested. "Yvonne won't tell us anything until she talks to you."

"Where?"

"The Dungeon."

Stanton stood. "Let's go."

The Dungeon was an after-hours club on Sunset Boulevard. It opened early in the morning, serving kids who didn't ever want the party to end. The black painted walls made day become night again.

When Stanton walked in, he found Kelly already perched on a bar stool, her arms around a guy Stanton had never seen before. Probably someone she was going to cross over. She let her soft, long hair brush tantalizingly against the guy's face.

Murray leaned against a wall, combing his hair. He let the girls come to him. He called it the James Dean method.

Stanton walked around two girls dancing together, bumping hips. Under the changing lights, their faces turned pink, then blue, then back to pink again.

He searched through the dancers until he saw Yvonne. She was wearing a blue see-through dress over lacy underwear. She had a perfect body and loved to flaunt it. She turned as if she had felt his stare. Her eyes invited him to join her. He started walking slowly toward her. She had become *lecta* last year and now she had her own league of Followers at Venice Beach.

"Hey, Yvonne," he whispered into her ear, drawing her away from the arms of the guy she had been dancing with. When the guy started to complain, Stanton shot him an insolent smile that made him back away.

He held Yvonne tightly against him, feeling the soft silk of her dress and breathing her flowery perfume. "What did you hear?" he asked at last.

"Where have you been that you don't know?" Yvonne replied, as if he had stood her up for an important date. "Last night we were all called together and you never showed."

"Halloween," he whispered into her ear as if that were excuse enough. He left a kiss on her temple. "Did everyone miss me as much as you did?"

She leaned back and glared at him, then laughed.

"You wear your emotions on your sleeve," he explained. "I don't even need to go into your mind to see how much you like me."

He glanced down at her body; she let his eyes linger. She loved to tease. She boldly moved her lips to his, begging for a kiss. He cautioned her lips away with the tip of one finger.

"What did you hear, Yvonne?"

It wasn't unusual for leading Followers not to

show up for important meetings and Yvonne had a responsibility to tell him what she knew. She was still subordinate to him.

She smiled coyly. "In only a matter of days the Atrox will have its key."

"Key?" He felt as if blood had drained from his head. Serena was the key, the goddess who had the power to alter the balance between good and evil.

Yvonne misread his face. She saw confusion, not apprehension. "You don't remember her? The goddess who stumbled into my cold fire ceremony down at the beach?"

The *frigidus ignis* ceremony was the ritual way the Atrox gave immortality to favored Followers who had proved themselves. That night Yvonne had stepped into the fire and the cold flames had burned away her mortality, bestowing eternal life upon her.

"Serena Killingsworth?" he asked. His chest tightened when he said Serena's name.

Yvonne tilted her head. "Sorry."

He looked at her carefully. "Why?"

"I know you were planning to take her to the Atrox." She spread her fingers through her long blond hair in a seductive way, making her glittering bracelets rattle on her arms. "You tried. That's good enough."

Stanton had lied to his Followers, even Tymmie, and told them he was trying to seduce Serena and take her to the Atrox. He had to tell them something after she had interrupted their ceremony down at the beach.

"I wish you'd been the one." Yvonne tried to cheer him, snaking her hands possessively up his back. "At least Zahi and his gang of goat-punkers didn't get her. That would have meant some bad stuff for us."

"Yeah." Stanton closed his mind and looked away, afraid that his emotions were too strong. Yvonne might pick up something, even though, as Stanton's subordinate, she would never violate his privacy.

Serena now filled his thoughts. He had saved her from Zahi, but in the end she hadn't needed his help. She was stronger than most Followers imagined, but she was also vulnerable, especially now. Could this be why he had been filled with such foreboding on Halloween that he had risked seeing her?

"What's the plan?" he asked at last.

Yvonne smirked. "If I knew that I'd be a member of the Inner Circle. They didn't tell us. But I know this plan is different."

"How so?"

"It's a member of the Inner Circle who came up with it, not a Follower," she explained.

Stanton stopped dancing. Malcolm's warning came back to him. Could this be the person he had warned him about? "What's his name?"

"Darius," Yvonne answered.

"Darius," Stanton repeated the name. He had never heard of Darius, and there was no way of confusing *Darius* with a name like *Lamp.*

Yvonne consoled him. "I know you're upset you didn't get her for your prize. So am I. We all are. We always thought that place in the Cincti would be yours."

Stanton nodded, but his thoughts were on Serena. He had to warn her. Then a thought shivered through him. Maybe he was already too late.

CHAPTER EIGHT

STANTON PARKED HIS car at Union Station and hurried across the street to La Placita. A fanfare of plastic flags with cutout patterns of skeletons flapped noisily in the air and overhead a piñata swayed, waiting for the hard blows of the breaking ceremony. He searched through the crowd lined up for the puppet show, then glanced down Olvera Street. The street had been closed to traffic for a long time now and looked like a Mexican marketplace, with stands selling boldly colored ceramics and paper flowers. He didn't see Serena, but her brother, Collin, had said she had gone to the Día de los Muertos celebration with Jimena.

He turned to see candy skulls with green sequin eyes and frosting lips staring back at him from a stall. When the vendor looked away, he grabbed three and tossed one into his mouth. The sugar dissolved with tangy sweetness.

He spun around, sensing other eyes. An old woman shook her head at him as she placed a bowl of spicy-smelling sauce on her *ofrenda*. Orange flowers, white candles, and faded snapshots of her dead relatives covered the altar. Stanton liked the way some people waited for the spirits of their loved ones to come back and visit, while others were terrified at the thought.

The old woman placed a sign on the table: SINCE DEATH IS INEVITABLE, IT SHOULD NOT BE FEARED, BUT HONORED.

"Not for everyone," he said softly.

She looked at him. "What's not for everyone?"

"Death." He smiled.

She waved him away. She didn't have time for

a thief and a liar. He wondered what she would do if she knew the other things he had done. Then her old eyes widened as if she had caught his thought in the air.

He left her and pushed inside La Luz del Día restaurant. He shoved his way to the front of the line.

A man glared at him. "It's my turn," he said.

Stanton entered the man's head and changed his thought about who was next. The man stepped back with a confused look. Then Stanton pressed into the counterwoman's thoughts and gave his order.

"One taco, right?" She handed him a paper plate. She had a beautiful smile and white teeth.

"Yes, I paid already," Stanton lied and the lady at the register confirmed his lie with a grin.

He backed out, pleased with how easy it had been to manipulate them. Good people were too trusting and easy to control. He sat at a table on the outside patio and bit into the taco. Heat and spice exploded in his mouth as red sauce ran down his chin. He wiped at it with a napkin while his eyes searched the crowd for Serena.

Then he saw Catty. He hadn't recognized her at first. She had painted her face white for the day and drawn black caverns around her eyes. Squares over her lips made skeleton teeth.

Children circled her, watching her paint a little girl's face.

Stanton popped the last bit of taco into his mouth, placed one hand on the iron fence surrounding the patio, and swung his legs over.

Like Serena, Catty was a Daughter of the Moon. She couldn't read minds; her gift was traveling in time. She could go back and forth in short spurts. When she tried longer jumps she got stuck in the tunnel—that was what she called the hole in time she used to travel from one day to the next.

"You'll look like a scary *calavera* now," Catty assured the young girl as she leaned back to admire the skeleton skull she had made on her face.

"Who's next?" Catty asked and pulled out another paintbrush.

Four hands shot up, but one little girl eased into the chair in front of Catty before she had a chance to choose. "My turn," she said.

Catty smiled and began smudging white over the girl's rosy cheeks. Suddenly her fingers stopped as if she sensed Stanton's approach.

He tried to ease into her mind to reassure her that his visit was not aggressive, but she blocked him and turned, her muscles tensing, ready to flee and warn the others.

Confusion rushed over her face when he didn't attack. She glanced down at her moon amulet. It matched the one Serena wore. Each goddess had one. The amulet wasn't glowing to warn her of danger. Still she stood and motioned the children behind her.

Stanton was a powerful Follower. Even though he had helped her once by taking her back in time to visit her real mother, she had never gotten used to him and Serena being together. She thought Serena was putting them all in danger by seeing Stanton. He could feel the distrust that surrounded her like a dark aura.

The children stared at him and some even backed away.

He stopped a short distance from Catty. "I need to find Serena."

"Why?" Catty narrowed her eyes.

"I have to warn her—"

"You tell me." Catty interrupted him. "I'll tell her."

Before he could say more, Jimena ran over to them, a papier-mâché skeleton in her hands. Three children raced after her, their shoes beating a rapid rhythm. Jimena stopped and handed back the skeleton, then whispered to the children to wait.

A boy with freckles glanced up and caught Stanton's eyes, then backed behind a booth selling freshly cut fruit.

Jimena marched toward Stanton. An ex-gangster, she considered herself the toughest of the group. She irritated him with her bold stares. She didn't understand his power or how he held back because of his affection for Serena. If she knew, would she still approach him with such attitude? He could feel her preparing to defend herself. Of all the Daughters, she disliked him the most, probably because she was Serena's best friend.

"He says he needs to see Serena," Catty told Jimena.

Jimena thrust her chin up. Her long luxurious black hair fell away from her face. "You said it was *demasiado peligroso*. Too dangerous," Jimena accused. "You told Serena you had to stay away from her because Regulators would terminate you both. "*¿Y ahora? ¿Por qué estás aquí?* And now you're here. Why?"

She folded her arms over her chest and smiled wickedly, the face of her wristwatch pointed at him. She knew the watch caused him discomfort. He hated timepieces, clocks, and sundials, anything that reminded him of his eternal bond to evil. All Followers did.

"I'm here to talk to Serena only," he said firmly.

Then the air filled with a sweet, musky fragrance and a delicate hand covered the face of Jimena's watch. He looked up into Serena's eyes.

She leaned against Jimena, her arm around her friend, and smiled at Stanton. She was wearing tight jeans and a sheer long-sleeved pink shirt over a thin T. Her hair was curled and glistened in the sun. She looked more beautiful than ever.

He smiled, wondering why he hadn't sensed her approach. Maybe she had learned some new skill to hide her presence.

She gently probed his mind without trying to hide her happiness at seeing him.

"I need to talk to you," he said, interrupting her before she could probe too deep. He didn't want her to see how much he had missed her. He offered her his hand and suddenly Vanessa was there, standing between them.

"What do you need to say to her?" Vanessa asked, her face worried. She dropped the marigold petals she had been holding in her hand to make a path for the dead. Specks of orange swirled around his legs and blew away.

"I have to warn her." Stanton frowned. He hadn't thought it would be this difficult to speak to Serena.

"If it's a warning, then it involves us all." Vanessa had dangerous eyes. He could see why Michael Saratoga had fallen for her.

"I think we all need to know," Catty joined in.

Serena devilishly reached for his hand. "I'll tell you what he says."

"Listen to me, Serena," Jimena cautioned, blocking her way. "If Stanton is such a good-guy Follower as he pretends to be, then why doesn't he ask us to bring him back from the Atrox?"

"Maybe he didn't know he could." Vanessa looked up as if the idea had never occurred to her before.

He sighed at their ignorance. "Do you think the Atrox would let that happen?" he asked, trying to keep annoyance from his voice. "A Follower who willingly asks to be released is destroyed. The release must be against his will for him to survive." He was careful to keep part of his mind closed to Serena. He couldn't let her see the real reason he could never ask them to break his bondage to the Atrox.

"Come on." Serena started to walk away.

Jimena's frustration was rising. "*¿En qué piensas?* What are you thinking? What if Regulators catch him when you're together? I don't know why you want to put us all in danger."

"Get real." Serena turned on her. "You're still mad at Stanton because he told you the truth about Veto."

"I am not." Jimena eyed Serena. "I've seen too many friends die. Don't be one of them. I don't want to have to say *que descansa en paz* every time I mention your name."

"You won't. I promise." Serena turned and looked into Stanton's eyes. The trust shining in her own made his heartbeat quicken.

"If it's a warning, we should all go talk to Maggie," Vanessa suggested. "She'll know what to do."

Maggie was their mentor and guide. She was still teaching them how to control their gifts.

"Maybe it's okay," Catty said softly. Vanessa and Jimena looked at her with surprise. She shrugged. "Stanton has helped us before."

"When it's self-serving," Jimena muttered under her breath.

Serena smiled. "It doesn't matter what any of you think. I'm going with him."

"How are you going to ignore all the premonitions I've been having about him?" Jimena asked.

That made Stanton start. So Jimena had received a vision. He wondered what she had seen. He started to probe her mind, but she blocked him.

"It's private," Jimena snapped, her eyes daring him to go into her mind. She was ready to attack.

He hated her arrogance. Did she really think she could defeat him? He turned back to Serena and held out his hand.

"Maybe you shouldn't," Vanessa whispered to Serena. "You know what Jimena has seen."

Stanton turned suddenly back to Jimena. Before she could close her mind, he caught a glimpse of a premonition. It made him shudder. Jimena had seen him bringing Serena to the Atrox.

CHAPTER NINE

"YOU'RE ALL BEING foolish," Serena told her friends. "You forget that I can read his mind. I know what's in his heart and I'm going to listen to what he has to say." She gave them a defiant look and started walking toward Stanton.

"No puedo creerlo." Jimena shook her head. "I don't even believe this. You think he can't hide stuff from you? He can. We all know it."

Serena took his hand anyway and they rushed across the street. They stood in the courtyard at Our Lady Queen of Angels Catholic Church and stared at each other in silence, then

Stanton pulled her into the shadows near a window and kissed her forehead.

He cupped his hands around her face. When she didn't resist his touch, he let his hands smooth gently down her neck over her shoulders to her back.

"I had to come see you," he whispered against her ear, breathing in her fragrance. His fingers stroked her back, and savored the silky feel of her blouse. He nestled his lips on her temple, her satiny hair tickling his cheek.

He drew back, wanting to kiss her, but hesitated, waiting for permission. She closed her eyes and let her arms slowly slip to his back, pulling him to her. He bent forward and when his lips touched hers, the sensation was electric. As they kissed, he weaved in and out of her mind, enjoying the luxury of sorting through her memories again and seeing what she had been doing. He lingered over her thoughts of him.

Finally, he pulled back and looked at her. She smiled, letting him see the truth; she still cared for him. He wondered what their relationship would have been like if her destiny hadn't stood between them. If she had been an ordinary girl, would he have taken her to the Atrox so he could bind her to him for eternity, or would he still have tried to protect her?

"But I'm not an ordinary girl," Serena whispered and held her face up for another kiss.

"I—" He started to say *I love you,* but the words felt too dangerous to express.

She smiled and he knew she had caught his declaration anyway. When he realized his confession hadn't turned her away, an unexpected smile spread across his lips that matched her own. He brushed his hands through her hair, then closed his eyes and kissed her again.

Dangerous emotions swirled inside him. This was too risky and too wrong. He tried to stop the ache that spread through his body. He was here to warn her. Do it and leave, he thought. He drew back and she looked up at him, startled.

"I have to warn you about the transition," he stated.

"What is the transition?" she asked with a

quizzical stare. "Maggie never mentioned it."

"The transition," he explained, "is what Followers call the period of time when the balance of power switches from good to evil."

Her look was doubtful. "We've stopped it before," she answered. "I just didn't know that's what it was called."

He shook his head. "This is different," he assured her. "It might not be so easy for you to fight." Guilt ran through him. He should be celebrating with other Followers, not warning the enemy. He pulled Serena closer to him. She didn't feel like an enemy.

"Why didn't you want to tell Jimena and the others?" She tilted her head up as if she were hungry for another kiss. "They need to know."

He nodded. "I lied when I said I could tell only you."

A stunned looked flashed over her face.

"I wanted an excuse to be alone with you again." He didn't need to add how much he had missed her. She could feel his longing. It was other dark compulsions that he had to hide from her.

"But the warning is real," he continued. "You're the key. The goddess who can change the balance between good and evil. I don't know the plan, but I know they will be coming for you."

As Serena considered what he was saying, he twisted inside her mind to read her thoughts. She had struggled between good and evil before, and knew the seductiveness of the Atrox. It had promised her the world, but once she had become pure evil she had only wanted to destroy with a hunger that even surpassed the one Stanton felt growing inside him now.

His hand rose to her chin and lifted her face to his. It would be so easy to take her now. She was too trusting. His evil side paced at the edge of his control. Then with a shock he realized that if he did something to Serena, *he* could destroy the balance. With rising dread, he wondered if it was possible that the Atrox had kidnapped him not to stop his father's crusade, but because it knew his love for Serena could one day be a catalyst for the transition.

"What?" Serena tried to push into his mind,

but he wouldn't let her. "Tell me. What's bothering you?"

She grasped his uneasiness so easily. Did that also mean she could sense the dark compulsion rising inside him? The one that made him want to turn her to the Atrox. He looked at her. She didn't seem afraid. Maybe he should tell her everything, even though he had never confessed the full story to anyone before. There was too much pain in remembering it all. Vanessa had seen a little and so had Catty.

"Then tell me," Serena whispered across his mind. "Trust me."

Her warmth and understanding flowed through his thoughts. He let her lead him to the bench under the window. A man eating a sandwich smiled at them and moved to a chair so they could have their privacy.

"My father," he started. He could take her into his mind and show her, let her live the memory, but that seemed too risky. The side of him that was bound to the Atrox felt too strong right now. He might trap her there forever even if that were not his intent. He didn't trust himself.

"Just tell me." Her soft fingers entwined with his. "I don't need to see it to believe you."

"One day when I was only six—"

"Before the Atrox took you?"

He nodded. "I still had hopes and dreams then. Everything in my life was perfect until that day. Then three monks walked up to the castle carrying something. They wanted to speak with my father. He took them in and they placed a manuscript on the table."

"The Secret Scroll?" Serena asked. "Catty told me that the Scroll had originally belonged to your family."

"It did." He took a deep breath. "I sat in the corner on a chair, alone and paralyzed with fear. They told my father about the Atrox. He argued with them. He said what they were saying was heresy, but if you looked in their eyes—" He turned away, remembering the stark fear he had seen on their faces. His father had argued with the men over the existence of such an unholy force, but Stanton had understood at once. "If you looked in their eyes you could see the truth. I know my father didn't want to see because he understood what it would mean, but in the end they convinced him that the manuscript was real."

"But the Scroll tells how to destroy the Atrox," Serena said.

Stanton nodded. "The priests explained that they had come to my father because the path was difficult and needed someone with a brave heart who would have the courage and fortitude to do what was required."

"And your father agreed?"

"Not then, but eventually he accepted the burden of the manuscript and organized a great crusade against the Atrox."

"You should feel proud of him," Serena interrupted.

Stanton sighed. "Yes and no. My father understood the danger to his family and he assigned his bravest knight to guard me. The priest had given my father a ring. They said it would protect him from the Atrox, but instead, he gave the ring to me."

Serena squeezed his hand.

"Not even the bravest knight or a charmed ring could protect me. The Atrox took me." Stanton pushed his hair out of his eyes. "Fear of losing his other sons stopped my father. I didn't see my father again until his death."

He felt Serena's sadness for him.

"By then I was an Immortal with the power to change into shadow. It was easy to slip into the castle late one night unseen and become whole again beside my father's bed." He remembered even now the quivering of his chin, the hot tears in his eyes as he leaned over and kissed the wrinkled skin and protruding blue veins on his father's temple.

"Was he happy to see you?" Serena asked.

"He told me I was no longer his son." He choked on the words. "He said I belonged to evil now." Rage swelled in his throat. He slammed his fist through the windowpane behind him. Glass exploded. Everyone in the patio turned to see.

Serena stood suddenly as blood-covered glass shattered on the cement.

"I was taken against my will," he said harshly. "My father knew. Did he blame me for losing a foolish ring? I was only a child."

People eating lunches in the serenity of the patio watched, eyes wide and vigilant, wondering if it was safe to stay.

Serena picked shards of glass from his skin, then took off her overshirt and wrapped it around his hand to stop the bleeding.

Blood seeped into the pink material as quickly as his anger grew. "He never tried to rescue me," Stanton whispered roughly as drops of his blood pattered onto the courtyard floor.

"But he searched for the Scroll after it was lost," Serena argued. "You've said so yourself. He went on a quest for the Scroll. I think that means he was trying to find a way to defeat the Atrox and bring you back."

"Then why did he deny me?" Stanton asked.

She shook her head.

He stared at Serena as the need trembled through him like an addict's mantra: *Find someone and kill the emptiness inside.* The duty to cross someone over was now a physical demand, the pain intense. He needed relief.

"You see what I am?" he asked, his voice harsh and grating. "Even my father rejected me because I'm pure evil."

"I see you've suffered." She tried to take his hand to comfort him.

He jerked it away. Already the bleeding had stopped and his skin was beginning to heal.

He handed back her shirt. "My father had other, stronger sons. Why did the Atrox take me? A child? Did it see something in my future? Some part I play?"

"It took you because it was easy to take a child."

"Why are you refusing to understand what I'm trying to tell you?" he asked.

"What is it you think I don't see?"

"The Atrox can see the future," he explained. "Maybe it looked into the future and saw my role in the transition and that's why it stole me from my father's castle."

"It chose you because you were vulnerable," she insisted.

Then a soft white glow caught his eyes. He glanced down and his heart lurched. Her amulet was radiant. Did it sense the part of him that remained loyal to the Atrox, the part that even now was gaining control? He started to back away.

"Where are you going?" Serena asked.

He turned and ran.

"Don't go!" she yelled after him.

The urge to go back was strong. His heart pounded with fury, pumping evil into every cell. He had to get away from her before he could no longer resist the need to destroy her.

Serena's quick steps tapped on the cement behind him.

He shot into oncoming traffic. Cars screeched to a stop. Drivers cursed.

Stanton pounded their car hoods and looked in their eyes, daring them to say more, his violence ready to explode.

CHAPTER TEN

AT THE END OF Olvera Street the rich smells of frying garlic, onions, and tortillas drifted into the air. Stanton paused and took three breaths. The compulsion had subsided. Still he was anxious to get back to his car and drive away before something happened that could trigger the urge to turn and destroy Serena.

A shadow moved inside the dark interior of the small restaurant Cielito Lindo. Cassandra appeared beside him, startling him. She had been apprenticed to him once, but he hadn't seen her since she had tried to betray him. He didn't want to talk to her today. He started walking.

"Hey, Stanton," she said as if nothing had ever happened between them.

When he didn't acknowledge her, she stepped in front of him and walked backward for a few paces, offering him a bite of her taquito. Her long skirt rustled about her.

He drew back and shook his head.

"It's good." Cassandra shrugged and pushed the last bite into her mouth, then licked the guacamole from her fingers.

He tried to push around her, but she stayed next to him.

"You seem to be in a bad mood," she teased. "Why are you so upset when you should be celebrating?"

He finally looked down at her. She had been so perfectly beautiful at one time, and wildly in love with him.

"I'm in a hurry," he muttered, and quickened his pace.

"Well, I guess I can see you're trying to outrun whatever is bothering you." She had a smug smile as if she knew something important. "Funny. I always thought you were the kind of guy who didn't have any problems. Guess I was wrong, huh?"

He stared at the parade of children ahead of them, faces painted like skeletons, and didn't answer.

She ran her fingers through her black hair. Streaks of maroon and blue flashed in the sunlight. He had loved her hair once. Her sultry eyes stared at him. She knew what she was doing, teasing him.

"It's been a while," she whispered and touched his cheek lightly. Her fingernails were long and painted black.

"A long while."

She giggled. "So you could at least slow down and talk to me."

There had been a time before when she could have let her words slip enticingly across his mind in a secret whisper. Stanton shuddered with the memory of how easily their minds had melded once.

"Don't you owe that to your favorite pupil?" she asked in a seductive voice.

He slowed. After Cassandra had been accepted by the Atrox, she had been eager to master the art of reading minds.

She seemed to know what he was thinking. "Love made me an eager student," she whispered, her voice filled with longing.

"Too eager," he added.

She made a face and looked quickly away. She had never attained the power of an Immortal because she had failed in her attempt to please the Atrox. Now she lived as an outcast.

"Maybe I was too eager." She shrugged prettily. "Nothing ventured, nothing gained and all that. What can I say? I tried."

"Where do you live now?" he asked. He had never really considered how she survived. She wasn't allowed in the squat, but she didn't look homeless.

"Around," she answered. "It's amazing how many friends you can find in this city." She shook her hair, and her long gold earrings jangled against her neck. Then she changed the subject. "I have something important to tell you." She closed her eyes and waited as if she were eager for him to enter her mind and read her thoughts.

"I don't have the energy to read your mind," he said with annoyance. He didn't want that kind of intimacy with her. Besides, she would have too many memories to show him, hoping to tantalize him with recollections he did not want to relive.

"It's easier if you just go inside my head and see."

"What's up?" His voice was firm. He could see the disappointment on her face.

"Everyone's talking about it." She peeled off her sweater as if the cool day had suddenly grown too hot. She wore a skimpy T under the sweater. She stretched luxuriously in the sun.

He glanced down, then away, but not before he saw the scars that spelled S T A on her chest. She had tried to slice his name into her skin with a razor blade once.

She caught his eyes looking at her body and smiled with triumph, then licked her lips and touched the pale white scars. One finger traced over the jagged T. "You remember this night?"

He remembered the blood trickling down from the cuts before Vanessa had stopped her from cutting the A. Stanton had taken the razor blade. But later she had added it anyway.

"Too bad I never got around to writing your full name." She pulled a lipstick from her pocket and brushed red across her full lips. "I tell people the S-T-A stands for Stalin." She laughed.

She had never finished the other letters because her emotions had changed from love to hate.

"You've seen the tattoo?" She didn't wait for an answer, but lifted her skirt high. Traffic honked as she exposed her thigh. His name curled on her hip inside a bleeding heart, pierced by a dagger. She took his hand and pressed his fingers onto the warm flesh. "It's what you did to my heart."

He jerked his fingers back. Maybe the tattoo was her strange way of claiming him and thinking it would keep others away. He had thought she was a cutter, and that she cut herself to escape not being able to feel. But now he wondered if it had been her way of showing love. She had his attention. He owed her that much.

She smirked as if she knew. "Let's not fight today." She hooked her hands around his arm and walked with him, her hips sinuous, slow and brushing against him. The silver rings on her fingers pressed hard into his skin. "Aren't you even going to ask me what I know?"

"Just talk, Cassandra." He pulled his arm away and checked the oncoming cars. He didn't want to be stuck at a traffic light with her.

"I've heard rumors," she whispered.

He didn't answer or coax her to speak. If she wanted him to know, she would tell him, but part of him understood that she was also trying to entice him into her mind. He suspected that there was something else she wanted him to see, something perhaps dangerous to know.

She inclined her head as if she were studying him. "Things are about to change."

"I don't need to hear about that from you."

He shook his head. "Did you really think I wouldn't have heard by now?"

He increased his step, anxious to get away from her.

"I know someone who wants to meet you." Her shoes made heavy raps on the street behind him as she hurried to catch up. "Someone who can help you be an important part in the new regime."

"You know where I live. Tell whoever it is to drop by."

"He can't be seen with you just like that. Not at a squat anyway."

Stanton turned quickly. "You know someone so powerful that he can't be seen visiting a squat?" He smirked. "That's a lie, Cassandra."

"It's not." She grabbed his arm and made him stop. "I know someone important who can make our dreams come true."

"*Our* dreams?" he said in disbelief. She was still attracted to him but he also knew that even if he liked her, it would be impossible to trust her now, no Follower could. She was an outcast and she would do anything to get her power and position back. "We don't share any dreams, Cassandra."

"We did once," she said, defiantly.

"Only in your daydreams."

She scowled. Her face seemed prettier when she was angry. Maybe that's why she was always on edge. She stared back at him as he checked the traffic again.

"I'm telling the truth," she insisted. "Someone powerful is going to help us."

He smiled. "Help you, you mean."

"Why won't you trust me?"

"Why would any Follower trust you or want your help?" He looked at her with scorn. "You're an outcast now."

"Not for long," Cassandra replied with determination. He could feel the promise in her words.

He saw a break in the traffic and ran into the wide street. Cassandra ran after him. A distant car bore down on them. It increased its speed. He grabbed Cassandra's hand and yanked her onto the curb.

Cassandra turned and yelled after the driver. "You could at least slow down! Dumbass!"

Stanton felt the anger burning inside her. A short time back when she still had her powers she would have pushed into the rude driver's mind and forced him to have an accident. She had liked being a Follower—the intrigue, the dishonesty, the alliances and deceptions.

She turned back to Stanton and tried to force a smile. "You trusted me once and you should trust me again."

"I can't, Cassandra." He stepped through the parked cars and headed for his.

"Because I'm an outcast? I thought you were tougher than that."

"No, because you betrayed me," he said flatly. She had gone to the Cincti with a plan to destroy the Daughters of the Moon. Her real plan had been to win a place of power higher than his.

"I wanted revenge then," she admitted.

Her confession surprised him. He stopped and looked at her to see if she was telling the truth. He could feel her inviting him into her mind and again he wondered why she was so eager to have him look inside.

"Well, if you won't look in my mind and see for yourself, I'll just tell you. I was a woman scorned and all that."

He leaned down so that he was in her face when he spoke to her. "Don't you understand, Cassandra? We never had that kind of relationship. We were never a couple. I couldn't have jilted you. We didn't have anything but friendship to cast aside and I remained your friend until you betrayed me."

She moved her head from side to side. "You don't need to lie to me, Stanton. I know how you felt about me once. I could go in your mind, remember? So I wanted to get even with you. When you stopped loving me—"

"I never—" He stopped and sighed.

A satisfied grin crossed her face. "But that was then," she continued. "I'm looking into the future now, not the past. I don't even care who she was."

He had known she had worshiped him, but

that frequently happened with Followers who were assigned to him. He had paid more attention to her than the others, perhaps too much, but he had never loved her.

Finally he spoke. "We were never more than friends, Cassandra. It's my duty to look after the Followers who are apprenticed to me."

"Friends?" she spit out the word and a tight smile crept across her lips. "You don't hurt friends the way you hurt me."

They reached his car. He unlocked the door.

"Stanton." Her tone had changed. She now sounded worried.

He opened the car door and turned back.

"Be careful. That's all." Her eyes looked surprisingly sincere, as if she still cared for him. "I've heard rumors about Regulators planning to destroy a Follower who is in love with a Daughter of the Moon as soon as they learn his identity. Any idea who that could be?"

"No." He got in and stuck the key in the ignition.

She leaned through the car window, her

breath warm on his face, but when she spoke her eyes were downcast. "If Regulators knew you were with another Follower, they would never suspect you. You'd be safe."

He touched the tip of her hair. "You're no longer a Follower, Cassandra," he reminded her softly.

She snapped her head back and stepped away as if she had been slapped. Her lips carved into a practiced smile, revealing perfect teeth that failed to mask her disappointment.

CHAPTER ELEVEN

TUESDAY NIGHT STANTON stood alone in the back of Planet Bang. It was hot, and smoky mist circled the room, waiting to reflect the lasers. The night before, worry had startled him from his sleep and he had decided that despite the danger, he needed to stay near Serena, unseen, eyes watchful and ready. Followers were saying that the transition was only days away.

He had listened to the rumors, hoping for a clue to help him understand Malcolm's warning. The name *Lamp* still meant nothing to him, but his foreboding had only grown stronger.

He scanned the crowd for Serena. She stood next to Jimena in silver hip huggers and a frosty top. Rhinestones and crystals sparkled in her hair like stars. Jimena wore a sequin-covered purple velvet dress. Their bodies glowed. He wanted to see a sadness on Serena's face that matched his own. Some sign that she missed him the way he ached for her.

The music started. Drums hit hard and blue lasers slashed the mist, mimicking the beat. Two guys asked Serena to dance. She laughed and twirled between them, her hands reaching over her head.

Raw pain spread through his chest. He didn't want to see more. He had come here to protect her, not to watch her have fun.

Jimena danced with Serena's brother, Collin. Collin was a surfer, sunburned with pale white-blond hair. You didn't need to be a mind reader to know how much he cared for Jimena. Stanton watched them jealously, then glanced back for Serena. She had disappeared into the crowd. He stepped around two kids kissing in the shadows, and tried to find her again. His throat tightened. Had she gone off with another guy so easily? He pushed through the people talking in the back and headed for the dance floor.

Someone grabbed his arm.

Irritated, he turned. Serena stood behind him.

"Serena?" He hadn't prepared himself for a chance encounter. He had only planned to spy.

"You could say hi, I guess," Serena teased, but her tone was caustic.

He nodded, but he still couldn't find his voice. This was chancy. The spirit of the Atrox claimed him tonight.

"I want to talk to you." Something in the pitch of her voice told him that she was giving him one last chance. "Just listen."

"All right." He dug his hands into his pockets and waited.

"I don't understand why you walked away from me on Olvera Street last week."

"I—" he started to explain, but she interrupted him.

"I know you've been visiting me at night when I'm asleep. Why?"

But before he could answer, she continued with a brusqueness that he had never heard in her voice before.

"My alarm clock. That's how I know. You always turn it to face the wall because you don't like to be reminded . . ."

He touched her lips with the tip of his finger. He didn't want to be reminded even now. His finger lingered on her chin until she pushed it away.

"So I know you've been visiting me," she continued. "That tells me you still care. Why else would you come?"

"I do care," he whispered, quelling the demon inside.

"You're either a masterful liar or you need to explain."

Her harsh answer surprised him.

She tilted her head. "Answer me."

When he didn't, she placed her hands on her hips and spoke low. "You were once willing to risk everything to be with me. Now I'm willing to risk everything to be with you and you're avoiding me."

The music changed to something sultry and the lasers flashed slow and easy in the smoky air. He glanced down at her moon amulet; its milky glow throbbed against her chest. She looked beautiful in the strange light.

A sudden rush of uninvited memories came from deep within him—memories of other times when he had lost control. Faces of girls flashed in his mind. It chilled him, remembering what they had become. Girls like Cassandra now dedicated to the Atrox and worshiping its evil.

He shuddered. "Get away from me, Serena."

She looked confused and hurt. "I know you love me."

"Once maybe, not now," he answered as his heart tightened with the lie. He bit his lips so that other words could not come out, then turned and threaded through the dancers toward the exit.

What's wrong? Her words traced across his mind.

His head snapped back. How had she reached his thoughts so easily? He didn't want her to venture there, not now, and see the truth.

With a burst of energy he pushed her from his head.

She staggered back as if she had been physically assaulted, then she looked up at him with shock. "You won't even let me into your mind? What are you trying to hide from me?"

Everything seemed to move in slow motion then, the dancers and lights became a whirling pattern of color and brightness around him. He wanted to tell Serena the real reason he couldn't see her anymore, but he was afraid that if he did she would only think it was something they could conquer together. She couldn't understand the pressure building inside him.

"I'm not trying to hide anything," he said finally. "Go back to your friends. Stay with your kind where you belong."

"Then why are you here?" Her voice was petulant again. "If you believe what you say, then you should be over at the Dungeon."

He shook his head. "Leave me alone."

She stood there, staring at him, so darkly beautiful in the patterned light. Why wouldn't she go? He wanted to tell her how much he'd been suffering, trying to control himself, hoping that if he could resist the urge long enough, he would finally have power over it. But he couldn't, not tonight, with his dark side so strong. He needed to go.

"Well?" she asked.

Her anger made him want her even more. Before he knew what he was doing, he had reached out and pulled her to him, pressing his lips against hers, so surprisingly warm and open. His tongue traced over hers. He felt a jolt of pleasure as he eased into her mind and she invited him to stay.

Then his resistance failed and the demon inside him took control. He reached deep into Serena and trapped her as he had always feared he would some day. She trembled, trying to escape his mind, but his power cut through hers easily.

He felt her struggle and part of him enjoyed the feel of it. He wrestled against the side that was anxious to turn her to the Atrox. Finally, he pushed it back, but just barely. It curled near the surface, patiently waiting for another chance to explode.

He grabbed Serena's wrists. "You see?" he said. "That's what will happen. If you ever cared about me, just stay away. I was trying to tell you that on Olvera Street. The reason the Atrox took me and not my brothers is because it saw the future even then. It knows what part I play in the transition."

She stubbornly shook her head. "No one can know the final outcome. Besides, if you truly believe that, then why are you here?"

"I wanted to protect you." He breathed, finally admitting the truth, "I can't stay away from you."

That seemed to please her. He wished he hadn't said it. Now it would only be more difficult to convince her.

"I'm the danger, Serena." The knowledge throbbed inside him. "I've always been the danger. I'm the one who will destroy you. It's my destiny."

She didn't seem surprised and she didn't back away. "I've always understood your fear," she said softly. "I've known since we first met that you were capable of destroying me."

He looked at her not believing what he had heard. "But what you don't understand is that I'm not always able to control it. Even now it's becoming stronger. I feel it." He touched his chest.

She smiled. "I'm not scared."

"How can you not be?" He took a step back. "Don't you know what just happened?"

"Nothing," she answered. "You were trying to pull me into your world, but you didn't, did you? You fought back. I could feel you protecting me."

He looked away. "This time. But maybe the next or the time after that . . ."

She stepped forward and touched his face. "Look at me, Stanton."

He turned but he was afraid to stare into her eyes. He was losing control again.

"I don't think your good side could ever let anything harm me," she explained. "That part the Atrox can't reach. You said it yourself. You're *invitus*."

He started walking away, going to the back corners where kids were making out. He quickened his pace. He was going to blend into shadow, leave, go to his car. Maybe disappear forever. It had been too close tonight. He raged against his own foolishness.

Serena ran after him and held tight to his sleeve.

Give me a chance. The words came softly across his mind. *Try. Please.*

She slipped her arms around his waist.

"Don't." He tried to push her away but instinct took over. He twisted into her head.

She was startled by his sudden attack. She sent all her force back in an attempt to stop him. That was a dangerous mistake. Now he kept her power inside him, leaving her vulnerable, with no defense.

She trembled and he thrived on her fear. It drove him deeper and deeper inside her until the music was gone and all he sensed was Serena around him. Slowly he pulled her deepest self back to the dark cold inside him.

“Meet the Atrox, Serena,” he whispered, turning her mind to the menacing shadows.

He could feel her soul turning and as it did a violent grief rushed through him. He had destroyed what he loved. He lifted his head and screamed until his throat was raw. The sound blended with the fast-moving music.

The Atrox had won.

CHAPTER TWELVE

HE GLANCED DOWN AT her, her green eyes already turning phosphorescent. His hand caressed her face. Shivers of regret ran through him as he realized what he had done. Still he didn't try to help her this time. He couldn't. She had to break free on her own now. He felt her struggling.

"O Mater Luna, Regina nocis, adiuvo me nunc." She repeated the prayer over and over. Her voice became stronger each time the words flowed from her mouth.

Finally, she spoke clearly, "I refuse to come

to you. The power balance shifts in favor of the dark if I become a Follower."

Then she blinked and shook her head. Her eyes looked normal again, but he could see the residue of fear in them. He felt disgusted with himself.

"Serena," he whispered and reached out for her, his fingers tentative as he touched her cold arms. He pulled her to him and hugged her tightly. "I'm sorry."

"Remember, I've met the Atrox before," she said with a shudder. "I'm not immune, but I know that its offers are empty."

He pressed his lips against her soft cheek.

"I was right," she said. "We can fight it."

"I don't think I could stand to witness that again," he uttered softly.

"I'll only get stronger each time," she insisted.

"Let me take you home."

She nodded and he took her hand. They shoved through the crowd of dancing kids and made their way to the door.

When they were at the entrance, Jimena

stopped them. Catty and Vanessa stood with her. They wore shiny elastic tube tops and heart-shaped crystal tattoos on their chests. Vanessa kept glancing at her moon amulet and looking at Stanton with wide-eyed worry.

"Why don't you let me have a moment alone with Stanton." Jimena smiled at Serena, but there was anger in her eyes.

Serena seemed unsure. She glanced at Stanton, then shrugged and backed away with Vanessa and Catty.

Jimena took his arm and pulled him to a far corner near the door. "Catty and Vanessa keep telling me that part of you is a nice guy, *un tipo simpático*." Jimena's voice was low. "But I've had enough premonitions about you lately to see your *diablo* side."

"Tell me what you've seen." He wondered if she had some clue about the meaning of *Lamp*.

She sighed. "*No puedo.* I can't. The premonitions are my gift to help me fight your kind. The images I see warn us. They're not meant for you."

"All right."

He could tell that she thought he had agreed too readily. She put her hands on her hips. "And don't try to go in my mind to see. It feels like worms are crawling though my brain."

She gathered her power like a storm, ready to strike any attempt to read her thoughts. He wondered if she really believed she could defeat him.

Then her hands went back to her sides. "But I can tell you this," she continued. "My premonitions show me that you're still the enemy. For Serena's sake I hope that isn't true, because I don't want her to get hurt." Then she looked at Stanton, her black eyes steady and sincere. "I can't stop the future from coming, but you'd better be careful with her. She's my very best friend."

Stanton nodded. "I care about her, too."

"I hope so, because I don't know what I'd do if something did happen to her." She tilted her head. "No, I guess I do know. Maggie says an Immortal can't be killed." She smiled menacingly. "But I bet I could find a way. Nothing can stop a homegirl from *el Nueve* once her mind is made up."

Her daring amused him. "I bet you could, too, Jimena."

She left him and he walked back to Serena. She was standing next to the concession stand alone, a Pepsi in her hand. She looked pale and tired.

"Did she tell you what she's seen in her premonitions?" Serena asked.

"No, she can't. Hasn't she told you?"

"No," Serena said as they walked outside. "She says it's better if I don't know." She answered his look. "She does that a lot. It's nothing new."

He nodded. "Jimena's a good friend." He opened the car door and helped her inside, enjoying the stretch of her body as she eased into the seat.

They drove to her home, then parked in front. A breeze had picked up, making the tree branches sway lazily overhead.

Serena wasn't anxious to go inside. She looked at him boldly.

"Goddess," he whispered and brushed a hand across her cheek. She closed her eyes as he savored the feel of her skin. He smoothed his hand down her neck, then leaned over to kiss her. His lips hovered above hers, feeling her breath and the warmth radiating from her skin.

"This moment feels too perfect," she murmured. "That scares me."

"Why?" he asked softly, lost in her sweet perfume.

"Because my best moments have always been followed by my worst," she whispered in a haunted voice.

"It doesn't have to be that way."

"I know, but for me it always has been." She looked off into the distance. "My best Christmas ever was right before my mother left."

He felt sad for her.

She turned back to him. "I guess she wanted us to have one great time to remember her by." She tried to laugh, but failed. "Maybe that's why I want to hold this moment forever. I'm afraid of what tomorrow will bring."

He felt a tremor of premonition of his own. When he spoke again his words were quiet and strong. “No matter what happens, always remember how much I care for you.”

“All right,” she answered.

“I better walk you up to your house.” He started to open the car door but she stopped him.

She pulled him to her and kissed him gently. “Now, we can go.”

They walked up the tinted stone sidewalk to the Spanish Colonial house, his arm tight around her waist. He stood near the spiked paddles of a cactus as she unlocked the large plank door.

He kissed her lightly, then waited until she was safely inside before turning and walking back to the street.

As he approached the car, he thought he saw something in the front seat. It had to be a trick of light and shadow. But when he stepped closer he saw Cassandra. She turned and gave him an icy smile.

CHAPTER THIRTEEN

CASSANDRA GLARED AT him as he slid into the driver's seat. Her eyes looked wet; for a moment he thought she had been crying.

He turned the ignition and pressed hard on the accelerator. The car shot away from the curb with a squeal of tires. Music pounded, making the dashboard shimmer.

"I told you about the rumors," Cassandra shouted over the music. "And you're still seeing her!"

He grabbed behind her neck and pulled her to him, forcing her to look into his eyes. "How long have you been spying on me?"

She tried to pull away but he wouldn't let her go. He pushed the accelerator harder and turned down Beverly Boulevard. Cars honked and screeched to a halt.

"Have you ever seen what becomes of a human body in a car accident?" He ran a red light.

"Slow down," she whimpered.

"Tell me your plan," he ordered.

"I don't have one!"

"Don't lie to me!"

"Go in my mind then," she offered.

He could go in her mind so easily, but the idea repulsed him. Instead, he sped into oncoming traffic to pass the slow-moving cars in his own lane.

"I'm an Immortal, Cassandra," he threatened. "I'll survive. But you're not even a Follower. You're an outcast. Imagine what will happen to your pretty face."

He could smell her fear. Still, she didn't back down.

"I don't have a plan!" she insisted.

"My body will already be repairing itself before the paramedics even arrive," he sneered. "But what will become of yours?"

She tried to pull away from his grasp. "Please stop." Her tears flowed freely now.

"Tell me," he demanded again. "That wasn't a chance meeting at Olvera Street. How long have you been following me?"

He let go of the steering wheel. The car lurched to the left, sliding dangerously close to the fender of an oncoming car.

"Three months!" she screamed, her face distorted by the glare from the headlights of the approaching cars.

He grabbed the wheel and swerved across the right lane, then continued with a shriek of tires onto La Brea Avenue.

"For almost three months now," she confessed, through ragged breaths. "Not always. It's hard because you can become a shadow. I haven't seen everything."

"To catch me with Serena, so you could turn us over to Regulators and win back your status?"

"Never," she answered quickly.

A police siren stirred the night air, followed quickly by another.

"Then what?" He glanced in the rearview mirror and saw flashing lights.

"I'd hoped you had stopped seeing her," she said bitterly. "But I wanted to make sure. I couldn't stand the thought of you being with her. We were always destined to be together, you and I."

"Jealousy? You expect me to believe that's all this is?" He released her.

"It's the truth." She fumbled with the seat belt and snapped it around her.

"What makes you think we could ever be together?"

"A member of the Inner Circle told me."

He jerked the steering wheel to the left and made a sharp turn onto Third Street. He shut off the headlights and music, then spun down Orange Avenue, the back end of the car fish-tailing. He parked in a driveway and shadows swallowed them. Then he turned off the ignition and waited.

The police cars sped down Third Street, and the sound of their sirens became more and more distant.

"Tell me the rest," he commanded.

"One of its members told me a prophecy." Her hands were shaking violently as she sobbed.

"What prophecy?" he asked.

"That you and I would be together for eternity."

Stanton started to laugh.

Her voice turned indignant. "That's why I never turned you in. You thought I wanted to get my own revenge, but that wasn't it. I never would have betrayed you because I knew you were going to be mine one day. I wanted to be an Immortal like you. I wanted you to love me. I never expected it to turn out this way."

Her mood changed to sudden sadness. "I'm an outcast and still I didn't turn you in." She took in a deep breath and let it out slowly, wiping the tears from her cheeks. "That's proof. You can look into my mind and see if I'm telling the truth, so why don't you?"

"I don't need to," he said finally. "I believe you."

She turned and even in the darkness he could see the rage in her eyes. "I didn't report you then, but I will now. I'm sure the Atrox would give me back my old status if I told it what you've been doing."

He studied her.

"I heard other rumors about a Follower betraying the group." She was regaining her composure now. "Someone trying to stop the transition. I never thought it was you, but now I have my doubts."

"I'm loyal to the Atrox," he sighed. "How can I not be?"

"I want to believe you, but I need to know." She sniffed. "I want proof."

That made him laugh. "An outcast is going to demand proof from me? I'll show you nothing."

"You will," she warned. "Or I go to the Atrox with what I've seen. You may not be concerned for yourself but I know that goddess has some kind of hold on you."

Her words were no idle threat. He had to

protect Serena. "What do you want, Cassandra?" he asked at last.

"How long has it been since you crossed someone over?" she asked. "I've been following you for three months and haven't seen you do it once."

"I couldn't."

She turned sharply. "*Couldn't?* Why not?"

"I've been trying to seduce Serena," he said, lying. "So I can bring her to the Atrox and win a place on honor for myself in the Inner Circle. She would know if I had harmed someone. I had to convince her that I was trying to be good."

She snorted. "Right. You expect me to believe that? You're taking an awfully long time."

"Maybe that's why the others failed—they didn't take enough time." His voice was soft and convincing. "I won't fail."

She studied him, considering what he had said. "Why didn't you tell me before now?" There was new anger in her words. "Do you know how much you hurt me?"

"I knew, but I had to make it look authentic." He could tell she was starting to accept his story. She desperately wanted to believe it. "Serena can read minds, so I couldn't tell anyone my plan."

Her mood seemed to lift for a moment, but then she bit her lower lip. "I think my duty is to report you. Unless . . ." The word hung in the air as tantalizing bait. "I haven't seen you recruit anyone for a long time. Do it and I'll believe you're still loyal to the Atrox."

He took her dare. "Let's find someone then." He started to turn the ignition but she caught his hand and pulled it to her.

"Not tonight," she murmured. "Tomorrow is soon enough. Tonight is for us."

She slid next to him and kissed his cheek, then traced a cold finger over his ear and whispered, "I never stopped caring for you, Stanton. You're my everything. Someday you'll love me and that's all I live for." Her hands brushed over the sides of his face and she bent his head to hers.

At last, he returned her kiss, thinking of Serena as he did. He had to keep her safe.

CHAPTER FOURTEEN

THE FOLLOWING NIGHT, Cassandra walked toward Stanton down Hollywood Boulevard, her smile easy and inviting. Her jeans were low, revealing the heart-and-dagger tattoo on her right hip. A gold chain hugged her slim waist and a skimpy top showed off her perfect arms and shoulders. She opened the car door and got in, looking at him as if she feared that he would change his mind.

"No chance," he said, answering her thought.

"Good." She let out a satisfied sigh, then spread her fingers through her hair, trying to work an old spell on him.

"Where to first?" he asked.

"Let's hit the club scene in Silver Lake," Cassandra suggested. "There's a new place I want to check out."

He did a U-turn into traffic and shot toward the east side of town.

Cassandra rolled down her window. Wind rumbled into the car and caught her hair. She was quiet, but when she looked at him he could feel her desire. "It's good to be back with you," she said softly. "I've missed you."

He nodded, but couldn't give her the answer she needed. He didn't feel the same. He was with her only because of Serena.

She seemed to understand his silence. "I've told you before," she said, not bothering to hide her pain. "I'm patient. I can wait." Then she leaned forward and turned on the music. She nodded her head with the beat as they continued to drive.

Finally, they parked and got out of the car. Stanton looked down the deserted street.

"Where's the club?" he asked.

"Don't be so suspicious," she answered. Her mood seemed cheerful again. She took his hand. "It's hidden."

She started walking, pulling him along. "No sign is going to advertise this club. You have to know about it to find it and," she added smugly. "You have to know the right people to hear about it."

Soon music filled the shady street. The thumping beat grew louder when they turned down a dark alley lined with newly planted palm trees. Spiky fronds bristled against their legs as they continued to a large open plaza. The music was loud now.

In a pit near the entrance B-boys in track suits and helmets did head spins and kung-fu flips.

A line had formed and kids waited restlessly behind red velvet ropes to go in. Two large men wearing black suits guarded the door.

Cassandra touched Stanton's chest lightly. "Work your magic."

They walked to the front of the line. Stanton darted into the mind of the larger security guard whose fist was filled with dollar bills.

The other guard frisked a thin white boy, checking his jeans for weapons.

The one with the money smiled suddenly as if he had just remembered an old friend. "Stanton, my man," he said and waved them in. He signaled the other not to do a weapon's check.

Both guards stood back with admiring smiles and let them pass.

The kids in line stared enviously, already assuming Stanton and Cassandra were record producers or music scouts.

"You haven't lost your touch," Cassandra smirked as they hurried through a dark hallway to a large room.

Inside the music hit Stanton hard, rocking through his chest. He liked the new sound. It was fast and heavy on the guitar. He scanned the crowd.

"All these hard-core rocker babes hanging out," Cassandra shouted in his ear. "It should be easy for you to find one who wants a little dark adventure."

He turned to her. "You're not jealous?" He taunted her spitefully. "I thought you would be."

She shook back her hair. Her earrings dangled against her soft throat. "Of them?" she asked with an arrogant snicker. "Open your eyes and look at me."

He nodded and couldn't conceal a smile. He couldn't deny that she was stunning.

"I knew you'd notice," she teased and ran a finger down his cheek, then touched his lip. "Fly high." She strutted away with a swing of her hips, knowing the guys lined against the wall were all staring at her.

Stanton laughed. When she had still been a Follower, the rich-looking guys in their silver-studded belts and clean, pressed jeans had been her target. She liked to play games with them. In the old days she had had the power to go into their minds and make them forget a few dollars on the table. Or sometimes she would send them out to buy her gifts. Now she had to outwit them, but that didn't look like it was going to be a problem either.

Stanton grabbed a Pepsi from a heavy-metal guy who had just purchased one at the canteen.

"Hey!" He thrust his skinny chest forward.

"You don't want to fight me," Stanton said simply, then plucked the anger from the guy's mind and brought forth false memories.

Finally, Stanton lifted the Pepsi in a salute. "Thanks, Gilly," he said, easily finding the guy's name.

"Sure, dude, any time." Gilly nodded and smiled as if he and Stanton were the best of friends.

Stanton found a table in the back. He sat down, flung his legs up, and rested his shoes on the table's edge. Immediately, three girls joined him, but his attention was on the next band setting up. Soon it began to play.

The girls sitting at the table looked at Stanton. He smiled, letting his mind tease around their thoughts. They had picked him out because they liked the way he looked. But he didn't pick up any fear or hesitation to awaken his desire.

"Want to dance?" the boldest one asked.

Stanton shook his head. When he didn't respond to their inviting looks, they left his table and pushed through the crowd.

Then a girl band in spandex and halter tops took the stage. The tousel-haired lead singer made his back shiver when she broke into song. Her tattoos seemed to crawl up and down her arms as she played her guitar.

Stanton thought about taking her and let his mind weave into her thoughts. She turned her head, eyes wide, and stared back at him with animal need of her own.

Girls in miniskirts and slinky tops danced near him, and he studied each one in turn, sliding into their minds briefly, reading troubles and woes, seeing broken hearts and boyfriends. None of them fired his imagination or his need.

A girl with braces and sweat glistening around her brow plopped into the chair across from him and daringly took a sip of his Pepsi. Her eyes looked at him with invitation. He eased inside her thoughts, then pushed deeper into her memories. He snapped from her mind. She was too eager. Let some Initiate find her. The girl seemed to sense his rejection and left.

Finally, Cassandra came back to him. "Girls have been flirting with you all night and you haven't done anything. Don't you even remember how?"

"I'm not going to," he stated. "I've changed my mind."

She tilted her head. A sly smile crept across her face. "I haven't changed mine."

"I didn't think you would." He resigned himself to what he was going to have to do.

She paused. "Just like the old days, you're waiting for angels. You're not going to find any here, so I'm going to choose for you. That one over there."

He followed her finger. She pointed to Maryann. What was she doing here?

Maryann waved. She wore a see-through dress, and a push-up bra. Even from across the room he could feel her discomfort and embarrassment over the way she was dressed.

"Doesn't she look wicked?" Cassandra teased.

"Did you tell her to come here?"

"I might have nudged her," she confessed.

Stanton realized then that Cassandra had followed him to the Halloween party in West Hollywood. Had she also seen Malcolm?

"Is she good enough?" Cassandra asked. Then she caught his look and shrugged. "I already told you that I've been following you. You liked her on Halloween night. Consider her my present to you."

He glanced back at Maryann and remembered her memories. She was a good person, the kind he liked to bend and turn. The other part of him awakened now with a slow lazy stretch. His heartbeat quickened. He had denied himself too long.

Cassandra caught the way he was looking at Maryann. "I had to show her how to dress," she said, laughing. "You can't imagine what she was going to wear—but that dress makes her sizzle."

She licked her thumb, pressed it on her hip and made a hissing sound.

Stanton stood. Already his body filled with fiery anticipation. He jostled through the dancers until he stood next to Maryann.

She looked up at him and smiled. "Hi, I was hoping I would see you again."

"I thought your father wouldn't approve." His eyes lingered over the thin green dress with beads sewn across the top. He turned her around to see the back of it. She was blushing when she faced him again.

She cleared her throat. "Did I actually tell you about my father?"

"No, I just knew." He brushed back her hair, then let his hand slide down her neck and rest on her shoulder, his thumb rubbing her collarbone. "You look good in that dress."

She relaxed and cast her eyes down before she looked at him again.

He loved her purity of heart. Memories of other nights breathed through him, making his craving stronger.

"You're looking at me funny." She giggled. He caught a memory of her pressing her face into her pillow the night before and pretending she was kissing him.

"You want a kiss?" he asked with a malicious smile.

She nodded, her face turning crimson with self-consciousness.

"You've never been kissed before, have you?" he asked, knowing that she hadn't.

Her eyes darted away. "Of course I have," she lied.

"Don't lie to me."

She started to deny it again, but changed her mind and shook her head. "No," she admitted.

The music stopped and the room filled with the sound of beer cans emptying. Kids shoved around them, heading for the bathrooms.

Stanton took her hand and pulled her back to a dark corner behind the tables where they could be alone. The singer on stage played a riff on her guitar. The notes vibrated through Stanton. He moved his feet in time to the beat.

Maryann watched him. "You're a good dancer." She seemed surprised. "I thought the other night you didn't know how to dance."

He put his hands on her waist and pulled her to him. "I can dance. There isn't anything I can't do. I'm a Follower."

"A Follower?" She smiled and danced close to him. "What's that?"

He let his hands slide up her sides. "I'm going to show you."

The night pulsed through him. He knew she saw something different in his eyes by the way she jerked back. He held her tight. "Don't you know when a guy wants to kiss you?"

She swallowed and seemed unsure.

"Put your arms around me," he ordered softly.

Her hands slipped tentatively up his chest and clasped his neck. He pulled her body next to his and she closed her eyes in anticipation.

What little resistance remained inside him slipped down into a cold abyss where his soul had once been. He eased into her mind with a suddenness that surprised her. Her eyes burst open with a shock and she stared at him. He saw the astonishment on her face and cherished the sensuous fear exploding inside her. She tried to break away from him.

"Too late," he whispered and held her with his eyes. Each time she tried to pull away, he drew her to him until he had her spellbound.

He could hear her whimpering, but it was as if she were far away.

Now sweet one, turn and face the Atrox. She struggled against his caressing, but soon she stopped fighting and her fear left her. The lies of the Atrox soothed her and filled her with promises.

Stanton smiled triumphantly and pressed his hand over her mouth so she couldn't cry out when she finally saw the bleak future that awaited her.

Her communion with the Atrox filled his emptiness, but he knew the ecstasy he felt from devouring her luxurious hope would only last for a short time. Soon, the aching need would return, but for now it was satisfied. He wondered now why he had denied himself for so long. He was a creature of night and he relished his evil existence.

"Soon," he whispered against her cheek. "Soon you will see the way and become a Follower. I'll guide you and help you."

She was too confused to answer him. Her eyes looked haunted. He caught a tear running down her cheek with the tip of his finger.

Then, a strange feeling came over him. He felt other eyes. He turned, and through the crush of dancers he saw Serena, staring back at him.

CHAPTER FIFTEEN

JIMENA, CATTY, AND Vanessa joined Serena and stood beside her, their amulets glowing.

Stanton hated the wounded look on Serena's face almost as much as he hated the smirk on Cassandra's. He knew in an instant that Cassandra had set him up. Anger spread through him like thick, hot tar.

"Serena," he yelled and tried to send a thought to her, but she repelled it. He had done this to protect her, couldn't she see? He tried to reach her again with his mind, but she slammed his thoughts away.

Dancers bobbed around him, getting in his way, but even from this distance he could feel the fierce anger building inside Serena. She felt betrayed. Then Jimena leaned against her and together their power crackled across the room. He deflected their hit. He was too powerful for them to fight, but he understood that they had to try to save Maryann and they wouldn't back down.

Serena, Stanton called again and opened his mind so she could enter it and see the truth.

Serena ignored him and shoved through the dancers, Jimena, Catty, and Vanessa behind her. When they were closer, all four stood together and locked arms. Their force exploded across the room in a blinding flash. Stanton split their barrage before it reached him. The room convulsed and hundreds of sparks spun in the air.

Kids stopped dancing and watched. Even the musicians were spellbound by the fiery lights.

"Light show!" the lead singer yelled into the mike.

Then the music started again. Dancers

crowded the floor as bits of fire continued flying around the room.

Serena stared angrily at Stanton through the shower of embers. He could feel how hurt she was. She glanced at Jimena, Vanessa, and Catty. They knew that they were no match for him, but the looks on their faces said they would not turn away.

All four pushed through the dancers with raw determination until they were almost beside him. Their moon amulets glowed in his eyes. He blinked and turned away.

"I'll never forgive you." Serena grabbed Maryann's hand and jerked her away from Stanton; then all four girls pushed through the crowd, pulling Maryann with them.

"Serena!" Stanton yelled. He tried to follow her, but dancers pressed tightly around him. He cried out her name again and when she didn't turn back, he elbowed through the crush of kids after her.

When he stepped through the front door he found Jimena waiting for him.

"I warned you," she whispered, and the air

split with a jolt he hadn't expected. It shattered into his head before he could block it.

Stanton staggered back, unable to regain his balance as Jimena's power came at him with another smashing wave.

Jimena glared at Stanton, daring him to attack, then she turned, ran through the break dancers and down the corridor, the palm fronds brushing against her jeans.

Stanton ran after her.

When he reached the street, Serena was helping Maryann into the back seat of Jimena's car.

"Serena," he pleaded. "Listen to me."

Her head whipped around. "I don't want to hear your lies."

Vanessa, Catty, and Jimena turned to face him. He could feel them preparing for battle. They were not supposed to attack first, but he knew they didn't always follow their own rules. He glanced warily at Jimena, then spread his arms wide and walked slowly toward Serena, his mind open, vulnerable, and begging her to listen. She wouldn't even look at him.

"Let me explain, Serena," he said. "You have the power to look in my mind and see what happened. Just look. You'll understand if you do."

"I don't want to," she answered simply, but he could feel the quiver of tears in her voice. "I'm done."

He stepped closer. A desolate ache spread through his chest. "Serena . . ."

"You heard her," Jimena shouted. "*Vete!* Get away. She doesn't want any more of your *mentiras.* All you've every done is lie."

He took one last step forward.

"Serena, I had to do it to protect you," he tried to explain. "That's the way it started. Cassandra saw us together. She was going to expose us to the Atrox."

Serena shook her head. "I don't want that kind of protection. That's not what I stand for."

He understood immediately that he should have been braver. "But that's what I am. What you saw in there. You've always known I'm a Follower and that's what Followers do. The Atrox demands it."

Tears shimmered in Serena's eyes. "Then I guess I couldn't have ever really liked you."

Vanessa looked at him with pity, but Catty seemed anxious to get away.

"It's over." Jimena stated flatly. "Leave her alone."

"Is that what you want?" Stanton stared at Serena. He had become her enemy again. Old battle lines were redrawn. "I'm lost without you, Serena," he pleaded.

Vanessa looked at him, then turned away, angered to think of the number of times she had stood up for him.

Jimena started to open the driver's side door but stopped suddenly, her hand flying to her forehead.

"Are you all right, Jimena?" Serena asked.

"Are you having a premonition?" Catty looked worried.

Jimena shook her head as if trying to rid herself of the image.

"What did you see?" Vanessa asked.

Jimena stood and looked over the car at

Stanton with new hate in her eyes. "I had another premonition about Stanton."

"Worse than the last one?" Vanessa's anxiety seemed to be increasing.

"Yes," Jimena said slowly. Her eyes held his in challenge.

Vanessa broke in. "Let's go then. Before any more start coming true." She slid into the car next to Maryann and Catty squeezed in after her.

Stanton tried to push into Jimena's mind to see her premonition, but when he did she shot a wave of anger at him. At last she jumped into the car and turned the ignition. The twin pipes roared.

Suddenly Stanton was afraid that he would never see Serena again. He ran to the car and pounded on the passenger-side window.

"Serena!" he yelled, then he glanced in the side-view mirror. His eyes glowed phosphorescent. He stepped back, defeated, as the car pulled away.

Serena turned and looked at him from the passenger's side window. He saw something new in her eyes. Contempt.

CHAPTER SIXTEEN

THE CAR SPED AWAY. Stanton watched until the taillights became invisible and only the exhaust remained.

Cassandra walked over to him and whispered with victory in her voice, "The one person you love now despises you."

Stanton looked down, defeated, and started walking.

"See how it feels?" Cassandra left the words trailing in the air.

He looked at the hate in her eyes and understood his fatal error. "What did you gain,

Cassandra? Did you think with Serena out of the way that I could start to like *you*?"

"I don't want your *like*," she snapped back furiously. "I want your *love*. I did this for us."

He shook his head. "Do you really think emotions are that easy?"

Determination settled over her face. "I'm patient," she answered coyly. "Besides, you liked what you did. I saw you with Maryann. That's what you are. A Follower. Why deny it for Serena? You'll never be like her no matter how hard you try."

He stepped into the shadows. He didn't want to hear the truth.

She ran after him and grabbed his arm before he could disappear. "Serena kept you from being true to yourself. Don't you understand? I needed to help you see what she was doing to you."

He thought of Serena again and the way she had looked at him with loathing.

Cassandra rubbed his arm. "Are you ready to come back to us?"

Stanton shook his head. "Leave me alone, Cassandra."

"There's more," Cassandra whispered softly. "I know someone who can convince you."

Stanton heard footfalls. It had to be his imagination, but the night seemed to thunder with the sound of the steps. He turned. A man wearing a hooded cape walked slowly toward him.

Stanton tensed. He felt afraid. How long had it been since he had felt that emotion for himself?

"Where did he come from?" Stanton asked. He should have felt the man's approach or seen him before now.

Cassandra smirked. "Hell."

CHAPTER SEVENTEEN

AS THE MAN STEPPED closer, Stanton recognized the Phoenix crest on his hood. Only the most powerful members of the Inner Circle were allowed to wear that emblem. The black wings and red flames on the chest of a beautifully plumed Phoenix represented the spirits of the netherworld. They were more enduring than Immortals. Even if something should happen to their bodies so that they couldn't regenerate, their spirits would live on. Stanton had never met anyone who had been allowed to wear the crest.

The man started to remove his cape. He was

taller than Stanton and had shoulder-length white hair. His hands were slender and long and there was something about the way his fingers gathered the silky cape that seemed familiar.

"This is Darius." Cassandra spoke reverently. "The one I told you about. The one who said our love was destiny."

The man turned, but his face remained in shadow. "Good evening," he said. His voice pierced Stanton like a dagger, releasing a flood of long-forgotten memories.

"Lambert," Stanton whispered with sudden recognition. The man standing before him might be called Darius now but his real name was Lambert Malmaris, the knight who had been charged with guarding him as a young boy.

Lambert stepped into the circle of light under the street lamp. A scar slashed down his right cheek. He handed his cape to Cassandra.

"So you still remember me after all these years, Stanton?" Lambert said in a soothing voice, a voice Stanton had listened to night after night as Lambert told him stories of great men and kings.

Stanton nodded, stunned. "The Atrox took you, too?" he asked carefully. "Is that why you couldn't protect me?"

Lambert smiled as if Stanton had said something amusing, his eyes deep and penetrating. "No, Stanton, I did what you've always suspected. I abandoned you and left you for the Atrox."

Stanton pressed his fingers against his chest, trying to ease the painful beat of his heart. "That can't be true." His words sounded jittery. "You were courageous and honorable—dedicated to service like all my father's knights."

Lambert walked closer to Stanton. "I decided to be dedicated only to myself." He breathed deeply. "The knights in shining armor must adhere to rules that give them nothing in return. I wanted the world."

Stanton shook his head. "The Atrox changed you. You weren't—"

"But I was," Lambert said darkly. "I became a Follower while I was still in service to your father."

Stanton studied his face. Lambert hadn't

aged, but his features had taken on a harder edge. "Why?" Stanton asked finally.

"The Ordene de Chevalerie only enslaved me," Lambert continued. "I knew the realities of knighthood. I joined with the Atrox to become a real member of the warrior elite. It was easy for me—you afforded me the perfect opportunity to become an Immortal."

"I can't believe my father trusted you," Stanton said. "Or that I cared for you."

Lambert nodded. "I know. You told me you wanted to grow up to be just like me . . . and you have." His laughter echoed into the night.

Stanton realized now that Malcolm had been trying to warn him about Lambert, but had only managed to mutter what had sounded like *Lamp*. But what plan could Lambert have that involved him? He glanced at Cassandra and wondered if she knew.

She smiled back at him insolently.

Lambert placed an arm around Stanton, the way a father would to a beloved son. "Now it is time for you to become a member of the Inner Circle."

Stanton pushed his arm away. "No," he said simply. He could never trust Lambert again.

"Listen to what he has to say," Cassandra coaxed. "You can't refuse such a position of power."

"You once valued my judgment," Lambert stated.

"Once," Stanton agreed bitterly.

"Think of the power you'll have." Lambert seeped into his mind and showed him a dizzy array of what he could become and do. His power of mind control was more than Stanton could ever have imagined. He felt hypnotized and fascinated. And then he saw a promise that pulled him deeper into Lambert's mind. The anxiety would finally be over—he would no longer have to struggle internally. Only one side would reign supreme. He saw himself free, without guilt or conscience to restrain him.

"*Invitus* is a hard life," Lambert said. "One foot in each world."

But there was still the lingering doubt. What had Malcolm wanted to say?

Lambert read his thoughts. "Perhaps Malcolm came to you out of jealousy."

"Jealousy?" Stanton started to laugh, but then something in Lambert's eyes made him stop.

"He was a powerful Regulator after all," Lambert went on. "But he failed to measure up. Perhaps he understood that you were next in line and he couldn't bear to see another take his place. So he went to you, trying to plant that seed of doubt that is growing inside you even now. He didn't want you to take what he felt was rightfully his."

Stanton wondered if that could have been it. He saw such certainty in Lambert's eyes. "But he died," Stanton mused. "He was an Immortal and now he's gone."

"So sad," Lambert said. "But enough of Malcolm. I see your thoughts. You're wondering what you would have to do to enter the Cincti."

Stanton nodded.

"Something so easy. So simple. The Atrox has been watching you. We all have," Lambert assured him, and suddenly his comforting arm was around Stanton again, but this time he didn't knock it away.

"We've all admired the way you've made the goddess fall in love with you," Lambert continued.

Stanton stiffened.

"Don't be concerned," Lambert said soothingly. "We don't plan to destroy you or your goddess. Not after you've worked so hard to gain her trust."

Stanton glared at Cassandra. "Serena no longer trusts me."

"But her infatuation with you is still strong." Lambert's words were hypnotic. "And she wants to trust you again."

"Does she love me?" Stanton wondered if Lambert had the power to go into Serena's mind even at this distance.

Lambert nodded. "If you want her, all you need to do is bring her to the Atrox." He gently placed a hand over Stanton's mouth to stop his protests. "Hear me out first. There is time to answer. An eternity of time. Think with me."

Lambert pulled Stanton into his mind. Suddenly, he saw everything so clearly. He knew Serena better than anyone. He had shared her deepest thoughts, her darkest memories and her best ones. Each weakness, each vulnerability. It would be so easy to take her to the Atrox. Isn't that what he had always feared he would do anyway?

A sound distracted him and he wrenched away from Lambert's gaze.

Cassandra was suddenly standing near them. "And me. Don't forget me. I'll be accepted back."

Lambert raised a hand, silencing her.

Her interruption cast a shade of doubt over Stanton again. Lambert seemed to sense his renewed struggle.

"Cassandra is worried only for herself," Lambert declared. "But you have more important concerns. You have to look at the entire universe, the balance between good and evil. Why must evil always be defined by good? Why not let it be the other way for once. Let people measure their good acts against evil ones. Shouldn't we reign? We can, with your help."

Stanton could feel the rightness in what Lambert was saying. His eagerness to obey seemed limitless.

"Think of Serena," Lambert encouraged. "I saw you with her tonight."

Stanton nodded.

"How can you love someone who doesn't trust you?"

Stanton glanced at him, considering.

"Even I understood that what you did to Maryann tonight was only your attempt to protect Serena. But Serena didn't even let you explain. Why is that?"

Stanton opened his mouth, but no answer came.

"You must remember that a goddess can never completely trust a Follower," Lambert continued.

"Yes." Stanton nodded.

"Deep down you have always known what you have to do, haven't you?" Lambert didn't wait for an answer but posed another question. "If she were a Follower and on our side, you would have her trust, wouldn't you?"

"Yes." Stanton had never thought of it that way before.

Lambert went on. "And she has always kept your relationship hidden. She has never introduced you to her father or brother. Is she ashamed of her feelings for you?"

"I don't know," Stanton wondered.

Lambert's voice was harsh. "Or has she been using you, Stanton?"

Stanton jerked his head around and stared into Lambert's eyes. "Using me?"

"She's the key," Lambert answered. "And it works both ways. Maybe she has been using you to find a way to vanquish evil forever."

"You think she's been using me?" Stanton asked again.

Lambert nodded. "Isn't it time to put aside your foolish infatuation with forbidden love and become a powerful leader?" Lambert asked, his hand reassuring and strong on Stanton's back.

"You were indomitable before you met her. Admired. Sought after. Strong."

Stanton nodded. How could he have been so foolish for so long? He nodded again. If Serena loved him, why wouldn't she turn to the Atrox? Then they could spend eternity together. It was such an easy solution. She was *lecta* already, chosen by the Atrox to receive its eternal life.

"That's right," Lambert whispered. "Once she is evil, you can have your bride."

"What?" Cassandra's anger abruptly split the air. "You said Stanton and I were destined to be together forever."

Lambert raised his hand to silence her.

"That's why I helped you!" Cassandra yelled furiously.

"Cassandra," Lambert said ominously.

"That's not what you promised me," Cassandra seethed. "You told me—"

Lambert did something to Cassandra. She became quiet and her eyes looked dreamy and faraway. A slight smile crept over her lips as if she tasted something sweet.

"You can have your Serena," Lambert repeated. "Once she turns to the Atrox. That is my promise to you. Bring her to me."

"And if I don't?" Stanton asked.

Lambert laughed. "Brave Stanton. You were always such a brave boy. If you don't, Regulators will destroy you both. You think she's protected because she's a Daughter of the Moon? The only way she is protected now is if you bring her to me."

Stanton turned the idea over in his mind but only for a moment. He could feel Lambert inside him searching through his turmoil.

Lambert read his thoughts. "You're right, Stanton. You'll lose her anyway if you don't act. You're an Immortal and Serena does not have much time left. And when she turns seventeen, what if she decides not to stay, what then? Why wait to see if she casts you aside?"

Stanton nodded. He didn't want to lose her.

Lambert pulled him closer. "If you love

her as you say, is there any other way?"

"No," Stanton whispered.

"Then bring her to me," Lambert urged.

"I will."

CHAPTER EIGHTEEN

JIMENA, SERENA, CATTY, and Vanessa walked together under the thin branches of newly planted trees, their faces passing from sunshine to shadow and back. Stanton followed over their heads, a dark rip in the thready light.

"I can't go with you today," Jimena explained to Serena when they reached the bus stop. "I have to go to my grandmother's house."

"It's all right," Serena answered. She buttoned her denim vest against the late-afternoon chill.

"I tried to get out of it." Jimena sighed. "But

she's making dinner for a *quinceañera* and needs my help."

Stanton settled in a cloak of dark cast by a large truck. All week the other three Daughters had stayed close to Serena. They had even taken turns spending the night at Serena's house. He hadn't been able to catch her alone once.

"Don't worry so much about me." Serena picked up her cello case as the bus rolled to the curb. "I've walked home from my music lesson a million times."

"But this is different," Catty whispered and turned slowly, scanning the shadows. She seemed more nervous than the others. "I wish I didn't have to go work in my mom's store."

"I'm okay," Serena reassured Catty, then she turned to Vanessa. "And I really don't need you to come with me to my lesson. If Stanton were going to do something, he would have already."

Vanessa looked doubtful. "I got my bus pass out so I might as well go with you," she stated. "I wish I could go home with you but I have to help my mom carry costumes over to the set where she's working."

"I can handle things." Serena was getting irritated.

"We know," Jimena answered, "but don't get tough on us and fight him on your own. Promise?"

Stanton smiled at their suspicions.

"See you tomorrow," Serena answered, ignoring Jimena's question.

Vanessa and Serena climbed on the bus and waved good-bye.

Satisfaction settled inside Stanton. Serena would be walking home alone.

When the bus pulled away, Catty turned to Jimena. "I don't like this."

"Don't say it," Jimena warned. "Don't even think it."

"But—" Catty stopped and pulled her long coat tightly around her. "You're right."

Stanton became immediately alert. What was it that Jimena didn't want Catty to say or even think? He pressed gently into the edges of Catty's mind. She had always been easier to read than the others, but now her mind was like concrete, her thoughts heavily guarded. He could use his power and force his way in, but then her moon amulet would sense his presence and begin to glow. He couldn't risk that, not now, when he was so close.

"I'll see you tomorrow." Catty turned and started walking away, her boots heavy on the sidewalk.

"Yeah," Jimena called after her. She sat down on the bench to wait for her bus and pulled her pink messenger bag onto her lap.

Stanton teased around her, flowing in and out of the shadows cast by others waiting for her bus. He needed to catch some tremor of thought. Then he sensed it. Her worry. Her face was set hard, her eyes not giving any emotion away, but he had found what he wanted. They had left Serena alone and Jimena felt concerned about it.

His heart filled with steely determination. Serena was his at last. He sped down Melrose Avenue, skating from shade to the deeper darkness along the north-facing shops. Papers fluttered and leaves trembled in his wake. Outside a dress boutique two girls turned, startled by the change in air he had caused. They glanced at each other and laughed.

The dark pretty one whispered, "Someone just walked over our graves."

That made them laugh again, but Stanton sensed more. He twirled back and savored their fear. He wanted to drop into his body and become solid in front of them but he didn't have time. Instead he whispered, "Death is riding on the wind."

Their eyes shot open and he sucked in their terror.

"That's not funny," the darker one accused her friend.

"I didn't say it," the other one answered in a shaky voice.

He left them arguing and cut up the side of the building behind them. Anyone looking would have seen only a sliver of black that was there, then gone. He continued across the rooftop like a fragment of night until he found a deserted alley, where he became whole again.

Then he started walking to his car.

* * *

Two hours later, he stalked down the street a block from where Serena lived. She would be coming this way soon. The sun had set but the moon had not yet risen. The nearby houses were still dark, waiting for their owners to come home. He kicked at a brick in a garden path until it was loosened, then he picked it up and hurled it at the nearest streetlight. After the second try the glass shattered and darkness exploded around him.

He listened. The soft sound of careful footsteps broke the quiet. He searched the street. Then he saw her. She stepped down the sidewalk on the next block, the cello case in one hand, music books in the other, her beautiful face glowing in the distant streetlight. He felt her mind reaching into shadows, scanning the nightfall for danger.

He leaned back in the air and released his body, then blended into the darkness beneath the low-hanging branches of a tree. "I'm your only danger now," he whispered.

Serena looked up, her eyes wary as she approached the next block. She crossed the street, her feet crunching over shards of glass, then stopped on the curb and looked at the broken streetlight. Finally she surveyed the night surrounding her.

Stanton skimmed over the jagged path of black shadows beneath the palm trees until he was over her head. Abruptly he slid back into himself and landed on his feet in front of her.

She gasped.

He let an indolent smile creep over his face and breathed in the sweet smell of her fear as his hand shot out and grabbed her before she could turn and run.

Soon you'll have nothing to fear. He pushed the words into her mind and added a pledge of love to make her his for eternity.

Her eyes flashed back with a promise of her own. The warrior-goddess emerged. At first he thought she was going to battle him. He opened his mind with eager anticipation. He wanted her to fight.

Instead, she surprised him. She dropped her cello case. It thudded on the concrete and glass. Then she flung her books at him. He batted the books aside as she darted across the street. Her skirt flapped wildly about her legs and her shoes smacked hard on the pavement.

He ran after her, his heart excited by the chase. *You can't escape me,* he whispered into her mind.

That's what you think.

He loved her foolish bravery.

She ducked under a bougainvillea. Branches snapped back and thorns scraped her forehead. Then she turned into the yard of an empty house and disappeared.

Stupid mistake, he sighed, feeling the words penetrate her mind. He grinned and stalked slowly after her. *There won't be any pain,* he promised. *Only an eternity together. Come back to me.*

He crept down the side of the vacant house into a backyard, overgrown with weeds and filled with wind-blown trash.

Her jagged breathing gave her away. She stood, a dark silhouette pressed against the trunk of a cottonwood tree. She was cornered in the yard. No place to go.

Sweet goddess, he traced across her mind. *I've only come to seal our destiny. You shouldn't feel so afraid of me.* And yet her fear was what he enjoyed. He savored it.

Her moon amulet shot white light across the dark.

He eased through the weeds until he was at her side. When his hand reached to touch her, she jerked back, and without warning leaped toward the redwood fence. Her hands grabbed the top as her feet worked rapidly to scramble up, but before she could slide over he caught her arm and stopped her.

She trembled as he pressed her closer to him, then touched her chin and lifted her face. A cold sweat covered her skin and a fiery gleam burned in her eyes but she wasn't preparing to fight or even read his thoughts. He felt disappointed. He didn't want her easy surrender. She was stronger than that. He wanted the warrior for his bride.

He pressed into her mind and examined her

thoughts, so open to him now, then caught an emotion that surprised him. She still cared for him.

"Then why didn't you let me explain?" he asked in a hushed voice.

But before she could answer he found a stronger feeling. His heart pulsed with her ache. He felt how much what he had done to Maryann had hurt Serena.

He started to apologize but anger ripped through him. *Then you should have let me explain.*

Her head jerked back as if his sudden temper had caused her pain.

It was too late now. There was no turning from his plan. He started to go into her mind again.

"I didn't trust you," she answered defensively.

You will soon.

"How could I?" she spoke rapidly now as if she understood his intent. "Jimena finally told me what she saw in her premonitions."

"So?" He didn't want her explanation now, he wanted to take her to the other side.

"Jimena saw you recruiting someone in her

first premonition. When that one came true, I assumed that the others would, too. That made it impossible to trust you."

"You should have trusted me," he answered. Again he entered her thoughts, but stopped. It wasn't fear that he had sensed in her earlier, but nervousness. That baffled him. Before he could consider it more he caught something in the corner of his eye.

He spun around. Nothing was there. He listened for the approach of footsteps, but the only sounds were branches scraping against the vacant house and leaves rustling overhead.

"Stanton." Serena touched his face softly, pulling him back to her.

"Do you sense anything?"

"Only the wind," she answered. "It's blowing papers around the yard."

He followed her finger and saw a yellowed page from the *Times* rolling like a tumbleweed. He held his hand up to check the breeze. The night was still. He started to walk over to investigate.

"Stanton," Serena called again, her voice more nervous than before.

He turned back to her but now he couldn't erase the feeling that someone was watching them.

She tried to bring his attention back to her. "Cassandra found me."

"I assumed she had." He studied the corners of the yard, wondering if the Atrox was there watching him. The shadows seemed normal enough.

"She brought me to the club in Silver Lake so I could see the truth about you." She stepped in front of him and tried to make him look at her.

"She set us up," Stanton answered and pushed her hands away. He looked behind him.

"At first I wasn't going to go, but I did and—" A sudden change of air made her stop.

Abruptly he was aware that someone was in the yard with them. And then he knew. A whirlwind rushed around him as Jimena, Vanessa, and Catty materialized beside Serena. Vanessa had shielded them with her power of invisibility.

"I'm sorry," Serena whispered.

All four stared at him. For a moment he felt confused.

But then he realized that everything they had said at the bus stop had been to set their trap. That's why Jimena had cautioned Catty not to speak or even think her doubts. They had suspected he might be near, trying to read their thoughts.

In a flash, their powers entwined tightly and struck with amazing force. He staggered back. A deep slow burn started inside his chest and spread outward to his arms and legs.

He tried to gather his strength, but before he could they sent another blast pushing back his power. This time he felt on fire. He understood that they weren't trying to destroy him. They were trying to release him from his bondage to the Atrox.

But they didn't understand that they could never release him. That was what he hadn't told them that day on Olvera Street. He had been evil too long to be freed. A Follower as purely evil as he was could only be destroyed.

Their moon amulets lit the backyard with a

white glow. They struck again. He could feel the light consume him. He had a strange awareness of something leaving his body and he became too weak to stand. He fell to the ground in excruciating pain.

He turned to look one last time in Serena's eyes.

She glanced at him and immediately understood.

"Stop!" she screamed.

But it was too late.

"What is it?" Jimena asked.

"We're destroying him!" Serena yelled as she knelt next to him.

"What do you mean?" Catty asked, rushing beside her.

Serena clutched his hand. He hoped she understood all the things he didn't have time to tell her. He hadn't wanted to harm her. He had only wanted to have her with him for eternity.

"I'm sorry," he tried to say but the words failed him.

"Stay," she cried softly. "Stay."

"Did we kill him?" Vanessa asked, her voice breaking.

The pain became a white fire burning through him, consuming his evil. When it was finished there would be nothing left of him. He would be like Malcolm, dust and bone. But like Malcolm he didn't feel afraid. He welcomed the peace that nothingness offered. It seemed blissful compared to the dark in which he had lived all these centuries.

I want this, he tried to tell Serena to ease the terrible sorrow he felt inside her. More than anything he wanted release from his enslavement.

Serena held his head on her lap. He could feel her pushing through his mind, trying to find a way to save him.

Catty leaned next to her. "Is he going to be okay?"

Serena shook her head.

"Maybe if I take him back in time—" Catty said.

"He only becomes our enemy then," Jimena answered softly.

Stanton looked one last time into Serena's eyes, then smiled, and drifted away.

CHAPTER NINETEEN

THE FIERY POWER of the Daughters of the Moon still burned inside Stanton. Slowly, the unbearable pain gave way. He realized he was no longer in the backyard of a vacant house in Los Angeles. He tried to move to see where he was but hot pain spread through him and he sank back to the ground, his muscles too tired to hold the weight of his head. He wondered briefly if this was the nothingness of death, but instinct told him that something else was happening.

"You're not dead, if that is what you are

thinking," a soft voice said to him from a distance.

"Hello?" he called out, his throat raw as if the top layers of tissues had been burned away. His eyes nervously searched the dark chamber in which he found himself. It seemed like a cave or a deep pit. The soft sound of water tumbling over rocks filled the air behind him.

Then a distant light appeared in the gloom and came steadily closer. He turned his head and watched the eerie glow. Before long, he made out the form of an old woman in a long black gown. She walked toward him carrying a lantern. The flame flickered as the lantern swayed from side to side, making her shadow jump and twist over the cavern walls.

"You're far from dead," she said, and set the lantern on a small outcropping of stone near the ground where he lay. Now his shadow joined hers.

"Where am I?" He wasn't sure what he expected her to say but he feared her answer. Dread settled over him, working its way to the bone. He felt lost and alone.

"You don't know?" She raised an eyebrow to a quizzical angle.

"I thought I was dead, but this doesn't feel right."

"How does death feel?" She laughed and her voice resonated in the hollow room, then she shook her head. "You're saved."

"Saved?" Stanton asked. "But I should have died."

"You're time isn't up." She stepped closer to him. Her long hair curled strangely around her body. Suddenly, he realized it wasn't her hair. A large black snake coiled about her waist. It slithered over her shoulders, its tongue flicking the air. Yellow eyes studied Stanton.

"You're—" he started to speak, but felt too stunned to continue. He raised himself up on one elbow, ignoring the dizzy feeling inside him, and studied her elegant face. He had heard rumors about the Dark Goddess, but he had never believed they were true. People once loved the Goddess of the Dark Moon and called upon her near the end of their time on earth to lead their soul through the passageway back to birth. But because the goddess was called upon only when people were dying, she became an omen of doom. Soon after people feared saying her name for fear of conjuring death.

"You're the death-giver," he whispered with awe.

"I prepare people for rebirth," she protested.

"Then why am I here if I'm not dead?" he asked.

"Because I understand the difficulty in being part Follower and part human. You have suffered for it."

Stanton smirked. "I haven't been human for hundreds of years."

"And yet you're here. Why is that?" She gave him a derisive grin that matched his own. She spread her gown and settled beside him. "Is it possible that some part of you is still human? Maybe something inside you never surrendered to the Atrox? Perhaps the piece of soul still within you that yearns for love."

"I don't understand," he said. "How can I

still be here? I'm an Immortal. I should have been destroyed when the goddesses tried to release me."

"You thought you were too evil to be brought back?" She took his hand. He felt comforted by her touch.

"Yes," he answered. "I know I was too evil. You don't understand what a Follower must do to receive the prize of Immortality."

"You must have committed horrible atrocities," she mused quietly.

He paused, remembering. "I have."

She placed her warm hand over the exact place on his chest where the pressure of regret spread through him. "I understand human nature. I see the cause of all mistakes and failures." She sighed. He sensed her compassion. "Some say I devour life, but I also cleanse people, so that, like the moon, they can be renewed."

"You're giving me a second chance?" he asked, and then he remembered Malcolm. "Malcolm prayed to you before he died. Had he come to you to be cleansed?"

She nodded. "Malcolm had come to me

after he failed to please the Atrox. That's when I see most of your kind—when they are terrified enough to consider extraordinary alternatives."

Stanton tried to sit up but the pain rocked him back. "You're the unthinkable thing that he did. He sought you out?"

"He knew the Atrox would terminate him for his failure, so he came to me, hoping to be purified and prepared for rebirth. But he had to pay a price. I made him prove his sincerity. I sent him on a mission to warn you."

"You gave him the ring?"

She took a cloth from her pocket and pressed it over his eyes. It smelled of lavender. "I knew if you saw the ring you would believe whatever he told you."

"He never finished telling me." As Stanton breathed in the flowery scent his lungs felt soothed.

She stood and stepped away from him. "Malcolm succumbed more quickly than I had imagined. He never gave you the full message. I hadn't seen that much evil in him, but then I tend to see the good in people, not the bad." She sat beside him again and lifted his head to offer him water.

He drank and the water eased the burn in his throat. "What caused him to die?" Stanton asked when he finished drinking.

"The ring," she answered.

"But how? The ring is for protection."

She poured the remaining water across his forehead. Tiny rivulets ran into his eyes. "The ring can't protect a Follower," she explained. "It can only destroy him, because the ring consumes evil. As you witnessed, Malcolm was evil, but not completely. There was enough of him left for me to save, and, thankfully, you took his remains to a consecrated cemetery where the Atrox could never reach him."

"How did you find my father's ring?" Stanton asked.

"Your father gave it to me after he found it," she explained. "He had hoped I could use it to free you, but you had already become an Immortal—"

Stanton held up his hand to stop her from saying more, knowing that by then he had been too evil to wear the ring.

"I knew the ring would grant Malcolm his desire for escape," she continued. "And I also knew it was the only way you would believe his warning."

Stanton thought back to the day his father had given him the ring.

"You were young then." She removed the cloth from his eyes. "Far too young to understand the power that had been given to you when your father gave you the ring or you never would have lost it in your sleep. The ring could have protected you from the Atrox."

Stanton laughed bitterly and pulled the ring from his pocket. He held it up to the light. "I can't even wear it now."

She took the ring, then slipped it on his finger. He gasped. There was no pain.

"But you can." She smiled and stood. "You are free."

He held his hand up and looked at the ring.

The stone caught the flame in the lantern and sent its light across the cavern walls.

"Your bondage to the Atrox is broken but you must never take off the ring. It is your only protection." She started to walk from him. "Rest now."

"But the warning. Malcolm never finished telling me."

"He was to warn you about Lambert." She picked up the lantern. "He has been planning to overthrow the Atrox and I had to stop him."

Her words surprised Stanton. "Why would you care? I would think you'd want Followers to destroy each other."

"Things are in balance right now," she cautioned. "And a war in the underworld could have consequences in the world of light. I needed you to stop Lambert before innocent people were harmed."

"I don't know how to stop him." Stanton felt a tightness in his chest as his apprehension deepened. "I don't have as much power as he does, especially now."

"I think you already have stopped him," she assured him. "He was using you to capture Serena. With Serena he thought he would have the power to overthrow the Atrox. Now he doesn't have either of you."

Her shadow bobbed over the cavern as she slowly walked away from him. The snake wrapped sinuously around her, its eyes on Stanton until the goddess disappeared into the dark.

As he closed his eyes, she whispered across his mind, *You have much to do before your final rest. Your trials have only begun.*

Stanton fell into a deep sleep.

CHAPTER TWENTY

STANTON'S WAKING BREATH exploded into his lungs with jagged pain. He opened his eyes and struggled to breathe. Serena leaned over him. His head rested on her lap. She smiled. He had never seen her look so beautiful.

He wondered if he had only been dreaming. He patted his forehead, then ran his fingers through his hair. His skin and hair were wet and he could still smell the lavender from the cloth. As he stared at his father's ring adrenaline surged through him. Had he really been brought back?

He tried to go into Serena's mind to see but

with a shock discovered he no longer had the power. Was it true then? His heart raced. Tentatively, he touched her moon amulet.

"You're not a Follower any more," Serena whispered. "If you were, the amulet would burn your flesh."

Stanton smiled back at her and balanced the amulet on the tips of his fingers. "Did I disappear? It seemed like I went away to another place."

"No," Serena answered. "You were here, but you scared us. We thought for sure we had lost you."

"She means we were afraid we had killed you." Jimena sat on the other side of him, her hands resting on his arm. "It wasn't like we could call the paramedics or tell *la chota* what had happened." Then she added apologetically, "We never meant to hurt you. We were only trying to free you."

He nodded. "I know."

Stanton glanced at the night sky and was overcome with reverence and awe. It had been a long time since he could gaze at the starry universe and not feel remorse, or uneasiness about the location and phase of the moon. Optimism surged through him. He touched Serena's cheek and wondered what their future might hold.

"Do you think you can stand?" Serena lifted his head and helped him sit.

He nodded and became aware of his body. He felt his arms, then smoothed his hands over his knees. Everything felt different. Strong, but not supreme. He had been an Immortal for so long that he had forgotten how frail mortals were. Now there would be no instant mending of a broken bone.

"Let's go celebrate!" Catty said, then stopped and looked at Vanessa. "Okay, what is it? You're being too quiet. You always have something to say."

"I was just remembering what Jimena told us about her premonitions," Vanessa remarked.

"Don't spoil this," Catty warned. "You said yourself that the premonition about battling Stanton could have been us bringing him back. So that event has already come and gone. He's not going to fight us. Okay?"

"But what about Jimena's last premonition?" Vanessa wondered. "How can you explain that?"

Stanton could feel Serena tense.

"You worry too much," Catty argued. "Maybe Jimena is like the rest of us and her power messes up once in a while."

"What did you see?" Stanton asked Jimena.

Serena answered before Jimena could speak. "Don't worry about it. We're here and we'll protect you."

He smiled at her, but felt uneasy. He didn't want Serena protecting him. He wanted to be able to protect her. Suddenly, he realized he no longer had that kind of strength. Would she still like him as much as she had before? He remembered the way he had changed them both into shadow and they had sped together across the night. Their relationship would be different now.

Jimena touched his shoulder in reassurance. The glitter on her forehead and cheekbones shone, making her look otherworldly. "Just because I saw it, doesn't mean it has to come true. *¿Entiendes?*"

But Stanton knew Jimena had never been able to stop any of her premonitions from coming true. "So what did you see?" he insisted. "If you're not worried about it coming true, then why can't you tell me?"

Vanessa stood and started pacing.

"What now?" Catty said with exasperation.

"It's just that he doesn't seem confused the way others have when we've brought them back." Vanessa folded her arms across her chest.

"What are you trying to say?" Serena demanded.

"Does he seem like the others?" Vanessa asked again.

Serena gently probed his mind. He could no longer rush to meet her thoughts and merge with her. The sensation now felt odd, a fuzzy tickle inside his head.

"He's not faking it if that's what you're trying to say," Serena answered. "He no longer has his powers. Any of them."

Stanton wondered if that would make a difference to her.

Vanessa bit her lip. "Just that maybe we can't—"

"Trust him?" Serena didn't try to hold her anger back now. She stood and faced Vanessa.

Before they could say more, Catty crowded between them. "We've never brought an Immortal back before. Maybe it's different, all right?"

"I went to the Dark Goddess," Stanton stated.

They turned and looked at him.

"Normally, you can't bring an Immortal back," he explained. "I should have been destroyed when you blasted me."

"We thought we had killed you," Jimena said.

"My body might have been here with you," Stanton continued. "But my real self was with the Goddess of the Dark Moon. She cleansed me and sent me back."

"The dark goddess?" Jimena asked, looking at the others.

"She's a force of good," Stanton added quickly.

"See?" Catty argued. "Does that cover all your doubts, Vanessa?"

Vanessa nodded but still seemed reluctant.

"So can we go now?" Catty threaded her arm around Vanessa's.

Jimena stood. "Catty's right. Let's go to Planet Bang."

"Yeah," Serena agreed and helped Stanton to stand. "Everything's okay for now. Let's just forget about it and go have fun."

"But . . ." Vanessa started.

"We're not going to change the future by worrying about it," Jimena told Vanessa. "Besides, how could my last premonition come true? Stanton's not even a Follower anymore."

"Yeah," Catty said happily. "Stanton's one of us now."

"A regular guy." Serena wrapped her arm around his waist and leaned against his chest.

Stanton smiled down at her. A sudden thought froze him. He wondered how long it would be before the Atrox realized he had turned traitor.

CHAPTER TWENTY-ONE

A NEON SIGN LIT the beige stucco wall with a flood of pink, blue, green, and orange lights. The colors seemed to vibrate with the rhythm of the music coming from inside Planet Bang. Serena and Stanton strolled arm in arm. Catty, Vanessa, and Jimena walked ahead of them, sharing lipstick, mascara, and a pocket mirror. The girls stepped to the back of the line, their feet impatient to go inside and dance. Stanton continued toward the entrance.

"Stanton, where are you going?" Serena asked.

He stopped, suddenly aware he wouldn't be able to hypnotize the security guards and enter. He smiled sheepishly and shrugged. "Being a Follower had its advantages." He placed his hands on Serena's shoulders and slid them down her arms. "But you could get us in. All you'd have to do is fool around with their heads and make them think they had already checked us through. It's easy."

Serena laughed. "No way. The line's not even that long tonight."

The line moved quickly and in a few minutes they were inside.

Vanessa surveyed the crowd. "Everyone got here early because Michael's band is going to play."

Stanton looked toward the back and wondered if any of his Hollywood Followers were hiding in the shadows waiting for their prey. Did they know yet that he was a traitor?

The deejay put on a song and the force of the music touched something deep inside of

Stanton. He put his hands around Serena's waist and stared into her eyes. Her hips found the rhythm and he enjoyed the slow movement of her body beneath his hands.

The song ended and the deejay picked up the microphone. "Let's give it up for Michael Saratoga and his band."

Kids whistled and clapped.

Michael's band had set up earlier. Now all four members ran on stage and grabbed their instruments. The drummer marked the beat and the energy in the room swelled.

Stanton took Serena's hand and pulled her closer to him, then leaned down and spoke against her cheek. "Everything looks so different to me now."

Her breath tickled his neck. "How so?"

"I'm no longer looking for the weaknesses in people," he confessed. "Or how to manipulate them."

He pulled back and saw the sympathy in her eyes. "It's okay," he reassured her. "I'm free now and I'm with you."

Serena looked at him with her large expressive eyes, making him wish he could go into her mind and read her thoughts. She seemed to understand. "I'm thinking about how happy I am that you're here."

He wondered if she had been in his mind all along. He ached, remembering how close they had been before.

"Don't feel bad," she answered. "You'll get used to the way you are now."

She leaned against his chest and he could feel her humming along with the music. Then she lifted her head and smoothed her hands up his body and around his neck. He took in a sharp breath and his heart raced. He felt a pleasant stirring inside him but it wasn't the old compulsion to turn someone to the Atrox. The feeling was sweet and pure.

He bent down and murmured against her ear, "You look so beautiful tonight. I don't want this moment to ever end."

"I know," she answered. "It's so much better now that we don't have to hide."

He caressed her face, longing to kiss her.

I want you to kiss me, Serena traced the words across his mind. She turned her face up, her eyes half-closed with expectation.

He hesitated, then bent his head until his lips hovered over hers. Their breath mingled and she closed her eyes. He kissed her soft warm lips, then her tongue brushed across his. A delicious longing spread through him. He loved the feeling of wanting her.

He pulled back and stared at her dark beauty before he nestled his lips against the curve of her neck and breathed the perfume in her hair. He felt happier than he could ever remember feeling, but he also felt tired. His knees trembled and his back began to throb as if the weight of his newly mortal body were more than it could support.

"You need to rest," Serena said.

Stanton looked down at Serena. "You're right. I think I'd better rest. I feel . . ." He laughed. How did he feel? Tired and more. They were all new sensations for him.

"But where will you go?" she asked.

He caught the concern in her eyes. He could tell by her expression that where he would live now was a detail she hadn't considered before. He didn't feel as concerned about it. He groped with a new emotion, overwhelming optimism. "I'll spend the night in my car."

"That could be too dangerous."

"I'll park somewhere near a police station. No one will mess with me there. Not even Followers."

She considered this. "All right. Do you want Jimena to drive you to your car?" Her eyes were already searching the room for Jimena.

"No, I want to walk and see the night. Everything looks so different."

"But you'll be careful."

He hated that she had to be so concerned about his safety now.

She started to walk him outside.

"Stay and party with your friends," he muttered softly. "You deserve a big celebration for what you did."

"You sure?"

He stroked her cheek. He cared for her more than he ever had. But he also understood the risks she faced. Followers would want revenge for what she had done. The Atrox would be unrelenting. He felt the weight of these dangers and knew they were greater than before because now she no longer had his protection.

"I knew the consequences, Stanton," she said simply, as if she had been in his mind again. "I understood what would happen before we decided to bring you back."

She seemed more goddess to him than she ever had.

She smiled and her words slipped across his mind, *You were worth the risk.*

He nodded, then watched her walk away and begin to dance between Vanessa and Catty, their faces sparkling and glowing in the flashing lights. Her eyes turned back and found him. She slid next to Jimena and moved her hips from side to side, her body responding to the music with a melody of its own. She never took her eyes away from him. Then her arms reached over her head, revealing her sinuous grace. His eyes lingered on her face, then slowly slid down her neck.

His heart lurched. Her amulet glowed opalescent. Rose-colored sparks shot into the air.

He shoved through the crowd, grabbed her wrists, and pulled her away from Catty, Jimena, and Vanessa.

They laughed.

"I guess you know how to tease the guys," Catty yelled.

"I thought you said you were going." Serena followed his look and touched the amulet. "It's nothing," she assured him. "Followers are around. Sometimes they come here."

Stanton hesitated, then on impulse he took off the ring his father had given him centuries ago and slipped it onto Serena's thumb. As soon as the ring touched her skin, her moon amulet stopped glowing and became a simple silver charm. She was safe now. He let out a long sigh.

"What happened?" she asked.

"It's the ring," he explained. "As long as you

wear the ring, Followers can't harm you." He clasped both hands around hers. "Wear it always. Promise me that no matter what happens you'll never take it off."

"But what about you?" she asked. "If the ring was given to you, you should wear it."

He gave her a tender kiss on the cheek. "I'm fine." Then he whispered into her hair. "I couldn't live without you."

"What?" she asked. "I couldn't hear you."

"It was nothing," he answered.

She tilted her head. "Tell me."

"I was just saying good night again," he lied. "That's all. Go back and dance."

She went back into the crowd, then found the beat and began dancing.

He bumped through the dancers and went outside into the cool night air. Fog was coming in. He stopped spellbound by the patterns it made. Before the cloudy mist had only been a convenient cloak to hide his approach. Now he stood in wonder, watching it curl around the street lamps.

Finally, he began walking. His footsteps echoed behind him. What lay before him? He felt more alone than he ever had, but at the same time he was at peace because he knew that he had a future now.

He wasn't sure where he would go tonight, probably sleep in his car, then find someplace tomorrow.

"Hey, Stanton."

He turned.

Cassandra stood in the fog, a long trench coat wrapped around her. She walked toward him. She didn't look good. She tried to smooth back her hair as if she felt embarrassed by her appearance. "I'm sorry, Stanton. I feel so stupid."

"Forget it," he answered and continued walking.

She stepped beside him, shaking her head. "I never would have helped Lambert, but he convinced me that we were destined to be together. He promised."

He could hear the regret in her voice.

"I guess I'll always be an outcast now," she

admitted. "What am I going to do? Lambert was taking care of me. Now I have no place to go."

He wondered if that was the reason she looked so bad. "Have you been living on the street?"

"I crashed over in Santa Monica. Not much better than the street, but at least the kids I'm living with have food and electricity." She looked up at him. "Can you help me?"

"I have nothing to offer you now, Cassandra."

"What do you mean?" She seemed puzzled. "You can use your mind and trick someone into giving me an apartment."

"I'm not a Follower anymore," he said simply.

"Right," she answered sarcastically. Then she grabbed his chin so he had to look down and into her eyes. "How?" Her voice quivered as she realized the truth.

"The Daughters of the Moon brought me back," he explained.

"Then why are you walking here? We've got

to leave and find someplace to hide. You know what's going to happen to you? You remember what the Atrox did to the last . . ." Her words trailed away and her eyes went cold with terror as if the memory were too horrible to recall. "Where's your car? We can drive someplace. Maybe Big Bear. I'm sure there are no Followers there."

He didn't know if he should trust her. He also remembered how the last Immortal had been used as an example to frighten others who might have been considering a change back. The punishment had been severe and long. Cassandra could be the one who was going to set the trap. He took a deep breath and when he let it out he only felt more tired and in need of sleep.

"You don't know what it's like not to have your powers." Cassandra seemed overwhelmed with frustration. "How are you going to survive? Now you're just another homeless kid on the streets."

He considered what she was saying. "I'll get a job."

"Great." She shook her head in disgust. "Who's going to hire you? And even if they do, you're not going to make enough to pay rent. You'll be living in a squat, but a different kind from the one you were in with the other Followers."

A distant sound made him alert. Something inside him froze. He tried to caution Cassandra to be quiet, but she continued talking. "How could you let this happen?"

He pressed his hand over her lips. Her eyes widened and he could feel the terror curl into her muscles as she became aware of other footsteps.

"Followers," she whispered and started to run.

He grabbed her. "Don't run," he said in her ear. "They'll hear you." He took her hand and led her across a yard and onto a porch. They waited behind a trellis heavy with roses.

Three milky shadows shimmered in the gray mists.

Stanton ducked and pulled Cassandra down with him. Muffled voices and stealthy footsteps filled the thick fog.

Cassandra trembled.

"Are they Lambert's Followers?" Stanton asked.

She shrugged and shook her head.

He peered from behind the trellis and wondered how Followers could be hunting him so soon. He tapped his head with one finger and knew Cassandra understood. They had to clear their minds in case one of the approaching Followers was powerful enough to scan the night and pick up thoughts.

Cassandra closed her eyes and he sensed she was concentrating on making her mind blank.

The fog was too thick for Followers to shape-change. There were no deep shadows to drift through and use as camouflage, only mist and gloom. Stanton felt sure that no one could sneak up on them. He would see their dark silhouettes first. Besides, not many Followers knew how to weave through the dark anyway. They would have to become Immortals first.

From gray silhouettes Kelly, Tymmie, and Murray stepped through the fog.

"He came this way," Kelly whispered. "I know he did."

"But we haven't found him and he can't just disappear into shadow anymore," Tymmie argued.

"I say go back the other way." Murray motioned with his head.

"This way," Kelly insisted, her voice ugly with anger. "We get him and take him to the Atrox before Lambert finds him and gets credit for it."

"How'd those bitch goddesses catch him?" Murray asked.

"It doesn't matter," Kelly answered. "We've got our chance now."

"Then we get Serena," Murray added hungrily.

Stanton smiled wryly. They had been apprenticed to him once and now they were intent on destroying him. They had been learning how to read minds. Tymmie had been the best, but their talking would distract him. He doubted they could detect him or Cassandra, crouched on the porch. But there were others, like Yvonne.

Ones with greater powers might also be looking for him.

He waited for them to pass.

"Come on." He took Cassandra's hand. It was cold with fear. "We'd better go."

As they stood up, Lambert appeared before them.

CHAPTER TWENTY-TWO

STANTON PUSHED CASSANDRA behind him and faced Lambert.

"Such bravery." Lambert mocked Stanton's effort to protect Cassandra, then without warning his hand shot out, gripped Cassandra's arm and took her from Stanton.

Stanton automatically reached for Cassandra, but Lambert sent an invisible burst of power at him. Stanton staggered back.

"Do you really think you can protect her

from me?" Lambert's eyes narrowed as he pulled her out into the yard. "Why would you want to? She betrayed you twice and would easily do so again." He shoved Cassandra to the ground near the sidewalk. "She's only an outcast, unwanted by either side."

Stanton hurried to Cassandra and helped her stand. She jerked away from him and sprinted up the street.

"So you see how loyal she is to you? She runs even now. Such sweet terror." Lambert breathed the air as if he enjoyed the feel of Cassandra's fear, then he turned and stepped to Stanton. "Why don't you run from me?" he asked. "You know what I will do to you."

Stanton stood defiantly still even though his nerves throbbed with the desire to turn and flee. "You love the chase, Lambert. I was once like you. I remember."

Lambert ran a cold finger across Stanton's neck, his fingernail scraping the skin. "So instead of trying to save yourself, you'd rather have a weak easy death."

Stanton remained quiet.

"How can you fail so miserably?" Lambert turned and paced impatiently, his cape fluttering behind him. "I gave you such a simple task to perform. You would have been rewarded with a commanding position in the Inner Circle. But not only did you fail, you were so weak, you let the Daughters make you a renegade."

"I might be a renegade," Stanton answered. "But what will happen to you when the Atrox discovers your treachery?"

Lambert whipped around. His cape slashed through the air with a loud slap. "So you've imagined some conspiracy?"

"You never wanted Serena for the Atrox," Stanton argued. "You were using me for your own gain. You wanted Serena because you thought that if you had her you could overthrow the Atrox."

"Silly lies."

"The Dark Goddess told me," Stanton replied.

"You're a fool, Stanton," Lambert sneered.

"Everyone uses you. The dark one has been an enemy of the Atrox for eternity. You believed her? What has she sent you back to do? Fight the Atrox? Fight me?"

"I believe her," Stanton answered.

"You're an *invitus* with divided loyalties." Then he smiled. "You were *invitus,* but no more. Now anyone can take you."

Lambert stormed into Stanton's mind and held him captive. The memories of what had happened to him as a child when the Atrox took him came rolling back. He remembered the cold rush of pain as if his body had been sliced opened and exposed to wind.

"How could you have so much pride that you thought you would destroy the Atrox?" Stanton forced the words past Lambert's control. "You could never win."

"Would the end of our world as we know it be so horrible?" He didn't wait for an answer. "Now your world will end."

Stanton held Lambert's eyes, determined that he wouldn't give Lambert the pleasure of his scream or struggle. He stared into the bottomless black holes with evil promise of his own. Some day he would meet Lambert as an equal and destroy him.

Lambert laughed. "You think you'll ever have my strength? I'm not here to bring you back but to terminate you. A renegade. A runaway. The worst kind of traitor. Then I'll take what is left of you back to the Atrox and show him how the fair one has betrayed his master."

"I know how to fight your control," Stanton insisted, but already Lambert's mental force pulsed through him, cutting down his resistance. His head throbbed with it as a bitter cold moved deep inside him. He thought he heard Serena calling to him, her voice distant. Impossible.

Suddenly, Lambert dropped his hold and Stanton fell to the ground. He shook his head and turned. Catty, Vanessa, Jimena, and Serena ran down the sidewalk, their footsteps thundering into the foggy night.

"No!" he yelled. "Go back." But he was too weakened. The words came out as a whisper.

Then he saw Cassandra running through the mist after them and he understood what had happened. She had gone back to Planet Bang and convinced the goddesses to rescue him.

The four Daughters stood together, their moon amulets glistening. Seen through a veil of fog, they appeared spectral.

"Goddesses," Lambert whispered, his eyes afire. "You look ravishing. I'm not sure which one of you I will destroy tonight."

"No chance," Catty answered with a wicked grin. Her eyes dilated as if energy were building inside her.

But before they could gather their forces, the air shuddered as Lambert fired a thunderbolt at them. The girls jumped away. Leaves on the low-hanging branches burst into flames and acrid smoke seeped into the overcast night.

Jimena smiled dangerously. "We've never fought a member of the Inner circle before," she threatened. "This should be fun."

The girls locked arms and the air around them glowed, then pulsed. An invisible wave smacked the space between them and rushed toward Lambert.

Lambert's cape flapped wildly from the force, but he didn't seem touched. He raised an eyebrow. "Goddesses, is that your best? I'm rather disappointed. I had hoped that this would be a challenge for me." He stepped toward them. His attack came like a demon howling from the center of the earth.

Stanton grabbed his ears.

Jimena and Serena stood perfectly still as if the sound didn't bother them but when the force hit, Jimena stumbled back, looking surprised. Serena seemed unfazed. Now the ring, not her amulet, sent fiery embers in a spiral around her.

Porch lights in the surrounding homes came on. Doors opened and faces peeked outside.

Catty and Vanessa confronted Lambert, their eyes focused. They hurled a piercing deluge. Electrical veins crackled through the fog.

Lambert looked pleased. He slapped another roll of power at them. The smell of ozone filled the air and bits of flame floated down to the sidewalk and grass. Small fires dotted the ground.

Stanton saw something on Serena's face that he had never seen in battle. She looked frightened. Jimena, always the warrior, didn't hesitate, but Stanton knew that was only because she had faced death before. Catty's hands were trembling. She took hold of Jimena's hand for reassurance. All four gathered together again, their eyes dilated, concentration intense, as their powers ran together. They held back and let the force build. When they released it, it tore through the air and hit Lambert with a jolt. His cape caught on fire. Orange flames singed the bushes behind him.

Lambert didn't smile this time. He looked angry. Then he pointed at Serena, his eyes expanded with savage rage. He flung out his hand and his power screamed through the air.

"No!" Stanton started running toward Serena.

The ring deflected Lambert's attack. Sparks showered from the stone as lightning smashed from the gem and screeched toward Vanessa.

"Look out," Serena yelled.

Vanessa turned and stared at the firebolt coming at her, as if mesmerized.

Lambert smiled and stretched his hand, taking aim. A spear of light emanated from his fingers and shattered the night. Thunder rocked the ground and the air crackled with jagged bits of flame as the force shot directly at Vanessa. Now two were coming at her.

Vanessa had her back to Lambert's charge. She was still trying to dodge the bolt deflected by the ring.

"Watch out," Catty screamed. She jumped in front of Vanessa and pushed her aside. Vanessa fell and rolled.

The blow from the ring and the new strike from Lambert hit Catty at the same time. Her eyes widened in shock, then her moon amulet exploded, and Catty disappeared.

CHAPTER TWENTY-THREE

THE AIR STILL RIPPLED from the explosion and embers continued to fall as Vanessa crawled to where Catty had stood only seconds before. Her hands patted the ground in disbelief.

Serena ran to Vanessa, knelt down and wrapped her arms around her.

Vanessa shook her head as flecks of ash settled in her hair. "Where is she?"

"She can't just be gone," Serena answered in shock.

"Catty!" Vanessa cried and turned her head, looking around as if she still thought Catty could be found.

Serena tried to soothe her. "We'll find a way to bring her back." But there was no confidence in her voice.

"When one Daughter is gone," Lambert taunted, "the power of the remaining three is greatly weakened."

Jimena stood protectively in front of Serena and Vanessa. She glared at Lambert, her eyes shiny with tears, and sent a surge of power at him. Her aim was off. It hit a tree and flames burst from the bark.

Lambert laughed. "Your power is weak now."

She wiped her eyes. "You haven't weakened us!" Jimena shouted back. "You'd better watch your back because no one hurts my friend and gets away with it. You're going down."

Lambert pulled his cape around him, the cloth still smoldering. "I'll destroy you each in turn. That is my promise, Jimena." He bowed deeply and disappeared into the mist.

Distant sirens filled the night. People in the nearby houses were stepping out on their porches now.

Stanton walked over to Jimena. "I'm sorry."

She turned on him. "Sometimes sorry isn't big enough to cover it."

"I wish I could have—"

"Helped?" she cut him off.

"Stopped Lambert," he finished.

"You've done enough," Jimena scolded. "Can't you see what you've done?" She sobbed, then took a deep breath and pulled her tears back inside. Her face looked stricken.

Stanton knelt beside Serena. "I didn't mean any harm to come to you or your friends." He rested his hand on her shoulder. More than anything he wanted to comfort her, but he could feel her muscles tense against his touch.

"Go away," Jimena whispered harshly.

"I didn't send Cassandra to get you," he offered in his defense. "I was willing to accept my fate."

Serena looked up at him, her face filled with anguish, but there was another emotion in her eyes, one she was trying unsuccessfully to hide—blame.

"I need to be alone with my friends," she explained, but she wouldn't look at him.

Her tone shocked him. His hand dropped to his side. He stood abruptly, then took a step away as a heavy ache spread through him. "I didn't want you to rescue me," he said. "That was never my plan."

None of them looked at him. Vanessa stared at the flickering flames on the ground, her eyes full of suffering.

"Come on." Jimena stood as the sirens grew louder and a fire truck turned the corner. Lights flashed across the yard. "We got to get out of here before the police show up. There's no way we can explain what just happened."

"I don't care." Vanessa voice was filled with bitter resentment. "Maybe it's time the world knows the truth. Why do we have to carry the whole burden?"

Jimena ignored her question. She and Serena helped Vanessa stand.

"We'll go back to Planet Bang," Jimena said, "and blend in. We can't waste time talking to cops. We have to figure out a way to get Catty back."

"From where?" Serena asked and wiped at her cheeks. "Where is she?"

Vanessa put her hands over her eyes as her shoulders convulsed with grief.

Stanton could see from the sorrow in her eyes that Serena didn't think it would be possible to bring Catty back. He felt burdened with guilt. The ring might protect Serena from Followers but it couldn't protect her from the horrible pain he saw on her face now.

"We'll go to Maggie's after things have settled," Jimena said. "This must have happened before."

"But . . ." Serena looked lost. "How can you be so sure?"

"There's no body," Jimena stated firmly as if she were trying to convince herself that Catty wasn't gone. "She must be someplace and there has to be a way to find her."

Cassandra came up behind Stanton and took his hand. Her sudden touch startled him.

"I'm sorry." Her voice seemed sincere. "We'd better get away, too."

He shook her off, annoyed by her presence. He didn't want her comfort or her help. If it weren't for her, none of this would have happened. "You shouldn't have gone to them for help," he snapped.

"I couldn't let Lambert destroy you," she defended herself.

"He wouldn't," Stanton argued. "He needs me. He was just going to turn me back."

Cassandra shook her head. "No, he was going to destroy you. I knew he was." She tried to draw him away as a fire truck pulled against the curb with a rumble of engines.

Stanton jerked his hand from Cassandra and looked for Serena. She was hurrying away with Jimena and Vanessa. He watched them disappear into the fog, the ache inside him growing.

He couldn't let her leave like this. He ran after her.

"Serena," he said softly, catching up to her. "Can I come see you tonight?"

She turned sharply and flung her words across his mind, *I said I needed to be alone with my friends.*

Jimena turned and glared at him, eyes narrowed.

He stared at the goddesses. He didn't need to read their minds to know that they were blaming him for the loss of Catty. He could see it in their eyes.

CHAPTER TWENTY-FOUR

STANTON WAS THE only person sitting at the counter inside Jan's restaurant. He leaned over his second cup of coffee, trying to forget what had happened, but there was no way to ease his mind. He sat near the pay phone so he could look out the front window. The traffic on Beverly Boulevard was thin. A homeless man pushed a shopping cart down the sidewalk.

It was somewhere past midnight. He knew

he needed to get out of Los Angeles and fast, but he couldn't leave Serena. He had waited for Serena, Jimena, and Vanessa outside Maggie's apartment. They hadn't spoken to him when they left her building, but he knew from the shattered looks on their faces that Maggie had offered them no hope of finding Catty.

He had wanted to comfort Serena. His feelings for her were deeper and stronger than they had ever been, but she had pushed him away. He had sensed the anger seething inside her, and even though he was no longer a Follower he knew the shame she felt for having cared about him. He wanted to go inside her mind and tell her that what happened to Catty wasn't her fault, but he didn't have that power now. Finally, he had watched them leave in Jimena's car before he had driven here.

He glanced at the night pressing against the window. No unnatural shadows hung in the darkness outside, but he had no doubt Lambert or other Followers would find him soon. It was only a matter of time.

"Are you all right?" the waitress asked as she

refilled his cup. Steam curled from the coffee. "You seem . . . I don't know . . . maybe you need to talk to someone."

Stanton shook his head. "No. I'm fine."

She rested her left hand on the counter anyway, the coffeepot poised in her right. "You sure?"

He wondered what she would do if he did tell her what was bothering him. To save Serena and her friends, he would have to battle Lambert even though there was no way he could win. Only as a Follower did he have the power he needed to protect Serena—but if he became a Follower again, then their love would be forbidden and he knew she wouldn't risk it this time, not after what had happened to Catty.

The waitress took his hesitation for a yes. "Girl trouble, betcha," she encouraged. "I'm an expert on that."

He nodded ruefully. "She doesn't like me the way I am now and she was ashamed of who I was before."

Satisfied, she patted his hand. "Don't change yourself to please a girl. One will come along who likes you just the way you are." She smiled, job done, and walked away.

The glass door opened and Cassandra entered, pulling a rush of cool air with her. She saw Stanton and waved, then walked along the counter, her hand brushing over the backs of the empty seats.

She sat down next to him. Her cheeks were flushed and her hair smelled of the night cold.

"I'm been looking all over for you." She was shivering as if she had been out walking for a long while.

He handed her his cup of coffee. She closed her eyes and sipped. When she finished, she set the cup on the saucer, took something from her pocket and handed it to him.

He looked down and saw the ring. "What did you do to Serena?"

She seemed puzzled. "I didn't do anything to Serena. Why would you think that?"

"The ring." He held it up. "How did you get it?"

"Serena's fine." She brushed his concern away,

but there was a trace of jealousy in her voice. "I followed them back to Planet Bang. I wanted to tell them I was sorry. I knew they'd think I had set them up, but I really hadn't this time."

He was surprised by her admission. "Be careful," he said. "Or you might become a nice person again."

"Like when you first met me?" she quipped.

A pang of guilt shot through him, but he nodded. "Like when I met you." She had been a good student with two loving parents. The kind of person he liked to bend and turn to the Atrox. He cleared his throat. "I'm sorry."

She looked at him oddly and shrugged. "I liked being a Follower. Anyway," she continued, "I found Serena in the bathroom. She took off the ring to splash water on her face and I just happened to be standing nearby."

Stanton realized he hadn't looked at Serena's hand when he had met her outside Maggie's apartment. He wondered why she had been so careless with it. He didn't like the answer that came to mind.

"I knew immediately it was *the* ring," Cassandra went on.

"*The* ring?" Stanton asked. "How do you know about the ring?"

She took it from him and moved it back and forth until the stone caught the light. "Lambert had been desperate to find it. He thought you must still have it. So when I saw it, I picked it up."

"Didn't Serena notice that the ring was gone?" he asked.

"No." Cassandra cocked her head, then took another sip of his coffee before she spoke. "She was too upset over losing Catty. Or," she added slyly, "maybe the ring became a symbol of someone she would rather forget." She stopped and stared at him. "Sorry."

Stanton nodded. "I know. You didn't say anything I haven't already thought."

"She shouldn't blame you. If she understood what risks you'd been taking—" She stopped and eyed the ring. "I thought you'd be happy to have your ring back."

"It's Serena's now," he said. "I'll give it back."

Cassandra seemed surprised. "Don't you want to know what the ring can do for us? If Lambert wants it so badly it must have huge power."

Stanton shook his head. "Not the kind of power you think."

"Then what?" she asked, staring at it. "Why is it so important?"

"He must think it has powers that it doesn't have." Stanton took the ring from her.

"But he said the ring could destroy his enemies," Cassandra insisted.

"It only has power to protect against evil," Stanton explained. "It will destroy any evil person who wears it."

Cassandra tilted her head as if considering. "So you're protected from Followers as long as you wear the ring."

"Even the Atrox can't harm you," he added.

"That's why Lambert wants it then," Cassandra concluded. "To protect himself from the Atrox."

Stanton looked into her eyes. "If Lambert

puts the ring on his finger, it will consume him."

"Kill him?" Her eyes seemed too eager.

Stanton corrected her. "Destroy his body only. Remember he's a member of the Inner Circle. He wears the Phoenix crest."

She shuddered. "I can't even imagine what it would be like if he were only spirit, unhampered by a body."

"We'll never have to find out," Stanton assured her. He put two dollars on the counter and started to stand. "I'm going to take the ring to Serena."

"You think she'll wear it?"

Stanton looked down at her. "I don't know. I hope so."

"I think you should wear it." Cassandra leaned forward and touched his finger lightly. "You're in greater danger than she is." Then she stood, took his hand, opened it, and picked up the ring gingerly. "At least keep it someplace safe." She dropped it in his shirt pocket and patted his chest.

"Good luck," he whispered and started to

leave, but she grabbed his arm and made him turn to her.

"It's dangerous for you here, Stanton." She ran her hands up his chest. "But if you wanted to go away, I'd go with you."

"Cassandra, what would you want with me now?" He felt baffled by her persistence.

"I like you, Stanton," she answered. "I always have."

"But I'm no longer an Immortal." He took her hands away from his chest. "I'm not even a Follower."

"So what?" she pouted.

"What use do you have for me now?" he asked.

"We have the ring," she offered. "It could protect us and if you'd just give me a chance, I know we'd be great together."

"You and I had our chance already," he explained, trying to keep irritation from his voice.

Tears crept to the corners of her eyes anyway. She didn't try to hide how much his rejection hurt her. "I'll miss you, Stanton."

He handed her a napkin from the counter. "Don't cry."

She wiped her eyes and lifted her head hopefully as if she were expecting a kiss.

"I'm sorry, Cassandra." He hurried away from her then and left Jan's. He walked out into the cool air, climbed into his car and drove over to Serena's house. She only lived a few blocks away.

He parked his car, then patted his pocket. The ring was gone.

CHAPTER TWENTY-FIVE

STANTON THOUGHT THAT maybe he had lost the ring. Then he recalled the way Cassandra had dropped it in his pocket and patted his chest. He was sure she had it. He could go back to Jan's but Cassandra would have left the restaurant by now. Instead he walked down the alley behind Serena's house. At the edge of her yard, he scaled the trunk of a beech tree, swung onto a branch, and climbed until he could see in her bedroom window. Serena and Jimena were leaning across the bed. Vanessa was lying between them, her face in a pillow.

Then a soft hiss filled the night air. Leaves bristled, caught in a strange magnetic storm. A silver-blue vapor poured from a shadow and Lambert landed on his feet near the tree, his cape settling around him.

Even in the thick darkness Stanton could see the merciless predator in Lambert's eyes. He clung to the tree and tried to control the look of prey in his own.

Lambert stretched one arm to his side, fingers spread wide. Ribbons of power arced from the palm, creating a whirlwind of light that circled Stanton, sucking him down. The tree shook from its intensity.

His feet slipped as his hands struggled to hold onto the branch above him but the force was too great. He fell, landing hard on his back with a thud. He felt numb with defeat before the battle had even begun. Then he remembered his father. He had told Stanton that a good knight never refused a fight simply because the odds were against him. In such times he was more likely to engage in combat. As a boy he had watched his father face four armed men at the same time. Stanton wondered where his father had found the strength.

"First you, then Serena," Lambert promised and looked up at the bedroom window. "She won't expect my attack tonight."

Stanton pulled himself up with new strength. He understood now the source of his father's bravery. It had come from his need to protect Stanton, the same way Stanton now wanted to save Serena. His knees felt weak and his back throbbed but he staggered forward. "Leave Serena alone," he said.

Lambent laughed at his feeble attempt. "Do you really think you have a chance against me?"

Stanton nodded, hoping to goad Lambert into attacking him. If he could, maybe the commotion would alert Serena and she and her friends could escape.

Lambert smiled derisively, but he didn't strike. Perhaps he had sensed Stanton's plan. He pulled Stanton back behind a line of oleander bushes.

"You won't get more from me," Stanton taunted him. "I won't show you the pleasure of a chase or show you fear. I can deny you that at least."

But instead of striking, Lambert stepped away as if he were trying to contain himself.

"I went to the Atrox tonight." His hate and anger made his breath shimmer in the air with a cold white glow. "I reported that you had become a renegade. That you had been so weak, the Daughters had been able to take you back to their side. I asked for permission to destroy you and make you an example to other *inviti*. In exchange I would bring in the key."

"Just destroy me," Stanton taunted him again. "I don't need to hear about your great triumph."

Lambert turned on him. "You should have been my reward for destroying the goddess Catty." His voice was low and filled with resentment. "That was all I wanted. Permission to do whatever I pleased with you."

Stanton wondered why Lambert hadn't been given permission, but before he could consider it, Lambert answered his thoughts.

"You wonder?" He smirked. "I've wondered all these centuries. I offered to deliver the key this very night but the Atrox wanted you! Is it any wonder I've had to make plans for my own fate?" He seemed suddenly aware of his treasonous words. His eyes darted around, searching the shadows.

Stanton looked, too, but the dark seemed natural. "Why would it want me back?" Stanton asked. This had to be more trickery. Some part of Lambert's plan to overthrow the Atrox.

"Why?" Lambert stared at him. "I ask myself the same. Why are you the protected son? Are you so critical to the cause? I'm the one who let the Atrox take you but it never rewarded me. It saved the position I wanted for you. Even now it's so eager to have you back. What secret do you hold?"

He clutched Stanton's neck, his fingers bitter cold. The nails dug into his skin, squeezing tighter as he told Stanton his plan. "I'll bring you back so the Atrox won't doubt my intent, but I'll leave you trapped in my memories until I've taken Serena over. Her allegiance will be to me, of course. Will that be enough to make you join me against the Atrox?"

Stanton struggled against his hold. "Serena will never be loyal to you," he choked out.

"I have my ways," Lambert countered confidently. "She will. I promise." His fingers pinched tighter and he drew Stanton closer, forcing Stanton to look into his eyes.

The dark pupils were compelling. Stanton was drawn in. He wanted nothing but the peace promised there. Without warning, he felt himself spinning through a black void. His hands tried desperately to grab onto something, but there was nothing to hold.

He fell and landed on hard stone. He shook his head and realized he was back in his father's castle. Lambert had trapped him in a memory. He wondered how long he would be held captive there and then another thought came bursting forward, one that made his heart swell. He could see his father again and his mother as well. He started running, when a voice spoke.

"You would like this memory, wouldn't you?" Lambert mocked him. "Let's find a more important one. Perhaps my memory of the night the Atrox stole you from your home."

The castle vanished and Stanton was drifting in the void again.

The sound of running footsteps filled the black space around him. He wondered where he was going next, but then Lambert released his hold. Stanton fell to the ground. He blinked and looked up. He was back outside Serena's house.

Footsteps crunched over the gravel in the alley. Leaves rustled and Cassandra stepped from the darkness.

"Stanton won't tell you his secret," Cassandra said rapidly. "But I will." She sounded as if she had been running. Had she followed him from Jan's?

Lambert turned and looked at her.

She held up the ring.

Light from his eyes shot through the stone and illuminated Cassandra's face with a pink glow.

"The ring," Lambert said with awe.

"The power of the ring is what made Stanton favored by the Atrox," Cassandra said boldly.

"That's not true," Stanton said, pushing himself off the ground.

Cassandra continued quickly, "He wouldn't have told you. He would have gone to his death first because he doesn't want you to have the power that the ring holds."

"Of course, the ring." Lambert lifted it. "How did you find it?"

"I stole it from Serena," Cassandra announced proudly. "Stanton had given it to her tonight."

Lambert considered this. "That's why my assault didn't harm her. The ring protected her."

Stanton suddenly understood what Cassandra was trying to do. He had to stop her. "Don't put it on," Stanton warned Lambert.

"You don't want me to wear it, Stanton?"

Lambert lifted his finger to slip on the ring.

"Don't," Stanton yelled. "The ring will destroy you."

"He doesn't want you protected the way Serena was," Cassandra coaxed. "With the ring you'll have more than enough power to overthrow the Atrox. Stanton knows that. He doesn't want you to succeed. He's jealous."

"She's lying!" Stanton tried to grab the ring away.

Lambert slipped the ring on his finger. Instantaneously, his mouth curled in pain. He tried to remove the ring but already his skin was melting around the band, gluing it to his flesh. His body began to wither.

"We won! We did it!" Cassandra laughed victoriously.

Stanton shook his head. "You don't understand what you've done, Cassandra."

"Won?" Lambert asked, his voice gritty now, as if it were difficult for him to speak.

"The ring can't give a Follower power, Lambert," Cassandra said gleefully.

Frightened eyes stared back at them from behind sagging lids that seemed to be fusing into his cheekbones.

"It can only destroy evil."

Lambert glanced up at Stanton with understanding. *"Protegas Innocentes et Deleas Malum,"* Lambert's voice rasped as his lips dissolved, exposing teeth and jawbone. "Your father's coat of arms. Protect the innocent and destroy the evil. The inscription in the ring only reads *Protegas et Deleas.* Protect and destroy."

Stanton nodded.

Skin and flesh shrank from Lambert's bones and his skeleton turned to dust. The evil that had been in human form spiraled into the night air with a horrible screech.

Cassandra and Stanton covered their faces against the sudden storm. Leaves, dust, and gravel swirled around them.

Lambert's spirit ripped into Stanton's mind. *I'll see Serena dead and use her body since you've taken mine. Then I'll also have the powers of the key. You should have joined me. Now it's too late.*

Then the night was still. Dust and leaves settled around them. Stanton grabbed Cassandra. "Do you see what you've done? You didn't destroy him." Stanton felt defeated.

Fear crept into her eyes. "What do you mean?"

"Lambert is part of the Inner Circle!" Stanton said. "He wore the crest of the Phoenix."

"So?" Cassandra looked confused.

"They are more enduring than Immortals or other members of the Inner Circle. Even if something happens to their bodies, their spirits live on." Then a sudden thought came to him. He stared at Cassandra in disbelief. "But you knew. You knew he wouldn't be destroyed and yet you urged him to put on the ring anyway. Why did you give him the ring? He's too powerful for us to fight now."

She hesitated.

"Tell me," he urged.

"I knew," she confessed finally. "But there was no other way I could get you back."

Stanton shook his head and waited for her explanation.

"With his body gone, he'd have to find a new one, and I knew his hate for you would drive him to take Serena's." Her eyes glistened with tears. "I want Serena out of the way because I need you, Stanton."

"You'll never have me!" Stanton snapped.

A startled cry made him turn. He ran around the oleander bushes and looked up at Serena's room. The French doors on the balcony blew open. He started running toward the house.

"Come back and find the ring," Cassandra yelled, as if she understood what he was going to do.

He ignored her and kept going.

"You can't fight Lambert's spirit as a mortal!" Cassandra screamed. "Not without the ring!"

"Watch me," Stanton yelled back.

CHAPTER TWENTY-SIX

ROSE THORNS STUCK in Stanton's palms as he climbed up the trellis next to Serena's balcony. Light from her bedroom cast a thin orange glow over the glossy leaves. He reached the railing and clasped it, but as he lifted his leg over, an explosive force stunned him. A bolt of air snapped his head back. He cried out and fell over the rail. As he tumbled backward, he grabbed onto a bar with one hand and dangled, his fingers slipping on the slick iron. He swung his body and his free hand found another bar and held on.

You're not a great knight like your father. Lambert's contemptuous voice filled his mind. *You should have been prepared for my attack.*

Stanton worked his feet back to the trellis, then his hands. The strike from Lambert left a fiery pain inside his head. He clung to the latticework and rested against the prickly vine until the dizziness passed, then he started up again. White rose petals fell over him.

The bedroom window above him shattered.

"Serena!" he yelled before he bent his face away from the shards of glass raining down.

No one answered his call. Quickly, he clambered up the trellis and over the railing. He peeked inside, searching for evidence of Lambert's presence. When he saw nothing, he eased into Serena's room. Her pet raccoon, Wally, brushed against his leg as if it needed comfort and reassurance.

He picked up Wally and petted him as he surveyed the bedroom. The Lava lamp lay on its side. Tarot cards were flung about the room and the leopard-print sheets twisted in a trail to the door. He heard another crash from downstairs. He set Wally on the bed and ran cautiously into the dark hallway. He paused, then headed for the staircase.

He started down, one step at a time, his breathing shallow and loud, his back pressed against the wall, not daring to rest his hand on the railing in case Lambert's specter were waiting at the foot of the stairs.

At the bottom he stopped and studied the shadows. The soft whimper of someone crying came from the back of the house. He turned and crept toward the kitchen. At the door, he pressed his ear against the wood and listened.

Fear made his hearing too sensitive. It was like a roar in his head. A car passed down the street and the noise of its rolling tires hid the simple sounds he needed to hear, ones that could betray Lambert.

His fingers found the doorknob and silently he turned it. Tumblers clicked. There was no way to muffle the sound. If Lambert's spirit was still in the house, the noise would tell him where

Stanton was now. He froze, waiting, and leaned his forehead against the door. The stillness that followed seemed complete. Maybe Lambert wasn't inside now, but waiting in the shadows by Stanton's car.

Finally, Stanton pushed open the door and crept inside. He had expected to be greeted by Lambert's energy but instead cool air hit him with the good smells of apples and bread. He let out a huge sigh of relief.

The moon had risen and its milky light filtered through the kitchen windows, making shadows around the counter and stove, pots and pans more vivid. Stanton breathed in, trying to sense Lambert. Now the silence felt too deep, the air too heavy, as if Lambert's spirit had somehow hushed the city sounds of ticking clocks, sirens, and traffic.

"Serena," Stanton whispered and waited.

When no one called back, he stepped through the kitchen to the dinning room and glanced in. A steady light from the moon cast a silver glow over the table and chairs, but he didn't see anyone or any signs of struggle. He turned and hurried back the way he had come toward the service porch, his feet padding stealthily.

As he passed back through the kitchen, a faint hissing made him turn. He took two steps toward the sound and smelled gas. Quickly he turned the knobs and shut off the gas. Lambert had somehow turned on the burners without letting the pilot light ignite. Stanton glanced around the room. He didn't think that Lambert had wanted to cause an explosion. More likely he wanted Stanton to know that his spirit had been in the kitchen with him all along. Then with a shudder Stanton realized that Lambert was probably watching him even now.

Another soft cry filled the house.

"Serena," he called again.

He left the kitchen, slipped through the dining area, and faced another door that led into the living room. He pushed through and stopped. His breath caught in his lungs.

Jimena stood in the corner between the couch and a large chair, her eyes wide with energy. A soft blue glow danced over her head. She tried to focus her power on the ghostly light, but when she sent out her force, the buoyant glare only bobbed away and sparks showered in the air.

She prayed to the moon goddess Selene. *"O Mater Luna, Regina nocis, adiuvo me nunc."* The prayer seemed to weaken the sapphire light.

Still, Stanton could tell its attacks were hurting Jimena. She whimpered with each bolt of light that struck her face. She sent another burst of energy at the phantom as Stanton crept across the room, the fall of his footsteps absorbed in the thick carpeting. He didn't know what he could do. His arms and legs were shaking violently, but he wasn't going to let Jimena fight Lambert's spirit alone.

He grabbed a crystal vase from a coffee table and continued forward, hoping that if he were lucky, he might be able to contain Lambert's apparition.

He charged and swept the vase into the air and caught the blue-gray glow inside.

"You caught it," Jimena yelled and rushed to

his side. "Do you know how to get rid of it?"

He held his hand over the top of the vase. The light inside turned a deep cobalt and flickered like fire, then the crystal exploded, sending glass splinters showering through the air.

Stanton shielded his face with his hands.

When he looked out again, the light stretched and vanished toward the front door.

"What was it?" Jimena asked as she picked a piece of glass from her arm.

"Lambert," Stanton answered. "He's a spirit now. Where's Serena?"

Jimena shook her head. "I don't know. Somehow in the confusion the three of us got split up. I locked Vanessa in the bathroom upstairs."

"And don't ever do it again," Vanessa ran into the living room, trying to catch her breath. She hugged Jimena tightly. "We have to stay together if we're going to win. It took me forever to turn invisible and escape."

Jimena nodded. "I was only trying to protect you."

"I know. You thought I was too upset to fight." Vanessa wiped away tears. "I think Serena's outside." Then she looked at Stanton. "Do you know any way to get Catty back?"

He shook his head. "I'm sorry. We have to think about saving Serena now. Lambert wants to settle his spirit in her body."

Jimena let out a sigh. "I hope she's running then because I'm sure Lambert went that way. The blue light did anyway."

Stanton's heart sank. "He'll find her."

Without hesitation, Jimena started toward the door.

Vanessa joined her. Stanton opened the door and they ran outside.

"There," Jimena pointed. Serena was sprinting down the sidewalk away from a strange coil of light that was gaining on her.

Vanessa went invisible, her dusty molecules swirled, then she sped after the light.

"Serena!" Stanton shouted and raced toward her. Jimena's footsteps pounded the sidewalk behind him.

Suddenly, the light chasing Serena changed into a streak of lightning. Thunder crackled through the night. The bolt shot through the dark with savage power and caught Serena. She stopped, stunned.

"No!" Jimena screamed.

A pale blue aura formed around Serena. Then the light stole her away.

CHAPTER TWENTY-SEVEN

"WHAT NOW?" JIMENA asked, blinking back tears.

Vanessa became visible again. "I couldn't get to her in time," she said to herself, wracked with guilt. "I wanted to make her invisible and take her away." She looked at Stanton tearfully. "Is she gone like Catty now?"

He shook his head. "I'll stop him," Stanton started to walk away, determined.

"We'll help," Jimena followed him, Vanessa close behind her.

"No!" Stanton yelled abruptly. "You can't help." Then in a quiet voice he added, "Just tell Serena that what I did, I did for her."

Jimena knew immediately what he planned. "Don't do it!"

Vanessa tried to grab his arm, but he darted away.

When he was hidden in shadows, he looked up at the night sky. He had no choice. He pressed his hands against his forehead, trying to think of another possibility. There was none.

He wiped at the hot tears stinging his eyes, then slowly he lifted his arms to the fathomless black sky. He could endure anything if he knew Serena was safe. Anything.

"Father of night and evil, I call you." A primitive vibration trembled in the air. He knew the Atrox was near.

"Allow me to cross over and become your servant again."

A deadly cold throbbed through him with the ancient rhythm of evil.

"I come freely," Stanton added and felt something collapse inside him. "Take me back to the night."

Spears of lightning crackled across the sky and a concussion boomed through the earth, releasing the sulfurous smells of hell. Then a raven-black cloud seeped up from the ground and hovered around him.

Stanton held an image of Serena's face deep inside him as he breathed the icy spirit of the Atrox back into his body. The chill seeped deep inside him, wintry tentacles reaching down to his bones. The Atrox embraced him and welcomed him back to its congregation. Its raw power surged through him and when Stanton opened his eyes, he again ruled the night.

The world around him seemed sharper now, as if he could see in the dark. His pain was gone and in its place he felt a dark joy. He grinned as the wild rapture seized him. This time he was no longer *invitus.* Evil pulsed through him without guilt or worry, consequence or remorse. He breathed in the feel of it, then leaned back and became a black mist, hissing into the air.

He didn't see with his eyes now but with a far more powerful vision inside his mind. He suddenly became aware, not of Lambert, but Serena. He rocketed through the shadows. Trees, houses, fence posts, and guard dogs blurred into blackness behind him. He slammed to a stop and became whole again. Anyone seeing him would have thought he had walked from a shadow.

"Serena," he whispered.

She was bent over, near a tree, gripping her stomach. Her breathing came in shallow gasps and her lips pressed tight together against the pain.

"What did Lambert do to you?" he asked but he didn't need an answer. Lambert had tried to enter Serena and take over her body.

Stanton soothed back her hair.

"It hurts," Serena moaned.

Stanton clasped her hand, trying to ease her pain. She dug her fingernails into his palm.

"Where is Lambert?"

Serena didn't answer at first. Her lips quivered. "You mean, the light? Is that Lambert?"

Stanton nodded.

"I'm not sure. It dropped me because it couldn't control me. That's what I think happened, anyway."

"You were too strong for Lambert. He didn't expect your resistance to be so great." Or, Stanton wondered, maybe Lambert had sensed that Stanton had returned to the Atrox. He put his arm around Serena. "You need to go to the hospital."

"No," she whispered. "Take care of Lambert first." Her eyes opened and there was a horrible sadness in them.

Stanton understood at once that she knew he was a Follower again. He glanced down and saw her moon amulet glowing. "I'm sorry," he whispered. "It was the only way."

"I'm sorry, too," she answered and now tears rolled from her eyes. "We could have done it without your going back."

He wasn't going to argue with her. "Hospital first," he answered and wrapped his arm around her waist.

She tried to walk but stopped. "I can't make it."

He swung her into his arms and she leaned her head against his chest. He started to carry her to his car when a piercing cry made him turn. Bluish lightning screamed after them. Stanton ducked, and held Serena cradled tight against him.

The bolt of light spun into a tree. Wood splintered and cracked. The light circled a street lamp. The globe popped and glass shattered onto the street. Then the light came back for another attack and disappeared abruptly.

Silence followed. Stanton knew Lambert's spirit was nearby, gathering power for another attack.

He hurried across a lawn, still carrying Serena. His car was parked on the street in front of him in full moonlight. The lunar glow made his eyes burn. They had almost reached the car when Serena dug her fingers into his shoulder.

"No!" her dry voice pushed into hysteria. "Please, no!"

He turned and saw the blue glimmer growing larger and coming at them. He opened the passenger-side door and eased Serena inside. Her head lolled against the back of the seat.

Stanton turned to face Lambert's spirit, but the blue light was gone. The moon's steady glow cast a thousand shadows under the trees, each one a potential hiding place for something that was only spirit.

Suddenly, electrical veins shot toward him. Instead of ducking the charge, Stanton turned to shadow and let Lambert's spirit flow through him. He surrounded the light and immediately struck with his mind control, taking Lambert's spirit deep inside him, imprisoning him in a memory of the Atrox.

Lambert's screams still vibrated through Stanton, as he became whole again and yanked open the car door. He fell behind the steering wheel. His hand searched under the floor mat for the key, found it, and started the engine.

He touched Serena. Her skin was cool and clammy.

"I love you, Serena." He turned onto Beverly Boulevard and sped toward Cedars-Sinai Hospital.

CHAPTER TWENTY-EIGHT

A WEEK LATER, STANTON walked into the fire. Sparks cascaded around him and formed a crown in his hair without burning. The cold blaze lashed around him, etching a frosty crystalline pattern of his arms and face.

He stared at the other members of the Inner Circle through the veil of flames as the fire burned his mortality away and he became an Immortal again. Their eyes looked more pleased than angry, more content than covetous. Stanton had destroyed the traitor Lambert, and the Atrox was pleased.

The fire became a maelstrom, shrieking up to the heavens in triumph. The crown of burning embers stayed on his head. Bits of fire showered the night and formed a pathway toward the blaze.

Three of the highest-ranking members stepped slowly forward along the fiery path, carrying a cloak spun of black, silky threads. Together they spread the fabric and set the cloak over Stanton's shoulders.

He stared at the emblem, surprised by what he had been given. He smiled, satisfied, and knew that Jimena's final premonition had come true. Only one was allowed to wear this crest. It was the highest honor given by the Atrox; two hands holding the eternal flame of evil. Stanton understood its significance. He had once been destined to be a prince. Now he was Prince of the Night.

Hours later, Stanton's car sped through the dark streets, its mufflers roaring against the pavement.

Winds had cleared the smog and the open, star-filled sky seemed an omen of good fortune.

He parked a block from Serena's house and slipped from his car, then walked into the alley until the shadows swallowed him. He blended into darkness and soared to her balcony. Nothing was forbidden to him now.

He became whole again inside her room and smirked at the line of alarm clocks on her dresser. Was she worried that he would return to claim her, or did she only want to know if he had visited her?

Her moon amulet cast a ghostly light around the room as he knelt beside her. He listened to her soft, rhythmic breathing and sniffed the sweet perfume that lingered in the air around her. Her wrist was still in a cast, her cracked ribs healing, the bruises fading. Doctors who treated her thought she had taken a fall after being slipped some new designer drug at a party. She was recovering well.

Stanton touched her lightly. He was no longer an *invitus*. He had gone freely to the Atrox, but he had never lost his love for Serena. He had kept that feeling safe inside him.

He spoke into her dreams. *I will have you.*

She murmured against her pillow and her amulet shot a barrage of rainbows across the room.

"So you sense that I am a threat now." He smiled wickedly. "I'm not, sweet one." She would be so easy to take. The real danger had always been from him. And now he had marked her. No one else could harm her.

"Tu es dea, filia lunae," he whispered.

He could wait. Her gift only lasted until she was seventeen. Then she would be his.

BOOK SIX

the lost one

PROLOGUE

A scraping sound came from the kitchen below the little girl's bedroom. She wondered if her parents were still cleaning up from dinner. She glanced at the clock on her nightstand. It was four in the morning. At this hour they should be in bed, deep in slumber.

Another, softer noise made her tense. It wasn't the natural creak and pop she sometimes heard at night. Thump. The noise repeated. She sat up with a start. Someone was walking up the stairs. She threw back her covers, crept to her door, and peered into the hallway.

Her heart lurched. Two shadowy figures pressed against the wall. She could scream for her parents, but caution told her to be still. Instead she slipped back across her bedroom to her open window, pushed out the screen, and crawled onto the thick branch of an elm tree. She had done this many times. She liked to sit there to think and write in her journal.

She had never clambered the length of the branch to her parents' bedroom before, but it looked possible. She tugged at her nightgown and struggled to their window, then stretched her arms out to pull off their screen, but suddenly stopped.

The streetlamp cast a beam of light across their carpet. Why were they sleeping, sprawled together across the floor? She bit her tongue hard to keep the scream in her throat from coming out, then she blinked rapidly, not allowing herself tears. She needed her strength to find her sister, Jamie.

With new resolve she reached forward and tore off the screen. It fell to the ground below, landing silently in a bed of pink and red carnations.

She mounted the windowsill and pulled herself inside. She didn't let her mind consider what made the carpets warm and wet beneath her bare feet as she crept forward. She crouched behind their door and looked out.

The two men were entering her room now. As soon as they did, she dashed on tiptoe across the hallway to where her sister slept. She rushed in and almost tripped over Jamie, lifeless and curled in a ball near the canopied bed.

Her knees were suddenly too weak to hold her, and she sank to the floor, realizing everyone in her family was dead. She knew that soon the men would be looking for her. She rose and started to hide in the closet, but something stopped her. Instinct told her the two men would find her there.

Quietly she raced across the hallway and down the stairs, stooping low against the banister. When she reached the landing, she heard the men behind her. She swung open the door as their footfalls pounded down the steps.

At last she ran out into the night, guided by the full moon.

CHAPTER ONE

SUNLIGHT CREPT OVER her face and she jerked awake, thinking the enemy had been shining the beam of a flashlight over her. She sat up, body tense, and searched for the danger. At first she thought it had only been a nightmare that had frightened her, but then she knew something was desperately wrong. She didn't know where she was.

She glanced frantically around the small, one-room apartment. A refrigerator hummed in the corner, but she was confident she had never seen it before. Water dripped into a sink near the only window. Not one dirty cup, spoon, or plate sat on the spare counter, and no plants gathered the sun's rays on the windowsill. There was nothing she could recognize as belonging to her.

A lone dresser leaned against the wall near the door. The top was bare, polished and reflecting sunshine. An oak table with two chairs sat in the middle of the floor, but there were no pictures or personal items anywhere. Everything looked stark and freshly cleaned, as if someone had tried hard to erase all traces of the people who had lived here before. Then she spied a blue backpack leaning against the door. It had to belong to her, but it didn't look familiar. Nothing sparked any feeling of recognition.

She pressed her fingers against her temples, trying to recall what had happened the night before, but her mind was like a huge void. She couldn't remember how she had gotten into the apartment or when she had arrived. The bed had not been turned down. She had slept on top of the thin bedspread and was still dressed in jeans and a leather jacket. The hems of her pantlegs were frayed and black with dirt, her socks worn. She glanced at her rhinestone-studded tee. It seemed like something she'd wear to a party.

A pair of knee-high slick black boots lay scattered on the floor. She swung her legs over the side of the bed to put them on, and when she did, a large rusted pipe slipped from her lap and hit the yellow linoleum floor with a loud clank. She gasped as if it had been a snake, then slowly bent over and picked it up. Her hands began to tremble. Why had she slept with a pipe? Perhaps she had felt in need of protection. The cold metal felt lethal enough to crush a skull. Her chest tightened, and she wondered how such a brutal thought could come to her.

She tried to calm herself, taking long, slow breaths, but the air in the closed room was stale and antiseptic, making her feel even more claustrophobic. She needed to leave before it was too late. She had no idea where this strange impulse came from, but the urgency she felt was strong and growing. She glanced at her wrist. She had no watch and saw no clock in the room. From the bars of sunlight slanting through the window, she was sure it was morning.

Somewhere in the building a door slammed and she jumped. Only then did she realize how terrified she felt. Yet she couldn't understand why. She was alone. The room looked safe. But a bizarre tension shimmered around her as if some-one or something threatening were present but not yet seen.

She closed her eyes, trying to bring back a memory from her past, and opened them again with a jolt of pure panic as realization struck. She didn't know who she was. She couldn't remember her name, her date of birth, where she lived, or who her parents were. As hard as she tried, noth-ing about her life before this moment came back to her. She glanced at the calendar hanging on the gray-green wall. It said November, but she didn't know the date.

Now instinct took over. The need to run was overwhelming. She glanced at the window as if she expected to see a threatening face staring back at her.

"Always trust your instinct," she mumbled, and stopped. The sound of her own voice startled her. It could have been that of a stranger talking to her.

She grabbed the boots, fell back on the edge of the bed and tugged them on, then stood. She had started walking toward the door when she felt something like a pebble under her right toe. She slumped onto one of the small wooden chairs, yanked off the boot, and shook out a soiled and crumpled note.

She unfolded it and read:

Dear LAPD,

It wasn't my imagination. Two guys were trying to kill me. If you're reading this, then they did. Now will you stop them?

Tianna Moore

A chill rushed through her and her body began to shake violently. Was she Tianna Moore? How could she be? It was like reading a name in the newspaper. It didn't feel like it belonged to her. She unzipped the backpack propped against the door, pulled out a notepad and pen, sat back at the table, and wrote *Tianna Moore.*

Her handwriting matched the writing on the note. Why would anyone want her dead? She couldn't have placed it in the toe of her boot recently. The paper looked old and stained. How long had it been there? A week? Two? Who was she running from? And if someone was trying to kill her, then why weren't the police willing to help? She should be able to remember something as important as that. She read the note again, then pulled on the boot, stood, stuffed the note in her pocket, grabbed the backpack, and rushed out the door.

In the hallway the smells of morning coffee, bacon, and burning toast made her stomach pinch with hunger. She wondered how long it had been since she had eaten. She felt starved. She rumbled down the stairs.

Her hand was on the front doorknob when someone called after her. Tianna let out a small cry and spun around.

CHAPTER TWO

"GOOD MORNING," THE voice called again. "I didn't mean to startle you."

Tianna turned cautiously. An old woman stood in the sunlight at the top of the stairs. She started down the steps, clutching the handles of two shopping bags. The bristles from a toilet bowl brush peeked over the top of one.

"I'm Hanna," the woman said, as if that should mean something to Tianna. She looked safe enough.

"Hi, I'm . . ." Tianna paused and cleared her throat. "Tianna." The name felt alien on her tongue. She pressed her back against the metal mailboxes and stifled the need to bolt and run. Maybe she could gain some useful information from Hanna. Anything would help. She didn't even know what city she was in.

"I haven't seen you here before." Hanna came sideways down the stairs as if she had pain in her hips and knees. Her movements were heavy and slow. "Did you just move in?"

Tianna didn't know what to reply. "Yeah," she muttered, and played with the strap on her backpack.

"Usually I meet the new tenants right away." Hanna had a big smile. Her teeth looked plastic, and when she stopped smiling, her lips worked as if forcing her false teeth back into place. "I try to make this a happy place to live. Knowing your neighbors is one way to prevent crime."

Tianna looked at the front door nervously. The urge to run was consuming her, and she wished now she hadn't stopped to talk to Hanna.

"There." Hanna grinned when she reached the landing, as if getting down the stairs were a major feat. She set down one bag and extended her hand.

After a second's hesitation Tianna took it. The knuckles felt like cold marbles, the skin slick and thin.

"Are you all right?" Hanna asked with concern. Her breath still smelled of morning coffee, and it made Tianna's stomach growl.

"Why?" Tianna's voice sounded on edge.

"Your hands are wet and you look pale." Hanna picked up her bags. "I bet it's because you didn't eat breakfast. You always should, you know."

"Yeah, but we can't always." Tianna brushed a hand through her hair. "I didn't sleep well last night."

"Who does anymore? Police sirens all night long." Hanna started toward the door. "I'm just on my way to work. Need a ride?"

"Why would I need a ride?" Tianna asked.

"You missed your bus." Hanna stepped outside.

"I did?" Tianna followed her onto the stoop,

eager to know more. The morning sun was hot already and felt good on her face.

Hanna nodded. "I heard the bus go by a few minutes ago. I'll drop you at La Brea High."

"How do you know I go there?"

Hanna turned and smiled with half her face. "You don't look like you go to one of those private schools over on the west side." She stared pointedly at the frayed jeans and soiled backpack. "All the other kids in the neighborhood take the city bus to La Brea High, so it stands to reason that you would, too."

Tianna considered this with rising hope. "Thanks, I could use the ride." She readjusted her backpack, feeling suddenly reassured. She'd go to school, find her friends, and get some answers. Maybe she had been slipped some designer drug at a party the night before. She didn't know how she would know anything about designer drugs, when she couldn't even remember the last time she had eaten, but the information was there, easy to pluck from her brain. She wished other things would come back as readily.

Hanna headed toward an old gold Cadillac with huge fins and tons of dented chrome. The windows were rolled down and the cracked leather seats inside had gathered the morning dew.

"The windows haven't worked in ages," Hanna explained. "And it costs too much to repair them, but the old Caddy gets the job done; she'll get us where we want to go."

Tianna glanced at the California license plates. "You buy the car here?" she asked.

"Sure did," Hanna answered. "Right here in L.A. in 1966."

That answered one question at least.

While Hanna took a rag from her shopping bag and wiped down the car seats, Tianna surveyed the neighborhood. Old stucco apartment buildings and massive trees stood on either side of the road. Cars lined the curbs, and bicycles were chained to porch railings. Nothing looked dangerous, but she couldn't cast off the ominous feeling that something was lurking in the bright sunlight, unseen.

"What does your mother do?" Hanna asked as she folded the rag.

The question caught Tianna by surprise, and she turned back. "She's a dental hygienist," she answered with the first thing that came to mind, then paused, wondering if she was.

"That sounds like something that will come in handy in our apartment building." Hanna opened the car door.

Tianna looked at her sharply to see if she was teasing. She didn't seem to be. "Why?"

"Not many people where we live can afford to go to a dentist." Hanna nodded. "Get in."

Tianna swung her backpack onto the floor under the glove compartment. It landed with a thunk, and the dashboard rattled. "Sorry," she offered, then slid in and slammed the door.

"What do you have in that backpack, anyway?" Hanna asked.

"I don't know—" she began, and caught herself. "Books, things." She'd have to be more careful with the answers she gave or people were going to think there was something seriously wrong with her.

Hanna only laughed. "I know what you mean—when I clean out my purse, there's no telling what I'll find inside."

Tianna lifted the backpack onto her lap and unzipped it. Maybe she would find something inside that would help her remember.

The Cadillac pulled away from the curb with a belch of black exhaust, and a faint odor of gasoline filled the interior.

First Tianna found a tube of toothpaste and gratefully squeezed a long line into her mouth, then used her finger to brush her teeth.

Hanna glanced at her, then away. "A dental hygienist, huh?" she muttered, then laughed. "Did your mother teach you that?"

Tianna shook her head. Her mouth filled with toothpaste foam.

"Funny, I haven't seen your mother around," Hanna continued. "I know everyone. How long have you lived in the apartment?"

Tianna was stunned. How long? She didn't

know. She wasn't even sure that was where she lived. She leaned out the window and spit.

"Stop," Hanna said. "It'll come back in the car."

Tianna jerked around. A glob of toothpaste foam landed on the backseat.

"Sorry." Tianna leaned over and wiped at the white mess with papers she found in her backpack.

"Put your seat belt on!" Hanna bellowed. "You want me to get a ticket? It's against the law not to have your seat belt on."

Tianna hunkered down, making a mental note not to accept morning rides from strangers anymore.

Hanna glanced over her shoulder. "It'll come out. Sorry I yelled." But her voice still sounded perturbed. She concentrated on the road ahead.

That was fine with Tianna. She dug through her backpack and pulled out three pairs of panties. She looked at them strangely.

So did Hanna. "Do you normally take your underwear to school?"

Tianna felt baffled, and then her hand reached in and took out a bra, socks, T-shirt, and pj's.

Hanna laughed. "Are you sure you didn't grab a bag of laundry? What else do you have in there? It's like you're packed for a trip."

Tianna took out three textbooks, a stack of papers, and a wallet. Her heart pounded as she opened the wallet and looked inside. She didn't know what she had hoped to find, but it only contained three twenty-dollar bills. The significance of what was happening finally came over her. How was she going to survive? Perhaps she should go to the police again. Surely a detective could help her this time since she couldn't even remember who she was. But another worry flooded through her. Maybe whoever wanted to kill her would be waiting for her to show up there. Somehow it didn't feel safe.

Tianna turned over the paper she had used to clean up the toothpaste foam. It was her class schedule. "What day is it?" she asked.

Hanna glanced at her. "Wednesday. You

sound as old as me. Don't you even know the day?"

"No, the date," Tianna asked impatiently. "What's the date?"

"The seventh." Hanna looked at her curiously. "Did you mess up on your homework?"

Tianna shrugged and stared at the class schedule. She had enrolled on Monday the fifth. She had only been going to the school for two days. This would be her third. Where had she lived before the fifth of November? Now her plan to find friends and have them explain what was going on wasn't going to work. She probably had only met a few people, anyway. Tears pressed into her eyes, and she quickly brushed them away. She didn't have time for an indulgence like crying.

"What?" Hanna asked. "Is something wrong?"

"Why should it be?" Tianna snapped, and sniffed.

"No, it's just, you looked . . ." She shrugged. "Scared."

"Scared?" That wasn't what Tianna had expected her to say.

"Here we are." Hanna pulled to the side of the road.

The school was huge and crowded. Kids stood on the concrete steps and more leaned against the chain-link fence while others lounged around the trees. A guy with red hair seemed to be waving at her. She wondered if she knew him.

"Well," Hanna muttered. "It's a sad day when schools have to look like armed camps."

Tianna followed her gaze. Security guards stood at the front gate, checking purses and backpacks before kids stepped through a metal detector. A large sign hung near the entrance, explaining the penalty for bringing a gun to school.

"Thanks for the ride." Tianna got out and slammed the door.

Hanna honked and pulled away. Tianna waved absently and started walking to the gate.

Guys turned and eyed her boldly, some of their eyes lingering longer than they should. Even girls looked her up and down. It seemed like more than the normal once-over. She glared back at them with unwavering eyes. She wasn't going to be intimidated by a bunch of kids she didn't even know, especially when she had real things to fear. She glanced down the street. The air around her felt unnaturally heavy and filled with dangerous promise. Instinct told her she needed to hide.

She stopped near the end of the line and watched the way the security guards were ransacking the backpacks and purses. She didn't want them fumbling through her stuff and accidentally pulling out her underwear. She didn't have time for this nonsense, anyway. She kept her head down and walked to the front of the line.

When a guard turned his back, she slipped around the metal detectors and ran across the blacktop toward the buildings. Kids applauded her audacity. She didn't even stop when a guard yelled after her. His footfalls followed for a moment, then fell away. Just as she had figured, he couldn't chase after her. He had to get back and examine the long line of kids waiting to enter school. She hurried around a corner, and someone grabbed her shoulder.

"Jeez—" The word whistled out of her.

"Startled you, sorry." It was the same guy with the long red hair. He leaned close to her as if he had known her for a long time. His deep blue eyes were piercing, and he had a scattering of freckles across his long, even nose. "You want to go hang out in the computer room?"

"No," she answered, and made a face. She might not have her memories back, but she wasn't going to trade sunshine for a dusky room and a glowing screen. Then she smelled coffee and looked down at his hands. He held a huge blueberry muffin and a paper cup of Starbucks coffee.

She considered. What did she have to lose? "Give me a sip," she said.

He smiled and handed over the cup. She held out her hand as she swallowed the sweetened brew and he passed her the muffin. She took a huge bite.

"This is the best I've ever tasted." She wondered if it were true. She didn't really care. She took another sip and this time let the warm coffee linger in her mouth.

"You can have it all if you want." He seemed to be laughing at her. "Didn't you eat breakfast at home?"

"No time," she muttered. "And thanks. This is heaven—sunshine, coffee, and muffin."

"You're so different from everyone else," he teased.

"How so?" she asked, and took another eager bite.

"Other girls are so worried about the way they look."

"What?" She sprayed out part of the muffin and coffee. "What's wrong with the way I look?"

"Nothing," he answered, but there was amusement in his eyes. "You look great."

She handed back the muffin and the coffee, wiping her mouth with the back of her hand. "Then why did you say I don't worry about the way I look?"

"I just mean other girls spend hours in front of the mirror and you obviously don't. You seem like the right kind of person to go on adventures with," he answered in a dreamy kind of way.

"That's what I want to do. Go on a dig, maybe. Wouldn't you like to uncover mummies or discover an unknown temple in the jungles of Cambodia?"

"Why?" she asked with a rising sense of uneasiness. "When you're safe and at home, adventures might seem like fun, but when you're living them, they're not."

"I thought you'd enjoy roughing it," he explained. "You don't seem to care about appearances."

He had said it again. What was wrong with the way she looked? Then a sudden thought came to her. Maybe that's why everyone had been staring at her. She hadn't looked in a mirror, and Hanna wasn't likely to tell her anything was wrong. Old people always thought young people looked cute. Perhaps the other students were staring at her because she looked awful.

"What's wrong?" he asked.

"Where's a rest room?" Her eyes were already scanning the buildings around her, looking for a sign.

"Over there." He seemed confused. "Don't you remember where the rest rooms are?"

"Is that really important?" she snapped, grabbed up her backpack and ran. She slammed through the rest room door and skidded to a stop in front of the mirror, expecting to see black mascara rings under her eyes and lipstick smeared to her ears or, worse, a long smudge of dirt or snot.

She let out a loud gasp.

Three girls sharing a cigarette in a stall turned and gawked at her. The girl standing next to her stopped brushing her long, sun-streaked hair.

Tianna gingerly touched her eyes, nose, and lips. She was startlingly beautiful.

"Wow," she whispered, and brushed her fingers through her long silky black hair. Not many people ever got to see themselves as a stranger would. There was no prejudice in her vision or modesty imposed from a lifetime of living with her face and body. She could honestly say she was stunning. No wonder the guys were turning their heads, and the girls, too. She was a knockout.

The girl standing next to her began to giggle.

"What's your problem?" Tianna glared at her.

The girl stopped laughing, picked up her lipstick and hairbrush and started to back away.

"Wait," Tianna called to the girl who was slinking away from her.

She stopped and tentatively looked back, her finger nervously stroking her dangling earring.

Tianna tilted her head and smiled. "I need some makeup. Do you have any I can borrow?" Silly question, she thought. The girl's eyes were caked with purple shadow and edged with a harsh black stroke, lips outlined in brown and glowing with too much gloss, and her cheeks were brilliant shocks of color. She looked like she owned enough makeup to paint graffiti on a stadium wall.

The girl nodded and pulled a large blue case from her oversized purse. "My mother says it's unsanitary to share makeup," she said, trying to argue. She seemed intimidated by Tianna.

Tianna gave her a friendly glance. "Do I look like I could give you anything?"

The girl considered, then handed over her makeup bag.

"What's your name?" Tianna asked as she drew black liquid eyeliner over the top lid of her beautiful eyes.

"Corrine," the girl answered, looking at her oddly. "I sit next to you in geometry."

Tianna turned her head and stared at the girl. There was nothing familiar about her. "We must be friends, then," Tianna mused as she added dusky shadow.

The girl raised one eyebrow. "I'd like to be, but . . ."

"But what?" Tianna rolled thick mascara on her lashes.

"You didn't seem to like me," Corrine answered.

Tianna wondered how she had acted on Monday and Tuesday. Corrine seemed afraid of her. She held out her hand for the hairbrush. Corrine handed it over.

"You know . . ." Tianna spoke as she brushed her hair. "I was just in a bad mood.

New school and all. I'd really like to be your friend."

"You would?" Corrine couldn't hide her surprise. "Yeah, starting a new school is tough, but you seemed to be having it pretty easy."

"Me?" Tianna handed back the brush and added gloss to her pouty lips.

"I mean, every guy has a major crush on you." Corrine dropped the brush into her purse.

"You think that makes life easy?"

"I guess." Corrine stared at her. "I like the way you look. I've never seen you bother with makeup before."

Tianna considered what she was saying. She was confident that normally she didn't wear makeup, but today was a celebration. She was seeing her face again for the first time.

"You look beautiful." Corrine sighed.

"You could, too," Tianna scolded, then tried to soften her voice. Why did she sound so on edge?

"I could?" Corrine seemed eager for more.

"You've got great style." Tianna complimented

her, and it was true. She wore a pale green top, jeans skirt, and incredible side-laced boots. "But you look like a doll with so much makeup. I mean, you're so vamped out. I bet you look better with bare cheeks, and definitely ditch the purple shadow."

"Take some off?" Corrine reached for a paper towel.

"Yeah, it makes you look desperate and insecure," Tianna answered absently, and turned in front of the full-length mirror behind her. Her reflection thrilled her. "When's geometry?"

"First period." Corrine gave her a questioning look.

"Lead the way," Tianna ordered. "Let's go."

"Sure." Corrine gathered all her makeup and put on her sunglasses.

Tianna picked up her backpack and started out to the hallway with a confident swing in her hips.

A sly smile crossed her face this time when she saw the guys stare. She walked down the unfamiliar hallways next to Corrine. The knot of anxiety was beginning to unravel, and she started to relax. She felt a rising sense of security here. She looked up and down the crowded hallway. Maybe it was because she wasn't alone, not with a thousand other students pushing past her. It wasn't likely anyone was going to kill her here, not with so many witnesses.

She stopped suddenly and Corrine bumped into her. She needed to find out who would want to kill her and why.

"What?" Corrine asked.

"Sorry, mood swing," Tianna muttered, disheartened again. She closed her eyes, trying to recall the morning's panic. It had been hot and raw. Maybe if she was patient, by the end of the day she'd have a memory or at least remember who was after her and why.

"Over here." Corrine guided her.

They turned down an outside corridor. When they passed room 103, four guys dressed like skaters ran to the doorway and leaned outside.

"Hey, Tianna," the first one shouted.

"Looking fine," the second one added.

"Thanks," she answered, and watched the other two admire her.

"I can't believe the impression you've already made with the guys." Corrine giggled and stopped in front of the closed door to a classroom.

Tianna slumped against the wall.

Corrine lifted her sunglasses. "You got that funny not-here stare."

Tianna leaned closer to her. "Sorry, I was drifting." Then she noticed three girls standing together in the sunlight staring at her. "What's up with them?"

That made Corrine laugh. "You act so casual about it. I don't even believe you."

"Casual about what?"

"Everyone's talking about it. I'm sure they're just jealous. Usually Jimena, Serena, and Vanessa get all the attention, but you were the one who all the guys wanted to dance with last night. So why did you leave so early, anyhow? Nothing could have pulled me away from all that."

Tianna raised an eyebrow.

"You didn't!" Corrine squealed.

"What?" Tianna didn't understand.

"Leave with some guy," Corrine gasped, already assuming that she had. "You left with Michael, didn't you?" she whispered quickly, and looked back at the three girls, who were still staring at Tianna. "No wonder they're glaring at you."

"I didn't," Tianna answered, but she didn't know for sure. Had she left with someone? That might explain what had happened to her last night, but it still couldn't explain the unnerving feeling of danger she'd had this morning or the note in her boot.

Tianna decided to tell Corrine everything. Maybe there was some way she could help. "Listen, I can't remember—"

Corrine squeezed her arm. "Look who's coming."

Tianna turned and caught the eye of an incredibly good-looking guy in a black long-sleeved shirt, Levi's, and a beaded necklace. She immediately liked his style.

"Hi, Tianna." He had a great smile and soft brown eyes.

"Hi," she answered back, loving the way he looked at her. She didn't know who he was but she was sure they had done more than talk. At least she hoped they had. She glanced at his sensual lips and bit her own. She wondered if she had ever been kissed, especially by him. She hoped she had, but without a memory it was impossible to know.

"I wanted to catch you before class." He ran a hand through his wild black hair as if talking to her made him nervous. She liked that she had that kind of effect on him. "I've been looking for you."

"You were?" she asked. Her stomach felt queasy and she took three quick breaths. She didn't mind this kind of nervousness.

"We missed you at Planet Bang last night." His hand rested over her head on the wall. She could feel the warmth of his body, and she wanted to slide her arms around his waist and hug him, right there in front of everyone.

"How so?" she asked, and considered. At

least now she knew she hadn't left early with him, whoever he was.

"You've got great moves—"

"Moves?" she interrupted. "What does that mean?"

He burst out laughing. She loved his laugh.

"Your dancing," he continued. "Everyone wanted to watch you some more, but you left so early." The bell rang, and he ran backward away from her as if he were reluctant to let her go. "See you, Tianna."

When he left, she turned to Corrine. "Who's that?"

Corrine opened her eyes wide. "Are you kidding? That's Michael Saratoga, and everyone is talking about the way you were trying to steal him from Vanessa."

"Who's Vanessa?"

"I don't believe you. She's only the most popular girl in the whole school." She pointed a finger at the girl in the middle of the three who were still watching Tianna closely. "Everyone knows Vanessa."

Vanessa had perfect skin, large blue eyes, and luxurious blond hair that curled over her shoulders.

"Are those extensions?" Tianna asked.

"All hers." Corrine sighed.

Vanessa was dressed in a funky white coat of fake fur that went down to her brown suede boots; underneath was a low-hanging party-girl skirt with two gold belts draped around her tan waist.

"Where'd she get the clothes? They're so cool." Tianna glanced self-consciously at her own jeans. The knees were soiled, and there was a long black mark on the side, as if she had skidded in dirt or oil.

"Her mom's a costume designer for the movies," Corrine confided.

Tianna felt a pang of jealousy—not for the clothes, but from the mention of Vanessa's mother. She wondered where hers was. Why hadn't she been with her this morning?

"What?" Corrine asked, as if sensing Tianna's emotions.

"Nothing." Tianna shook her head.

"Don't compare yourself to her if that's what you're doing. You're glamorous in your own way."

A man walked toward them carrying a briefcase. That had to be the teacher, Mr. Hall. He drew a handkerchief from his pocket and wiped his nose, then stuffed the hanky in a back pocket and took out keys to the classroom.

Everyone started toward the door.

"Who's that other girl with Vanessa?" Tianna asked. "The one with the teardrops tattooed under her eye?"

"That's Jimena." Corrine spoke in a lower voice. "Don't mess with her. Everyone says she's been in a camp twice."

"Camp?" Tianna asked.

"Youth authority," Corrine muttered, as if Tianna ought to know. "I can't believe you didn't hear. It's all over school. She used to be in a gang."

"And the one staring daggers at me?"

"The one with the cello case is Serena," Corrine answered wistfully. "You should hear her play. I'm so jealous of her talent. She'll be famous someday."

Serena wore a fedora and a tie-dyed shirt with studded jeans. She had a beautiful face and compelling eyes.

"She also can tell your fortune with her tarot cards," Corrine whispered. "She read mine once, and it was spooky, everything she knew. I never went back for a second reading."

Corrine and Tianna edged closer to the door and joined the line forming to go inside the classroom. That's when she noticed that Serena, Jimena, and Vanessa each wore matching silver charms.

Corrine caught what she was staring at.

"They never take them off," she whispered. "Not in P.E., not for dances. Never. They had another friend, Catty, who wore the same amulet, but she's gone now. Someday when we're alone, I'll tell you what happened to her."

Tianna looked at the face of the moon etched in the metal on the charms. Sparkling in the morning light, the charms didn't seem silver but more like a strange stone that reflected a rainbow of colors. She glanced up to find Jimena staring at her, her black eyes intense, as if Tianna had done something wrong by looking at their charms.

She waited for the three to go inside, then spoke to Corrine. "Are they witches?"

"What?" Corrine asked, and her head shot around, eyes wide and frightened, then she glanced nervously back at the three girls.

Tianna was sure Corrine had heard her. She wondered why she seemed suddenly so afraid, but instead of repeating her question, she shrugged. She wasn't intimidated by them.

"Too bad for Vanessa," she whispered to Corrine. "I'm not going to let some old girlfriend stand in the way of my getting Michael."

"You are incredibly wicked," Corrine joked, and Tianna sensed the admiration in her voice.

CHAPTER THREE

AT THE END OF THE school day Tianna sat alone, writing her name over and over on a piece of paper, hoping to stir a memory. She had discovered very little about herself. Several times she had felt on the verge of recalling something, and then the feeling slid away. She could remember some things like the taste of coffee and potato chips, but she couldn't say what had been her favorite snack. Simple things like that had made her feel cut off from everyone else. It had been difficult to join in conversations, even though most of the kids had seemed friendly enough.

A hollowness filled her chest, and she pressed her fingers under her eyes. Crying wouldn't help, but even as she tried to push the tears away, her vision blurred.

She supposed that she should go back to the apartment where she had started this morning, but she didn't know how to get there. She had left in a rush, and instead of looking at the streets while Hanna drove, she had been rummaging through her backpack, searching for clues.

Her hands began to tremble again. She felt unsure. She had been vacillating between plans all day. Everything seemed too chancy. But that wasn't the worst part. The loneliness was. If she only had a parent or a close friend she could confide in, someone to comfort her and tell her that things would be okay.

The note she had found in the toe of her boot this morning had made her leery about going to the authorities, even the school vice principal. If the police wouldn't believe that someone was after her, then why should a teacher or principal? Maybe the best plan was to head for the Greyhound bus station in Hollywood and get out of town until she came up with some plan, but she was reluctant to leave. She felt safe here on the school grounds.

A shadow stretched over her, and she turned with a jerk.

Michael smiled down at her. He had taken off his shirt. Tattoos decorated his tan arms.

She wiped at her eyes carefully. She didn't want him to see the tears. And she definitely didn't want his pity.

"Hey, Tianna." His lips curled around perfect white teeth as he swung his backpack onto the table. He seemed happy to see her.

"Hi, Michael." She tried to keep the excitement from her voice, but already her heart was beating wildly. She wondered if he could tell how much she liked him.

"You okay?" He sat down next to her, and she caught the scent of spicy deodorant before he slipped on the long-sleeved black T-shirt.

"Sure," she said. "The sun was making my eyes water." She breathed deeply, disappointed that he had put on his shirt.

"I was trying to find you over at the gym." His dark eyes looked at her openly, and a pleasurable shiver raced through her.

She smiled, pleased that he had been looking for her, and studied his lips, imagining what they would feel like pressed against hers. Then with a shock of excitement she realized that she might already know if she could only remember.

"And why did you need to find me?" She leaned closer to him flirtatiously.

"I wanted to give you this." He dug into his backpack.

Eager anticipation flooded through her. She wondered if he had bought her a gift. A crystal, maybe, that she could hang on a silver chain, or a shell bracelet that matched his necklace.

He handed her a blue piece of paper. She took it and hoped he didn't see the disappointment on her face. "What's this?"

"My band's playing at Planet Bang on Thursday," he explained. "I hope you'll come listen to us. We don't go on until nine."

"Sure." She let a smile creep over her lips as she stared into his deep-set eyes. She had no idea where Planet Bang was, but she had been hearing kids talk about it all day and she knew if she went there, she'd be able to dance with Michael. She pictured his hands around her waist, his lips settling gently on hers. "I'll be there."

"You're a great dancer." Michael's body seemed to press closer to hers, and she wondered if he was doing it on purpose.

"I am?" she asked coyly, wanting to continue their conversation from this morning. Michael had watched her dance, but had that been while he was dancing with her? She liked the feel of his eyes on her, the way he was looking at her now.

"You know you are. You don't need for me to say it. You got enough compliments." The flyers fluttered in his hands.

"Your compliment is the one that matters." She let her finger stroke the top of his hand. He had the long fingers of a musician. She wanted to clasp his hand and bring those fingers to her cheek.

He smiled, teasing. "You want to hear more about how awesome you were?"

She wished she could remember what had happened. "Did you think I was?" She tilted her head and let her fingers trail up his hand, until all four entwined his wrist. She liked the warm feel of his skin beneath her palm, the rapid race of his pulse. She had a sudden desire to slide her fingers up his shoulder, circle her hands around his neck, and pull his face to hers.

"So how's everything going?" He stuffed the flyers into his backpack.

"Okay." How could she tell him that she had awakened this morning with no idea of who or where she was?

"It seems like something's bothering you." He watched her carefully.

She bit her lip. Did she dare tell him? It didn't seem right, but then, maybe he would have some idea of what to do. "Just things, you know."

"How could you feel down with every guy in school trying to hook up with you?" he asked.

She looked away. "A guy's not always the answer," she said with a sigh. "In fact, I don't think it ever is."

"All right, I said it wrong," Michael continued. "Have you met any guys yet that you think you could like?"

"I met you, Michael," she said softly.

"I'm talking about guys you might like, you know, for more than just a friend," he corrected her.

She eyed him slyly. "Why wouldn't I like you that way?"

He blushed beneath his dark tan and started to say something, but before he could, Vanessa ran up to them. She was wearing yellow baggy shorts, a white jersey, cleats, socks, and shin guards.

"Tianna," she called impatiently.

Tianna knew girls sometimes confronted each other over a guy, but this was ridiculous. She certainly wasn't going to have a shouting match with Vanessa in front of Michael. She stood and placed her hand possessively on his shoulder. "What do you want, Vanessa?"

But Vanessa didn't seem jealous. She didn't appear to notice the way Tianna's hand rubbed across Michael's back.

"Why aren't you over at the gym?" Vanessa raked back her thick blond hair and clasped it in a ponytail with a rubber band.

"Because I'm here." Tianna felt completely confused. This was definitely not the fight she had expected from Vanessa, but her answer made Michael laugh.

Vanessa shot Michael a warning look. He raised an eyebrow and stopped laughing.

Then Vanessa put her hands on her hips in frustration. "The soccer game is about to start."

Tianna looked at her dumbly. "So?"

"You're not even suited up," Vanessa continued, annoyance rising in her voice. "And we still have to do warm-ups."

Tianna didn't understand.

"You're my lead player." Vanessa seemed overwhelmed with frustration. "Come on."

Tianna choked. "How did I get on the soccer team so quickly?"

"Would you stop playing around? This is no joke. Decca High is our biggest rival, and I want to beat them." Vanessa was angry now. Her face flushed, and Tianna could see the vein in her neck throbbing. "Either you play or you don't." She turned and ran away.

"Come on." Michael took Tianna's hand. "We all want to watch you play, and Vanessa needs you."

Tianna bit her lip. How was she going to pull this one off? She wished now she had left school after the first bell. "I don't really think I'm going to help the team, and I sure don't understand what's got Vanessa so upset."

"Don't get too aggravated with Vanessa," Michael explained. "She gets crazy over soccer now. She and Catty used to play when they were little and she doesn't like to be reminded of it anymore."

Tianna looked up at him. She wanted to say "So?" sarcastically, but she had a feeling that there was something important in what he was trying to tell her. "Who's Catty?" she asked. "And what doesn't Vanessa like to be reminded of?"

He turned and looked at her. "You didn't know?" Michael had a curious expression on his face. "I thought Vanessa would have told you. That's the girl you're replacing on the team. She and Vanessa were best friends and then . . ." His voice drifted away.

"And then what?" Tianna needed to know.

"Catty went away," Michael explained.

"You mean ran away?"

"That's what I thought at first, but Vanessa insisted it wasn't so. Rumors started, but Vanessa won't really talk about it. She and her friends act like Catty's dead. So does Catty's mother."

"How do you know if they won't talk about it?" Tianna studied his face.

He leaned in closer as if he didn't want anyone to hear what he was going to say next. "I saw them putting flowers on the street a few blocks from Planet Bang as if they were making a *descanso*. It gave me the chills to watch them. I never told Vanessa that I saw them."

"What's a *descanso*?"

"It's where people mark the place where someone has died by laying down flowers and candles. Usually it's from a drive-by or a car accident." He looked up, and his eyes followed Vanessa as she disappeared inside the gym.

"You think she was killed and they're not telling anyone?" She had a sudden mental flash of the note she had found inside her boot. Maybe she wasn't the first one who had been chased down.

"If she was, a body was never found," Michael answered.

"That's terrible." Tianna suddenly felt sorry for Vanessa.

Michael shook his head. "You've got an important game to play." He seemed determined not to stay down. "You need to suit up."

"Are you going to watch me?" she asked.

"I wouldn't miss it for anything." He smiled down at her.

"Great," she answered with faked enthusiasm. She was going to be the joke of the school after this was over. Even if she strained, she couldn't remember how to play. Why had they put her on the team in the first place?

CHAPTER FOUR

TIANNA ENTERED THE gym, her boots scuffing on the cement floor. The steamy smells of damp towels and sweat confronted her as she looked down the long line of gray lockers. She didn't know which one was hers. She had cut P.E. earlier in the day for the same reason; it felt too embarrassing to ask someone to help her find her locker, and she wouldn't have remembered her combination, anyway. Besides, she hadn't been in the mood to play. She had spent the hour sitting in the warmth of the sun.

"Hola." The word echoed around her. She turned. Jimena sat on a bench, putting on her

shoes. She was wearing fluorescent blue shorts and a shirt; her long black hair was braided and stacked on her head.

"Aren't you and Vanessa on the same team?" Tianna asked, eyeing the uniform. She dropped her backpack and slouched beside her.

"I'm the goalie," Jimena answered, and pulled long white socks over her shin guards.

"And?" Tianna ran her finger over the graffiti scratched into the bench.

"Goalkeeper's uniforms don't match the team," Jimena explained impatiently. "You know that." Then she looked at her oddly. "Are you all right?"

"Of course I am," Tianna lied.

"Then why aren't you suited up?" Jimena rubbed sunblock on her face. "This is the big game."

"I can't remember my combination," Tianna confessed. She didn't bother to add that she also couldn't recall which locker belonged to her.

Jimena tossed the tube of sunscreen. It hit the back of her locker with a loud metallic clank.

She turned and gave Tianna a derisive grin.

"What?" Tianna asked.

"Just strange you can't remember your combination," Jimena retorted. "Because we have key locks here."

Tianna bit her lip. "Can you show me my locker, then? I can't remember which one is mine."

The scowl dropped from Jimena's face and she laughed with understanding. "Yeah, this school is really big. I was overwhelmed when I first transferred in, too. Don't worry about not remembering. I had to carry my class schedule with me for an entire week."

Tianna smiled gratefully and followed Jimena down the row of lockers. Jimena's cleats made a clicking sound on the floor.

"You were assigned Catty's old locker, right?" Jimena asked as she turned and they walked down another drab line of metal boxes.

"Right," Tianna answered, even though she had no idea if that was true.

Jimena stopped in front of a locker near a floor-length mirror.

"This one was Catty's," she said softly.

A watercolor painting of the full moon rising over an ocean was taped to the front. A beautiful woman hovered behind the moon, her purple robe billowing into the starry sky behind her. The image was haunting.

"Did she do the painting?" Tianna asked. "It's really pretty."

Jimena nodded. "She was a good artist."

"I guess the locker is a hard one to miss. I should have gone up and down the aisles until I found it," Tianna said, even though she knew she still wouldn't have been able to recognize it as belonging to her.

"That's okay," Jimena answered with a shrug, and continued staring at the picture as if she missed Catty a lot.

Then another problem occurred to Tianna. "Is my uniform inside, or do I get it from another place?"

Her question jerked Jimena from her reverie. "You forgot that, too? Vanessa gave you Catty's shirt and shorts. You're the same size. I hope you kept them in your locker. You can't play without a uniform."

"What happened to Catty?" Tianna asked.

Jimena's mood changed abruptly, and Tianna knew she had trod in forbidden territory.

"Long story." Jimena tried to smile, but her look was more guarded now than friendly. "So I'll see you out on the field."

"Yeah." Tianna tossed her backpack on the bench, unzipped it, and started looking for a key.

Jimena turned back. "You don't have your key?" There was exasperation in her voice now.

"I have it," Tianna answered. "I just have to find it." At least she hoped she did.

"Hurry, then," Jimena answered, and turned to leave.

"I will." Tianna found a key chain with a couple dozen keys jangling from the ring. She stared at it, perplexed, and wondered what the keys were for.

"Why do you have so many keys?" Jimena asked, as if the same question had occurred to her.

Tianna shrugged. "Just things."

Jimena stepped back to her. "You don't remember which key?"

"I don't." Tianna tried the first key.

Jimena sat down beside her. "Are you doing this on purpose?" she asked. "The game with Decca High is really important."

"I'm doing my best," Tianna assured her, and pushed the next key into the padlock.

"I hope you're not trying to make the game start late." Jimena seemed dismayed. "We'll get penalized. *¿Sabes?*"

"I'm not trying to make us late," Tianna answered. "And if you're so worried about it, get a substitute."

"Engreída," Jimena muttered.

"What does that mean?" Tianna jerked around and glared at Jimena.

"It means you got a big head. You know we're counting on you for this game Maybe Vanessa will beg you to play, but I won't."

"Leave me alone," Tianna said, and the padlock snapped open. She unhooked the lock and pulled out a white jersey and yellow shorts that matched Vanessa's. She placed the shoes with cleats on the bench beside her, then took out a clean pair of socks, a sports bra, and shin guards. She wondered if all these had belonged to Catty or if she had purchased some of them. The shoes looked new. She stared at them in wonder but couldn't remember ever seeing them before.

"Warm-ups are starting," Jimena reminded her. "I'll see you out on the field."

"All right." Tianna took off her boots, then her jeans, stripped off her T-shirt and then her bra. She was about to put on the sports bra when she caught her naked reflection in the mirror.

It might as well have been the face of a stranger that stared back at her, but that wasn't what was bothering her. Her body was covered with bruises as if she had been in a major fight. A thick black knot the size of a shoe was bleeding a pale green color into her ribs, and another long red welt crossed her back as if someone had hit her with a stick. *Or a pipe.* She felt suddenly chilled, and her skin broke out with gooseflesh. How could she not remember such a brutal attack? And then another thought made her wonder. Why didn't the police believe that her attackers were real? Hadn't they seen the bruises? She touched another one on the top of her thigh. It felt hot beneath her fingers, and she wondered if she was getting an infection as well.

Maybe she had been mugged. She had heard of people getting amnesia from blows to the head. Where that information came from she couldn't say, but she knew it was true. That might also explain why she had such a strong feeling of impending danger. That would be natural after such a fierce attack, but it couldn't explain the note. Unless whoever had done this to her had been trying to do more than mug her. Her heart raced.

Something moved behind her, and she caught Jimena's reflection in the mirror.

"What are you staring at?" Tianna asked angrily as she grabbed the sports bra and tugged it on.

"You want to talk?" Jimena's voice was gentle now, and she sat down as if there was all the time in the world before the soccer match would begin. "I'm sorry for getting upset with you. I know what was going on in your head now."

"No, you don't." Tianna pulled on her socks, then the shoes.

"Who beat you up?" Jimena asked softly.

"I fell," Tianna answered curtly, and slipped the jersey over her head.

"You think I haven't seen what a kick to the ribs looks like the day after?" Jimena's hand reached out to comfort her, and Tianna jerked her shoulder away.

"I don't remember what happened to me," Tianna replied. "Just forget about it.

"Whatever you say stays here with me." She pointed to the two tears tattooed under her eye. "I won't go to the cops."

Tianna stepped into her shorts. "Like they could help, anyway."

"But maybe I can," Jimena offered.

"Right." Tianna started walking away. "I got enough problems. Just leave me alone."

She could hear Jimena's cleats clicking after her.

"What?" Tianna turned on her.

"You forgot your shin guards." Jimena handed them to her.

Tianna grabbed them. She sat on the nearest bench and put them on, hating the way Jimena hovered over her.

Finally she stood. "I don't want your pity," she said through clenched teeth. She grabbed up a ball and ran.

Outside, she set the ball on the ground and stared down at it. This was really bad. The game was going to be a total disaster if the team was in any way counting on her, and from what Jimena had said, she suspected that they were. She nudged the ball with the tip of her toe.

"Hey!" someone shouted.

She glanced up, and suddenly the guy with the red hair from this morning ran toward her. His foot kicked the ball, and he dribbled it away.

She had started after him when Vanessa yelled from the field, "Tianna, would you stop playing around? Bring the ball and get over here for warm-ups."

Tianna whipped around, ready to scream *I quit!* But then she saw Michael standing next to Vanessa. He waved at her, his big, gorgeous smile covering his dark, perfect face.

Tianna turned back to the guy. "Just give me the ball."

He grinned at her as if daring her to steal it back.

"Look, please." Tianna frowned, her anger growing. "Do you want Vanessa to get more upset with me than she already is?"

"You're her star player," he teased. "You can be late."

"Tianna," Vanessa called again. "If you don't get out here, I'm going to kick you off the team!"

"Like I care!" Tianna shouted back. Then she remembered Michael and how much he didn't want to upset Vanessa because she was still getting over the death of her friend Catty. "I mean, I'll be right there!"

She looked at the guy. Anger seethed inside her. "Give me that dumb ball. This has not been a good day, and I really can't take any more."

"Come get it, then." He smirked and ran away from her, kicking the ball lightly with the inside of his feet. He didn't look down, and he never lost control over it.

Tianna sighed and shook her head.

"Come on." He taunted her, and picked up speed. "You afraid you can't get it back from me?"

Something exploded inside her. She felt it like a hot fire flashing up to her face. She dashed after him and caught him in seconds. He seemed surprised by her speed but also delighted.

When she reached him, he darted away, changing direction, but it seemed as if her body had anticipated where he was going to go and she ran parallel with him, her feet tipping in and trying to steal the ball.

He laughed and shifted his weight in one direction, then took off running in the other, using the inside of his foot to roll the ball.

"Wrong thing to do," she shouted angrily. This time her feet went on automatic. She ran alongside him, then swung her leg in front of him and struck the near side of the ball. It popped away from him.

Her foot shot out again. He tripped and fell flat on his back.

She picked up the ball and sauntered back to him, then held out her hand to help him up.

"You don't have to smile so big," he said with a matching grin. He took her hand. His felt warm and strong.

She couldn't help but smile. No wonder they put her on the team so quickly. Her feet had talent. She was a master.

"Say, what's your name?" she asked as he stood.

He looked at her oddly but didn't let go of her hand. "Derek," he answered, and he seemed hurt. "You're teasing me, right?"

She didn't know his name, but suddenly there was no doubt in her mind that they had known each other before she lost her memories.

"Of course, I'm teasing," she lied, and ran out to the field.

CHAPTER FIVE

"¡PUENTA!" JIMENA SHOUTED, and dove for the ball. Her defenders cleared away and Jimena made another save. She punted the ball, and it went flying past midfield.

"Got it!" Tianna cried out. She threw out her arms and hit the ball with her forehead. It shot at the goal. The keeper tried to grab the ball, but it hit the net.

Jimena screamed, "Gooooaaaalll!"

Serena cupped her hands around her mouth and joined in from the sidelines. "Way to go,

Tianna!" Then she threw her hands over her head and gave a loud, "Woo-hoo!"

Tianna smiled at Michael, standing next to Serena and Derek.

"That was awesome!" Vanessa ran to Tianna and hugged her. "You're the best striker I've ever seen." She got a funny look on her face. Tianna wondered if she felt as if she was betraying Catty by saying that.

"Thanks." Tianna turned back as the goalkeeper threw the ball in a javelin pass. It hit her hard in the face.

"You did that on purpose," Vanessa yelled at the goalkeeper.

"Sorry," the girl called back. "It was an accident."

"I know you better than that, Michelle," Vanessa answered angrily. "You've done things like this before."

Tianna grabbed her nose and sat down on the grass, then leaned back and pinched hard, trying to stop the flow of blood. Her eyes teared; she felt sharp pain in her head.

Without warning a memory streaked across her mind, as if the impact of the ball had loosened something inside her skull. Someone dangerous wanted to destroy her, and it wasn't some ordinary pervert or stalker. The two guys who had been chasing her had feral eyes that glowed like a cat's in the dark. They also had mysterious powers of mind control.

"Tianna, are you all right?" Vanessa leaned over her.

She didn't answer. She was vaguely aware of the pounding feet of her teammates, running up to her, but she studied the memory. No wonder the police didn't believe her. She could barely believe it herself. Yet she knew it was true. She must have told the officers that her attackers had tried to hypnotize her with their glowing yellow eyes. She shuddered. How was that possible? She concentrated, but her mind gave her no more.

Vanessa knelt beside her. "Do you think she broke your nose?"

Tianna shook her head and looked at the blood on her hands.

"Oh, no, what have I done?" Michelle asked with mock sincerity. "I hope you don't have to sit out the game, Tianna."

"Not a chance," Tianna answered.

"That's not very nice, Michelle," Vanessa shot back.

"Especially since you did it on purpose," Jimena added.

"What do you mean?" Michelle asked innocently. "I'm just worried about her. Do you think I want you to lose your best player? I hate a game when there's no competition."

"Somebody get me a towel," Tianna said. "I want my penalty shot."

"No way." Michelle smirked and pulled her dark, curly hair away from her face. "I'm still in the game, and no one's called a foul."

"Tianna should get a free kick." Vanessa glanced over her head and waved for the referee.

"She got in my way," Michelle argued back. "I was only trying to get the ball down to midfield for the kickoff. Besides, even if the referee called a foul, which she didn't, you're not going to get another shot past me."

The referee walked over to them. "What is it?"

"Michelle threw the ball at Tianna on purpose," Vanessa said.

Michelle folded her arms across her chest. "She got in the way."

The referee looked at Michelle and shook her head. "I didn't see it," the referee said to Vanessa, then asked Tianna, "Can you still play?"

"Sure." Tianna nodded.

The referee didn't look convinced. "Your nose has to stop bleeding before I can let you back in the game."

"I'm fine." Tianna pinched her nose and glared at Michelle. "Nothing's going to keep me from playing."

"I'll get a towel." Vanessa hurried away.

The referee picked up the ball and started back to midfield as the other girls drifted back to their positions.

Michelle waited until everyone was far

enough away, then she leaned over Tianna. "Decca High hasn't lost a game all season," she said. "And we're not going to start with getting beaten by a loser team like La Brea High. It's not even fair that they let you play."

"What are you trying to say?" Tianna asked.

"What do you think?" Michelle sneered. "With you out of the game we're going to win. No way La Brea can beat us then." She turned and started to walk away.

"I hope you break an ankle," Tianna shouted after her.

"Fat chance." Michelle laughed, but then she tripped. She screamed and grabbed her ankle, then turned and looked back at Tianna accusingly. "You did that!"

"What?" Tianna asked, and spread her hands wide. "I was back here."

"You did something." Michelle searched the ground around her as if she were looking for the thing that had tripped her. "What did you do?"

"I didn't do anything." Tianna felt terrible.

She knew it was silly. A thought couldn't make something happen, but she couldn't squelch the guilty feeling that it was her fault Michelle had fallen.

CHAPTER SIX

THE REFEREE RAN back to them. "What happened now?"

"She tripped me," Michelle squealed.

"How could I?" Tianna said. "I was sitting here the whole time. She's ten feet away from me."

The referee looked from one girl to the other. "She couldn't have tripped you, Michelle; she hasn't moved since I was here before."

"But she did," Michelle protested, her forehead twisted in pain, and when she protectively placed her hands around her ankle, she let out a small moan.

Vanessa came back and gave Tianna a towel. "What's wrong?"

"Michelle fell and she thinks I did it." Tianna pressed the towel against her nose. It was still bleeding badly.

"You'd both better go to the nurse," the referee announced. "Tianna, can you help Michelle get there?"

"Yes," Tianna answered, not bothering to hide her disappointment at being unable to finish the game.

"I don't want her to touch me," Michelle yelled.

"Michelle, she couldn't have hurt you," the referee said. "She was lying on the ground."

Tianna stood, walked over to Michelle, and offered her a hand.

Michelle slapped it away. "Don't touch me."

"I'll get someone." Vanessa waved, and Derek and Michael ran onto the field. "Can you take Michelle to the school nurse?" she asked them.

"Sure," Michael answered, and cast a quick glance at Tianna. "Awesome play."

Derek and Michael locked their hands and carried Michelle to the nurse's office between them. Tianna followed, holding back her head.

At the nurse's office Derek lingered near the door. "You want me to stay?" he asked. "And give you a ride home?"

Tianna shook her head.

He gently moved the towel away from her face. "It doesn't even look swollen."

"But Michelle's ankle is," Michael said. "It looks really bad."

The nurse suddenly appeared at the door. She was a short, fat woman with a cropped pixie cut and happy gray eyes behind purple frames that were too large for her face. "Thank you for your help," she said. "Now, you boys go on so I can take care of the girls."

Tianna mouthed good-bye and reluctantly followed the nurse inside her office.

A few minutes later Tianna sat on a stool under a buzzing fluorescent light, holding an ice pack to her nose as the nurse examined Michelle's foot in the other room.

Tianna glanced idly around the nurse's office and stopped at the desk. The nurse had left her computer on and open to confidential school files. Her eyes shot back to the door to the examining room. The nurse was still busy with Michelle.

Cautiously she set down the bag of ice and crept over to the computer. She grabbed the mouse and scrolled down through the health files marked CONFIDENTIAL until she came to the one for Tianna Moore.

Her heart beat rapidly when she read her own name. She opened the file, then studied the information on the screen. Born 1986 in Los Angeles, California. Normal immunization records and illnesses. The last line surprised her. *Habitual runaway. Paranoid tendencies. Recommend counseling at Children's Hospital.*

Tianna read the last line again. Had she said something to the school nurse about being chased by strange men with glowing eyes?

Then she heard movement in the next room.

"I'll be right back," the nurse told Michelle. "I'm going to call your parents. You need to go to the hospital for X rays. I'm sure your ankle is broken."

"No!" Michelle moaned. "I'm the goalkeeper. How's my team going to play?"

Tianna had started to close down her file when something caught her attention. She saw her home address. She picked up a pen from the desk and hurriedly copied it onto her palm.

The nurse's shoes squeaked on the polished linoleum floor, coming closer now.

Quickly she grabbed the mouse, closed down her file, and turned away from the computer.

The nurse entered the room and eyed Tianna suspiciously. "Was there something you needed?" she asked, and scanned her desk, then looked at the computer screen. Tianna hadn't taken the screen back to where it had been before, but she hoped the nurse didn't remember what had been there.

"I think I'm okay to go home now if that's

all right with you." Tianna stepped away from the desk.

"Let's see." The nurse held either side of Tianna's head with gentle hands and moved it from side to side, then pushed it up and looked inside her nose again.

"All right," she said with an overworked smile. "But make sure you rest, or your nose will probably start bleeding again."

Tianna headed for the door.

"Wait." The nurse gave her four forms to take home and fill out and another one with instructions for her home care. "Read it carefully just in case."

Then Michelle yelled from the other room, "Has everyone forgotten about me?"

"I'm calling now," the nurse yelled back.

Outside in the hallway Tianna stared at the address written on her palm. That took care of one problem at least. She'd know how to get back to the apartment building. Maybe someone would be waiting for her, like a mom or a dad. Perhaps her parents had had to leave for work early this morning. It was comforting to think she wasn't alone.

She had started walking quickly back to the gym to pick up her backpack and change into street clothes when another thought alarmed her. The guys with the yellow burning eyes could also be waiting for her. She slowed her step. She had a sudden impulse to run, but she didn't know where to go.

CHAPTER SEVEN

THE LATE-AFTERNOON sun cast orange light at a low angle and long black shadows swept across the street. Tianna stared at the house in front of her and compared its address to the one written on her palm. The address was correct, but this large brick Tudor home with its massive chimney and steeply pitched roof was definitely not the apartment building she had left earlier this morning. She wondered if this was where she lived. She studied the tall, narrow windows. Perhaps one belonged to her bedroom.

She couldn't help but hope her parents were

inside. Maybe they had been desperately looking for her. Her heart pounded crazily as she unzipped her backpack and pulled out the chain with the dangling keys. Did she have the right one to get inside? She glanced back at the dark house. More than anything she wanted to be home and feel the comfort of a parent's arms around her.

She took a deep breath and hurried across the street, stepped up a short flight of stairs between two thick ornate iron banisters, then followed a brick path to the porch, where she skipped up the steps and rang the doorbell twice.

No one answered.

She hadn't really expected anyone would. Her hands trembled badly, making the keys jingle like wind chimes as she stuck the first one in the lock. The looseness of the doorknob surprised her. She tried one key, then another. Finally a bronze one slipped in. She turned it and smiled when she heard the click.

She opened the door, stepped quickly inside, and called, "Mom! Dad!" trying to keep the tension out of her voice. She closed the door behind her and waited. The air smelled of lemon oil and rose blossoms. She wasn't sure what she expected to hear, running footsteps, maybe, or the relieved yell of someone who loved her.

Finally she stepped across the tiled entry to the living room. Golden bars of sunshine shot through the windows and reflected off the polished wood floors and heavy, dark furniture. But the room felt too cold. In the overwhelming silence, the ticking of the clock seemed to echo around her.

Comfortable brown-and-gold chairs faced a huge stone fireplace. She turned around, looking for a picture of herself. Anything that would tell her she belonged here. She found nothing.

At last she went back to the hallway and found the stairs that curved up to the second floor. She took the steps two at a time, her backpack banging against her, and almost collided with a wheelchair on the landing. She touched the cold metal handles. It looked too small for an adult. Maybe she had a brother or a sister who had been seriously injured.

Then she glanced down the hallway. Three open doors spilled fading sunlight onto the hall runner. A fourth door at the end was closed. She tiptoed past a long table decorated with crystal vases. The house was deserted, yet she couldn't shake the feeling that someone was there, watching her. She paused and listened before she entered the first room.

Inside the air was thick with disinfectant and medicine smells that seemed incongruous in a room with bright yellow-and-green wallpaper. Games and stuffed animals lay on a hospital bed in the corner. Syringes, pumps, and monitors sat on a long counter next to coloring books and crayons and a tattered game of Monopoly. This room must belong to the brother or sister who used the wheelchair.

She started to step back into the hallway but paused. Something was wrong. The air seemed to be growing colder and her body was filling with a sense of impending danger.

She eased inside the next room. Posters of skateboarders hung on the wall. She smiled. She touched the skates, bats, baseball gloves, knee pads, and helmets lining the shelves. On the desk she spied something that made her heart lurch; doctor's instructions written on Children's Hospital letterhead, and on top of that a long line of brown pill bottles. She picked up the first one and read the name: *Shannon Culbertson.* The last name was different from hers.

Maybe she didn't belong here after all. She glanced at the address on her palm again, the letters and numbers now blurred. The school records said this was her home. Perhaps Shannon was her half sister, or the nurse's records were outdated.

A loud creaking sound made her head jerk around. She waited and listened. Had someone opened a door downstairs? The big house was silent again. She hurried inside the third room and carefully closed the door. This one had to be hers. It definitely belonged to a teenage girl, but she didn't like the decor. The full-size bed was covered with a flowery emerald comforter and lacy pillows, and she felt no sense of familiarity with the white furniture or the pink fabric flowers in the green vase. Was she really the type of girl who would have decorated her room like a flower garden? She didn't think so.

Then she saw the computer. She set her backpack by the nightstand and pressed a button. The computer whined on. Maybe she could find something in the documents stored in the hard drive. She sat down at the desk and stared at the screen, then worked the mouse, but she didn't find any files. There were no e-mails, and it looked as if she had never sent any out. Odd. She shut down the computer, then went to the closet and walked inside. She patted her hand along the wall, searching for a light switch, found it, and turned it on. Her breath caught.

"Wow," she whispered. The clothes definitely looked like something she would wear. Scoop-neck tops and slinky skirts, hipster flare jeans and a leopard camisole. Even the shoes were perfect: Mary Janes with thick, chunky soles, bungee sneakers, and boots. She slipped off her leather jacket, tore off the tag on a fuzzy hooded sweater, and pulled it over her head. She liked the way the sleeves came down to the tips of her fingers. Automatically she poked her thumbs through the weave and smiled.

She stepped back into the bedroom. The tastes in clothes and bedroom decor were too different. She glanced back into the closet, then went to the laundry hamper and lifted the lid. It was empty. She scowled. The clothes looked new and unused. Most still had the sales tags hanging from the side. Even though she couldn't remember her life before this morning, she knew there should be at least one pair of ratty sweats or some dirty clothes.

She started looking through the dresser. In the third drawer, hidden under socks and bras, she found a lined notebook. It looked like a diary. Her hands trembled as she lifted it and opened it to the first page. *Tianna Moore* was written across the top. Her heart began beating rapidly. At last she would have some answers. She had only begun writing in it two days before—the same day she had enrolled in La Brea High. She stretched out on the bed when a sound made her stop. She held her breath and listened.

Stealthy steps quietly crossed the wood floor downstairs. Someone was trying hard to hide their footfalls. That made her alert. A parent or sister wouldn't need to sneak around.

Her hands went cold and she set the diary on the nightstand, careful not to make any sound.

The person was climbing the stairs now. She thought she heard a furtive whisper. She stood and walked silently to the door, paused, and listened, trying to hear what they were saying.

The steps halted on the other side of her bedroom door. A hand brushed against the wood, and then she heard someone squeeze the doorknob. She froze as she watched it slowly turn.

Always trust your instincts. The words came to her suddenly. Who had told her that? No matter. She frantically looked around for a place to hide, then walked back to the bed and slid under it as the door opened.

If the person turned out to be a parent or sibling, she was going to feel very foolish. The comment about paranoid tendencies written on the nurse's computer screen rushed through her mind. Perhaps this was what the notation had meant. Then another thought came to her. Maybe paranoia was sometimes a sane response to what was going on.

She held up the edge of the bedspread with the tips of her fingers and watched as two guys entered the room. They looked about sixteen, not much older than that. The first guy was tall and thin with jagged scars on his bony face. He wore black wire-rim glasses, but the glasses couldn't hide his spooky eyes, which looked piercing enough to penetrate steel. Three silver skull earrings hung from his left ear, and his face was a pincushion: three rings in his nose, two in his lips, and a barbell through his eyebrow.

She felt a shudder of recognition. He was the same guy she had seen in her flashback this afternoon after the ball slammed her face. He looked human enough, but there was also something supernatural about him.

The second guy had the same intensity in his eyes, but he wore a scraggly goatee. A green snake was tattooed on his broad neck, and his dark hair was streaked with orange and yellow. He remained at the door while the bony-faced guy continued into the room.

He stopped near the bed. Her heart lurched. Had he sensed her presence?

Suddenly he leaned over and picked up her backpack.

She banged her head on the thick carpeting, angry at her stupid mistake. How could she have forgotten her backpack?

He lifted the bedspread, and their eyes met with full recognition. She knew him. He wanted to kill her, but she still didn't know why. Her heart beat fiercely.

"Hello, Tianna." He spoke in a sweet, silky voice, as if they had known each other for a long time. His blue eyes sparkled with yellow lights and seemed to bore into her head. His lips curled, but not exactly into a smile—there was too much hate and contempt in it.

"I knew we'd catch you one day, Tianna, I just never expected it to be this easy. You always gave us such fine combat and chase." He seemed truly disappointed.

Instinct told her not to look in his eyes, but it was hard to pull away. Then she realized he had made one big mistake. She smiled, enjoying his sudden confusion. His face was too close to the toe of her boot. She edged her foot back, but something stopped her. Was he controlling her? She didn't think so. It was more a feeling that she couldn't attack, she could only defend. Where had that come from? Some mysterious force inside her seemed to have taken control.

"Come out now." His hand reached for her ankle, and in a flash she made her decision. She knocked his glasses off with the tip of her boot, then kicked again, batting them away. While he was patting the floor, searching for his glasses, she scrambled out the other side of the bed, jumped over it, grabbed her backpack and diary, and ran toward the door.

The guy with the snake tattoo blocked her exit. "Where do you think you're going?"

There was no way she could get around him.

He was enormous, like a football player. She glanced at his face. His eyes held hers, and his thoughts pushed right through her skull. She blinked and shook her head, but she couldn't get rid of the feeling that he was still inside her mind, telling her to go back and sit on the bed.

He laughed at her struggle.

"Sorry," she whispered as she made her decision.

"Sorry?" he repeated.

She brought her leg back as if ready for the goal, but at the last second the mysterious force held her back again and kept her from completing the kick. Instead, she pushed him hard, knocking him off balance. That gave her enough time to dart around him.

He lunged for her like a nose tackle, arms stretched in front of him, and fell flat on his stomach behind her with a loud *oof* as he grabbed her ankle. The table in the hallway skidded and a crystal vase on top rocked back and forth.

"I knew I could count on you to make this fun, Tianna, you always do," the one with the snake tattoo said as he squeezed her ankle tightly.

"Do I know you?" she asked, trying desperately to kick off her boot.

A startled expression crossed his face. "You don't remember, do you?"

"Remember what?" she yelled back with a surge of adrenaline.

"Justin," he shouted. "She doesn't remember."

"I told you, Mason." Justin's excited voice came from the other room. "You said you hadn't been able to take anything from her, but I knew you got her Tuesday, and you did."

Mason was distracted for an instant, and he loosened his grip. That was all she needed. She yanked back and as she did, her hand accidentally batted the table. The crystal vase tumbled and hit him hard on the top of the head.

"Whoops," she said, even though she knew it couldn't be her fault. She scooted backward, then got up and ran.

He was too large and awkward. She was already at the top of the stairs when he finally stood. At the front door she heard his footsteps thundering behind her. She swung open the door and it hit the wall with a bang. She reached back and closed it, hoping to stall them for precious seconds.

She bounded down the front steps.

A loud crashing sound made her glance back. They had knocked open the door and were following her, eyes glowing.

She tasted fear, her mouth so dry she couldn't swallow, and then she felt their combined mental attack. Against her will she slowed her pace. What kind of creatures were they? She tried to run faster, but her legs begged her to stop. She didn't know how much longer she could fight them. She wanted to surrender and stare into their compelling eyes.

Already she could hear their heavy breathing. They were too close. She was not going to make it.

CHAPTER EIGHT

AT THAT MOMENT Tianna spied a skateboard. Her hand acted on its own, and before she knew what was happening she had grabbed the board, sent it rolling, and jumped on. Two strokes with her right foot, then she pumped, moving her knees from side to side. She curved down the front sidewalk, bumping over the bricks, and just before reaching the front steps, she turned a high ollie and landed on the thick iron banister. She tailslid down the rail, then bent her knees to cushion her landing and kept going.

"Awesome," she breathed, impressed with herself.

She jetted down the middle of the street, the breeze rushing through her hair. She dodged around traffic and eased up on the sidewalk and back out into the street again.

When she was a mile away, she slowed. She didn't know where she was and she didn't care. At least she had gotten away, and apparently she had gone far enough so their powerful mind control couldn't reach her. Why would they want her? There was nothing special about her.

She continued past a parking lot and a taco stand, then looked up and saw that she was at the crossroad of Hollywood Boulevard and Vine. Kids in front of a bar started an impromptu rap. Pedestrians hurried around the hat the kids had set on the sidewalk for tips. She passed a tattoo-and-piercing parlor, a movie memorabilia shop, and a doughnut stand.

Tianna turned the skateboard and wove through tourists gathered around a pink granite star embedded in the sidewalk. She hopped off the curb and sped down the middle of a side street, pumping. She glanced back. No one was following.

When she faced forward again, a black Oldsmobile was racing toward her, engine roaring. She jumped and rode the board over the top of the car, down the back windshield, and off the trunk.

The car screeched to a stop.

She did a one-eighty, whirling around to face the driver and see what kind of damage she had caused, then she did a wheelie stop near the back of the car.

Mason stepped out and grinned at her.

She grabbed the skateboard and heaved it at him, then ran. She ducked behind a line of parked cars and scurried forward, her breath coming in rapid gulps. She scrambled across a parking lot as the sun balanced on the horizon, then crouched low behind a delivery truck. She felt as if she were drowning in her own fear.

She peered from behind the bumper. She couldn't see either of them, but she had an inexplicable feeling that they were close. With a shudder she understood why. An eerie prickling sensation rolled inside her head, and she wondered if they could send out brain waves like some kind of mental radar, searching for her. She knew that she needed to get farther away.

She dodged into an alley that smelled of rotting garbage and kicked through newspapers and broken beer bottles, then climbed a Cyclone fence. The gate swayed back and forth like a snake trying to shake her off. She jumped from the top and landed in the trash that had swept against the bottom of the wire mesh.

She sprinted past a rusted Dumpster and stopped, then twirled around, the stench unbearable. She had boxed herself in. She heard a sound and turned. Justin had the toe of his shoe in the wire mesh and started to climb the fence.

"Hi, Tianna." Mason stood beside him, casting a huge shadow down the alley.

CHAPTER NINE

JUSTIN GRINNED AT HER as his hand reached the top of the gate. She let out a sigh. This was it. She wished the mesh in the fence were too small for his feet.

Abruptly he slipped. He slid down the front of the fence and landed on the ground. He looked back at her, surprised, then over at Mason. "I thought you said you got her."

"I did," Mason explained.

"Well, then, did she get her memories back?" Justin asked.

Mason cautioned him to be quiet. "Shut

up!" He scowled and looked back at Tianna.

Justin tried again to push the toe of his shoe into the mesh, but this time it didn't fit. "We still have you," he shouted angrily.

"She has to come out this way," Mason agreed, and motioned to Justin. They walked back to the entrance of the alley.

"We'll be waiting for you, Tianna," Justin said, taunting her.

She knew he was right. That was the only way to get out, and already she could feel their thoughts piercing through her mind, telling her to surrender.

She took refuge behind the Dumpster. Those guys weren't ordinary people, but then she smiled to herself. She was beginning to think that she was no ordinary girl. For the second time today, she had thought something and it had happened. She hated to think that she had actually broken Michelle's ankle. That had never been her intent, but she had desperately wanted the mesh to become smaller, and it had. Could it have just been a coincidence? She hoped not.

She leaned against a brick wall and studied a stack of old newspapers next to a crate of blackened lettuce leaves. In her mind's eye she pictured the edges moving.

She watched in wonder as the stale newsprint fluttered.

She sucked in her breath. Had it only been her imagination? Now she let her mind expand. She pictured the pages opening, and they did.

"Cool," she whispered, and smiled. "Now dance around the alley."

The papers wavered, then glided about in a strange collage, flapping like the wings of giant cranes.

She turned away, and the papers fell to the ground again. She saw an apple core. She imagined it flying over the fence and landing at Justin's feet.

The apple core zipped away. She peeked from behind the Dumpster as it landed in front of Justin.

He picked up the apple core and turned. In the instant their eyes met, he knew.

"Good luck catching me now!" she yelled at him.

He nudged Mason and they both started walking down the alley toward the fence. The air shimmered in front of them with purple heat waves seeping from their eyes.

"Too late," she said. "You had your chance." She darted behind the Dumpster. She had heard about telekinetic phenomena. Where she had heard about it she didn't know, but she knew telekinesis was the ability to move objects by thinking about them. She felt thrilled with the possibilities of her newfound power.

She wondered if she could move larger things, too. She glanced at the Dumpster, narrowed her eyes in concentration, and strained. The side of the Dumpster buckled with a sharp pop. She gasped. Could she bend objects, too?

A noise like rattling chains startled her, and she peered back down the alley. Justin and Mason were shaking the double gate in the fence as if they were trying to break the chain lock. She turned back to the trash piled at the dead end and raised her hands like a great conductor of an orchestra. Soon lettuce leaves, orange peels, coffee grounds, and papers were flying everywhere. With a flick of her wrists, the garbage bounced away from her, heading for Justin and Mason.

Without warning she let everything fall. Trash and garbage rained down on them. She laughed, and even though she could feel the sting of their minds, she didn't turn away yet.

Windows above her opened and people leaned over their sills, staring down into the alley.

"What's going on?" a woman screamed.

Tianna looked up. That's when she saw the fire escape over her head.

When the woman ducked back inside her apartment, Tianna concentrated and willed the iron ladder to lower. It did. She picked up her backpack, swung it over her shoulders, grabbed the rung, and climbed up to the fire escape. She continued up the stairs until she found an open window.

Cautiously she climbed inside a stranger's apartment and tiptoed toward what she thought must be the front door. She had her hand on the doorknob, twisting it, when a young woman came out from another room, carrying a baby in her arms. She stopped and stared, speechless, at Tianna.

"Oops, wrong apartment." Tianna hurried out the door, then continued down the long hallway to the fire stairs and outside.

She walked in the cool evening air and took a deep breath, feeling safe at last. She had started to pass a storefront when someone grabbed her arm and yanked her inside.

CHAPTER TEN

TIANNA TURNED, READY to defend herself. "Jimena," she sighed, and let her hands drop back to her sides.

"Estás escamada," Jimena whispered, and her eyes darted outside as if she were searching for the danger. "What scared you?"

Tianna shook her head. "I'm not afraid."

"*Mentirosa.* Why do you always lie to me? Your fingers are cold and trembling. What happened?" Jimena gazed at her with her witching eyes, all dark and smoldering as if she were working some kind of black magic on her, then the moment ended and Jimena shook her head and scowled. "What's with you? Don't you know how dangerous it is out there? What were you doing walking down those streets alone, anyway?"

Tianna searched for an excuse, then drew back. What made Jimena think it was any of her business? "I was just taking in the sights like any tourist," she lied defiantly.

"Well, don't," Jimena warned her. "Not in this part of town. You don't understand how *peligroso* it is at night here."

"Are you talking about gangbangers or drug users?" Tianna snickered. "I'm not scared of them." She wondered what Jimena would do if she knew what kind of strange creatures had been chasing her.

"You think I'm talking about some *vato loco* or a *tecato*. You don't even know."

Jimena's dismissive manner angered Tianna. She started to say something and stopped. She couldn't tell Jimena what had really happened, and even if she did, there was no way Jimena would believe her.

"Maybe you'd better rest here for a while." Jimena softened suddenly.

"Do I look like I need to rest?" Tianna glared at her.

"After the way you played soccer today, you deserve a rest." Jimena smiled, her charm rekindled, and once again there was something captivating about the way her eyes sparkled. "You were awesome. Come on. You can't go back out there now. I'll give you a ride home after."

"After what?" Tianna asked.

Jimena lifted a heavy black curtain and Tianna looked inside, surprised. She had thought the storefront was vacant, but she was in some kind of performance bar.

Kids were crowded around a foot-high stage. Serena stood there under the only light in the entire room, reciting poetry. She looked beautiful, all in black, her eyes sad and cast down, reading from a sheet of paper, her lips against a mike.

Tianna nudged through the crowd behind Jimena, then squeezed into a seat at a table and shoved her backpack underneath. Graffiti with disturbing messages covered the tabletop.

A girl with multiple piercings and red eye shadow around bleary eyes set a bowl of gummy bears on the table and handed Tianna a menu.

"Go ahead and order." Jimena sipped an oversized latte. "I'll treat."

"I've got money," Tianna lied. She didn't really have any that she could spare. She needed every dime to run away.

"Yeah, but you need your *plata*." Jimena looked at her knowingly. "I can recognize someone who's on the run."

She started to protest but stopped. "Thanks. I'll have a mocha."

"De nada." Jimena smiled.

Minutes later the waitress brought back a cup the size of a soup bowl filled with steaming chocolate-flavored coffee and topped with whipped cream and chocolate shavings. Tianna realized she hadn't eaten anything since the bite of muffin early in the morning.

She sipped the brew, enjoying the rich, sweet taste, and listened to Serena recite a poem about her demon lover. It made Tianna think more than ever that Serena was some kind of witch or worse. How could she know so much about temptation and choosing between good and evil? The words sent chills through Tianna. She glanced around the room. Celebrities in sweats and baseball caps trying to be inconspicuous sat next to punks, goths, gangbangers, and students from UCLA. All of them seemed captivated by Serena's words.

Tianna liked the artsy vibration. Canvases of new art hung next to poems kids had written on the walls in large letters with Day-Glo felt markers.

Serena started another poem about the moon and hope.

"She's good, huh?" Jimena whispered.

Tianna started to say yes, but a guy with a safety pin through his eyebrow shot them a warning look, and instead she only nodded and glanced back at the stage.

Finally Serena finished and walked back toward Tianna and Jimena. Kids were shaking her hand and asking for copies of her poetry.

Jimena stood. "Come on, we'll meet her out front."

When they got to the door, Jimena opened it and looked cautiously up and down the street.

"Who are you looking for?" Tianna asked, wondering what Jimena had expected to see.

"Just being careful." Jimena smiled. "My car's parked a block away."

They started walking, and soon Serena caught up to them.

"Great game," she congratulated Tianna.

"Thanks. I loved your poetry." Tianna returned the compliment, then she looked at Jimena. She had forgotten to ask. "Did we win?"

"Decca never got a goal past Jimena," Serena announced proudly. "She was incredible."

"Yeah, but we needed the goal Tianna made," Jimena added, and then her mood became more serious. "What did you see out here tonight that frightened you, Tianna?"

"Nothing." Tianna wasn't in the mood to answer questions. Maybe she should go to the bus station. "Look, I live close by," she lied. "I think I'll just walk."

"It's safer if you stay with us," Jimena said as they passed a Laundromat with its smells of bleach and detergent drifting into the air.

"Why?" Tianna asked, wondering what they knew. "What's so dangerous in this area of town?"

"Just your normal freaks and perverts," Serena answered with a grin. "They like to hang out here."

Tianna glanced at her to see if she was teasing. She looked dead serious, but Tianna had a feeling that there was more she wasn't saying, and then her eyes changed. It was startling the way her pupils opened and dilated. At the same time Tianna felt a black wave rush across her mind, followed by a tingling, as if worms were crawling through her brain. Had Serena done that? Or were Justin and Mason back? She studied the old storefront buildings behind her, lit up by blue, green, and pink neon lights. Nothing looked menacing, and the odd feeling in her head was gone now, anyway. Maybe she was only supertired and hungry.

"Was someone chasing you?" Serena asked unexpectedly.

Tianna looked back at her. "Why would you ask that?"

"Just if you were afraid, I thought maybe someone had been bothering you." Serena glanced behind them as if she were checking the street for danger.

At the same time Jimena seemed to study the shadows in an odd way.

"What are you looking for?" Tianna asked nervously.

Serena grabbed her arm. She had that same enchantress smile as Jimena. "You know, don't you? Do you want to talk about it?"

Tianna stopped. What did Serena mean? She felt a rush of confusion, and then anger took over. "I just wish you'd both go away and stop bothering me."

They looked at her, surprised.

And in an instant she realized she had made a wish. "I don't mean it," she added quickly, terrified that her thought might make something happen to them. She hated to think she could actually make people disappear, but she didn't understand her power yet and she didn't want to harm them accidentally the way she had hurt Michelle.

Jimena and Serena looked at her oddly, and under the streetlight a gold aura seemed to flutter around them and billow out into the cold night. Then suddenly Jimena stared at her, sightless, as if she were in a trance.

Tianna felt the blood rush from her head, and she had to grab the fender of a parked Toyota to keep from swaying. What had she done this time? Jimena looked bad. She glanced at Serena. She still seemed normal. At least she hadn't harmed them both.

"I'm so sorry," Tianna whispered. "I didn't mean to hurt her. I just didn't want you to ask me any more questions."

"Hurt who?" Serena stepped closer, her eyes compassionate.

"Jimena," Tianna blurted. "Look at her. I didn't want to do that."

Serena turned slowly and looked at Jimena. She acted as if she were used to seeing Jimena stare sightless into the night.

"What do you mean?" Serena asked.

"I put Jimena in some kind of stupor," Tianna confessed with growing panic. "Can't you see? She's not moving. Maybe we should get her to the hospital."

Serena snickered. "She's fine." But then she turned back with a swiftness that made Tianna flinch. "But why would you think you had done that to her?"

Tianna leaned over the back of the car, trying to gather her thoughts. The metal felt cold and comforting against her flushed cheek. "I did it. You don't understand what I can do."

Serena patted Tianna's back as if she were trying to comfort her. "Why don't you tell me what you're talking about."

"I broke Michelle's ankle," Tianna confessed.

"You couldn't have," Serena answered. "I was watching the whole time. You were too far away."

Tianna pushed herself up, ready to explain everything, but before she could, Jimena shuddered and a smile crossed her face. She glanced at Tianna, then Serena, as if nothing strange had just transpired.

"Did you see something?" Serena asked Jimena in a low voice.

Jimena nodded. Happiness seemed to bubble inside her and spill over into the night air.

"I can't wait to hear." Serena's eagerness matched Jimena's.

Tianna felt relieved. She hadn't done anything to Jimena. But then she felt flustered. If she hadn't put Jimena in a trance, what had just happened? Quickly, new apprehension took hold. Jimena must have been working a spell, trying to divine something, and Serena had known all along what she was doing. Apparently the spell had worked. Jimena had seen something, but what? Tianna had a creepy feeling it involved her.

"Okay, here's the car." Jimena pulled out a key on a silver chain and stepped to an '81 Oldsmobile that sparkled as if it were new.

"Nice car," Tianna said.

"It belongs to my brother," Jimena explained. "He lets me drive it when he's home from San Diego even though I don't have a license yet."

"You don't?" Tianna wondered if it was safe to ride with her.

Jimena smiled and seemed to read her thoughts. "I'm safe. I learned how to drive jacking cars."

"So it's true what I heard about you?" Tianna stared at her in disbelief.

"It's not like she does it anymore," Serena put in, and then she changed the subject. "Tianna was worried she did something to you, Jimena."

Jimena glanced at Tianna, her eyes laughing. "Why would you think that?"

"You looked odd," Tianna answered. "That's all." She really didn't want to say any more. She wanted to get away from them.

"I'm sorry you were worried. I'm fine," Jimena reassured her.

"She thinks she broke Michelle's ankle." Serena opened the car door.

"I wished it," Tianna mumbled. "But I didn't really want it to happen."

Then they both laughed.

"You're so superstitious," Serena said. "Is that all?"

"Yeah, a wish can't make something come true," Jimena added. "If it could, half the people walking around would be dead."

Tianna didn't say more. Let them think whatever they wanted. She was never going to see them again after this night, anyway.

If she'd had any doubt before, she was convinced now that Jimena and Serena were witches. She wondered if the guys chasing her could be some kind of warlocks who belonged to the same clan. She didn't think so. Jimena and Serena seemed too nice, and Justin and Mason had an aura of evil about them.

"Get in," Jimena said. "I'll give you a ride home."

"Come on," Serena coaxed. "It's safer with us than on the street."

Tianna looked back at the night. She wanted

to go to the bus station and leave now, but it might take her hours to find it. Besides, she felt too tired to walk, and she definitely didn't want to run into Justin and Mason again. Reluctantly she opened the car door and slid inside.

Jimena turned the ignition. Music boomed from the speakers, making Tianna's heart vibrate with the beat.

CHAPTER ELEVEN

"DON'T YOU REMEMBER where you live?" Jimena asked after traveling down Wilshire Boulevard between the La Brea Tar Pits and Ralph's grocery store for the fourth time.

"It's nearby," Tianna answered. She could picture the apartment clearly in her mind. She just didn't know where to find it. "Someplace around here. I just moved in."

Serena glanced at her watch again. "It's getting late. I promised my dad I'd be home before eight."

"I think if you just turn right at the next

block." Tianna wished she hadn't taken the ride with them. Why had she assumed she would be able to remember enough to find her way back to the apartment building? Los Angeles was huge.

"Serena, would you find out?" Jimena asked impatiently, and shut off the music.

The silence made Tianna's ears ring.

"How's she going to know?" Tianna started to ask, but stopped suddenly.

Serena leaned over the car seat. There was something uncanny about the way her eyes dilated, as if some kind of power were building inside her. Tianna wanted to look away, but she felt compelled to stare. It wasn't frightening, but warm and soothing in a dreamy way, even though she didn't like the inexplicable feeling of fingers wiggling through her brain.

Then suddenly the feeling was gone and Serena looked at her with fascination. "It's one of the old apartment buildings over by Ralph's on Wilshire," she said to Jimena. "We've passed the street already."

Tianna braced herself as Jimena made a big

looping U-turn and started down Wilshire in the opposite direction.

"How did you know?" Tianna asked, amazed. "You saw . . . did you read my mind? You did."

Serena laughed, and the sound was magical. "No one can do that."

"But you did," Tianna said, dismayed. "I felt something when you looked at me."

"You couldn't have," Serena insisted. "Because I didn't."

"Then how did you know where I live?" Tianna didn't believe her. She wondered what else she might have seen. Did she know she couldn't remember anything before this morning? Or that she planned to run away?

"That one." Serena pointed.

Jimena pulled the car over to the side of the road in front of the same apartment building that Tianna had left earlier that day. She pressed the brake hard and turned off the car engine.

"Thanks." Tianna grabbed her backpack and hurried to get out. She had had enough of these two. They were nice, but way spooky. Before she could open the door, Serena turned back and locked it. She kept her finger on the lock, pressing down.

"Now we need some answers, Tianna." Serena spoke softly. "What are you running from?"

"That's a strange thing to ask," Tianna answered.

"If you knew everything about us, you wouldn't think it was," Serena explained. "Jimena and I can help you. Do you know why they want you?"

"No one's chasing me," Tianna insisted.

"I'm pretty sure I know who is after you," Serena said. "But I don't understand why."

"Couldn't you see?" Jimena asked, looking baffled.

"There was nothing to see," Serena explained to Jimena.

"How can that be?" Jimena jerked around and stared at Tianna in amazement.

Serena shrugged. "Everything was blank. She only has a few memories."

"You did read my mind." Tianna accused her angrily.

Serena smiled sheepishly. "Only because we want to help you."

Tianna used the moment to bat Serena's hand away, unlock the car, and scramble outside.

"Hey!" Serena called after her. "Come back."

"No way!" Tianna yelled.

Jimena opened the car door and shouted after her, "You need our help, Tianna."

"I don't want you to help me."

Their offer to help only made her uneasy. How could she trust them after the strange way they had behaved? Besides, all she wanted to do was eat, sleep, and run. Tomorrow at dawn she was going to be on a Greyhound, waving goodbye to L.A. and all its crazy people.

Tianna rushed into the apartment building and slammed the door, half afraid Serena and Jimena would chase after her. She glanced out the side window and watched Jimena's car pull away from the curb. She let out a sigh. She was starving and hoped there was something good in the refrigerator.

Her excitement was building as she ran up the stairs. Maybe there would be someone waiting for her inside with a big cheese pizza, chocolate-chip cookies, and a huge glass of milk. And if someone were there, then she wouldn't have to run away. She would have a home and someone who loved and cared for her.

As she reached the landing, Hanna stepped in front of her.

"There you are." Hanna popped a green olive in her mouth. "I've been waiting for you." The smells coming from inside Hanna's apartment made Tianna's stomach grumble. She breathed deeply, inhaling in the warm spicy smells.

"Why?" Tianna asked impatiently. Her stomach felt as if it had acid in it.

"I have a favor to ask." Hanna smiled.

"Sure," Tianna said. "Right after dinner. I'll come back."

"It's really quite urgent," Hanna insisted. "My friends and I need a fourth person for our séance."

"Séance?" Tianna couldn't believe what she was hearing. This day wouldn't get any weirder.

"Won't you join us?" Hanna pleaded. "We have to have a fourth person to make our circle complete."

Tianna shook her head. "Sorry." That was the last thing in the world she wanted to do. With everything else that had happened today, she didn't need to see a ghost, too. "No, but thanks for asking."

She started to dart away, but Hanna grabbed her hand.

"I made my beef brisket," Hanna coaxed. "Everyone says it's delicious. After dinner we'll pull out the Ouija board. The séance won't take longer than an hour. You'll still have time to study."

"Another night. I think my mom's waiting for me," Tianna said, eager to get away.

"If you change your mind," Hanna yelled after her, "there's still time. We won't start until after we eat."

"Okay," Tianna called over her shoulder.

The door to her apartment was unlocked. She didn't remember locking it when she ran out that morning. She entered and quickly closed it behind her. The interior still smelled of Pine-Sol and looked the same as when she had left it earlier. She tossed her backpack on the bed and opened the refrigerator. It was empty except for a box of baking soda. She quickly looked through cupboards and drawers. All were barren.

The truth hit her, and she sat on the bed with a heavy sigh. She was a squatter. She didn't somehow rent the apartment. This had never been her home. She had broken into it.

Now the aromas of onions and coffee coming from Hanna's apartment were more than she could bear.

CHAPTER TWELVE

HANNA'S APARTMENT WAS larger than the one Tianna had claimed. There was a small kitchen off the living room and a bedroom in the back down a long hallway. Tianna sat at a round dining table, eating off sparkling white china. A small oscillating fan on the sideboard swung lazily back and forth, making the edge of the red tablecloth float up, then down.

"That's the best brisket I've ever made, if I do say so myself," Hanna announced.

Tianna nodded and scooped more gravy onto her potatoes. "You're a great cook," she repeated for perhaps the fourth time. "Everything's delicious."

"It doesn't look like you're going to have any problem with leftovers." Hanna's friend Sylvia smirked. She had red hair like a flame and wore a long gray dress with three strings of pearls.

"I used to eat like that when I was young," Hanna's sister, Trudy, put in. She was a short chubby woman with a walker.

Tianna glanced up. They were watching her. Then she realized she was the only one still eating.

"Do you want some more peas, dear?" Hanna asked, and handed her the bowl.

"No, thanks." Tianna put down her fork.

Hanna slapped the sides of the table, making the silverware jingle. "Let's get this cleared and into the dishwasher, then we can start."

Tianna stood. Her stomach felt stuffed, but the feeling was a good one.

After the table was cleared and the dishes neatly stacked in the dishwasher, Hanna placed candles about the room, then arranged more in a circle in the middle of the table around a Ouija board.

"So who are you trying to contact?" Tianna pushed her hair back.

Hanna turned and smiled at her, eyes misting. "Skinanbone."

"Skinanbone?" Tianna asked.

"My Chihuahua, may he rest in peace." Hanna reverentially placed a tiny black dog collar with silver studs on the table near the Ouija board. A small gold heart and dog license tags were attached to a metal clasp near the buckle.

Then Hanna and Sylvia each took a book of matches and started lighting the candles. Wicks sparked and wisps of smoke made serpentine patterns in the air. The flames bent sideways each time they caught the breeze from the fan.

Trudy sadly pointed to a picture on the piano of a Chihuahua wearing a red sweater. "That's Skinanbone."

"What happened to him?" Tianna asked as Hanna turned off the lights.

Sylvia pulled out her chair and sat down.

"Another dog just grabbed him up and stole him away."

"That's horrible," Tianna said.

Trudy pointed to a corner of the room and whispered, "Hanna still hasn't been able to clear out his things."

A red pillow sat next to a comfortable chair. Dog toys were piled high in a basket.

"That's where Skinanbone slept while I watched TV," Hanna added as she joined them.

Sylvia nodded. "They always watched the nightly news together. They both loved weather."

"Shall we hold hands and begin?" Hanna had a solemn look. "We do the séance first," she explained to Tianna, "and try to call up his spirit. Then we use the Ouija board and see if he has anything to communicate."

Tianna nodded and Hanna clasped her hand tightly, then Sylvia grasped her other hand and their circle was complete.

There was a moment of silence. Tianna wasn't sure what to do.

Hanna looked up, took a deep breath, then

closed her eyes and whistled, loud and long. "Here, Skinanbone," she called. "Here, boy, come home to Mommy."

Tianna bit her lower lip and glanced around the table. Sylvia's eyes were closed and her head was back, lifted toward the ceiling in total concentration, and Trudy gazed upward with a hopeful expression.

"Say something, Trudy," Hanna urged. "He was always close to you."

"Come here, Skinanbone." Trudy spoke dramatically. "Your mommy's been crying for you."

Tianna could sense how much the women missed Skinanbone. Maybe she could make them feel as if they had contacted him. It would be her thank-you for such a tasty and generous dinner. That was the least she could do.

She concentrated on the dog collar until it lifted into the air to where she imagined Skinanbone's neck might be if he were standing on the table. Then she jiggled it from side to side as though the dog were shaking his head.

Hanna's eyes burst open. "Skinanbone!"

"Is it really him?" Sylvia asked, and opened her eyes. "Oh, my."

"What?" Trudy looked from one woman to the other.

"Look," Hanna shouted.

Tianna wiggled the dog collar again.

"He's back," Trudy declared. "Praise be."

"We miss you, you sweet little puppy," Hanna said in a babyish voice. "How is doggie heaven?"

Tianna concentrated again. This was harder to do, but finally she made the dog collar fly from the table in a natural arc as if Skinanbone had leapt from it. Then she moved the collar over to the doggie bed in the corner and used her power to press into the red pillow below the collar to make it look as if tiny paws were walking over it.

"Hanna, look!" Trudy motioned with her head.

"What?" Hanna asked.

"His box!" Sylvia shouted. "Look at his box!"

Tianna focused, trying to make the tiny paw

prints circle the way dogs do before they settle for a nap.

"He always made me dizzy when he did that," Trudy said in a wistful voice, then she sighed. "He was such a sweetie."

Tianna slipped deeper and deeper into herself as she concentrated more. She made the collar rush to the box of dog toys, then tried to make it appear as if a very small dog ghost had bitten into a ball and was dashing away with it.

The women squealed.

"He wants to play," Hanna exclaimed happily.

Suddenly the voices of the women became fainter, then Tianna's vision blurred and the room seemed to shift as though she were hovering over it and far away. Reality wrinkled, and it was as if Tianna were looking at everything through pebbled glass.

She blinked and shook her head, but that didn't make things move back the way they had been before. She could no longer hear Hanna, Sylvia, or Trudy. There was only a rushing sound like wind or water.

At last the glass rippled and broke apart, and she was alone in a cold and murky place. It was like being in the middle of nowhere, but something about it was familiar, as if she had seen it before. She felt on the verge of recalling some important memory.

Then the air around her stirred and a white cloud formed from churning mists and came toward her. A girl about her age floated in the delicate vapor. She sensed something good about her and thought perhaps she was some kind of guardian angel, one that had no wings.

The girl looked at Tianna with frightened eyes, but the fear only made her beauty more divine. Tianna wondered if she had known her once in this life before something tragic had happened and she had passed on to the other side.

"Go," the girl mouthed, and waved her hands as if warning Tianna away.

She looked behind her. Where could she go? Nothingness surrounded her. She wondered if she had broken into heaven, but then behind the girl a black-night shadow formed. Crimson waves shimmered from the dark form, and Tianna knew it was more likely she had fallen into hell. There was something unholy about the dusky shape, and the cold emanating from it. She began to shiver.

The black vapor twirled, then swept toward her. The girl tried to stop it, but the demon shadow twisted around her and shot at Tianna with a speed that made the air vibrate.

Tianna shrieked and screamed again, knowing it had her.

Then she felt warm hands touching her cheeks. She shook her head, and suddenly she was back in Hanna's living room and everyone was staring at her.

Sylvia held her arm and Hanna patted her face.

"Don't be scared," Hanna said, "Skinanbone was a loving little pup." There were tears in her eyes. "He would never, ever hurt you. I promise, dear."

"You'd love him if you ever met him in real life," Trudy added.

But Sylvia continued to stare at her oddly.

"Tianna has some kind of special power," Sylvia remarked.

"What do you mean?" Tianna asked in a shaky voice.

"We've never been able to make contact with Skinanbone before," Sylvia said. "But tonight we could because you're here."

"And what happened, dear?" Hanna asked. "You were in a trance or something. We had a hard time waking you."

"Mediums always do that," Trudy said. "You know that, Hanna. They have to go into a trance to call up the dead."

Tianna's heart beat rapidly, and she wondered if she had actually made contact with the spirit world. She glanced about her. The shadows in the living room all had a bloodred cast now and a strange texture as if they were solid and warm.

She knocked back her chair and rushed from the room.

Chapter Thirteen

Tianna cautiously entered her apartment and looked around. A sudden scraping sound startled her. She glanced at the window and thought she saw a face staring back at her, but quickly realized it was only the limb of a tree. The twiggy branches continued to grate across the glass. She shut the door and flicked on the light. Everything seemed normal, but she couldn't stop the shaking of her hands.

Footsteps in the hallway made her alert. She listened carefully to the voices, but the people didn't sound as if they were trying not to be heard.

She pressed her ear against the wood anyway. They walked right by. Fear was clouding her thinking and making her too edgy. She tried to convince herself that she would be secure here for the night. At least she hoped she would be, but she wondered if she could ever feel safe anywhere again.

"What am I going to do?" she said aloud, trying to give herself comfort, but the tremor in her voice only made her more afraid.

She considered what had happened in Hanna's apartment. It felt as if she had lifted some kind of barrier and uncovered another world. She shuddered. The shadow had felt completely evil.

Slowly she took off her boots and wiggled her toes. Maybe that other world was the dimension she belonged in. Could it be that Mason and Justin were only trying to take her home? She shook her head. She didn't think so.

The bed looked inviting. She needed to lie down and sleep. She felt exhausted, but she was afraid to stay in this tiny, enclosed space. It could too easily become a trap. She stared at the dark shape of the hulking tree pressing against the window. Maybe that was a possibility. She opened the window. The screen was already gone. She looked down. It rested in the lawn under the bluish light of a security lamp. She must have crawled in through this window the night before. She leaned out now and looked up.

It felt safer to sleep on the roof, and she thought she could use the tree to crawl up there. Within minutes she had rolled a pink blanket and the bedspread into a tight ball, then tied them to her backpack, swung both onto her back, crawled out the window onto the branch, and used the tree limbs to climb to the roof.

Her body began to unwind. It felt safer here under the stars. She curled into her blanket and rested her head on her backpack, gazing up at the moon. She noticed that it was on its waning cycle and almost dark. Her heart started beating rapidly. She didn't understand why the ebbing moon should fill her with such a growing sense of urgency, but it did. She felt that there was something important she was supposed to do, but she couldn't remember what.

CHAPTER FOURTEEN

TIANNA WOKE WITH the gentle feeling of sunshine warming her face and an opulent deep turquoise sky over her head. She stretched and smiled, recalling yesterday. As horrible as the day had been, it was still a sweet pleasure to be able to have some memory of her life before this moment.

The aromas of biscuits and coffee drifted up to her, and she wondered idly what Hanna was fixing for breakfast. She thought about last night. Now, in the daylight with a soft breeze caressing her face, what had happened in Hanna's apartment seemed unreal. She tried to recall how dead scared she had felt, but the feeling of terror had slipped away in her slumber. Maybe she had fallen asleep at the table after all and only conjured the girl in her dream. She had been in a torpor from such a big meal. She had probably dozed off. Maybe she should try again and see.

She rolled up her blanket, grabbed her backpack, and crawled down the tree. Everything inside the small apartment looked the same. She shut the window behind her and threw her bundle and backpack on the bed. She wanted something to eat, but first on her list was a long, hot shower. She stepped into the small bathroom, turned the spigot, stripped, and climbed under the luxurious spray.

It felt too dangerous to stay in Los Angeles, and fortunately she had enough money to buy a bus ticket, so as soon as she dressed, she was going to leave. She didn't know why Justin and Mason wanted her so badly, but she didn't need to stick around and discover the reason.

She turned off the water and stepped out.

There were no towels in the bathroom, so she pulled the sheet from the bed and wrapped it tightly around her. She sat in the sunshine cascading into the room and worked a comb through her hair. She thought again about the strange sensation yesterday of going into another dimension. She was more curious than afraid now and wondered if she could make it happen again.

Maybe it was part of her power. She tried to ignore the compulsion to return to that other world and focused instead on untangling her long black hair. It could be risky. Last night Hanna had been there and she had pulled her back somehow, but now she was alone. What would happen if she couldn't get back to reality?

She flipped the comb aside. Why was she hesitating? It wasn't like she had anything to lose. She couldn't recall her family or her friends, and just possibly what had happened to her had something to do with that other place. More than anything she wanted to remember so she could get back home. It was worth a try. Besides, how was she going to learn how to leave that realm unless she went there and came back? She'd only stay for a moment. It had probably been a dream, anyway, so why wait? Find out now.

She stared at the wall. The wind sighed and brushed through the tree branches outside and made spangled sunlight sway back and forth across the apartment in a mesmerizing way. She concentrated and tried to use the same mental energy she had used last night to put the paw prints in Skinanbone's pillow.

Soon the gray-green paint bubbled. Then the plaster buckled and crumbled away, exposing the laths. The thin boards snapped and a swirl of dust climbed into the air. At last her vision blurred and the world seemed far away, as if she were looking through gritty textured glass. It wavered, then shattered, and Tianna was no longer in the small apartment but back in that other place.

Almost immediately she saw the same girl floating toward her. She didn't look as frightened as she had the night before, but something still seemed wrong with her.

"How did you get here?" the girl whispered, and looked behind her as if she were scared the shadow cloud might appear again. She seemed weakened and languishing, as if this dreary place was stealing her strength.

"Are you all right?" Tianna asked.

"You shouldn't be here," the girl warned her, and Tianna had the impression that something bad was happening to her. Her eyes, so bright the night before, looked joyless now.

"Where am I?" Tianna looked at the gloomy mists roiling around the girl. Were they sucking energy from her?

The girl started to answer, but then the fear crept back in her eyes. "Leave!"

"I'm not sure I know how," Tianna answered, and realized she had made a foolish mistake. She had never really believed she'd be able to get back here, and now that she was, she didn't know how to go.

"You can't stay," the girl insisted.

"Why not?" Tianna glanced nervously around her, but she didn't see anything to suggest danger, and she wanted to find out if the girl knew anything about her past. Maybe she held the key that could unlock Tianna's memories.

The girl seemed panicked now. "Don't you feel it? It knows you're here and it's coming for you."

"What knows I'm here?" Tianna asked, and at the same moment Tianna felt her body collapse under a heavy weight that filled the air with a pernicious chill.

"Leave!" the girl repeated harshly.

"How?" Tianna rubbed her arms against the cold.

The girl shrugged. "If I knew, I wouldn't be here."

"How did you get here?" Tianna asked, and reached for her hand. "Maybe we can escape together."

The girl jerked her hand back. "It's too late for me. Just save yourself."

The air closed in tightly and Tianna started to tremble as dread spread through her. She didn't see anything, but then she heard a loud whoosh and the shadow funneled into the murkiness.

The dark form hovered briefly, undulating as it grew. Tianna felt awestruck, unable to pull her eyes away. The strange cloud was beautiful in its own evil way, like a fierce approaching storm. Then suddenly it soared at her as if it had a will and a vicious human intent to destroy her.

"Run!" the girl urged. "Go. Don't let it catch you."

"Where?" Tianna looked around her. Everywhere appeared exactly the same. It was like being in the middle of the ocean without a sun. She dashed away, wanting to scream, but her mouth felt too dry.

The sheet she had wrapped around her hampered her speed. She had only gotten a little way when hands reached from the shadows and held her tight.

"No!" she screamed, struggling against the warm arms circling her.

Suddenly, it was as if a veil had ripped

between the two worlds and she was back in reality. Sunlight glared in her face.

She glanced around, still filled with panic, and was surprised to see that she now stood in front of the apartment building. When she had run from the menacing cloud in that other realm, she must have somehow changed location in this world as well. She was about to start back to the apartment when she realized someone's arms were still wrapped tightly around her. Her head whipped back to see who held her.

"Derek!" she shouted, and realized suddenly that she only had the sheet covering her.

"You were out here running like crazy," he explained, and released his hold. "You didn't hear me when I called your name. I figured something was wrong, so I caught you. What were you running from?"

She felt grateful and embarrassed at the same time. He had pulled her back and saved her from the shadow. She tightened her hold on the sheet, and Derek didn't bother to take his eyes away.

"I thought I heard a woman scream that

someone had taken her purse," she lied. "So I came outside to help."

"Like that?" He smirked.

"I sleep in the nude." It was the first thing that came to mind and it was also the worst thing to say. She rolled her eyes at his silly grin. "Look, in an emergency you don't have time to put on clothes."

He snickered. "Get dressed. I'll give you a ride to school." He pointed to a blue Ford Escort parked at the curb.

They started walking back to the apartment building. Her knees still felt shaky and twice she cast glances behind her just to make sure the shadow hadn't left its world and followed her here. She wondered what it was.

Then she stopped suddenly and eyed Derek suspiciously. "How did you know where I live?"

"I asked Michael," he explained.

"Michael knew?" She felt surprised and elated at the same time.

"Not at first," Derek said. "Michael asked Vanessa and Vanessa asked Jimena."

"Michael did all that to find out where I live?"

"For me," Derek added as they started up the steps.

"For you?" She stopped at the door and looked at him.

He blushed and didn't answer her.

"Wait here, Derek." She went inside and left him on the porch. "I'll just run upstairs and change and I'll be right back down."

"If you hurry, we can stop at Starbucks for a muffin and coffee," he offered.

"I'll hurry." But she had no intention of coming back. She was going to dress, then climb out using the tree and head for the bus stop. By the time Derek realized she was gone, she would be drinking coffee on a Greyhound.

She ran up the stairs, the sheet tangling behind her, and passed Hanna, leaving for work, the same two shopping bags clasped in her hands.

"Morning," she said, then she tried her door. It was locked.

She heard Hanna's kind laughter and turned.

"You have to be more careful," Hanna explained. "It's too easy to lock yourself out of these apartments. And look at you! What were you trying to figure out? How to fix a sheet for a toga party or something?"

Tianna nodded, but she had no idea what a toga party was.

"I didn't even think they had them anymore."

"Mom already left," Tianna said. "Can you help me?"

"I've got an extra key," Hanna explained, and started to unlock her apartment door. "The last tenant asked me to hold on to it for emergencies just like this. It might still work. I'll be right back."

Tianna waited patiently as Hanna disappeared into her apartment. When she came back to the hallway, she pinched a brass key in her fingers.

"I wanted to thank you for last night," Hanna announced as she slipped the key in the lock. "I hope you're not too afraid to try it again."

"No, I'd love to." Tianna felt bad for lying. She really liked Hanna.

"Thank you," Hanna answered softly, and worked the key. Then she pushed open the door.

"You're a lifesaver, Hanna." Tianna felt like giving her a kiss, but instead she hurried into the room.

"You'd better keep it." Hanna tried to hand her the key.

Tianna smiled. "I won't be needing it again. I promise."

"Then I'm off." Hanna turned and started toward the stairs. "See you tonight," she called back.

"Yeah," Tianna answered sadly, and shut the door.

She quickly slipped into the clean underwear from her backpack and had started pulling on the same clothes she had worn yesterday when a scratching sound made her stop. She looked around, expecting to see a mouse or a squirrel that somehow had gotten into the room from the tree.

But what she saw made her freeze in terror. She watched with alarm as the letter *H* slowly appeared on the wall above the dresser. Something or someone was writing a message. Instinct told her it wasn't a ghost. It was someone or something trying to communicate with her from that other realm.

Slowly the words *Help me I'm Catty* appeared on the wall.

Catty must be the girl she had seen. The name was unusual. It had to be Vanessa's friend, the one Michael had told her about who had disappeared. Could she have somehow been trapped in that other dimension? It had to be.

Then another scraping sound made her tense. As she stared at the first message other words were scrawled over it. *Stay away.*

CHAPTER FIFTEEN

FOR A MOMENT TIANNA sat dumbfounded, unable to move. She couldn't leave Los Angeles even if it was dangerous for her to stay. She had to help Catty. She wouldn't be able to live with herself if she ran away now because she would always know she had been a coward. She had to act even if she failed. She dressed rapidly, grabbed up her backpack, and hurried outside, her hair still wet against her back.

Derek looked up, surprised. He was sitting on the steps. "That was fast."

She walked right past him. "Hurry," she commanded.

He stood and started following her.

"Give me the keys," she ordered.

"You want to drive?" he asked.

"I'll get us to school faster," she said as she opened the driver's-side door and tossed a stack of travel magazines into the back.

"I brought the magazines for you to look at," Derek complained.

"Later." She held out her hand for the keys.

He hesitated. "Do you have a driver's license?"

"Of course," she said, not knowing if it was true or not. She was already sitting behind the steering wheel.

He tossed her the keys and she turned the ignition as he climbed into the car.

She pressed hard on the gas pedal and the car shrieked away from the curb. The back end fish-tailed. She needed to get to school quickly and find some answers. She had a feeling that Catty wasn't going to last long in that place.

The light turned yellow ahead of her.

"Slow down!" Derek shouted as the car in front of them stopped for the light.

She didn't let up.

"You're going to rear-end it!" Derek cried, and his foot pressed the floor as if he were trying to work an invisible brake.

She jerked the steering wheel, swerved smoothly around the car, and blasted through the intersection, ignoring the flurry of horns and screeching tires.

Derek snapped his seat belt in place. "Why are you in such a hurry to get to school?"

"Geometry test," she answered, and buzzed around two more cars.

At the next junction she needed to make a left-hand turn, but the line of traffic waiting for the green arrow would delay her too long. She continued in her lane, and when she reached the intersection, she turned in front of the car with the right-of-way. Angry honks followed her as she blasted onto the next street.

"We've got time, Tianna!" Derek yelled. "School doesn't start for another fifteen minutes."

Would fifteen minutes give her enough time to get the answers she needed? She didn't think so.

She pressed her foot harder on the accelerator. The school was at least a mile away, but if she ignored the next light and the next, then maybe she could get there with enough time to question Corrine. She didn't think her powers were strong enough to change the lights and she didn't want to chance endangering other drivers, but she was sure she could at least slow down the cross traffic.

She concentrated on the cars zooming east and west on Beverly Boulevard in front of her without slowing her speed.

"Tianna!" Derek yelled. "You've got a red light!"

She squinted and stalled a Jaguar in the crosswalk. Cars honked impatiently behind the car, and when a Toyota tried to speed around it, she stopped it, too. She could feel the pressure building inside her as she made a Range Rover and a pick-up slide to a halt. She shot through the busy intersection against the light.

Derek turned back. "You've got to be the luckiest person in the world."

"Right," she answered with a smirk. "I have the worst luck of anyone you can imagine."

"You?" he asked in disbelief.

"Me," she answered, and glanced in the rearview mirror. Traffic had started to flow down Beverly Boulevard again.

She sped around the corner in a tight turn.

"We're here," she said, and pressed hard on the horn to let kids in the parking lot know she was coming through.

She parked with a jerk and slammed on the brakes.

Derek bounced forward, then back. He turned and looked at her with shock in his eyes. "Where'd you learn to drive?"

"I made it up as I went along." She opened the car door and tossed him the keys. "Thanks for the lift, Derek." She grabbed her backpack and ran.

She didn't recognize Corrine at first, sitting outside the geometry classroom, legs stretched in front of her, doing some last minute cramming. She wasn't wearing makeup and her eyes looked clear, her skin fresh and beautiful.

"You look good." Tianna squatted beside her. "Tell me about Catty."

Corrine stared at her briefly, surprised, then she nervously looked around her as if she were afraid to speak. Finally she closed her geometry book and began. "I was there that night at Planet Bang," Corrine whispered. "When this girl came running inside. I didn't know who she was, but she was asking for Vanessa, Catty, Serena, and Jimena. She found them and they all went charging outside. Twenty minutes later they're back, minus Catty, and you could tell something was really wrong. They hid in the bathroom, except Jimena, who was all tough and lying for them."

"What do you mean, lying for them?" Tianna asked.

"When the police questioned them," Corrine confided. "She told the police they hadn't gone outside, but they had. I saw them. I was too afraid to say anything."

She paused as if something had made her hesitate. Tianna glanced up. Serena, Jimena, and

Vanessa were walking down the hall toward them.

"Go on," Tianna urged.

Corrine's voice was lower now. "A few blocks away all these fires had broken out and there were fire engines and police cars and all the people in the neighborhood were saying that teenagers had been playing with firecrackers and explosives."

"Is that what you think?" Tianna asked.

Corinne shook her head, and her eyes never left Serena, Jimena, and Vanessa. "I don't think it was explosives. I think the fireworks were from some kind of magical power because they never found Catty's body. I think they did something to her."

"Like what?" Tianna felt tense.

Corrine turned and looked at her. "I think they killed her."

"How?" Tianna glanced back at Serena, Jimena, and Vanessa. They might act strange, but she definitely knew they weren't capable of murder.

"I think they cast a spell and it went wrong."

Corrine finished. "There, I've said too much already."

Could Corrine be right? Maybe they were witches and they had cast a spell. But that didn't feel right. Modern witches, like wiccans, were loving and kind. It was only superstition and misunderstanding that made people think they used their charms malevolently.

She wondered if they could have done something to their friend. Maybe it had started out as fun, but a fatal mistake had been made. Then another terrifying thought came to her. Maybe they weren't witches at all but kids who dabbled with magic of a darker kind. Did they have power enough to conjure up a demon? Was that what the shadow had been?

Tianna needed her memories back now more than ever. If she could go into that other realm, then there must be something she could do to help Catty, but what? If she could only remember.

Corrine touched her arm and she jumped.

"Are you all right?" Corrine looked worried.

Tianna nodded.

"Can I borrow a pencil for the test?" she asked. "I forgot mine."

"Sure." Tianna opened her backpack and saw the diary. With everything that had been going on yesterday, she had completely forgotten about it. Now she'd have some answers. Her heart beat fast with anticipation. Maybe she'd even learn about that other dimension and then she could find a way to help Catty.

She handed Corrine the pencil and stood. "See ya."

"You'll miss the test," Corrine called after her.

"Like I care," Tianna muttered. She charged down the hallway, then ran across the blacktop to the metal detectors. She didn't want some hall monitor snooping around and sending her back to class. The best thing to do was to leave campus. The security guards at the front gate were too busy checking purses and backpacks to notice anyone running back outside.

As soon as she was away from the campus, she stood near the curb and started to read.

The social worker claims I ran away again. Of course, I didn't. Mason and Justin found me, so I had no choice but to leave. They almost caught me, too. They're getting closer. Time is running out—

Before she could read more, a hand grabbed the diary away.

CHAPTER SIXTEEN

TIANNA TURNED QUICKLY to see who had stolen her diary.

Derek opened it, then glanced up at her with a sly smile. "Does it say anything about me?"

"Give it back." She leaned her head to the side and started walking toward him with her hand outstretched.

"I want to see if you're as good at keep away as you are at soccer," he teased.

"I'm not in the mood," she snapped, and charged after him. She leaped for the diary as he started to hand it back, and accidentally knocked it from his hand. It skidded across the sidewalk. She tried to use her power to stop it before it slid into the street, but she was too flustered, and instead she made the gutter water slosh against the curb and slop onto the sidewalk.

She dove into the oncoming traffic, trying to retrieve it.

Derek grabbed her arm and pulled her back as a huge UPS truck rolled over the diary and smashed its binding. Pages soared in a circle, then fell into a pothole filled with muddy water.

"That could have been you under the truck wheel," Derek said. "What's wrong with you, anyway? I was going to hand it back to you. You're acting like it was a matter of life or death."

"It was." She sighed and watched the wet pages flap and tear apart as car after car whizzed by and rolled over what might have been her life. She could use her power to bring the pages back, but they would be unreadable now.

She and Derek fell into a strained silence. Then he spoke. "Why did you run away from me back at the parking lot?"

"Geometry test," she mumbled, and watched the soggy pages become no more than a soft, pulpy mass under the steady stream of tires.

"For someone so worried about her geometry test, you've already missed the first bell." He looked at her. "Why did you lie to me?"

"You'd never understand." She shook her head. What was she going to do? That was her only chance of finding a way to save Catty. Her only hope now was to get her memories back. No chance of that.

Derek started to say something and she stopped him.

"Derek, I just need some time alone, okay?"

"I think we need to talk." There was a seriousness in his eyes that she didn't understand.

"Not now." She started walking away from him. She hadn't gone half the block when footsteps ran after her and someone grabbed her shoulder.

"Derek," she said angrily. "I need to be alone." She turned with a scowl.

Michael stood behind her.

"Hi, Michael." She hoped there wasn't too much eagerness on her face. Just looking into his dark gentle eyes made her feel better.

"Were you looking for Derek?" His lips curled in an infectious smile.

"No." She grinned foolishly. "Are you cutting school today?" And then she added too quickly, assuming that he was, "Want to hang out?"

"I don't start until second period," he explained.

"Oh." She didn't bother to hide her disappointment. She would have loved some time alone with him.

"I saw you walking and I wanted to remind you about Planet Bang tonight." He stepped closer.

Her hands went automatically to his chest and played with his shirt button. "I'll be there." She looked at his lips. She bet he was a great kisser, and she was determined to find out for herself. She breathed deeply and took in his spicy aftershave. What would he do if she put her arms around him right here and pulled his face down to hers? She looked up at him, wondering if she could use her power to bend his will to hers.

"See you tonight, then." He pulled away. Was there promise in his eyes, or had that only been her imagination?

She watched him walk toward school. She loved the way his black hair fell in curls around his neck. She sighed. Michael was the only thing going right in her life. No matter what else happened, she was resolved to have some fun tonight. She was going to get that kiss. She didn't care how bold she had to be.

But first she had to do something.

CHAPTER SEVENTEEN

TIANNA CREPT THROUGH a patch of ivy and hid in the shadows near a stone wall. It was past dusk, and cars were pulling into driveways. She watched with yearning as children raced up to porches to escape the cool air, their backpacks and school papers clasped in their hands. Soon the dark windows swam with warm golden lights and acrid smoke filled the air from hearth fires in the homes up and down the street. She stared at the thin gray wisps circling from the chimneys and envied the people who lived inside. She imagined them cozy in front of blazing flames.

Her eyes went back to the two-story Tudor home. It stood alone, back from the street, its entry porch dark. The windows indifferently stared back at her, reflecting the amber color from the streetlamps.

She didn't think Mason or Justin lived there, but she prayed whoever did might have the answers she needed. A car turned the corner. The beams from its headlights swept over her. She pressed back into darkness as it spun into the drive of the Tudor home and the automatic garage door opened. The car went inside and the door slowly closed after it.

With quick, even steps Tianna crossed the street. She didn't go up the front walk but to the side of the house. She glanced behind her. If anyone happened to look out their window and see her, they would think her movements were furtive and probably call the police.

She scurried into the shadows along a wall and crept to the back, then scaled the fence and fell into the yard of the Tudor house, trampling a bed of red gladiolas. She hurried around a swimming pool, shaded by Mexican fan palms, then stepped quickly across a long patio crowded with potted plants.

Her breath was too loud now. She waited until it came in slow, even draws again. Then she found a rock and hit the plastic covering on the sliding door latch. She wondered how she knew so much about breaking and entering, but she never questioned what her hands were doing. She had discovered in the past two days that if she didn't think and just let her body act, there were a lot of surprising things she could do.

When the plastic cover fell to the patio floor, her fingers released a metal hook inside. One click and the Tudor home was no longer safe from an intruder.

She paused, nerves on end, then as silently as she could she slid back the door and entered. A television played cartoons loudly somewhere in the house. She stole her way across the dark family room to the lit kitchen and peeked secretively inside.

A woman in pink slacks and a white sweater

spooned ground coffee into a coffeepot. A young girl of about twelve with a bald head and swollen face stared into an open refrigerator. Behind her a thin boy in a wheelchair rolled to the table and spread peanut butter onto cut pieces of celery.

The girl took an apple, and as she closed the refrigerator door, their eyes met. "Tianna!" Her smile was huge. She dropped the apple and ran to her, arms spread wide.

Tianna stepped into the kitchen, baffled, and embraced the young girl.

"I knew you'd come back," the girl said.

The boy grabbed the gear on his wheelchair. Its motor whirred and he twirled around, his smile crooked but his happiness showing through.

Then the woman shot a worried glance at Tianna, and her forehead wrinkled as if seeing her had brought on sudden distress. "Thank God you're all right."

Tianna blinked. "Mom?"

"Mom?" the girl repeated, and laughed.

The woman patiently hushed her. Then she turned to Tianna. "You can call me that if you want." She put a cautionary finger to Tianna's lips. "But don't say anything more."

"Is the house bugged?" Tianna asked.

"I wish it were that simple," the woman explained. "They can read minds."

Her answer sent a chill through Tianna. "You know?"

"Now I do. I didn't believe you, either, at first, but then they came here." She looked at Tianna with mounting concern. "What happened? No, don't tell me." She shook her head. "If I know, they'll find out. I can't stop them from getting inside my head."

"I don't remember anything," Tianna confessed. "I know I should know you, but I don't."

"They must have done something to you." The woman didn't act as if Tianna's confession was strange at all. "I'm Mary, and this is Shannon."

"You really don't remember?" Shannon asked.

Tianna shook her head.

"And Todd." Mary smiled lovingly at the boy.

"You didn't forget me, did you?" Todd waved. "We played Monopoly."

"Sorry." Tianna shrugged.

"Sit down." Mary pulled out a chair. "I'll tell you everything I know, but it's not a lot." That look of fear shot across her face again. "I don't think they'll come back now, but if they do, run. Don't worry about us. It's you they want."

"How do you know?" Tianna felt Shannon's comforting hand on her arm.

"Because when they go into your mind to read," Mary explained, "they leave a residue of themselves. I can't say how I know, but I do."

Tianna sat down. Her knees felt too weak to hold her any longer, and her fingers began trembling.

Shannon took her hand and squeezed it tightly. "We're here for you, Tianna. We're family now, just like Mary said."

"You were an emergency placement—" Mary began.

"Placement?" Tianna asked.

"I'm a foster mother," Mary explained.

"I have no home?" Tianna felt her heart drop, but it wasn't as much of a shock as it should have been. Part of her had known she had been running for a long time. Still, she had hoped.

"I'm sorry," Mary answered with true concern. "They called me two weeks ago and asked if I could take . . ." She stopped.

"What?" Tianna asked, wondering if there was something wrong with her.

Mary regarded her kindly. "The social worker wanted to know if there was any way I could handle a problem teen."

Tianna waited for Mary to explain.

"She said you kept running away from your placement homes and she thought maybe I could make a difference because I had been so successful with others in the past."

Tianna knew immediately that there was something Mary wasn't saying. "So the kids and I went shopping and got everything for your room," Mary continued. "We were excited to have one more in our home."

That explained one mystery at least, Tianna

thought. Now she knew why the decor and her style of clothes were so different.

"And then you arrived." Mary brushed back a strand of hair that had fallen into her face.

"In a really bad mood," Shannon added.

"Yeah." Todd rolled his eyes.

"Sorry," Tianna whispered.

"You had no clothes, no personal belongings," Mary remarked. "You said everything had been stolen. So we went shopping. You have great taste, by the way."

Tianna smiled.

"It seemed like everything was going to be fine," Mary went on. "But then, you became nervous and kept checking the locks. That didn't seem too odd, considering we live in L.A. Twice during the night on Sunday you woke me up but it was as if you were checking to make sure I was okay. I had been home-schooling you so I thought maybe it would help if you went to high school and made some friends."

The coffeepot gurgled and the smell of freshly brewed coffee filled the room.

"Would you like a cup?" Mary asked as she stood and poured herself one.

Tianna shook her head.

Mary sat down and took a sip before she continued. "Monday morning I enrolled you in La Brea High, and then I took the kids over to the hospital for their treatments. When we got home, you were already waiting for us. You told me that the two guys who had been chasing you were back. I wanted to call the police, but you told me not to. You said the police department had never believed you before. I called them, anyway, of course."

Tianna thought of the note in her shoe. "And they didn't believe me this time, either, did they?"

"You told them the guys had big shining yellow eyes," Shannon put in. "Nobody believed you. Not even me."

"Me neither." Todd shook his head.

"I felt sad that such an athletic and intelligent girl like you had lost touch with reality again. The social worker had told me that you had delusions. But then . . ." Mary looked at the children, and Tianna could feel their fear. "Tuesday night we found out it wasn't a delusion at all. Everything you said was true."

"How?" Tianna was worried now that Justin and Mason might come back and hurt them.

"You had gone to Planet Bang. Maybe I shouldn't have let you, but you seemed to like this boy so much and I thought it would be helpful for you to get out with . . ."

"Normal kids," Tianna finished the sentence for her.

Mary's eyes looked sad as she nodded. "There was a horrible pounding on the front door."

"Like someone was trying to break it down." Shannon's eyes widened.

"I thought something had happened to you," Mary said. "I swung open the door and two boys a little older than you were standing on the porch. They were evil. I have no other explanation for the strange feeling they gave to the air around them. They looked at me, and I could feel them prowling inside my mind. They were trying to find you."

"Their eyes were glowing yellow, too," Todd said interrupting. "Just like you told the cops."

Mary nodded. "They read my mind and ran off to Planet Bang to find you. We got in the car as quickly as we could and drove over to warn you."

Todd made a noise imitating a jet plane.

"But you were gone when we got there," Mary went on. "I didn't tell the social worker or the police about the two boys. I knew they wouldn't believe me, either. I barely believed it myself. I just prayed that you had gotten away. We would have run, too, but we couldn't. Shannon and Todd needed to go to Children's Hospital for their treatments."

"We all slept together in my room." Todd made a face. "Shannon snores."

"I do not," she argued, and slapped at him playfully.

"You weren't scared?" Tianna asked, and then felt foolish. It looked as if Shannon and Todd were facing death every day from other sources.

"Of course they weren't as frightened as I

was," Mary said proudly. "They are extremely brave."

Tianna looked at Mary. "Did they come back?"

She nodded. "The next day. I'm not sure why. When we came home, the front door was open and they had broken a vase in the upstairs hallway. Odd—why that vase?"

Tianna didn't bother to explain that she had done it accidentally.

"They came back that night," Mary continued. "They seemed angry that there was nothing new to dig from my mind. I was thinking that I should take the children to a hotel, but then I overheard the one with all the piercings say it was going to be over soon, so I decided to stay."

"Do you know what the *it* was?"

Mary shook her head. "Sorry, I don't have any idea. Although . . ."

"What?" Tianna leaned forward.

"It's not based on anything. It's more a feeling I had after they left my mind."

Tianna nodded.

"They were trying to stop you from doing something, and if they could hold you off for just one more night, it would be too late for you to do anything."

Tianna wondered what it could be. If only she had her memories. She stood and scraped back the chair. She liked Shannon and Todd and Mary. She wished they really were her family.

"Well, I'd better go." Then she remembered the clothes upstairs. She needed something to wear to Planet Bang. It didn't sound as if she was going to live long, anyway, so she might as well enjoy the little time she had, and more than anything she wanted that kiss from Michael.

"Can I take some of the clothes?" Tianna asked.

"Of course," Mary answered. "They're all yours. Take anything you need."

CHAPTER EIGHTEEN

AN HOUR LATER Tianna was walking toward Planet Bang, wearing a sweater shell with sequins and an ankle-grazing skirt slit up the sides to the top of her thighs. She glanced at the waning moon and stopped. There was something important she had to do before the moon turned dark and it was in some way connected to Justin and Mason, but what? She stared at the sky as she continued, hoping the memory would come to her the way soccer and skateboarding had.

When she rounded the corner, the music grew louder. A neon sign throbbed pink, blue, green, and orange lights over the kids waiting to go inside. She recognized some of them. It seemed as if everyone had come with a friend or friends. Their heads turned and watched her as she walked to the end of the line.

She spread her hands through her hair and arched her back. As long as they were going to stare, she might as well give them a show. She twisted her body and stuck one long leg out from the slit in her skirt. Guys smiled back at her as she stretched her arms in a sexy pose. The girls mostly turned away, pretending they hadn't been checking out their competition.

The music coming from inside excited her. She could hear kids whoop and stomp in time to the beat. She couldn't wait to dance. She wanted that at least, especially if it meant dancing with Michael. She breathed out, trying to calm herself. If only . . . Life could be so perfect here. She tried not to think about Mason and Justin, but her eyes nervously scanned the nearby shadows anyway and she wished the line would move faster.

Finally it was her turn with the security

guards. She handed her backpack to the first one. He smiled at her, and there was no doubt in her mind it was intended as a flirt. He couldn't have been much older than she was. His hands went rapidly through her things.

"What are you doing?" he joked when he saw her underwear. "It looks like you carry your whole life in here."

"I do," she answered with a tilt of her head, then she took her bag and went inside.

She liked the feel of energy that was coming off the crowd. Lights flashed and shimmery clothes sparkled around the room. Girls wore full-on body glitter and some had diamond-sparkle tattoos on their faces and arms. She set her backpack on the floor in the corner near bags, sweaters, jackets, and shoes.

The music beat through her and she started to dance, her eyes searching for Michael. She found Michelle instead, leaning on crutches, her foot in a cast. She wore slacks with cutouts on the side that revealed the bare tan skin of her hips and thighs. Her hair was in ringlets clasped back with diamonds away from her face.

Tianna walked over to her. "Great outfit. I like your hair, too."

Michelle jerked back and almost tripped.

Tianna caught her. "I'm sorry about your ankle."

"Stay away from me," Michelle warned, and hobbled away.

Tianna saw Corrine on the other side of the floor and waved. She wore a funky tiara with stars and only a little makeup. Tianna had started to push through the crowd toward her when a hand touched her back. She turned, hoping to stare up into Michael's beautiful eyes, but instead Vanessa, Serena, and Jimena circled her.

"Hi," Tianna said, and pushed through their circle. She had other plans for the night, and it didn't include being with witches. She shoved into the crowd and started to dance.

Jimena twirled after her with a laugh.

"We overheard you talking to Corrine about Catty." Jimena spoke above the music. She was wearing big hoop earrings and a sequined mesh dress with gold sandals.

Tianna knew she was lying. She couldn't have overheard her talking to Corrine. They had been whispering, and Jimena and her friends had been too far away.

"So?" Tianna answered, wondering if she could get more information from them about Catty. She glided beside Jimena, hips touching hips, enjoying the way Jimena danced.

"We didn't exactly hear you," Serena confessed. "We found out another way."

Tianna wondered who had spied on her. Derek hadn't been around. The only other person would have been Corrine herself, but she seemed too frightened by them to say anything and Serena had been too far away to read her mind, or had she?

Suddenly Vanessa stepped in front of her. She wore a spaghetti-strapped red dress, with a red leather jacket over her shoulders.

"We'd like to know why you were asking about her," Vanessa said. "That's all."

Tianna didn't think they'd believe her if she did tell them why she had been asking about Catty. Besides, she had questions of her own. "I just wanted to hear what happened the night Catty disappeared." She watched them closely to see if there was any reaction, and there definitely had been one in Vanessa's eyes. "Maybe you should tell me."

Vanessa stepped closer. "Is there a reason why it's important to you?"

Jimena stopped dancing and stood beside her, arms folded over her chest with determination. "Something happened to our friend, and if you know anything, we'd like to hear it."

Tianna stopped dancing and looked back at her. She didn't like the strange way Serena was staring at her.

"Don't believe everything you hear at school about us or Catty," Serena warned. "We're not witches, and we can't cast spells."

"Who said you could?" Tianna answered defensively.

"More than anything we want to get Catty

back," Vanessa put in. "We really miss her. If you know anything, please tell us."

Her statement surprised Tianna. That didn't sound as if they thought Catty was dead. She wondered if they knew their friend was trapped in another world. "Then tell me what happened that night." Her eyes held a dare and she waited for Vanessa's reply, but before she could answer, warm hands touched Tianna's shoulder and pulled her away. She turned and looked up into Michael's eyes.

His hands smoothed down her bare arms to her wrists, making a pleasant ache spread through her.

"I was hoping I'd find you." He guided her deeper into the crowd away from Vanessa, Jimena, and Serena.

When he stopped, she lifted her hands over her head and started to dance, teasing him. Her hips moved sultry and slow, the beat of the song echoing her intense desire. He smiled as if he knew she was playing with him. Then his arms circled her waist. Sweet anticipation spread through her, and she brought her hands down slowly and entwined them around his neck.

"I'm glad you came," he said at last.

"Me, too." She inched closer until she could feel the movement of his leg against her thigh.

He bent down, his face close to hers. She liked the feel of his breath against her neck. She closed her eyes and let her lips rest on his cheek.

"Normally I don't get into matchmaking," he said into her ear.

She pulled back abruptly. "Excuse me?"

"I think you and Derek make a great couple." He smiled at her as if he were embarrassed for being so bold. He seemed to sense her confusion. "I was hoping you'd give Derek another chance."

"Did I ever give him a first one?" She glanced over Michael's shoulder and saw Derek staring back at her.

"He's got a big crush on you, and it did seem as if you liked him until Wednesday," Michael explained. "What happened?"

"Derek?" She looked back into Michael's beautiful eyes. Was that the only reason Michael had been so affectionate? For Derek? She felt heartsick.

"Did you talk to Tianna yet?" Vanessa suddenly stood next to them and started dancing, her body sinuous and easy.

Michael nodded.

"You and Derek are good together," Vanessa added. She looked so sincere.

Tianna wished she'd smirk or give her the slightest reason to hate her. She wanted to, but she couldn't. Vanessa was too genuine and good for anyone to dislike.

Someone tapped her shoulder. She slumped. She didn't even need to look behind her to know who it was. She sadly watched as Michael pulled Vanessa close to him and they danced away.

At last she turned.

"Hi," Derek said, his eyes sparkling with optimism. "I hope you don't mind that I had Michael speak for me."

She glanced back at the dancers. Michael caught her looking at him and gave her a thumbs-up.

"I thought everything was going so well until Wednesday." Derek put his hand tentatively on her waist. "Then you acted like you didn't even know me. I didn't understand. I thought we'd hooked up."

"Yeah, well, things happened." She looked at him. She knew he'd never believe her even if she did tell him that she woke up that day and couldn't remember her own name.

"Let's dance." He pulled her to him.

She stared into his eyes. He was sweet and likable. She'd never hurt his feelings, but he was no Michael Saratoga. She glanced over his shoulder, but Vanessa and Michael were gone now.

"You know, I don't feel very well," Tianna said, and made a mental promise to herself that if she got through this night, she would never lie again. "I've got a headache."

"Are you getting headaches since that hit you took in soccer?" He looked concerned.

"Yeah, from the soccer hit." She started to pull away.

He squeezed through the dancers after her.

"You'd better see a doctor," he suggested. "I'll give you a ride home."

"It's all right." She stopped at the door. "I can walk. I don't want to take you away from the fun."

But he had already left the building without getting his hand stamped. He kept glancing down at her legs as they peeked out from beneath her skirt.

She sighed. In trying to get away from him she had left her backpack inside. She started to ask him to go back and get it for her, but he spoke first.

"I'm sorry about the way I treated your cousins the last time we were here. I thought maybe that's why you were upset with me."

"What cousins?" She put her hands on her hips and studied him.

"Those weird punker dudes." He shrugged. "It's hard to imagine they're related to you, but they said—"

"Derek, what are you talking about?" She was getting a real headache now. A strange buzzing in her head made her squint.

"I just felt bad about the way I treated them," Derek replied. "I didn't know they were related to you. They explained everything to me when I saw them at Starbucks today."

It dawned on her. "Mason and Justin?"

"Yeah. I told them you'd be here tonight." He smiled and pointed. "There they are."

Justin and Mason slowly walked toward her. Their eyes flashed with red and gold sparks as if a fire burned inside their heads.

"They're not my cousins, Derek." She needed to do something and fast, but she didn't want Derek to see her use her power. Somehow she felt that the less he knew, the safer he would be. The best thing to do was flee. She started to run, but Derek grabbed her hand and stopped her.

She turned and stared into Derek's eyes. They seemed triumphant. Was he one of them?

CHAPTER NINETEEN

TIANNA WOKE UP AND blinked. She was lying on her side, arms behind her, face pressed against a cold, damp concrete floor. Slowly, thin bars of pale orange light came into focus on the wall above her. It looked like the outline of a door. Another grayish glow to her left appeared to be a dirt-streaked window. She must be in a cellar. That explained the foul odor of mold and mildew.

She couldn't remember how she had gotten here, but at least she still had the memories of who had captured her. Justin and Mason wanted her for something. She was sure they had kidnapped her so they could turn her into one of them. Her chest tightened as her apprehension deepened. What were they?

Then she recalled how Derek had stopped her before she could escape. She wondered if he had always been part of their group. He had seemed like such a nice guy.

A scuttling noise made her heart drop. It sounded like tiny feet dragging a long skinny tail. She hated rats, and she wasn't waiting until one was in her face; she was leaving now. She tried to move, but something stopped her.

"No," she moaned. Her hands and legs were tied. She stretched her fingers and felt the ropes and knots binding her wrists, then concentrated her telekinetic powers to loosen them.

"Tianna?"

"Derek?" Her head jerked around. She couldn't see anything but shadow.

"Are you down here, too?" His voice seemed shaky.

"Yes." She tried to sound calm to reassure him.

"Those dripping water sounds are driving me crazy," he complained.

She listened. She hadn't noticed the constant ping and drip of water coming from the corner. "Yeah, I guess it would have bothered me, too, but I just woke up." She hadn't been sleeping, exactly, but it was close enough to the truth. Her mind continued working on loosening the knots that held the ropes around her wrists.

"I thought I was alone." His relief was obvious.

She was grateful he wasn't in league with Mason and Justin, but at the same time her heart sank. It was going to be harder to escape now. She would have to protect Derek. Then she remembered that her last thought before blacking out had been that he had betrayed her. So what was he doing here?

"Why did you stop me when I tried to run away?" she asked, not bothering to hide the accusation in her tone. She felt the ropes loosen and now tried to uncoil them with her mental energy.

"I thought you should speak to your

cousins," he explained in an embarrassed voice. "But I guess they weren't your cousins after all."

"How could you think they were?" She started to scold him but stopped. Anger was a waste of time, and she needed to conserve her energy.

"I'm sorry I believed their story about your family squabble. I swear I thought I was bridging a gap so you could all be together for Thanksgiving. I didn't know it would end up like this."

"It's all right," she sighed.

"I should have been suspicious," he countered. "I'm such a dunderhead."

"No, you're not," she reassured him.

"But I knew better," Derek insisted, "I saw what they were doing Tuesday night, and then I went ahead and believed their story. They said you were stubborn." He stopped, and when he continued, there was a light tease in his voice. "Okay, maybe that part of their story is true."

"Thanks," she answered sarcastically as the ropes around her wrists dropped free. She brought her hands in front of her. They prickled painfully as the blood flowed back to the tips of her fingers. She shook them, and when they were no longer numb, she examined the ropes around her ankles.

"What did they do to me?" she asked. "Why was I unconscious?"

"You won't believe me if I tell you," he answered.

"Right now, I'd believe anything," she assured him. "You can't begin to imagine everything I've seen in the last two days."

"Their eyes turned yellow," he answered finally. "And they used them to make you pass out."

When she didn't laugh, he continued. "You don't think it was my imagination?" He didn't wait for her to answer. "You know about them. What are they? Something supernatural? They look it. So tell me."

"I wish I knew," she answered as the first knot tying her ankles came loose.

"Maybe they escaped from a genetics lab? I mean, you see it in the movies all the time—maybe the government really is working on some kind of superhuman." He took in a deep breath and was silent for a moment as if considering what he was going to say next. "Do you think they're Martians?"

"Martians?"

"You know, guys from outer space. They can . . ." He started, then stopped as if he was still in awe of what he had seen.

"What?"

"Talk right in your head." Derek let out a long breath. "I know you can't believe me—"

"But I do," she answered bluntly.

"You do?" He seemed relieved.

"Yes, they've been chasing me for a long time, and somehow on Tuesday night they stole my memories."

She could hear him moving as if he was trying to get closer to her. "That's why you acted so strange Wednesday morning at school?"

"Yes."

He was silent a moment. "And you're not really a runaway. I mean, you are, but you have a reason to be on the run."

"I guess I've been running for a long time." She felt sad and quickly changed the subject. "Did you hear anything that could help us?"

"Yeah, I overheard them on the car ride over." He stopped as if something had suddenly baffled him.

"What?" she asked, sensing it was important.

"They're waiting for a third guy to show up so they can take us down to the beach. They're going to cross us over, whatever that means."

"I know it can't be anything good," Tianna answered.

He sighed. "There's no way to escape, so I guess we'll find out."

"How can you be such a pessimist?"

"We're both tied up," he answered. "The ropes are too tight. I've been trying to loosen them, but they won't budge."

"They didn't tie me up," she lied. She figured he couldn't have seen her working the ropes in the dark, anyway.

"They didn't tie you up?" He sounded surprised.

"I guess they thought I'd remain unconscious."

"Untie me, then," he urged.

"All right." She stood and tripped over something in the dark, then stumbled and fell on Derek.

"Ouch," he moaned.

"Are you all right?" she whispered, and realized she was lying on top of him. She liked the way his body felt so familiar and comfortable beneath hers. She rested her head against his chest and closed her eyes, suddenly regretting all the mean things she had said to him.

"Aren't you going to get up?" he asked.

"Sure," she answered, and let her hands smooth down his chest and then his arms. She was surprised by the feel of his rock-hard muscles.

"I work out," he murmured unexpectedly.

"What?"

He snickered. "The way you're feeling my chest and arms—"

"I am not." She jumped up, indignant, then knelt beside him. "I was searching for your ropes."

"Liar," he whispered.

She felt a blush rise to her cheeks and was glad it was dark so he couldn't see.

"The ropes are tied around my ankles and wrists," he said, but there was still laughter in his voice.

Her fingers traveled down his jeans leg and found the rope. The knots were too tight. It would take her forever if she picked at them. Instead she imagined the coils wiggling free. Within moments she tossed the ropes aside.

Derek stretched his legs. "Thanks. Get my hands."

She pushed a stack of boxes aside, then felt the ropes that held his hands behind his back. The tips of her fingers touched his palm and lingered there as if they had memories of their own.

"Is there a problem?" he asked.

"No, why?" she answered, not wanting to take her hand away.

"Just that you're taking so long."

She used her telekinetic powers to undo the ropes. As soon as his hands were free, he waved them in the dark, searching for her.

"You okay?" he asked. His fingers brushed across her cheek and settled lightly on her chin. He leaned closer. She drew in air. His warm breath caressed her lips.

"Come on," he whispered. "We've got to get out of here." He grabbed her hand and helped her stand.

She wondered if she would have let him kiss her if he had tried. She didn't understand her disappointment that he hadn't. She liked Michael, didn't she?

Then she froze. Hollow footsteps pounded on the floorboards overhead.

"They're on the move," he said cautioning her.

"Do you think they heard us?" She used that as an excuse to put her arms around him.

"It sounds like they're going outside." He started forward again.

The distant sound of a door opening and closing came to them.

"Yes, definitely they went outside," Derek said. "Hurry, let's get to the stairs.

"Stairs?" She followed him blindly through puddles and over stacks of wood and pipes.

"Since the door is up so high," he explained, "there must be stairs."

"Yes," she answered with a sudden rush of excitement. If they could get up to the door, she could use her powers to open it. She hurried after him.

"That's odd." He seemed perplexed. "They must have removed the stairs."

"Why?" She waved her hands in front of her, searching. Nothing was there. Not even a ladder.

She sat down on the floor in total frustration. That's why Justin and Mason had been so careless. Even if she had come to and used her power to untie her ropes, there was no way she was going to get up to the door. She couldn't fly. "There must be another entrance. How did they get us down here?"

Derek was silent for too long.

"What's wrong?" she asked.

"Do you think it's possible that they took

away some of my memories?" He seemed distressed. "I remember the car pulling up out front and the next thing I recall is being tied up alone in the basement, but I don't remember how I got down here and I don't remember them bringing you down here, either."

"Anything's possible." She stood and touched the wall. Water seeped over the bricks. Then her fingers felt something marshy and soft. Her hands jerked back. "Yuck."

"What now?"

"The wall. It's covered with some kind of creepy mold. It feels totally gross." She wiped her hands down her skirt.

"We're in a basement." He laughed. "I didn't think you'd be so squeamish."

"You touch it," she said.

She heard him shuffle forward.

"Jeez. What is this stuff?"

She took off her shoes and handed them to him.

"What are you doing now?" he asked.

"I'm getting us out."

"How?"

She didn't like the disbelief in his voice.

"I'm going to scale the wall." Already her mind's eye had started working a brick to make it stick out a few inches so she would have something to step onto. A soft squishy grating noise let her know she had been successful.

"What was that?" Derek asked.

"What?"

"That sound."

"My hands slipped," she explained. "I'm trying to find protruding bricks." That was partly true. She ran her fingers along the wall. The mold and moisture made the bricks slippery, and even after forcing them out at an angle the surfaces were hard to grip.

Derek stood next to her. "You think you can do it?" he asked hopefully. "Be careful."

"I will." Her fingers grabbed hold of another ice-cold slimy brick. She paused to make sure she had a strong hold, then felt with her foot for something to step on. It was worse feeling the gummy mildew squish between her toes. She had to struggle for balance until she could find another brick.

A few minutes later she was almost there. All she had to do now was use her power to open the door, then climb onto the floor and help Derek out. She clasped the jutting edges tightly, her fingers slipping, and concentrated on moving another brick out. A sludgy scraping sound followed, and a glop of squashy stuff fell on her face.

"Yuck," she moaned.

She blinked, then reached up and felt along the wall for a brick that was sticking out. She wrapped her fingers around it and too late realized it was completely covered with spongy mold. Her fingers slid off and she fell back, plunging to the basement floor.

CHAPTER TWENTY

DEREK TRIED TO BREAK her fall but only succeeded in tumbling to the basement floor with her. Tianna landed on her back, her head hit the concrete. Hot pain rushed through her skull with the roar of a train as dark clouds pressed into her vision. She sighed and let go.

When she opened her eyes again, Derek was beside her, calling her name and caressing her cheek softly.

She didn't answer him because all at once her life was coming back to her. The fall had somehow released her memories. So many forgotten moments were flowing back into her consciousness at a frightening speed.

Justin and Mason had captured her on Tuesday night. She felt again the strange sensation of Mason inside her head, controlling her thoughts.

Mason had tried to steal her sense of self and make her one of them. He had shown her a menacing black shadow. The same one she had seen in that other dimension with Catty.

She had felt mesmerized by the whirling dark cloud, and when he had told her to go toward it, she had wanted to even though part of her knew if she did, she would lose herself forever.

But someone had torn her away from Mason and she had run. She tried to recall who, but that memory hadn't come back to her yet.

Mason's power had been strong and continued absorbing her memories even after she had escaped. That was why she couldn't remember until now all the hours spent running and hiding with Justin and Mason on her trail. She had run for miles, slipping into shadows and sprinting down dark alleys. They had almost caught her once and she had fallen down an embankment to escape them. That was why she had so many bruises the next day. She had managed to get away, and finally she had lost them and scrambled up a tree next to the apartment where she lived now. The window had been unlocked, so she had gone inside and crashed.

Then she remembered Pete. That's how Justin and Mason had caught her. Pete had asked her to dance at Planet Bang. He had seemed like any guy her age, except for the way his hands had been all over her, uninvited. She had tried to break away from him, but before she could, Justin and Mason had grabbed her. She had been able to escape because Derek had come.

"Derek," she said with surprise. "You saved me."

"I didn't. I should have been able to catch you."

"No, Tuesday night." The memory shot through her. "You grabbed my hand and jerked me away from those guys."

And then she had run.

"Yeah, I was jealous of the way all three were dancing with you." There was still anger in his voice. "I didn't know they were your cousins." He paused. "Well, they're not your cousins, but you know what I mean."

Earlier on Tuesday a mysterious force had been directing her to run. The same voice that had guided her since that first night when she had escaped the murderers in her parents' home. That's why she had taken her backpack with her to Planet Bang. She had never intended to go back to Mary's house. But before she ran, she had wanted to see what it would feel like to be an ordinary kid, hanging out with guys her age.

"Derek." She called his name softly this time.

His lips were close to hers now. "Yes," he breathed.

Why not tell him the truth? She had gone to Planet Bang hoping to see him and had foolishly flirted with Michael Saratoga only because Derek had been dancing with another girl when she got there.

"Who was the girl with the long hair you were dancing with on Tuesday night?" she asked.

"Who? You mean, Sara?" He laughed. "That's my younger sister."

She lifted her arms and wrapped them around his neck. She had liked him from the moment she had met him Monday at school. No wonder he thought she had been acting weird on Wednesday when she couldn't even remember his name.

But other memories came to her now. Ones that filled her with sadness. She saw her mother, father, and sister. Tears burned into her eyes. Having her memories suddenly restored made it feel as if they had died all over again.

"You're crying." Derek pressed her against him and rubbed her back soothingly.

She remembered the way she had struggled through the woodlot that first night and finally found shelter in the trashed boxes behind a liquor store. She had fallen into a deep sleep and was awakened the next morning by the woman who owned the store.

That began her first foster placement. More than anything she had wanted a home. She had lived in so many different houses and towns. West Covina. Ontario. Long Beach. Wilmington. She had kept a key from each one. That's why there were so many on her key chain. She felt suddenly sorry for herself, sorry that she had lived like a stray.

"Tianna." Derek spoke softly. "Why do those guys want you so badly?"

The answer came to her with sudden force. They were trying to stop her from bringing back the lost goddess before the dark of the moon. Was that tonight?

"Can you see the moon out tonight?" she asked suddenly.

Derek chuckled. "I haven't really noticed."

"Try," she told him. "It's important." Justin and Mason didn't want her to make the three become four again. Now she remembered what she was supposed to do, but it still felt like a puzzle.

"How 'bout the window?" she asked.

"You want me to see if there's a moon?" His

shoes scraped on the cellar floor as he started to move.

"No. I'll climb up there and get us out."

"I don't know." She could feel him shake his head. "The window looks like it hasn't been opened in a zillion years."

"It'll open for me." She stood and had started to walk to the wall under the window when an unexpected sense of doom struck her. What if she didn't survive the night? She turned abruptly and knocked into Derek. She wanted to know what a kiss felt like before she died.

"Derek, kiss me." Her heart was beating so hard, she was sure he could hear it.

"I've wanted to kiss you since the day I first saw you," he admitted. His hands caressed her shoulders, then glided down her back and pulled her closer to him.

"Then do it," she urged and rushed her tongue over her lips so they wouldn't be dry.

He leaned over her and cradled her against him. She was aware of the warmth of his body.

Then his lips touched hers. The feeling startled her and she took in a sharp breath.

"It's your first kiss." His lips spoke against her ear.

"No—" she began. "Yes."

He brushed her hair back with his fingers as if she were fragile and precious, then he took her hands off his chest and placed them around his neck. He wrapped his own hands around her waist and kissed her again for a long time.

"Thank you." She sighed when he finally pulled away. "Now I have to rescue you."

"Because I kiss so good," he teased.

"That and because I got you into this mess in the first place."

They walked over to the wall beneath the window, holding hands.

"I'll climb up, then open the window," she ordered. "As soon as I'm outside, you follow."

She could feel his skepticism before he even spoke. "I don't know. That window looks like it's frozen shut. You'll never get it open."

"Trust me," she answered, and didn't bother to

hide her annoyance. "Just because I'm a girl . . ."

"I didn't say because you're a girl," he corrected her. "I said the window looks frozen shut. Some things are impossible."

"Nothing's impossible," she said. "Just watch me."

She touched the wall. It was covered with a slimy growth. Years of leaking water and damp earth had created a garden of fungus and mold over it. The smell was so strong, she could almost taste it on her tongue.

She focused her mind on moving the first brick out just a few inches so her toe had something to perch on, then she reached as high as she could and willed the brick beneath her palm away from the wall as well. She stepped on it, and felt the wall slump. Mud oozed from a crack, pushing out the mortar, and covered her foot.

"What's that sound?" Derek asked.

"The foundation is unstable," she explained. "From the water. I think there's a river of mud behind the bricks."

"We'd better hurry, then."

This time she used her telekinetic powers to move the brick more cautiously. A grinding sound filled the cellar as it scraped out a few inches.

Derek stood next to her, his hands on the wall, as if he were trying to hold back the flood of slimy soil. "Hurry," he repeated.

"So you believe I can do it now?" she asked, trying to make her voice come out teasingly, but her words sounded strained and filled with fear.

"I know you can," he encouraged.

She hadn't counted on the bricks being so old and the mortar decaying. She climbed up two more steps, then glanced at the window. She willed it open.

The frame protested with a shudder, then screeched against the side jambs as rusted hinges slowly pulled the window up.

"How'd you do that?" Derek asked. "You're not even close enough to reach it."

"I was," she argued. "You must have looked away."

"But even if you stretched, you couldn't touch it now."

"I was closer and I slipped," she said, exasperated. "Do we have to discuss it now? Just climb."

"But—"

She cut him off. "Justin and Mason could come back after us any minute."

"All right."

She took a deep breath and perched her toe on another brick, then pulled herself up and grabbed onto the windowsill. She struggled and wiggled into thick gluey spiderwebs. The cobwebs stuck to her face, and the more she wiped at them, the more they seemed to cling to her cheeks.

"What now?" Derek asked from below.

She didn't answer but rolled outside under a hibiscus bush. Low-hanging branches scratched at her back. She wiped her hands on the grass, then turned and looked back into the basement. She couldn't see a thing. "Can you feel the protruding bricks?"

Derek patted his hands along the wall, making a wet slick sound. "It feels like grabbing a handful of slime," he muttered.

"Thanks for sharing that," she whispered back. "I already cleared part of it away, and you won't even have to deal with the spiderwebs." She stretched over the windowsill to guide Derek. She could feel the bricks shift beneath her.

"This might not work," Derek said. "I'm heavier than you are by maybe thirty pounds. That would make a difference. It's like the whole thing is ready to collapse. Maybe you should just run for help."

"And leave you? No way. Try again."

This time as he started up, she used her power to force the bricks to stay.

He grasped a brick and pulled himself up. The foundation seemed to hold. "I can't believe it," he said with bafflement in his voice.

She felt her strength wavering, as if she was losing control. She wondered if there was a limit to her power. She focused until her forehead ached.

"Tianna," Derek called from below her. "I think we have a problem."

"What now?" she rasped, not hiding the exasperation in her voice. She could see the dim outline of his head. He only had a little way to go. She leaned in farther.

The marshy soil was sweeping through the bricks with a squishing sound. The odor was nauseating.

She concentrated, not sure if she had enough strength left to suppress the cave-in.

Silence followed.

"Start again," she said as a spider scurried over her face on feathery feet. When she turned to brush it away, she saw Mason and Justin. They were leaning against the front corner of the house about fifteen feet away, near the porch light, smoking cigarettes and talking.

CHAPTER TWENTY-ONE

"JUSTIN AND MASON are right out here," Tianna whispered down to Derek. "Be quiet."

"That's kind of hard to do with these bricks," he answered with frustration. His hand clutched the windowsill, and she rolled back to give him room to climb outside.

As he pulled himself through, her mental hold gave way. The sludgy mess of bricks and mud collapsed, emitting putrid smells of wet, brackish earth and decay.

She looked at Derek with complete surprise. "It hardly made any noise."

"There must have been so much mud that it insulated the sound of the bricks falling." Derek wiped his hands in the grass to get rid of the mud, then peered under the bobbing branches of the hibiscus to where Mason and Justin stood. "They didn't hear anything, at least. Maybe because of the traffic sounds."

Tianna listened. They were near a freeway or highway. The constant roar from cars and trucks could mask almost any sound.

"Now let's just hope the house doesn't collapse." New worry stirred inside her, but the frame of the house looked solid.

"Yeah," Derek agreed, and his hand went protectively to her back. "And hope they don't see us."

"Too late." Tianna cursed under her breath.

Mason and Justin threw away their cigarettes and started to walk toward them. The red embers made twin arches as they flew across the night sky.

"They're coming." She had grabbed Derek's arm, ready to run, when a resounding boom like distant thunder made her stop. "What's that?"

A '57 Chevy with dual exhaust pipes rumbled into the drive, its fenders ablaze with red and yellow metallic flames. It skidded sideways to a stop, the motor died, and Pete stepped out, dressed like a hipster in khakis, a white T-shirt, and an Armani jacket. Other than his clothes, he looked the same as he had when he had asked her to dance at Planet Bang. Then he turned and his face caught the porch light. She shuddered. His eyes had an unnatural glow.

Mason and Justin continued walking toward the car. They spoke in loud voices now, as if they were boasting. Pete whooped. The howl of his laughter made her skin crawl.

"They're pretty freaky guys," Derek said, as if he had felt the same shiver.

Then all three turned and strolled toward the front of the house. Under the harsh glare of the porch light Justin and Mason no longer looked young but cadaverous and wan. She wondered how old they really were.

"What are they?" Derek asked, as if he had also seen the hideous change in their faces.

As soon as the door closed, she took Derek's hand. "Now's our chance."

They scrambled out from under the hibiscus bush, then ran across the lawn toward a long line of eucalyptus trees.

"Go toward the traffic sounds." Derek indicated with his head.

"Where are we?" Tianna asked.

Derek took a deep breath. "It's got to be somewhere near the beach. You can smell the salt air."

They stepped over a bed of dried eucalyptus leaves, then slid down an embankment until they were on a busy street nestled against the beach. Derek pointed to a road sign. "Pacific Coast Highway," he read.

"But where?" she asked. "PCH runs up and down the entire California coast."

He shrugged. "We'll worry about that later. Let's go."

They ran along the shoulder of the road toward the bright headlights of the oncoming traffic. Their clothes flapped and their hair blew about their faces as air currents from the speeding cars breezed around them.

Soon they were at a strip mall. The smells of garlic and lemon came from a small Italian restaurant that had eight-by-ten glossies of celebrities on the wall.

"We can slow down now," Derek assured her, and let go of her hand. He wrapped his arm around her, and they strolled down the sidewalk. "We're on the strand and they're not likely to bother us here."

She wished she could feel so sure. She tried to steady her breathing as they walked past a long line of stores selling souvenirs. Sunburned kids, surfers, bikers, and tourists pushed through the stores, eating churros and hot dogs on sticks.

They had started to pass a pricey hotel with twenty-four-hour armed security guards when Derek clutched her hand and pulled her down a delivery driveway that curved behind the building.

"Why are we going here?" she asked, and started to go back. "It's a dead end."

"I got an idea." He smiled broadly.

Men were wheeling crates of vegetables from the bed of a truck onto the loading dock. Derek climbed onto the dock, then walked over to one of the men. She wondered if he was begging for something to eat.

In a few minutes he came back to her. "They're going to give us a ride back to L.A."

"Thanks." She rested her head against his chest. She liked him a lot, and that was precisely why she couldn't see him again. She had to find a way to tell him they couldn't hang out. It was too dangerous. She sighed. It was going to be hard. She loved the way he made her feel, but she couldn't think only about herself. Besides, he was probably searching for an excuse to break up with her right now. No guy wants a girl who has monstrous humanlike creatures chasing her down.

"Come on," Derek said, and they hurried onto the loading dock, then into the bed of the truck. They sat next to the cab on lettuce leaves, bits of broccoli, and carrot tops that had fallen from the crates.

She looked into Derek's deep blue eyes and wished she didn't have to tell him good-bye.

The driver closed the tailgate and gave them a thumbs-up and a big smile. In moments they were rolling up the driveway and onto the coast highway toward Los Angeles. Tears blurred her vision, making the traffic lights and taillights smear together into one reddish glow.

She took a deep breath, turned to Derek, and started to speak, but before she could say anything, he broke the silence. "I really like hanging out with you, Tianna."

"What?" She wiped her eyes. "After tonight I thought you'd never want to see me again."

"Are you kidding?" He seemed as surprised as she felt. "I've never had such an exciting night."

"Are you making fun of me?"

He shook his head. "From the first moment I met you, I knew you were the kind of girl who went running off the high dive into the deep end of the pool before you even knew how to swim."

She laughed.

He pulled her closer to him. "I like that rush of adrenaline I felt tonight."

The truck turned with a swerve in the road and she slid closer to him. She didn't move away.

"My adventures before have always been from reading books. I mean, look at me, Tianna."

She did. What did he have to complain about? His life seemed so perfect. Everyone at school liked him. He had tons of friends, and he got good grades.

"What about you?" she asked finally.

"I'm the only guy in the high school whose mother refused to sign a permission slip so I could play football. She said it was too dangerous. You can't believe the things I'm not allowed to do. Do you know that when I go snowboarding with Michael, I have to lie to my mother and tell her I'm going to visit his grandmother in Pomona?"

Tianna felt a sudden pang of jealousy. She wished she had a mother who cared about keeping her safe. "It's just that she loves you. That's the way she expresses it."

"Sure." He nodded. "But I have an adventurer's spirit," he went on. "More than anything I want to live a life like the one you showed me tonight."

Suddenly she felt annoyed. "It seems like fun to you because you've only had to deal with Mason and Justin for one night and now you can go home to your safe bed and remember all of this like a dream. But if you were always on the run from them, I can guarantee it wouldn't seem so great—" She stopped. How could she ever make him understand? "It's really unsafe for you to hang around with me. They're not going to stop until they destroy me, and they don't care who they take with me."

He put his arms around her. "How long have they been after you?"

"A long time," she answered, but she didn't elaborate. She didn't want his pity.

He held her tightly. "We've got to do something to stop them, then. Let's go to the police."

"I've tried that," she answered. "They don't believe me."

"Then we'll capture them ourselves and take them to the cops. They'll have to believe us if they see them."

"It's not that easy." She shook her head. "They have powers you don't understand."

"But we have to find a way to stop them so you don't have to be on the run. Then you could stay here and go to La Brea High." He kissed her temple. "That's what I want. I hope you do, too."

"More than anything," she murmured, but she had to face reality. It wasn't likely she was going to be able to do that.

The truck jerked to a halt. Derek tapped on the cab window and mouthed a thank-you to the driver, then they climbed over the tailgate and jumped off.

"We're only a block from my apartment." She started walking.

When they reached the stairs, she turned and faced him. "We're safe for right now. Let's get some rest and then tomorrow we'll make a plan." She looked at him and hoped he couldn't tell she was lying. She was going to leave Los Angeles tonight. Maybe go to Seattle. She didn't think she could pull Catty back from that other realm, and the longer she stayed here, the more she put the people she cared about in jeopardy.

"I'll pick you up first thing in the morning," he promised.

"Sure." She looked at him and wondered why now more than ever she didn't want to say good-bye.

"I really like you, Tianna." He tentatively slipped his hands around her waist, then bent closer as if he were going to kiss her.

She pulled abruptly away, afraid that his kiss would destroy her resolve. She turned, and as she hurried up the steps, she glanced at the night sky. The moon, only the thinnest crescent, was now a reminder that she had failed. Tomorrow night would bring the new moon and it would be too late.

"Tianna," Derek called. "What's wrong?"

She glanced back at him as she opened the door. She hated herself for the wounded look on his face. "I'll see you in the morning," she said.

CHAPTER TWENTY-TWO

BACK IN THE SMALL apartment, Tianna washed her hands, neck, and face, then glanced at her skirt. It was torn and covered with a black moldy mess from the cellar walls. She seemed to have a knack for destroying clothes. She wanted nothing more than to take a hot shower and to slip into bed. She had started toward the bathroom, nerves throbbing, feet sore, when she caught something from the corner of her eye. She whipped around.

It looked like a huge swarm of gnats in the corner near the sink. She watched in wonder as the swirling cloud became denser and the dots seemed to come together and take form. Then Serena, Jimena, and Vanessa became visible in front of her.

She stumbled back, astonished. "You really are witches," she exclaimed, but she didn't feel afraid of them; she felt awestruck.

"We had to do something drastic to make you believe us," Serena said. "Because we need your help."

Tianna took another step away from them. "Look, if witchcraft is your thing, it's okay with me, but really I'm not into magic or spells."

They laughed as if she had said something funny.

Serena stepped forward. "You move objects with your mind and go into other dimensions, but you don't believe in magic. You are magic."

"How do you know that's what I do?" Tianna felt even more amazed than she had the moment before.

"Because we each have a power like yours." Vanessa pulled out one of the chairs from the table and sat down.

"But I'm not a sorceress," Tianna retorted. "I don't work any magic, and I can't cast spells. If I could, my life wouldn't be such a mess."

"I read minds," Serena confessed. "That's my gift, and I've gone inside your head. I know what you can do."

Tianna felt lost in wonder, but she believed Serena. That explained how she had figured out where she lived and how they had known that she and Corrine had been talking about Catty. "But how did you get here?" Tianna fell down in the chair opposite Vanessa. "Was it some kind of teleportation?" She was ready to believe anything now.

"No, we used my power," Vanessa explained. "I can make my molecules expand until I'm invisible. We waited outside until we saw you come back with Derek, then I made us all invisible so we could follow you inside."

Then Serena took Tianna's hand. "We're on

the side of good, like you. We battle the Atrox. That's what you've been running from, but you didn't even know it."

"Atrox?" Tianna shook her head. "I've never heard of it."

"It's an ancient evil," Jimena put in. "And Justin and Mason are two of its Followers."

"You know about them, too?" Tianna asked, stunned. "But how do you know? If you're not witches, then what are you?"

"Let me explain," Vanessa started. "In ancient times, when Pandora's box was opened—"

"Pandora?" Tianna laughed. "Don't tell me that myth is true."

Jimena nodded solemnly.

Then Serena continued, "The last thing to leave the box was hope—"

Tianna interrupted her. "I know the story."

"But there's more," Vanessa cautioned. "Listen."

Serena continued. "Selene, the goddess of the moon—"

"She's real, too?" Tianna knew at once that

Selene was the mysterious force who had directed her to run. That also explained why her internal guide was strongest during the full moon and weakest during the dark of the moon.

"Selene saw the creature that had been sent by the Atrox to devour hope," Serena said. "She took pity on the people of earth and gave her daughters, like guardian angels, to guard hope. We're those daughters. We're goddesses."

"Goddesses?" Tianna answered with a mocking grin, but this time when she looked at them, their faces seemed to glow.

You know what I'm saying is true, Serena breathed into her mind.

Tianna's derisive smile fell from her face. Serena had been able to speak to her by using her mind. The same way Justin and Mason could go inside her head. She felt staggered by everything they had told her, but even as stunning as it was, she believed them. Too may things had happened in her life for her not to.

"We need your help." Jimena's black eyes stared at her.

"What can I possibly do?" Tianna wondered aloud.

"Help us get Catty back," Vanessa urged.

"Catty was a goddess, too, wasn't she?" Tianna suddenly understood. "The three I'm supposed to make four again. I was supposed to bring Catty back to you."

"We hope you can," Vanessa coaxed. "Jimena had a premonition. That's her gift. We need to know if it's come true. Have you made contact with Catty already?"

"Yes. I think it was Catty, but the girl didn't wear a moon amulet like you three do."

"That's because hers exploded the night she disappeared," Serena explained.

"Can you contact her again?" Vanessa asked eagerly.

"The Atrox and its Followers have sworn to destroy the Daughters of the Moon because once we're gone, they will succeed," Serena put in. "Catty vanished when we were fighting a powerful member of the Atrox's inner circle. Our powers are weakened now that she's gone."

"But that's not the only reason we want her back," Vanessa added. "She was my best friend, and I miss her too much."

"But I tried already, and I couldn't bring her back," Tianna explained. "She's in a different dimension."

"How did you get there?" Vanessa asked.

"I was using my telekinetic powers and—"

Serena interrupted. "Can you try again and take us there?"

"I can go there, but I don't know how to get back," Tianna explained. "Twice I've gone, and both times I've only been able to return because someone on this side pulled me back."

Suddenly they all clasped onto her and she knew she had no choice.

"Take us," Jimena ordered.

"It's too dangerous," Tianna argued. "I don't know how to get back. Maybe I should practice a few times with just one of you."

"We'll figure out a way to get back once we're there," Vanessa said. "We have to get Catty. The dark of the moon starts tomorrow night, and then it will be too late. If we don't get her back tonight, she'll be a sacrifice."

Serena smiled. "We're willing to take the risk. All of us together will find a way back."

"I'll try." Tianna narrowed her eyes in concentration and pushed with her mind against the dresser. The wood warped and her vision blurred. She felt the girls' fingers gripping tighter and knew they had also experienced the change. Then the walls of the small apartment furrowed and became ridged as if she were looking at them through wavy glass. At last the glass shattered, reality fell away, and they stepped into that other realm.

"Wow." Vanessa sighed. "It's like being in the middle of an endless desert."

"Something's wrong," Tianna cautioned. "Don't let go of me." Her eyes darted around the strange gloom. She had an overpowering sense of danger.

"This is where you found Catty?" Vanessa asked, and stepped away from her.

"Yes. She's usually floating in some sort of

cloud." Tianna tried to hold on to Serena and Jimena, but already she could feel them pulling away. "Don't!" She tried to stop them, but it was too late.

"Don't worry so much." Suddenly Serena dove away from her, swimming through the curious air that was as buoyant as water.

Tianna looked at them. Maybe the only danger was in her mind. They didn't seem concerned, but instinct told her something was terribly wrong, and she always trusted that inner voice. "It doesn't feel right."

"What do you mean?" Jimena flapped her arms and a capricious smile crept across her face. *"Estoy volando. Mírame."*

"Don't go so far from me." Tianna wondered what had happened to them. It was as if they had forgotten the reason they had come here. She tried to keep her mind centered, but she could feel something seeping into her brain, trying to tranquilize her. Was someone manipulating their thoughts so they couldn't feel the danger hovering in the air? Tianna shuddered as realization took hold. The Atrox had used her to set a trap. The girls were going farther and farther from her, lured by a false sense of safety and euphoria.

"Come back!" she yelled, and her voice echoed around her in a taunting tone.

"Come on and join us, Tianna." Serena did a somersault like an underwater swimmer. "This is so cool."

"Your moon amulet," Tianna called back. "It changed colors. What does that mean?"

The amulet hanging around Serena's neck was shimmering with light. She glanced at Vanessa and Jimena; both their amulets were also glowing.

Tianna jumped, caught Jimena's arm, and jerked hard. "We have to go back," she said.

Jimena blinked suddenly as if she had snapped back from a dreamlike state. She looked at Tianna, then glanced down at her fiery amulet and understood immediately. "*¡Oye!*" she shouted. "Serena! Vanessa! Come back!"

Vanessa and Serena continued frolicking. Tianna watched in panic as the black mist began spilling into the air.

"The Atrox," Jimena breathed. "Get us out now."

"I told you I don't know how," Tianna said with panic.

"Then just do what you do to get in," Jimena said. "I'll get Serena and Vanessa." Jimena dove up into the air and jetted away as billowing shadows gathered over Tianna.

She narrowed her eyes in concentration, trying to penetrate the veil that divided the worlds.

Suddenly the shadow charged toward her. It hit her with the strength of a fist. She staggered back, then tripped and fell. The black vapor whipped around her.

She steadied herself and concentrated, using the full force of her mind to leave this realm. Her eyes went out of focus, and suddenly she was back in reality. She hit the side of the cupboard in the small apartment and fell, then sat up with a gasp.

"We did it," she yelled with excitement, and looked around the room. She was the only one who had made it back. Had she accidentally trapped the others?

A loud rap on the door made relief flood through her. Maybe they had come back and landed in another location, the same way Derek had found her running outside the apartment this morning.

She hurried to the door and swung it open.

"Derek?"

Derek had an odd look on his face, and then she glanced behind him. Justin and Mason were there.

CHAPTER TWENTY-THREE

TIANNA AND DEREK stood on the cliff above a public beach, Mason and Justin beside them. A fog bank sat offshore, seeming to sweep in closer with each rising swell. The phosphorescent breakers tossed spray as they crashed over the rocks below, and distant lights on a pier reflected off the black water.

Mason stared at Tianna. "I didn't need to bring you here, Tianna," he said. "You already failed."

Justin snickered.

"But with you it's personal," Mason explained. "You made me look like a fool too many times."

Tianna glanced at the sky. "I still see a sliver of moon," she said.

That made them both laugh. "You think you can do something now, when we have all the goddesses?" Justin asked.

"Down the cliff," Mason ordered.

Tianna looked at the edge. "Where?"

"A path over there." Justin shoved her back. "And don't try to use your fancy mind stuff because you don't want anything to happen to Derek."

She nodded and started down the path.

"I'm sorry," Derek whispered behind her. "I wanted to play the big hero, so I went back to Planet Bang to get my car and they found me there."

She smiled ruefully at him.

Derek sighed. "They got your address by going through my mind."

"Thanks, Derek!" Mason laughed.

Tianna pushed through the chaparral and walked cautiously over the jagged rocks. Because it was almost a new moon, the tide was at its lowest, and she sloshed through a small tide pool that normally would have been much deeper, then stepped onto wet sand where a wave had left bubbling foam. Another wave hit her ankles with a shock of cold. When the water receded, she felt tingling on the soles of her feet from tiny mole crabs burrowing back into the soupy sand.

Fires down the beach caught her eye.

"Toward the light," Justin ordered.

She tottered in the sand and walked around a tangled bed of kelp, then headed up the shore with an increasing sense of doom. As she got closer, she saw that the fires were actually torches set in the sand. The flames at the end of the long poles waggled in the ever present wind, the tips radiating an uncanny whiteness that seemed different from any fire she had seen before. Ice-blue sparks spit into the cold night air and continued to glow until they spun out of sight. The fires were breathtaking and left a slight odor of sulfur in the air.

Followers standing on the beach looked at her with hunger, as if they had waited for Tianna a long time. Suddenly, she realized why they wanted her. With her gone, there was no chance that the four goddesses could ever be united again.

She glanced into Justin's eyes as he took off his shirt and stood under the first torch. The flame flapped and the standing goat tattooed on his arm seemed to move.

She stopped, startled by the tattoo. There was something familiar about the shape, and then she knew. She had seen it on the arm of the men who had stolen into her home when she was a little girl. She glanced up and Justin understood her look.

"So you remember now," he said with a smirk.

She nodded. She felt weak and powerless. The same way she had felt that night so many years back when they had invaded her house. She wondered what they had wanted with her even then that could have made them commit such an atrocity.

"Sit," Mason ordered.

She collapsed onto the sand with a childish desire to cry.

Derek sat beside her. "Tianna, what's going on?"

"Some ceremony. I don't know. I guess they're getting ready to cross us over."

"Who are the goddesses they kept talking about?" he asked.

"I'll explain later," she hushed him.

"Later?" he exclaimed. "You think we're going to survive this?"

"I am," she said with determination. "And I'll save you."

"Right," he scoffed. Then he looked at her with his deep blue eyes. "You know, Tianna, I think we're going to die, so if you know, then it's only fair you tell me."

Tianna looked at him. "You're right. I can tell you what I know, but that doesn't mean it's going to make sense because it still isn't clear to me. Most of it I just learned myself about an hour ago."

She started to explain as more Followers arrived at the beach. They didn't look like kids coming to the beach for a picnic. Some guys wore tuxedos, others stepped out in painted and patched jeans, but all looked glamorous.

Tianna continued telling Derek everything that had happened. He seemed to accept all that she said. She told him about accidentally trapping Jimena, Vanessa, and Serena when they tried to rescue Catty.

"So now instead of saving one goddess and making the Daughters of the Moon four again, I actually lost all of them." She finished.

"Space is a funny thing," Derek mused.

"That's not exactly the reaction I expected."

"The universe is constructed of atoms," he continued.

"Derek, I know that, and I really don't feel like talking about science in my last moments on earth. Can't you think of some way to get us out of this?"

He grinned and went on, "Spaces exist between these atoms, and within these spaces are other atoms that create a parallel universe, one existing simultaneously with ours."

"Okay." She smiled. "Now you've got my attention."

"That other realm and this one are woven together," Derek said.

"So," Tianna concluded, "if Vanessa, Jimena, and Serena are being held captive in another dimension and if the ceremony is going to take place on this beach, then they're probably right here behind the veil that divides the worlds."

"That would be my guess." He nodded. "Now do something."

"Say no more." Tianna leaned over and kissed his cheek quickly. "Don't forget to pull me back like you did this morning when you saw me running, wrapped in the bedsheet."

His eyes sparkled as if he enjoyed that memory. "I'm ready," he announced, and glanced at his watch. "Five minutes is all I'll give you, then I'm going to yank hard."

"That's all I need," she agreed. "Either they're there or they aren't."

She gazed at the fires and narrowed her eyes in total concentration.

CHAPTER TWENTY-FOUR

THE FLAMES ON THE torches trembled, and then it was as if she were looking at the ocean through a crumpled sheet of plastic. The roar of the surf became distant, and at that moment the membrane dividing the two worlds rippled and swelled before bursting.

She found herself standing in that other realm. It was eerily still and a strange gentle radiance filled the air, although she couldn't see the source.

"Vanessa," she called. "Serena. Jimena. Can you hear me?"

Then she felt a change in the air and looked cautiously behind her, sensing something evil hidden in the gray nothingness. She cursed silently and called their names again.

Where were they? Derek's explanation had seemed so reasonable. She had been confident she would find them here. She had expected to see all four of them tied up together. Now she wondered if she had walked into another trap. Maybe this was even part of the ceremony.

She had taken only a few steps when she had to stop. She realized with a grateful sigh that Derek had taken her hand and was keeping her bound to the real world.

A soft fluttering sound made her look around. "Hello," she called. "Is someone there?" Her words fell into the air with a tremor of fear.

A flapping noise made her look up. Jimena waved and dove toward her.

"You did it!" she yelled. "I knew you'd find a way to get us back."

"I almost didn't." Tianna spoke softly. "And we're not safe yet. I still have to get us out."

"What is this place?" Vanessa yelled as she soared into view. "It's like being in a huge tank of water without the water."

"Another dimension." Tianna shrugged. "Where are Serena and Catty? We don't have much time." How many minutes had gone by already?

Catty and Serena appeared from a roiling mist. Serena was pulling Catty by her arm.

"This is Tianna," Vanessa said to Catty. "The one who first saw you in a séance."

"It wasn't really a séance," Catty insisted. She still seemed weak, but not as weak as the last time Tianna had seen her. "And how do you know she's not one of them? After all, she trapped you in here with me."

"She's not," Serena insisted. "I told you, Followers killed her parents." Then she glanced at Tianna. Her eyes seemed worried that what she had said might upset her. "Sorry, I read it in your mind back in your apartment."

"How did you know they were Followers?" Tianna asked. "I didn't even know until just a few minutes ago."

"I recognized the tattoo," Serena explained.

Jimena took Vanessa's hand. "She's going to get us out of here. Hold on."

As they joined hands, Tianna had an uneasy feeling. It was as if the mysterious force were alerting her to danger again. She glanced around, wondering if that deadly shadow were about to filter into the air.

"What's wrong?" Serena asked.

"It shouldn't be this simple," Tianna answered. "Why did the Atrox trap you only to let you go so easily? I'm starting to get a weird feeling. I always trust my instincts, and something's telling me this isn't right."

"Why does everything have to be hard?" Vanessa asked. "Maybe for once we're getting a break."

"It never works that way," Jimena answered.

Tianna felt a tug on her hand. "We're going back," she said. She had forgotten that Derek had agreed to pull her back in five minutes no matter what.

Suddenly they were sprawled in the cold, foaming surf.

Derek yelled, "Look out!"

The Followers bolted toward them, kicking up sand. There was nowhere to go but back into the other dimension. Even the ocean seemed too forbidding. The high tide had now started to come in.

"What are we going to do?" Tianna said.

"Stay and fight." Jimena laughed dangerously as the Followers slowly circled them.

Justin took a step forward, his eyes glowing. The Followers crowded beside him

"We're outnumbered." Tianna realized now she had made another foolish mistake. "Maybe we should go back to the other side."

"No way," Serena argued.

"Not a chance." Catty looked strong again now that she was back in the real world.

Tianna wondered what they were doing. They didn't seem afraid. Didn't they understand how dangerous these guys could be? Instead they stood together, their amulets glowing, and a golden aura wavered around them, coloring the beach with inexplicable rainbow lights. Then their eyes seemed to dilate as if energy were building inside their heads.

"They look like the guys from Zahi's old group," Catty said with disgust in her voice.

"You're right," Serena agreed.

Tianna stood motionless. "You've fought them before?"

"We tried to tell you," Vanessa said.

Their eyes flashed with anticipation.

Tianna wondered why they seemed so eager to fight. There were too many Followers, and before she could even start to consider how many, Mason stepped forward with a twisted grin on his bony face.

"We have never fought so many at one time before." Jimena looked directly at Mason. "It's been something we've been wanting to do for a long time."

Mason raised an eyebrow. "You won't win."

Suddenly Jimena, Catty, Vanessa, and Serena locked arms, and the air around them glowed, then pulsed and rushed toward Mason with amazing force. He staggered back.

"Justin," he called. "Time to show them the strength of the Atrox."

"I hear you." Justin stepped next to him.

This time when the girls sent an attack, Mason and Justin pushed it back. The force exploded in electrical waves around Serena and Jimena. Their moon amulets sparkled, then glowed weaker. Tianna could feel something happening.

She glanced back at Justin.

"Serena," Tianna yelled too late. Justin attacked. Even at this distance she could feel the heat of his power.

Small fires bobbed on the surf before going out and the dry chaparral smoldered.

Then Jimena and Serena leaned together and Catty and Vanessa joined them, all four locked arms again, and their power crackled across the night.

Justin deflected their hit, sending sparks like a million fireflies swirling up and around.

Tianna felt spellbound by what she had seen. Derek grabbed her shoulders and pulled her back.

"You're too close," he cautioned. "Can you believe this?"

"I don't think they're winning," Tianna said, worried.

The air smelled of ozone, smoke, and sulfur. She stared at Mason through the shower of embers. A strange light covered his face, and then she realized it was coming from the moon amulets. His eyes flashed with evil anticipation, as if he enjoyed the fight. The others Followers gathered close around him, with the same hungry look in their eyes.

She moved in front of Derek, ready to protect him but not sure how.

"For the first time," Justin said, "all four goddesses will join the Atrox at once. Think what that will do to the world."

The others pushed forward.

Tianna was doubtful the Daughters could

fight so many by themselves, and she didn't understand her fierce need to protect Derek. Then an idea came to her. She had already made the three four again. Her mission was accomplished. Why not just take Derek and flee?

"Come on." Tianna grabbed Derek's hand and started to pull him toward the jagged rocks.

"Where?" he asked, eyes wide.

"Back to the road." She motioned with her head. "It's not our fight."

They scrabbled up the rocky cliff.

She heard Jimena, Serena, Vanessa, and Catty reciting an incantation or prayer. *"O Mater Luna, Regina nocis, adiuvo me nunc."* They chanted the words over and over.

Justin scoffed. "Look at the moon tonight, goddesses. It's only a crescent, soon to disappear. The queen of the night won't help you now."

Tianna glanced back. The power emanating from Jimena, Catty, Serena, and Vanessa made the air waver and glow, but not as brightly as before. Their strength seemed to be fading.

Derek took her arm. "Do something."

"Me?" Tianna said in exasperation. "I don't have the kind of powers they have. The best I can do is save you."

The air rocked as Mason and Justin attacked again. Serena staggered back from their smashing blow, her moon amulet on fire. Jimena caught her.

"They're not going to be able to defeat them without your help," Derek insisted.

She turned to him. "But what can I do?"

CHAPTER TWENTY-FIVE

"USE YOUR POWER," Derek encouraged.

An idea came to her, and slowly she made her way back down to the rocks. Waves crashed over her. She stood on a boulder and concentrated until she had created a breeze. She made the wind swirl around her, and when it had enough momentum, she sent it charging down the beach. The tempest slashed through the sand and scooped it up, then whirled like a dust devil, surrounding the Followers.

They covered their eyes as the sandy winds screeched about them.

Justin stopped his attack.

Mason looked around, his baggy clothes flapping wildly as the squall circled him.

Then Justin caught her eyes, and in a flash she understood that he knew what she was doing. She felt him piercing her mind. His mental force throbbed through her, forcing her to stop. She could hear Derek say something, but his voice was too far away.

She tried to fight Justin with stubborn determination, but then Mason joined him. Their power was too strong, and her head ached until the pain became intolerable. She collapsed and released her power as they cut through her resistance.

The wind went out of control and blustered around the beach. It tore into her lungs, smothering her with air too thick to breathe. What had she done? She was going to destroy them all.

She grabbed onto a rock and pulled herself up. Sand scraped her face and arms, and the night turned an odd coppery dark. She squinted, eyes tearing from the grit, and held her hand over her nose and mouth while taking a stumbling step forward.

Sand gummed her mouth, coated her tongue, and clogged her nostrils. She spit and coughed. With laboring steps she continued up the cliff.

Then through the swirling whirlwind a hand grabbed her shoulder and pulled her onto an outcropping of jagged rock. The air was clearer there. She sneezed and brushed the sand from around her eyes.

She looked back at the strange roiling clouds below her.

"You did that." Derek looked down at the howling winds with amazement.

"I think I killed them all." She started to cry.

Then Jimena, Catty, Vanessa, and Serena pushed through the sandstorm and climbed on the rock.

"You did it!" Serena yelled, and spit sand from her mouth.

"You saved us." Vanessa hacked.

"I almost suffocated us all," Tianna argued.

"No, you didn't," Catty replied. "You still gave everyone a way to escape. It's just that the way the winds were blowing, the Followers had to run away from us down the beach."

"Yeah," Vanessa agreed. "Very smart."

Tianna smiled.

"Let's get away from here, anyway," Catty urged.

Vanessa hugged her, obviously glad to have Catty home.

They started up the cliff, brushing sand from their hair and ears.

"How did you get in that other dimension?" Tianna asked Catty when they were safely on the street and walking down the strand.

"Long story." Catty shook her head. "We were fighting this powerful Follower."

"And Catty got hit because she was trying to save me," Vanessa added. "She's such a good friend."

"So what happened?" Tianna asked.

"I saw that he was going to have a direct hit

on me," Catty explained. "So I tried to escape, but when I opened the tunnel—"

"That's Catty's gift," Vanessa interrupted. "She travels in time, and the tunnel is what she uses to get from one place to the next."

"His force hit me just as I opened the tunnel, and it threw me into that other dimension," Catty continued. "I figured I was going to be sacrificed at the next dark moon. So I was just as shocked as you were when I first saw you. I tried to warn you then."

"But you wrote 'Help me' on my wall," Tianna said, confused.

Catty shook her head. "The Followers wrote that. They were trying to lure you to stay. I'm the one who scratched 'stay away' because I knew it was too dangerous for you to rescue me."

Then all four turned as if they had suddenly become aware of Derek. "Should we fix his mind so he doesn't remember?" Serena asked.

"No." Tianna jumped in front of him. "Please don't. He loves adventure."

They all looked at her curiously.

"I'm not going to tell anyone," Derek promised. "If that's what you're worried about. No one would believe me, anyway."

That made them all laugh.

"Let's go home," Vanessa said.

Tianna sighed. More than anything she wanted to go home, but she didn't have a place to go. She walked slower and fell behind the others.

Derek took her arm. "What's wrong?"

She couldn't look at him.

"After what we've been through tonight, I can't believe you have a secret you're not going to tell me." He put a comforting arm around her.

She looked up. "I don't have a home to go to. I guess I can go to a shelter or the nearest police station."

He thought about it. "My older sister is away at college. I bet my mom would let you spend the night in her room."

Jimena was suddenly beside her. "You can stay with me. My *abuelita* would love to have someone living with her who hasn't heard all her stories."

"Or you could live with me," Vanessa offered

quickly. "We'll clear out the bedroom where my mom stores all her clothes. She could use another daughter as a model for her dress designs."

"We have room, too," Catty put in. "My mom will say yes to anything once she sees that I'm okay."

"See?" Vanessa said. "You have plenty of homes."

Tianna took a deep breath. "Thanks."

"But there's someplace we have to take you first," Serena said.

"Where?" Tianna asked, baffled.

"You'll see." Catty smiled mysteriously, then she glanced at Derek. "Sorry, Derek, this is one place you can't go."

"That's okay." Derek laughed. I've had enough adventure for one night. I'll catch a bus home."

He pulled Tianna away from the others and whispered against her cheek. "It looks like you're going to be staying in L.A. I'm glad."

"Me, too," she said and softly kissed him good night.

CHAPTER TWENTY-SIX

"WHERE ARE YOU taking me again?" Tianna asked suspiciously as they walked through the massive Cedars-Sinai complex. Nurses going off duty turned and stared at them, covered with sand and scrapes.

"Don't worry." Vanessa smiled. "You'll like it."

The fragrance of night-blooming jasmine filled the air as they stepped up to the entrance of a gray apartment building and Catty pressed a button on the security panel.

"Yes," a voice answered.

"It's Catty."

A loud hum opened the magnetic lock.

They entered and immediately caught their reflections in the mirrors and started laughing. Even though they had brushed at the sand, they were still covered with a fine layer of dust on their faces and arms. Their eyes were bloodshot, and their hair looked as if it had been moussed with Play-Doh. They continued laughing as they crowded onto the elevator and rode up to the fourth floor.

When the doors opened, they walked down a narrow outside hallway.

A woman wearing a white silky gown stood in the open door of her apartment. She was short, with long gray hair that curled thickly to her shoulders. "Look at you! Whatever happened?" She embraced Catty and hugged her tightly.

"Is that Catty's mother?" Tianna asked.

"No, this is Maggie," Serena replied.

Maggie smiled at Tianna. "So this is the friend you told me about." Her amiable eyes glanced over her, and then she motioned them to come inside.

Candles blazed, and the flames reflected in mirrors and gilded frames. It gave everything a fairy-tale feel.

"Why don't you each take a shower while the others talk," Maggie offered. "You'll find clean robes and towels, oils and soaps in the back bathroom."

Tianna was the first one to shower and dress in one of the silky robes. When she came out, Jimena went in.

"Come join us, please." Maggie offered her a chair and a cup of tea.

Tianna sat down as Serena, Vanessa, and Catty continued to tell Maggie all that had happened.

Finally they had all finished showering and sat together, hair wet and wrapped in towels. Maggie pulled out a moon amulet that matched the ones Serena, Jimena, and Vanessa wore. She handed it to Catty.

"You lost yours," she said simply.

Catty slipped it on. "Thanks." Immediately it turned an opalescent color and reflected the candle flames with multicolored sparks.

Then Maggie walked around the table until she stood behind Tianna. "And now, my dear, I have one for you, too."

"Me?" Tianna looked at her in disbelief.

Maggie clasped the amulet around Tianna's neck. The silver stone felt good on her skin and gave her comfort.

"Thanks." Tianna touched it. "It's pretty."

"It's more than style," Vanessa said.

"You'd better tell her, Maggie," Jimena coaxed.

Maggie moved a candle to the middle of the table and stared across the flame at Tianna, her blue eyes intense. "Selene has looked down and decided to make you a goddess because of the courage and fearlessness and the talent you have shown in using your telekinetic powers to fight evil."

Tianna laughed and held up her hands. "Does a goddess have cuts and bruises and ripped fingernails?"

Maggie nodded. "*Tu es dea, filia lunae.* You are a goddess, a Daughter of the Moon."

Tianna stopped laughing.

"We told her the story already," Serena put in.

"And about the Atrox, too," Vanessa added. "But I think that was a little harder for her to believe."

Maggie nodded. "The greatest strength of the Atrox is that people no longer believe that the demonic walk among us. So you see why it is so important that you help fight it."

"Me?" Tianna whispered.

Maggie nodded. "Catty, Vanessa, Jimena, and Serena have no choice. That is what they were born to do and it is my responsibility to guide them and to help them understand their powers. But you are being offered a choice."

Tianna felt happy. Since she had lost her family, she had wanted to belong somewhere.

"That mysterious voice that seemed like an inner guide," Tianna asked. "Was that Selene?"

Maggie nodded. "Selene was always guiding

you. She looked down on you that first night and felt pity for what the Followers had done and for what you were going to endure. And now because you have proved yourself, she is allowing you to become—"

"A goddess," Tianna whispered.

"A Daughter of the Moon." Maggie corrected her with a smile.

"But what about Justin and Mason?" Tianna wondered if she would always be on the run. "Will they still be after me?"

"No," Maggie assured her. "You have succeeded in fulfilling what you were meant to do. You brought the four Daughters of the Moon together again."

"And now we're five," Catty added.

"But why did they have to take my family from me?" Tianna asked.

"Evil doesn't have a rational explanation. I do know the Atrox sent them into the past to correct what it had seen happening in the future. But by altering the past, they actually created the future that was always meant to be."

Tianna looked down. "So the Atrox saw me saving Catty in the future and it sent Justin and Mason back into the past to destroy me."

"Yes," Maggie said. "Now all of you must go home. You have families who are worried about you."

Tianna looked down.

Maggie's soft hand cupped her chin. "You most of all, my dear. Mary and Shannon and Todd care about you very much. You need to go home at once and let them know you're all right."

"Home?" Tianna repeated the word so softly, she wasn't even sure she had said it aloud.

"Yes," Maggie answered. "I'll come with you, if you like."

Maggie and Tianna stood outside the large brick Tudor home. A line of smoke wafted from the massive chimney.

"I believe Mary is sitting up waiting for you," Maggie encouraged. "I'll wait here until you go inside."

"I'm nervous, " Tianna said. "What if the

things she said about me coming back were just talk? Maybe she doesn't really want me."

"She does," Maggie answered simply. "She lost all the family she had, and now she desperately needs you children."

Tianna looked up at the window, then took a deep breath and walked up to the house.

Mary answered the door tentatively, looking over Tianna's head, then up and down the street. "You're alone?"

"They're gone," Tianna said. "Can I stay here?"

In response, Mary smiled and opened the door wide. Tianna walked inside. Flames flickered in the hearth, and the smell of popcorn wrapped around her.

Shannon and Todd looked up in surprise when they saw her. Shannon ran to her with arms spread as wide as wings, and Todd did happy wheelies around the room.

Hours later, stomach filled with popcorn and Pepsi, Tianna crawled onto the soft cotton-flowered sheet and pulled the comforter over her head. Her bed smelled fresh and new, and she had a cozy feeling that she hadn't felt for a long time. Tears stung her eyes. She missed her parents and Jamie, but now at least she had a chance to start to live a normal life after so many years of running and living on the street.

She stared out the window at the dark night sky and touched the amulet hanging around her neck.

"Goddess," she murmured. The word felt so right.